A NOISE TO HER LEFT STARTLED HER FROM HER THOUGHTS. A PANEL in the wall began to slide open. The first thing Eve could see was a pair of scuffed hiking boots. Her gaze drifted upward. *Oh my, powerful thighs, a huge cock, if the ridge in his jeans was any indication.* His waist was trim, his stomach flat. A chest wide enough to spread out over, thickly muscled arms. It just kept getting better and better, even if he was a kidnapper.

He had a wild mane of red-gold hair, almost an identical match to her own untamed locks. But it was his face that made her heart thump uncontrollably. Or, more accurately it was his eyes. His golden cat-eyes glittered. She could see their sparkle from half a room away. His lips were full but not overly so, kissable lips. Firm, high cheekbones. His features looked almost Asian, but he was a pure *Lionese* man. There was no doubt of that.

It had to be her imagination. It looked like he was thinking of sex. Hot, sweaty, bone-melting sex. Was she to become some sort of sex slave? Was he setting up a harem?

That couldn't be right though. He didn't look at the other women, didn't pay them the slightest attention as he raked her body from head to toe.

Eve squirmed. Her pussy clenched. She could feel the heat of his passion blaze at her. He looked at her as if she belonged to him — his own personal nirvana. She swallowed, taken aback by his attention.

How could she feel attracted to someone who went around stealing women? Was she going into heat a couple months early? Hell, nothing would surprise her now.

Worlds Apart

Taken

By

Bonnie Rose Leigh

This book is dedicated to three very special people, my husband Chris, my critique partner, Tianna Xander and my Beta Reader, Fedora. Without their support, advice and shoulders to cry on, my stories would never have seen the light of day.

TALIFF'S CURE

Chapter One

"You can't send him, your highness. How will it look?"

"I don't care how it looks, Curran. He's the only one qualified to fly deep space. He's going and that's final."

"I really think…"

"I know what you think. You've been telling me nonstop since I announced my decision at the council meeting two moons ago." Hunter Shi'Lan stood, pushed away from his highly polished Senach wood desk and headed for the nearest door. Time grew short and he wanted to wish his brother a safe and successful journey.

The halls were empty as Hunter made his way to his personal transport. It left him free to think about the possible repercussions of his actions. The truth is they didn't have enough women to go around. Drastic action was necessary. If he lost his throne, then so be it. He'd made his decision.

Guards followed on his heels, determined to keep him safe despite their disapproval of his actions. Every man on his security detail was without a mate, due to the genetic flaw that prevented most female cubs from taking root in their mother's womb. *Chantrean* scientists had yet to determine the cause, hence the need for this mission's success.

When he finally approached the landing pad where his personal transport hovered, he breathed a sigh of relief. He hadn't missed him after all. Taliff, his brother and head of his personal guard, slouched against the craft, a ready smile on his face. "I was beginning to think you'd miss seeing me off."

"Not a chance, little brother." Hunter grasped Taliff by the forearms, then pulled him into a hug. "I shall miss you. You take our hope with you."

"I won't fail. If there is another colony of *Lionese* out there, I will find them."

Hunter nodded, then stepped back. "Everything is ready aboard the *Wanderer*?"

"The only thing it needs now is its pilot."

Hunter knew he had to let his brother go. He took a deep breath and looked him in the eye. "Come home in one piece. I'm giving you one solar cycle, then I'll come after you myself." With one last glance at his brother, Hunter turned around and went back inside the palace. "Goddess speed, my brother. Goddess speed," he muttered. Hunter shook off his melancholy and went back to his chambers. Pressing matters awaited him.

TALIFF SHI'LAN WATCHED HIS brother walk away. Somehow, he didn't think Hunter would need to come for him. Times were too unsettled here on *Chantrea* right now for his brother to leave anyway. He knew his duty, and so did Taliff. Find the *Lionese* that disappeared from their home world millennia ago and bring them home.

Or at least bring the women. His mission, scouting for the lost colony, was too important to let petty political squabbles get in the way. If he happened to find his own mate along the way, all the better.

Well, no time like the present. With one last glance at his brother's retreating back, Taliff turned on his heel and headed to the *Wanderer*. His ship, a star class cruiser, usually held a complement of over a hundred men, but with the urgency and need for secrecy behind this mission, he would be traveling on her alone.

He'd arranged to have the ship stocked with supplies, the energy core inspected and charged to full capacity, and his personal effects placed on board, while he conferred with his second in command and met with Hunter. Everything appeared ready when he arrived at the spaceport. The only thing left to do—clear Central Space Command.

He ignored the massive size of the vessel he'd inhabit alone and boarded quickly. His footsteps echoed down the silent halls as he made his way to the command deck. He placed his palm on the identity pad, leaned into the laser recognition device to allow it to scan his features and gave his authorization code. "Authorization code Shi'Lan seven-six-three-four-eight-seven."

"Authorization approved," the computer purred. "Welcome home, Commander Shi'Lan."

"Thank you, *Shoshoni*." He glanced around the empty deck, sighed. "*Shoshoni*?"

"Yes, Sir?"

"Have you analyzed the data from the ancient records?"

"Affirmative."

"What have you concluded?"

"Probables suggest *The Adventurer* headed toward deep space, quadrant four."

"Possible locations?"

"I've narrowed it down to ten possible solar systems."

"Which is the most likely?"

"System Omega Three."

"*Shoshoni*, plot a course to system Omega Three. We might as well start there."

"Yes, Sir."

"Oh, and, *Shoshoni*?"

"Yes, Commander?"

"How long will it take us to arrive there using the star drive?"

"Approximately four moon cycles."

"Thank you, *Shoshoni*. After we clear the defensive shield, I'll be heading down to the stasis chamber. Wake me on approach to Omega Three."

"Yes, Sir. Course plotted."

"Engage engines. Let's get out of here." Taliff walked over to the main viewscreen and watched as the planet below slowly disappeared from view. "*Shoshoni*, follow Deep Space Protocol and interrupt stasis at the first sign of trouble."

"Understood, Commander Shi'Lan. Deep Space Protocol established."

IN THE MONTH THAT Taliff had spent investigating the planet called Earth, he'd discovered many things. Not the least of which, humans appeared to be a bloodthirsty lot, warring amongst themselves with no regard to the sanctity of life.

He also learned that his species here on Earth had no idea how to treat their women. They didn't take a mate but procreated with any female who would accept them. They didn't cherish them, protect them as they deserved. So he had no regrets about the thirty-five women now aboard his ship, some in stasis, some happy with their situation and therefore free to roam the ship.

With this one last trip down to the surface of the planet, he'd be ready to head back to *Chantrea*. So far, none of the women he'd abducted was a mate for him, but others on his home planet might get lucky. His mission had indeed been successful. The *Lionese* on Earth had none of the problems reproducing females that the women on his planet did. For that, his people could rejoice. They now had hope for their future.

Taliff sighed and glanced at the control panel of the shuttle. After setting the new coordinates, he leaned back and put his hands behind his head. He missed the sweet air of *Chantrea*. He'd been gone nearly five moon cycles now. If he didn't leave soon Hunter would worry and there were enough troubles for him to deal with back home. Now wasn't the time for him to leave just to look for his little brother.

Now that the survivors of the *Adventurer* had been located, Hunter would order other expeditions to travel to Earth. Maybe next time they could negotiate the removal of the women rather than resort to abduction. It would certainly make things easier all the way around.

He'd gone out of his way to choose wisely. He'd made sure that none of the women left behind loved ones and in some cases, he managed to take not only the woman but her children as well. He didn't want their lives on *Chantrea* to begin with heartache. An unhappy mate made for tough times.

He shook his head, amazed at his musings. How would he know what it was like to live with an unhappy mate? He was just going off what he'd overheard among the few mated males he knew. One thing was for sure, his mate would be happy about her situation. He wouldn't allow for anything less.

"*Shoshoni?*"

"Yes, Commander Shi'Lan?"

"Give me all the data you have on the settlement we're heading to now."

"Settlement Anora. It's located on the eastern seaboard of the Northeastern United States. Population is currently at two hundred ten. Of that, one hundred and thirty are female. There are twenty-seven infants. Eighteen of them female."

"How many women below are without children?"

"Data unknown."

Taliff removed his hands from behind his head, sat up and looked out the viewscreen. They were just entering Earth's atmosphere. This would be the fifteenth raid he'd performed in the one moon cycle he'd been in this solar system. "What kind of defenses are we looking at?"

"None that I can detect, Commander."

"That's odd. The other settlements at least used shielding technology. Have you drawn any conclusions as to why this one is defenseless?"

"Yes, Sir. Probables say they are unaware that they are descendants of a race from another planet."

"What, they think they just spawned themselves from ameba?"

"Data unknown."

"I was just kidding, *Shoshoni*. Begin descent. Land the shuttle five miles from the settlement."

This was definitely a complication he hadn't expected. At least at the other settlements, oral history passed down from father to son spoke of the first ones who crashed on the planet. Each settlement had variations of the theme, but whether they believed the old tales, they were aware of them.

If the women of this settlement assumed they were descendants of Earth, there were bound to be problems ahead. People of this planet were thousands of years behind *Chantrea* in technology. Even getting them aboard the ship could be problematic. He rubbed his face in frustration, then stood up and walked to the beverage dispenser. "*Shoshoni*, give me a mug of water."

He watched the mug materialize in front of him. Even this would be foreign to them. Oh well, at least they'd be on their way back to the home world within a few hours. He'd put the Anoran women in stasis and keep them there until they reached *Chantrea*. Then it would be someone else's headache.

"Arrival at the coordinates in thirty seconds."

"Thank you, *Shoshoni*."

Taliff walked back to his seat, buckled in and took over the controls from the computer. Time to finish his mission and get his ass back home where he belonged. He found a clearing about five miles from the village and after scanning to make sure no intelligent life forms were in the area, took the ship down. All he needed to do was land in the middle of a *Lionese* hunting party.

He grabbed a backpack, filled it with supplies and headed out of the ship. If anyone spotted him walking in the woods toward the village, they would just assume he was just another hiker who'd gotten lost.

It didn't take him but thirty minutes to find the settlement. It looked like any other small town he'd seen. A pub stood on the first corner he came to, people loitered out in the streets, couples holding hands looked through shop windows and antique shops seemed to be bustling with activity.

It appeared that not only did they not have the shielding technology as the other settlements, but they lived as humans, too. Very peculiar. He'd like to learn more about why they lived so differently than the other descendants, but now wasn't the time.

The first order of business—locate the residential area and mark the houses that *Shoshoni* had pinpointed as being perfect for his needs. Then he'd scope out the rest of the town, find somewhere to wait out the hours until he could put his plan into action and pray that nothing went wrong.

He was just passing the pub when the crowd began to part in front of him. Within seconds, *Lionese* men surrounded him. Some looked like they, what did the Americans say again? Ahh, yes, looked like they bench pressed Buicks. At least he'd come prepared and had masked his scent so they wouldn't know he could shift. It was the only advantage he had in situations like this.

There could be only one reason the males were acting so territorially to a stranger right off the bat. Some of their women must be in their yearly heat cycles. As if he didn't have enough complications as it was, he had to add one more.

Taliff wondered which one of these guys was the ringleader. There always was one. Maybe he could reason with them, but the way his luck seemed to be going, it didn't look likely. He had to try though. "Hello. Can one of you gentlemen point me in the direction of a diner and a place to clean up?"

A burly man with a row of earrings in each ear, a mane of greasy black hair that hung past his ass and the belly of a swine, approached him first. Ahh, he found the ringleader. As if any of the woman would willingly lay with such a creature. Taliff's thoughts were confirmed when the man twisted his mouth and spit a wad of tobacco juice onto the street. "Don't think we can help you, stranger. You might want to head back where you came from."

"Look, I don't want to cause trouble. I just want something to eat and drink. Maybe somewhere to rest for a few hours, then I'll move on." The men started to move closer as they tried to box him in. All they really managed was to piss him off, especially their self-appointed leader.

"Fine, I'll leave." Taliff backed slowly away from the mob, turned around and headed back the way he'd come. He'd have to come back and reconnoiter after the town bedded down for the night. After he made sure that no one had followed him, Taliff headed for the shuttle. He needed to get some rest before he returned. One never knew when the shit would fly and he might have to fight his way out.

It was almost three in the morning when Taliff returned to Anora. He crouched just on the edge of the tree line and looked at the quiet little town. All clear. He was just about to step out of his hiding spot when he smelled it.

Chantrean legends say that you'll know your mate by the unmistakably inviting scent. Your blood will pound in your veins, your heart will race and your libido will explode when in proximity to her.

The strange scent once again drifted his way. His body reacted immediately. His cock jerked in response, his pulse leapt in his throat. Shocked, he stood up, visible to anyone who bothered to look his way. He didn't care. How could he have found her so quickly?

Before he could rejoice, he detected another scent layered over hers. The pungent musk of another male. His every territorial instinct went on alert. His hackles rose, his mane of hair rose and expanded. This would not do.

Time to take action. Taliff ducked back into the trees and waited for his unsuspecting prey to approach. It was time for a mate hunt.

Chapter Two

"All men should rot in hell. If one more man grabs my ass, accidentally touches my tits, or fondles my crotch, I'm going to geld him." Eve Roberts was not a happy woman. She didn't mind being woken up to deliver a child in the middle of the night. It was her job, as healer. She shouldn't, however, have to put up with the groping shit from the expectant fathers. They were *Lionese*, though. What did she expect? Not a one could keep his dick in his pants. They were worse than rabbits when it came to fucking.

God, she was pissed. It was bad enough half the damn women in town were in heat and being bitches because of it. She'd be damned if she'd spread her legs for a man because her hormones were getting the better of her. But would they take no for an answer? Fuck, no. The men just had to go ahead and try to force themselves on her anyway. What she wouldn't give to be able to leave this place, just disappear forever. Unfortunately, the women here needed her and she never turned her back on someone who needed help.

Lost in thought, Eve didn't notice the stranger until she'd barreled over him. Before she could apologize, the world began to grow dim. She felt him place something against her heart. Lights flashed, blinding her. She blinked, then opened her eyes, only to find herself stuck inside some kind of glass coffin.

"What in the hell?" Panic tore through her. A scream stuck in her throat. This couldn't be happening. What in the hell was going on?

Sweat beaded on her brow, her pulse skittered. She looked around, desperate to find a way to escape her prison. She looked to her left, her right. Women in glass containers like hers were all around. There had to be at least a couple dozen.

None of the women moved so much as an inch. They weren't dead, were they?

Dear God. How many women did this creep need, anyway? "Oh, God...Oh, God...Oh, God. I shouldn't have wished to disappear." Panicked, Eve kicked at the lid of her box, slammed her fists against the sides. It didn't as much as crack. What in the hell was this thing made of?

"Let me out of here, dammit."

No one answered. No one came to see what all of the racket was about. That was the scariest thing of all. There was simply no one there to hear her at all. "Please, let me live through this so I can kill the son of a bitch." With no one there to witness her breakdown, she finally let the tears flow.

Over the course of the next two hours, Eve's mood went from pissed off to lost, then curious and finally, back to pissed off. As more women, ones she knew, suddenly appeared in previously empty containers like hers, concerns for her own situation dimmed. She had to take care of the others, make sure they were all right and that they stayed that way.

Along with her determination, there were questions. Why was it that she was the only one awake? Did he want her to suffer for some reason, to be aware enough to fret about her fate? She wouldn't give him the pleasure. She'd face this head on like everything else she did in life.

This *Lionese* woman wouldn't cower to the bigger beast.

A noise to her left startled her from her thoughts. A panel in the wall began to slide open. The first thing Eve could see was a pair of scuffed hiking boots. Her gaze drifted upward. *Oh my, powerful thighs, a huge cock, if the ridge in his jeans was any indication.* His waist was trim, his stomach flat. A chest wide enough to spread out over, thickly muscled arms. It just kept getting better and better, even if he was a kidnapper.

He had a wild mane of red-gold hair, almost an identical match to her own untamed locks. But it was his face that made her heart thump uncontrollably. Or, more accurately it was his eyes. His golden cat-eyes glittered. She could see their sparkle from half a room away. His lips were full but not overly so, kissable lips. Firm, high cheekbones. His features looked almost Asian, but he was a pure *Lionese* man. There was no doubt of that.

It had to be her imagination. It looked like he was thinking of sex. Hot, sweaty, bone-melting sex. Was she to become some sort of sex slave? Was he setting up a harem?

That couldn't be right though. He didn't look at the other women, didn't pay them the slightest attention as he raked her body from head to toe.

Eve squirmed. Her pussy clenched. She could feel the heat of his passion blaze at her. He looked at her as if she belonged to him — his own personal nirvana. She swallowed, taken aback by his attention.

How could she feel attracted to someone who went around stealing women? Was she going into heat a couple months early? Hell, nothing would surprise her now.

He entered the room, locked his gaze with hers and stalked her way.

"I'll have your name," the sex-on-a-stick demanded.

Just like that, her attention shifted from her overeager libido to her current situation. How could she have forgotten that this man held her prisoner? She wet her lips, shifted in her prison and prepared to blast him with her anger.

"Please," he whispered, a plea in his voice, "your name?"

She found herself answering, despite her anger. Maybe the desperation in his eyes made her do it. She really didn't care why, just felt the need to answer him. Hell, she just needed, period. She wanted to screw him senseless. What in the blazes was wrong with her? "Eve. Eve Roberts."

Was that throaty voice hers? Did she sound as desperate for him as she thought she did? Could she be any more humiliated?

"I'm called Taliff Shi'Lan. You're aboard my ship, the *Wanderer*."

Okay, she could handle this. Oh, hell no she couldn't. "Ship. I'm on a freaking ship?"

His eyes, once filled with savage passion, were now wary. Good, let him sweat. Not that he had much to worry about with her trapped the way she was.

He nodded, shifted his stance and moved closer. "Yes, a ship. A star class cruiser to be exact. Does any of this sound familiar to you?"

Wariness flooded her. Where was he going with this? "Familiar how?"

He answered her question with one of his own. "Have you never wondered why you are what you are or where you came from?"

"What are you talking about? Look, can you let me out of here?" She tried to sound innocent and afraid. She'd say anything at this point to get out of her crystal prison. It must not have been believable because all he did was quirk an eyebrow in response.

"I didn't think so," she mumbled.

He ignored her outburst and continued as though she hadn't said a word. "You're *Lionese*. Where do you think your kind originated?"

"What do you mean, where we originated?"

She could tell she was frustrating him, but she just didn't want to believe what he had implied. That they weren't human, not even a little bit. That Earth wasn't their natural home.

"Millennia ago, a ship called the *Adventurer* disappeared while doing deep space exploration. Historians assumed that all hands on board were lost. I found the descendants of those men and women. I found you."

"Uh, huh. If they assumed everyone died, then why did you come looking for us? I assume you didn't just stumble upon us by mistake?" Despite the seriousness of her situation, of the likely danger she and the others were in, her curiosity needed to be appeased.

"The simple truth? We're desperate."

She waited for more. For some kind of explanation, but none came. "That's it. That's all you're going to say?"

Taliff nodded. She turned her head away, afraid for him to see that even though she feared him, feared what might happen to her, she still wanted him. She was such a slut, and a fool, because she was going to help him.

She sighed, looked into his eyes. Yes, she was a slut. That had to be the reason she was about to offer her assistance in any way she could. She opened her mouth to speak, hesitated and tried again. She felt like she was about to give up her very life to the man.

"What can I do to help?" There, she said it. She wasn't selling her people out. She was helping them. At least, she hoped so.

She watched as Taliff pressed a button on the lid above her. It slid silently open. "Thank you."

Eve scrambled to sit up, thankful she could do so. "But I want some explanations." When she thought he would object, he just smiled. The twinkle was back in his eyes. Her clit twitched. Oh, she was in serious trouble here.

It's not as if she'd spent her youth on her back. Hell, she'd only had sex once. It wasn't even something she enjoyed. Well, she hadn't before, anyway. This guy looked like he'd know exactly what to do to make her scream.

"I'll tell you everything you need to know. Would you like to see the command deck? I need to give the computer instructions for takeoff."

"Takeoff? We're leaving?" Eve ignored the outstretched hand he offered her. If she touched him, she just might jump him, no matter how upsetting his words were to her. He expected her to leave everything she knew behind? Everyone?

"Of course."

"We can't just leave like this." Eve swept her arms out to the sides, "And what about all of these women. What exactly is going on?"

"Everything will be explained. First, we must leave your atmosphere. I've been circling your planet for too long as it is."

Taliff turned his back and headed for the door. "Come, there is much for you to see." When he reached the door, he stopped and extended his hand once again. His eyes were patient now, as if he knew just what it would cost her to place her hand in his.

Eve swallowed the spit in her mouth and shifted from foot to foot. Almost involuntarily, she approached him. After only a slight hesitation, she squared her shoulders and placed her hand in his. She closed her eyes to center herself, then opened them to find him staring at her. She closed the last remaining distance between them. Her last thought before she exited the room was, *let my new life begin.*

TALIFF COULDN'T BELIEVE THE faith she'd placed in him. When he had first walked into the room and saw her, his heart stopped. For one second it stuttered to a standstill. Her beauty mesmerized him.

She was so small and delicate compared to his massive build. The stasis chamber looked half-empty with her lying in it. Her eyes were the brilliant amber of the crystals in the Mating Chamber on *Chantrea*. But it was her wild mane of hair that had stopped him in his tracks. The same red-gold as his own—it was a sign that they were destined mates. A matched pair in every way. To have his body's reaction confirmed left him speechless and a little humbled. What had he done in his life to deserve such a treasure?

He couldn't have stopped his cock from rising even if he wanted to. He wanted, no needed, to show her what effect she had on him. She needed to understand that she was his. That could wait though. He didn't want to ruin the peace they'd seemed to establish so easily. There would be time enough later to tell her what she was to him, to explain the mating and all it entailed.

He looked down at her hand clasped in his, heaved a sigh of relief and tugged her out into the hall.

"What about them?" She pointed back toward the room they'd just left. "You can't just leave all those women in there. They deserve to know what's happening."

"All of the women aboard are aware of the situation. Most have accepted that their lives are to be different. Those who wouldn't accept their circumstances, who caused mischief and dissent among the women, are in the stasis chambers."

"How many women do you have on board?"

"Including you, forty-six." Taliff waited for her to digest the information he'd already given her before he continued to speak. "Only those I transported after you are unaware of what is going on. It will be your job to tell them."

Eve stopped walking and pulled on his hand, until he, too, stopped. He looked down at her, waiting for her to say what was on her mind. He didn't mind that she had a strong will, but she needed to learn to show it only in private. The women on his planet were submissive and it appeared his mate was anything but. It would be his pleasure to teach her all about submission and all that it involved.

"My job? Why the hell is it my job?"

"Would you rather I told them, the stranger who abducted them? I assumed you'd want to spare them as much trauma as you could. Am I wrong?"

"No, dammit. But some of those women you took don't exactly look upon me with favor."

Taliff nodded, then pulled on her hand. It was time they started their voyage back. He didn't know his mate, her likes, her dislikes, but perhaps she'd enjoy the view of her planet from this vantage point. It truly was a beautiful sight. "Come. There's something I want to show you."

Taliff was conscious of Eve the whole way to the command deck. The mating scent wrapped around his balls and squeezed. If he didn't get to sink himself into her soon, the pain might kill him. How was she going to react once he showed her where she'd be sleeping? Would she scream at him, demand her own quarters? Would she willingly stay with him?

He hoped to hell she stayed with him without having to beg for her company. Should he tell her why she'd be sharing his living quarters, would that make a difference? He usually wasn't so uncertain, but this was completely new territory for him. He'd just have to improvise.

"So, where is the rest of your crew? We've been walking these corridors for ten minutes and I have yet to spot anyone."

"There is no crew. The ship can pilot itself."

"No crew at all? With all these women on board? Aren't you the lucky one," she scoffed.

"Don't make assumptions on my character based on what you've known on your planet. The men of *Chantrea* don't treat their women how your men have treated you."

"I'll believe that when I see it."

"Yes, you will." He'd show her personally just how well a real *Lionese* man treated his mate. She'd have no doubt just how cherished and desired she was.

Taliff ignored the odd look she gave him and stopped in front of the portal to the command deck. "Watch me, Eve. You need to know how to get in here if there is an emergency."

He once again placed his palm on the identity pad, leaned in to the laser recognition device to have his identity confirmed and gave his authorization code. "Authorization code Shi'Lan seven-six-three-four-eight-seven."

"Authorization approved."

"Thank you, *Shoshoni*." Taliff turned to his mate and gave her a long look. "If you need anything, just speak aloud and the computer will hear you."

"*Shoshoni?*"

"Yes, Sir?"

"Eve Roberts is to have full access to this ship and all its systems."

"Access granted."

From the stunned look on her face, Eve was just beginning to realize how much power she now wielded. He once again tugged on her hand and pulled her over to the viewport. "This is what I want you to see."

Taliff watched as Eve saw her former home in the distance. "*Shoshoni*, engage engines. Change current heading and plot a course for *Chantrea*."

"Course plotted."

It filled him with a great deal of satisfaction when he finally uttered, "Take us home."

While the planet Earth faded in the distance, Taliff took the next step in binding his mate to his side. The time had come to perform the hand fasting. "Would you like to see our quarters?" What would she say? All he could do was hold his breath and await her answer.

Chapter Three

"Our quarters?" She couldn't possibly have heard him right. He expected her to share living space with him. Eve was torn. Her inner slut was yelling, *Yes! Yes!* while her sensible self wondered just how she'd gotten into this situation.

What should she say? Hell, what should she do?

"Yes. Your place is with me now."

Glancing at the viewscreen on the bridge, Eve stood mesmerized by the sight of the Earth as it hung in space. As the ship moved out of orbit, she watched as her home grew smaller and smaller, until eventually it disappeared altogether. Reluctantly, she turned to face Taliff, knowing that there was no way she could talk to him without facing him. "I think you should explain that to me."

"I'd be happy to—in our quarters."

There didn't seem to be a way to get around the fact that she would have to follow him to his room. Did she really want to fight him on this? She honestly didn't know.

Well, she wouldn't find out anything just standing here. "Lead the way."

As they made their way through the ship to Taliff's cabin, Eve kept her mind blank. It was easy to do, what with her having a splendid view of his ass the whole way there. His jeans hugged him so perfectly it left nothing to the imagination. By the time they reached the room, Eve couldn't say what route they'd taken or how long she'd stared at his bottom.

She was in no shape to have a serious conversation while practically sitting on the man's bed. There had to be a better place to go. She was afraid she'd tackle him if she got within five feet of his bedroom.

Before she could protest their destination, Taliff stopped in front of a silver door, keyed in a code on the lock pad and held the door open for her. She couldn't tell the difference between it and any other door on this ship. If she stayed here with him, how was she ever going to find it again?

Eve shook her head. Now wasn't the time for her thoughts to wander. Whatever Taliff had to say must be damned important if it had to take place in private. Praying she wasn't about to do something foolish, she stepped past Taliff and entered his cabin.

She jumped at the snick of the door locking shut. It sounded ominous to her in the heavy silence of the room. She glanced around the room, looking everywhere but at him.

Some sort of black silk fabric covered the walls, hiding the steel beneath. Bookshelves filled to capacity lined three of the four walls of the sitting room. A doorway led off to the right. The bedroom perhaps. Two sofas sat in the middle of the cabin, facing each other. A coffee table made of some silvery wood material lay in between them. In the far corner, sat a table and matching chairs. Overall, it looked quite homey.

The silence stretched, becoming painful in its intensity. She couldn't stall any longer. She'd hear whatever he had to tell her and make an informed decision. She turned to face him for the first time since she entered the room. Her eyes glazed over. Her heart stuttered.

A god stood before her.

A very naked god.

"What are you doing?" she screeched. Her composure disappeared. What was she supposed to do now? She couldn't have a serious conversation with him with his shaft standing at attention, bobbing against his rock hard stomach. Moreover, he was huge. Hung like a horse, huge. It could have its own zip code. No way in hell would that thing fit inside her.

"I'm following the traditions of our people."

"By getting naked?" Did she sound as prudish as she thought she did? But holy crap, what else could she say?

"It is customary for a mated pair to spend their bond night unclothed. Do earthlings not have such a custom?"

"Uh, not exactly." And then what he said hit her. "What do you mean, a mated pair? I'm not mated. We're not mated." She didn't care if her voice rose with every syllable. She would have her say in this.

He laughed—a full-bodied belly laugh. His dick bobbed with every chuckle. She had to force herself not to watch. She couldn't afford the distraction.

"Of course we are."

"What, I don't have any say in this?"

"Do you deny the heat you feel when you are near me?"

"No, but that doesn't mean we're mates. Besides, the *Lionese* don't mate."

"No, the *Lionese* on Earth don't mate. *Chantrean Lionese* take one mate during a lifetime. Once mated, we seek solace only in her arms. Only my mate can carry my child. Only you can carry my child."

Eve backed up a step, turned away. She needed to think. What Taliff spoke of was exactly what she'd always wanted for herself. How could she turn her back on this? On him? But what if it was all a lie? Then what? She'd be stuck in a relationship she'd never be able to escape.

She hugged her arms to her body, hunched her shoulders and dropped her chin to her chest. What should she do? "How do I know you're telling the truth?" she whispered.

"Why would I lie?"

"I don't know." And she really didn't. It wasn't as if he didn't have his pick of women on board the ship, even before he had taken her from her life.

"Then there's the answer you seek. Turn around, Eve. There's no need to hide your fear from me."

Eve shrugged her shoulders, took a deep breath and turned to face him. Yes, he was still naked. She was afraid of that. "I'm not afraid exactly."

He quirked a brow in response.

"Okay, I'm a little scared. I never wanted a mate. I don't want to be treated like I'm nothing but a broodmare while my mate screws everyone with two legs and breasts."

"The only way you'll know if I speak the truth is if you let me prove it to you, Eve."

"I don't know if I can."

"Then we'll take this one step at a time. You live with me as my mate. And when you feel you can trust me, trust in us, we'll go through the formal bond ceremony in the Mating Chamber on *Chantrea*, agreed?"

She thought about it for another minute, before coming to a decision. Rather than tell him her choice with words, she'd do so with her actions. With infinite slowness, Eve slipped the top button of her shirt free from its buttonhole. She worked her way down, letting her top gape open to give him a small peek at what he would get by mating with her.

She couldn't be more nervous if she tried. The one time she'd been naked in front of a man, it'd been full dark and clouds obscured the moon.

She could feel Taliff's eyes burn as they watched her every movement. It made her feel sexy, desired. When all the buttons were undone, she shrugged, letting the shirt fall to the floor in a heap.

Her eyes locked onto his. She licked her lips. His eyes dilated and he gasped in response. She'd never acted so brazenly before. It was liberating. She had Taliff's full attention. Slowly she reached in front of her and popped the front clasp of her bra. Her breasts spilled free from their confinement.

She allowed her gaze to roam his body as she worked the button on her jeans. His cock bobbed under the attention. Pre-cum leaked from its tip. She gripped the edge of her waistband, eased the jeans down past her ass and let them fall to the floor in a puddle. She never wore underwear so she stood in front of him bare.

Eve took the last of her courage in her hands, stepped over the pile of clothes and held her hand out to Taliff. "Make love to me, Taliff."

"It will be my pleasure, mate."

She waited for Taliff to close the gap between him. Her courage only went so far. The next move was his.

She didn't have to wait long.

Instead of pulling her in his arms as she expected, he grabbed her hands in both of his and gave a slight tug. "Follow me. I have a surprise for you."

Hand in hand, the pair walked toward the arched doorway on the right. "This leads to the sleeping quarters and bathing chamber."

Eve licked her lips. Her pulse jumped. If what Taliff said were true, a real *Lionese* man would finally make love to her. But he didn't head for the massive bed that took of the majority of the room's floor space. Instead, he led her to a smaller door and into a hedonist's paradise.

Eve gasped. She'd never seen such a beautiful room in her life. The chamber was easily twice the size of the bedroom. The bathing pool dominated the room but it was in no way the centerpiece of it. On a raised dais, lay a pallet covered in luxurious furs and decadent pillows of red and gold. Surrounded by candles, it, too, screamed luxury. But it was the walls that held her spellbound. Cream-colored tiles covered every square inch of the walls and on each one, there was a pictograph etched in some kind of red dye.

"Is that the history of your people?"

"Our people," he murmured. "And yes it is."

She heard the pride in his voice and wondered what it would be like to grow up believing in the strength of your people. How would it feel to know your history and learn from your mistakes rather than repeat them?

"Will you teach me about the tiles? About what they say, what they mean?"

"Of course. I'll teach you all you need to know."

Eve wasn't sure why that statement sounded ominous to her, but it did. She gave herself a mental shake. She wouldn't start this new relationship questioning the meaning behind his words. At least, not intentionally, she qualified. She wouldn't lie, even to herself.

"This room is breathtaking."

"I'm glad you like it. I spend much time in here on shorter voyages. In here, I feel closer to *Chantrea*. Come, let us enjoy a bath together." With her hand still clasped lightly in his, she followed where he led.

Everything about tonight seemed surreal. She'd been abducted, brought aboard a spaceship, told of her people's true origins and was about to become her kidnapper's mate. It sounded like a sci-fi based soap opera.

Already filled with steamy water, the sunken tub called to her more feminine side. She loved to take long baths after a stressful birthing. She'd had an especially difficult one just a few hours ago. It had been an eventful day to say the least and it wasn't over yet.

While she'd been lost in thought, Taliff had turned on the jets in the bath. It worked just like the hot tubs back home. Eve embraced this little piece of normality and stepped into the tub. Taliff stepped in right behind her.

She fidgeted, dropped her gaze and caught sight of his engorged cock. Her head snapped up and a blush spread across her body. She noticed the twinkle in Taliff's eyes and sighed. He was obviously trying not to laugh at her discomfort.

"Sit. Rest easy. Nothing will happen until you're ready."

Eve breathed a sigh of relief and sank into the deliciously warm water. Taliff moved up behind her, picked her up by the waist, moved to the bench seat and sat down with her atop his lap.

She squeaked, went to jump up. He caught her and eased her back in place. "I thought nothing would happen."

"I didn't say I wouldn't try and convince you."

"But..."

"No buts. You need to learn my body, get used to the feel of it pressed against yours."

Slowly, she eased back, rested her weight against him. His arms came up and wrapped around her, held her close to his heart. Her discomfort disappeared as they sat together and enjoyed the bubbling water. Her tense muscles relaxed. She curled into the curve of his body and his arms tightened around her.

Hesitantly, she said, "This is nice."

"Hmmm...yes it is."

His heartbeat throbbed against her ear. Its rhythm matched her own. "Why do our hearts beat the same?"

"I've told you this already. We're a genetically mated pair. Our bodies know this. Our souls will soon follow."

"You have such confidence."

"Of course."

Eve rubbed her cheek against his chest and started to purr. Embarrassed that she couldn't control her animal nature, she tried to sit up.

"I like to hear you purr. It proves you're feeling comfortable with me."

Taliff loosened his grip around her waist. One hand slid down her taut stomach to the swell of her hips. The gentle message sent currents of desire through her. Her thighs clenched. She could feel her clit swell. How could a simple touch inflame her body so easily?

Blood pounded in her veins, her knees trembled. Her entire body felt electrified. She began to shake as his hands drifted lower, over her mound. His fingers lightly brushed her clit and she arched against him. "Oh, God," she moaned.

"That's it. Just lay back and let me pleasure you."

The brush of his fingers against her pussy sent another jolt of pleasure through her. His other hand began an exploration of its own, lightly touching her hardened nipples, before it moved on. He picked up a lock of her hair and caressed it gently, used it to turn her head toward his.

He bent his head, looked into her eyes and paused as though asking permission to taste her. When she nodded her approval, his mouth covered hers. His kiss was surprisingly gentle.

Parting her lips, she raised herself to meet his kiss. Their tongues met, twined together in passion. She wrapped her arms around his neck, twisted her fingers into his hair and held on for dear life. Nothing in her life had prepared her for the feelings this man inspired in her. Her response to his touch shocked her. It was a kiss for her tired soul to sink into.

She couldn't take anymore. If he didn't make love to her soon she'd die. "Make love to me, Taliff. Please."

"As you wish."

With incredible ease, Taliff stood, wrapped her legs around his waist and carried her over to the pallet. Gently he eased her down on to the makeshift bed. His hands lightly traced a path across her skin. He bent his head, took a nipple in his mouth. She arched under his touch. Her body sang from the attention.

She wanted to touch him, to explore his body as he was exploring hers.

Just as she was reaching for him, an alarm blared through the cabin. The lights flickered.

Oh, God. This could not be happening.

"Commander Shi'Lan?"

Taliff rested his head against her chest, took a deep breath and answered the computer.

"Yes, *Shoshoni*. What has happened?"

"We are under attack. You are needed on the Command Deck immediately."

"Understood and acknowledged."

Taliff looked at her with regret and eased his body away from hers. "I need you to keep the women calm. Can you do this for me?"

She nodded. "Just find out what the hell is going on. They'll want to know. And I really want to finish what we started," she admitted.

"I'll walk you to the common room. You should find the women there."

As they walked to the sitting room, Eve noticed their scattered clothing. She bent over, went to reach for her clothes.

"What are you doing?"

"I'm getting dressed."

"No. You must remain unclothed until the next rising. Remember?"

"You have got to be kidding me?"

Taliff shook his head, reached for her hand and dragged her reluctant body out into the hall. How in the hell was she going to face a bunch of strangers butt ass naked?

Chapter Four

Five steps outside their door, Eve skidded to a stop. "No. I won't go in there naked, and dammit, neither will you."

"Tradition states..."

"Look, we're under attack, the women don't know me and I'll be damned if they'll use my nakedness as a reason to gossip."

"We don't have time for this, Eve. I must appear on the command deck now."

"And how intimidating are you going to appear to the people who fired on this ship with your dick hanging out?"

"That isn't the point."

"Well, it's *my* point." After giving Taliff a pointed stare, she slipped from his grasp and turned back to the door.

It didn't take Taliff long to respond to her taunt. Out of the corner of her eye, she watched as he entered his security code into the lock pad. "You won't always get your way, Eve."

She blew out a breath and nodded, fully aware she'd just overcome her first hurdle of the relationship. Taliff could and would bend when she felt strongly about something. Perhaps this mate thing wouldn't be so terrible after all. Especially if it involved some more body-on-body action.

As soon as the door slid open, she ran for the pile of scattered clothes. She really should be embarrassed about her apparent lack of morals, but she wasn't that big a hypocrite. Eve dressed quickly, careful not to let Taliff see her disappointment when he covered his own nudity. She had no idea why all she could seem to think about was raunchy, sweaty sex, but it appeared to be the case all the same.

Once dressed, she moved to the door to wait. She had pushed Taliff enough for one day. She wouldn't try his patience further by dallying.

Less than five minutes later, Eve stood in front of the Common Room door, alone. What should she say to the women? Hell, would they even listen to her? It wasn't as if Taliff had the time to introduce her to the group. He had just walked her to the door, squeezed her hand and taken off down the corridor. Not that she blamed him. He still needed to ascertain the nature of the threat.

"Computer?"

"Yes, Eve Roberts?"

"What is the proper protocol to assume the leadership mantle of the women here on board?"

"You must enter the Challenge Ring. There you must prove you're the best to lead by winning the challenge?"

"What's the challenge ring and how is a winner determined?"

"A Challenge Ring is an arena where challenges are fought in front of a panel of judges."

"And the winner is determined how, *Shoshoni*?"

"Two ways, Eve Roberts. The victor is determined by drawing first blood or the death of the opponent as a result of the challenge."

"Thank you, *Shoshoni*."

Well, no sense standing outside the door like an ass. With more grit than courage, Eve punched the code she'd watched Taliff use and opened the door.

Gathered around the table and scattered on furniture throughout the room were dozens of women. They varied in age from late teens to early forties, and came in every shape, size and color. No one could say that Taliff made his choices based on any certain characteristic. In fact, it looked as though he gone of his way to choose woman of every nationality on the planet.

Eve observed them unnoticed for nearly a minute before a girl no older than nineteen looked her way. The teen wasn't a great beauty, but her jade eyes and strawberry blonde hair gave her a delicate, ethereal glow. "Hi. I'm Amy. You must have come aboard the last time they locked us in our quarters. I'm so happy to see a new face in here," she gushed.

Taken aback by the young girl's enthusiasm, Eve nodded, speech beyond her right now. She'd expected to find the women traumatized, or at least worried about their current situation. These women looked excited about their journey and not in the least concerned about their fate.

What had Taliff told them? Hell, *she* didn't even know why he kidnapped them except that it was out of desperation. She should have asked more questions, dammit, instead of jumping him as soon as they were alone. That was what she got for letting her hormones rule her brain. Now she was at a disadvantage and among a pride of women that was the last place you wanted to find yourself.

Time to assert her dominance over the others, otherwise she'd find herself at the bottom of the social structure. And at the bottom, she'd be no help to Taliff or the women. Eve stiffened her spine and turned back to Amy. "Who seems to be in charge of the women?"

"What do ya mean?"

"Out of all the women in here, who has stepped in as the spokeswoman for you?"

"Oh, you mean Myra the bitch."

"I take it she doesn't treat you well?" Not that she really needed the answer. She could tell by the way Amy's hair lifted from her shoulders and the pure venom in her voice that she sat at the bottom of the food chain. It wasn't a comfortable position to be in, especially for one so young and unable to truly defend herself.

"You could say that. It's like I'm her personal servant or something. She won't even try to figure out the food machines, just orders me and the other girls to fetch for her."

Eve nodded, fully aware of the attitude some wannabe alphas use to treat others. She wouldn't allow it to continue. But first she had to make her stand, prove her dominance to Myra and the others. Then she'd set things right.

"Which one is she?"

Amy turned toward the crowd gathered around the table and pointed toward the *Lionese* woman sitting at its head. She should have known. The woman's sense of superiority wafted off of her like cheap perfume. It was downright nauseating.

Blonde, blue-eyed and buxom, the middle-aged woman sat in her chair as though she owned the world itself. The others sat around her, some in awe, others with fear etched across their features. Yes, something definitely needed to change around here. Miss Myra's reign of terror was at an end.

"Stay back, Amy, this might get a tad nasty."

"No. You might need me...or something." Her voice trailed off. She couldn't blame Amy for her nervousness.

Eve didn't argue with her, simply nodded instead and headed toward the crowd paying tribute to the alpha from hell. She waited until she became the center of everyone's attention before she addressed Myra. "I believe you're sitting in my seat."

Dead silence greeted her statement and then a feline snarl reverberated throughout the room. "You think you can challenge me?" Myra snickered. "You're nothing but another little girl playing grown-up. Talk to me after you've won a few challenges."

She couldn't help but laugh. "Lady, I'm just going to skip to the head of the line—unless you think you can't handle a little upstart like me."

Apparently tired of the insults, Myra pushed to her feet and towered over everyone at the table. "I think you might want to watch what you say to me. I will not back down from a challenge."

Eve knew it was impossible for the alpha to back down now that she issued a challenge, no matter her posturing. Until settled, Myra's orders were questionable. By challenging her openly, Eve prevented her from using unscrupulous methods to win the confrontation.

"Anytime, anyplace."

Myra paused, looked around the table at the expectant faces. She'd let her mouth get her into a situation she couldn't talk herself out of. She knew it, Eve knew it and every woman in the room knew it.

She waited until it was obvious Myra had made her decision, then said over her shoulder to Amy, "Push the tables and sofas against the walls. I have something to take care of." She made sure not to break eye contact with Myra. It wouldn't do to leave herself open to attack because of carelessness on her part.

Within minutes, the center of the room stood bare as the others in the room pitched in to clear a space for the challenge. Excited chatter filled the room. It wasn't very often a newcomer succeeded in taking control of a pride. Eve heard the gossip fly around the room as speculation spread. That was fine by her so long as no one interfered.

While she waited for Myra to come forward to the makeshift Challenge Ring, Eve started to undress. It seemed she didn't need to come to the room with clothes on after all. At least this way no one had the opportunity to see Taliff without his. Just the thought of the size of his cock as it bobbed in front of her was enough to make her wet.

By the time Myra entered the ring, Eve stood in proper battle-ready stance—unclothed, with her legs spread shoulder width apart, her hands down by her sides, palms outward. This wasn't her first battle and it sure wouldn't be her last. Myra underestimated her abilities when she called her a little girl and she was about to prove it.

Once the pair stood ready before the crowd, Amy stepped into the center of the ring. "The rules are as follows. No one will shift until told to. The person who draws first blood will assume the leadership mantle until we reach *Chantrea*. There are no appeals."

Amy turned to both of the women. "Do you comply?"

Eve nodded. "Yes."

"Yes, I agree," Myra sneered, her gaze locked on Eve. "Be prepared to lose a paw, bitch."

The threat meant nothing to her, so Eve ignored it. In the end, there would be only one winner and it wouldn't be the cocky beauty queen with entitlement issues.

Amy stepped from the center of the ring. Above the din of the crowd, Eve waited until she heard her say, "You may shift." She didn't stop to think, just called to her other self. Heat rushed through her body. Her heart stuttered, then increased its pace. Her form shimmered. Brilliant white light shone through her pores. In a sudden flash of brightness, Eve disappeared. A lioness now stood in her place.

With the signal given, Eve expected Myra to attack fast and dirty. She didn't disappoint. Before she could shake off the effects of the change, Myra came in low, her claws extended. Eve leapt over the attacking cat and landed ten feet away.

Myra, off balance, tried to swing around to lash at Eve again. By the time she faced Eve, it was too late. Eve launched herself at Myra, raking her left side with her claws. Blood dripped from the deep furrows and pooled onto the oatmeal colored carpet.

The crowd grew quiet. Eve shook her head and roared. As she padded out of the Challenge Ring, Amy's voice echoed around the room. "Look out!"

Before she could turn and face the defeated feline, Myra lunged for her throat. She tried to dodge Myra's gaping jaws but the warning came too late. Eve shook her head from side to side but the lioness held on. Blood dripped down her throat and coated her fur. Weakness spread through her limbs. Her thoughts grew sluggish as more blood rushed from her wounds.

Eve knew that to defeat the attacking cat, she needed leverage. In a sudden move, Eve dropped to the floor and rolled onto her back. Though it left her belly exposed, it also gave her the leverage to use her hind legs to thrust Myra away.

She knew that she could not show Myra mercy. It would undermine her authority with the other women if she didn't retaliate. Myra scrambled to her feet and leapt through the air. Eve was not about to let the treacherous bitch pin her down. She met Myra's leap with one of her own. Rather than swipe at the lioness, Eve clamped her fangs on her throat and dragged her down to the blood-soaked floor.

Myra tried to fight her off, twisting savagely in an effort to toss Eve away. All she succeeded in doing was sealing her own fate that much quicker. With no choice left, Eve pinned Myra to the ground, using her own body weight to prevent the cat from bucking her off. When the cat tried to swipe at Eve with her paw, she bit down on it, severing it from her leg.

Disgusted that it had come to such drastic action, Eve spit the paw to the floor and padded out of the ring. She didn't even bother to look at the defeated lioness. The others could clean up the mess. As far as she was concerned, Myra had brought this upon herself.

Eve limped over to her pile of clothes. She needed to think and she couldn't do that in here. There was nothing to celebrate, nothing to roar her satisfaction over. Taliff would probably be pissed when he found out she had to take the other woman's paw, but what other choice did she have? Perhaps she could have showed more mercy and given her death instead. If she had to do it over again though, she would still make the same decision. Her mate would just have to deal with it.

Although weak, Eve still managed to gather enough energy inside her to initiate the change. Heat raced through her, her image grew translucent, and in a flash, Eve the woman crouched over her pile of clothes.

She reached into the pile and grabbed the first thing her hand touched. Eve stood to her full height and looked over the room. Other than the two women who had gone to Myra's aid, all eyes were on her. It wasn't a comfortable feeling.

She slid her legs into her jeans. She could barely get her fingers to obey her command as they fumbled with the zipper. She was almost too weak to bend over for her shirt. Amy was there with it in her hand before she even made the attempt. "Here, let me help you."

She nodded to Amy, grateful for the help. Once dressed, she walked over to the beaten woman sprawled on the bloody carpet and looked down on her. "You ever try to challenge me again and I will do more than take a paw. It will cost you your life. Is that understood?"

Eve didn't wait for an answer. She turned her back on Myra and walked over to the group of people gathered around the conference table, in effect showing everyone gathered in the room she felt no fear of her defeated opponent. With all the poise and determination she could muster, Eve sat down at the head of the table in the chair Myra had claimed as hers.

God, she hurt. She needed to get this over with and have her and Myra's wounds tended before they bled to death.

She looked over the women, her eyes steady and sure. She could show no signs of her ever increasing weakness. "Do any others wish to challenge me?"

When no one responded, Eve looked to Amy, then met each woman's gaze with her own. "Amy will be my Beta, my second in command. There will be no discussion about my choice. You will all return to your quarters until told otherwise."

When no one moved, Eve straightened her shoulders. "Did no one hear me? Move. Now."

The women scrambled to their feet and headed for the door, all but the ones still crouched over Myra. "You two have trouble understanding or do you need help in that regard like your friend there?" she said, her gaze quickly flicking toward Myra, then back.

The women looked across the room to where Eve still sat. She could feel the hate they felt for her like a slap. It seared her with its intensity, but she wouldn't let that faze her. It appeared she had more than one enemy aboard ship to watch her back for.

She knew she'd get no verbal response from the women so she addressed her question to the computer. "*Shoshoni?*"

"Yes, Eve Roberts?"

"Just call me Eve, *Shoshoni*."

"What is it you require, Eve?"

"Where is the infirmary? Myra and I are injured and in need of medical care."

After a few seconds, the ship's computer responded. "I have taken control of the lighting along the floor of the corridors. Follow the red lights. They will lead you to the infirmary."

"Thank you, *Shoshoni*. Oh, and, *Shoshoni*?"

"Yes, Eve?"

"I would prefer that Taliff not find out about this yet, if it's all the same to you."

"It will be as you request. For now."

Eve looked over at Amy. The computer's implied threat was not lost on either woman. She just hoped Taliff was too busy with his own concerns to worry over her until after her wounds were treated.

Chapter Five

By the time Taliff made it to the deck that housed the Command Center, nearly ten minutes passed. In that time, he felt the ship shimmy nearly half a dozen times as the defensive shields reflected the Laser-Cannon fire. He should have ensured Eve would be fine without him, but he had to worry about the safety of all the women, not just his mate.

The ship shimmied again. The shields wouldn't hold out against the attack much longer. He ran down the last two corridors, rushed through the security station and entered the Command Center just as another blast rocked the ship.

"*Shoshoni?*"

"Yes, Commander Shi'Lan?"

"Open the front viewport. I want to take a look at the bastards firing on us."

"Yes, Commander."

Taliff watched as the seemingly solid wall turned translucent, then clear. He should have showed Eve this. She had no idea just how advanced the *Chantrean* civilization had become. This ship had the very latest in hologram technology. In fact, he couldn't wait to show her the Pleasure Chamber so she could experience that technology for herself.

"Have you identified the ship, *Shoshoni?*"

"Yes, Commander Shi'Lan. It's the *Warrior.*"

"The *Warrior?* You're sure?" Stunned that one of their own ships would attack and without provocation, Taliff closed his eyes. It saddened him that treason entered the hearts of his people.

"Have they tried to establish communication?"

"No, Sir."

"Open a communication channel. Tell Commander Dav'Ren to cease his attack or I will retaliate. He has two minutes to stand down or I will carry out my threat."

"Yes, Commander." There was a minute pause while the computer did as requested. "Message relayed."

When a full minute passed, Taliff asked, "Is there a response from Commander Dav'Ren?"

"No, Sir. What are your orders?"

"Do you have sample DNA from all of the officers on board the *Warrior*, *Shoshoni*?"

"Yes, Commander."

"Good. Locate Commander Dav'Ren's DNA signature and transport him to the confinement cells on deck ten. If the ship continues to attack, transport the rest of the officers to the vacant cells. Allow no contact between the prisoners."

"Yes, Sir. Commander Dav'Ren is in holding cell Omega. It is shielded to prevent the *Warrior* from attempting retrieval."

"Very good, *Shoshoni*. I'm heading down to deck ten. If the ship continues to fire on us once her officers transport to our holding cells, open fire. Blast it from the sky if you must."

"Understood, Commander Shi'Lan."

As he started to walk from the room, Taliff stopped and turned back to the viewport. "Send the following message, *Shoshoni*. 'Your Commander is my prisoner. The charge is High Treason. Cease fire before your ship is destroyed. This is your last warning.'"

Taliff shook his head and left the Command Deck. What could possibly prompt his best friend into committing such a foolish act? Why attack one of their own ships? It made no sense.

He'd left *Chantrea* many moons ago. Anything could have happened since then and they wouldn't be within communication range with *Chantrea* for another two moon cycles. Taliff worried over his brother's political situation the entire trip down to deck ten to the holding cells.

Maybe Shivo Dav'Ren could explain why he'd attacked *The Wanderer*. Taliff doubted the reason would stay his friend's execution though. He'd signed his own death warrant by attacking a member of the ruling house of *Chantrea*. At this point, Taliff could do nothing to save him.

Five minutes later, he stood outside Commander Dav'Ren's cell. His longtime friend gripped the bars. His eyes blazed his defiance. What happened to the man he'd looked up to for most of his life? Five years his senior, Shivo was like an older brother to Taliff. In fact, Shivo talked Hunter into letting him tag along on their adventures. When Hunter heard of Shivo's betrayal, it would crush him. Taliff sighed and then faced his friend.

Taliff held Shivo's gaze until the traitor lowered his head. What could he say to the man? He couldn't consider their shared personal history. He needed answers. "Why, Shivo? You're my family."

"Ha! I was never your family. I'm nothing but an insignificant man you allowed into your lives to show others you didn't think better of yourselves. But we know different, don't we, Taliff? You always have and always will think you're better than those beneath you."

Frustrated, Taliff ran his fingers through his hair. "How could you possibly believe that any of the royal family feels such a thing? You have been a part of our lives since we were boys."

"Why else would Hunter send you, the head of his personal security, on a mission such as this? Your family and the Council want the women for themselves and to hell with the rest of us who are without mates."

"Even if that were so, you cannot justify the actions you took. I have no choice but to return you to *Chantrea* where you will be executed, Shivo."

"That's what you think. You've underestimated me for the last time, Taliff."

He quirked an eyebrow at Shivo's boast. "What do you think you can possibly do while locked behind unbreakable, platinum-alloy bars and a high-energy containment field?"

"Only this." Shivo smirked, then quickly pressed a button on what Taliff had initially assumed was just a timepiece.

Before Taliff could react, Shivo disappeared and in his place sat a neutron bomb, something that his people banned centuries ago when their world had turned toward peaceful coexistence rather than forceful negotiations. "*Shoshoni?*"

"I am aware of the unauthorized transports. Am attempting to remove the weapon from the ship, however, the *Warrior* has sent a computer virus through the communication relay and it is making it difficult to get a lock on the weapon."

"I don't care how you get a lock on it or where you send it, but do it, and do it now."

"Working, Commander."

He watched as the timer on the bomb started to tick down. "Cancel previous order, *Shoshoni*. I have a plan. Drop the containment field and open the cell."

"Yes, Commander."

The shimmering energy field disappeared just as the cell door slid open. He ran to the cylindrical bomb, lifted it into his arms and exited the cell. "Lock on to my transmitter, *Shoshoni*. Transport me to the nearest airlock."

"Understood. Standby for transfer."

Taliff closed his eyes while he waited in the middle of the penal deck for *Shoshoni* to transport him to his destination. A sudden wave of heat seared his skin. When he next opened his eyes, he stood in the center of the airlock with the bomb clutched in his hands.

He glanced at the timer and swallowed the fear that bubbled in his throat. He placed the bomb in the center of the room and quickly backed out. After he secured the airlock doors that led to the interior of the ship, he entered the code to release the outer doors and watched as the bomb drifted into space.

No sooner had the doors closed than the ship rocked from the force of the explosion. Taliff had to grab the wall to keep his feet from sliding out beneath him. He needed to get back to the Command Deck and he didn't have time to race down the corridors to get there. "*Shoshoni*, transport me directly to the Command Center. Shivo won't miss this opportunity to attack now that his primary plan failed. Also, as soon as time permits, find out how Shivo managed to get a locator beacon signal through the containment field. I'll need an answer right away if we are to counteract such a scenario in the future."

"Understood, Commander. Prepare for transfer."

Once again, heat seared his skin as the computer transported him directly inside the Command Center of the ship. "*Shoshoni*, blast the *Warrior* out of space. I want nothing but space junk left when you're through."

"Yes, Commander Shi'Lan."

He watched dispassionately as the green laser-cannon fire targeted the enemy ship. For several minutes, the ships exchanged fire, each trying its best to destroy the other. How Commander Dav'Ren hoped to keep the women to himself if he destroyed the *Wanderer*, Taliff had no idea. Perhaps Shivo's goal was to disable the *Wanderer* long enough to remove the women before he destroyed it and Taliff. Well, it wouldn't happen.

"*Shoshoni?*"

"Yes, Commander?"

"I need you to target the Command Deck of the *Warrior*, specifically the main viewport. It's the weakest part of the ship's infrastructure."

"Targeting the viewport now."

More laser fire hit the enemy ship. Taliff hoped his plan worked because the energy in his own shields was drained to a dangerously low level and continued to drop with each successful blast from the *Warrior*. Until Dav'Ren and his ship were destroyed, Taliff could not divert energy from the weapons to re-power the shields.

Commander Dav'Ren's ship managed to get off another shot. It hit the *Wanderer* with enough force that Taliff lost his footing. "*Shoshoni?*"

"Yes, Commander?"

"What is our shield strength down to?"

"Our shields have dropped to below ten percent of their maximum strength."

"*Shoshoni*, pull the rest of the energy from the shields and increase weapon strength. I want that ship destroyed before it takes us with it."

"Complying. Energy transfer complete."

"Focus all weapons, both lasercCannon fire and our entire supply of neutron torpedoes on the Command Deck of that ship."

"Weapons ready."

"Fire all weapons, *Shoshoni*."

"Weapons locked on enemy vessel. Weapons away."

Taliff looked on as the weapons converged on the *Warrior's* Command Deck. Blast after blast rocked the ship. Its defense shields wavered, then fell. Several torpedoes blasted a hole through the ship's thin metal skin. The vacuum of space continued the damage the torpedoes started as it ripped the ship to shreds. An explosion from deep inside the enemy ship sent a shock wave that rocked the *Wanderer*.

"*Shoshoni?*"

"Yes, Commander?"

"Redirect power from weapons to shields. When that ship blows apart, I don't want to be caught in the crossfire."

"Energy transfer complete. Shields are at ninety percent power. Weapons power is at forty-five percent.

"Reverse the engines. Put as much space between our ships as possible."

"Yes, Commander."

Taliff felt the engines shift into reverse. He continued to watch through the viewport as the *Warrior* grew smaller as *Shoshoni* increased the difference between them. Seconds later, a massive explosion rippled through the crippled ship. It sent a colossal shock wave through space.

When Taliff's ship passed through the shock wave, he peered out of the viewport to witness the evidence of the *Warrior's* destruction. All that was left of the *Warrior* were thousands of pieces of metal that drifted aimlessly through space, some no bigger than his fist. All that was left of his childhood hero was vapor dust and a slew of decades old memories.

A wave of sorrow washed over him. He would miss Shivo, though he'd never forgive him for his betrayal of their people. How many men just lost their lives because one man and his officers felt they should just take what they wanted? The saddest thing about the whole situation was that Shivo's mate might already be aboard the *Wanderer*. His own impatience caused his death. Impatience and envy.

"*Shoshoni*, did anyone manage to escape the ship before it exploded?"

"No, Commander. All escape shuttles were still aboard The *Warrior* prior to the explosion."

"And there is nowhere for the crew to transport either?"

"No, Sir. Not that I'm aware."

"Thank you, *Shoshoni*." Taliff leaned against the nearest bulkhead. His legs felt weak. His hands continued to shake. He didn't have time to rest, but he couldn't force himself to move. He needed to ensure his ship remained in top condition as Shivo might not have planned this attack alone. But what he really needed was his mate.

"*Shoshoni*?"

"Yes, Commander Shi'Lan?"

"What is the current location of Eve Roberts?"

"Eve Roberts is in the infirmary."

Taliff straightened from the wall, his every thought now focused on the welfare of his mate. "Why is she at the infirmary?"

"She is currently receiving medical treatment for several injuries, Sir."

"How is it that she received these injuries and why wasn't I informed right way?" Before *Shoshoni* could answer, he'd already started for the door. He needed to see Eve's injuries for himself. He'd find out later why his computer failed to notify him of her condition. "Never mind,

Shoshoni. I'll ask Eve myself. I'll be at the infirmary if there are any more problems."

"Yes, Commander."

Taliff made his way to the infirmary in record time. When he entered the room, his gaze immediately zeroed in on her location. He was by her side an instant later. Eve lay silent and unmoving in the enclosed bed. It looked similar to a newborn's incubator, but sized for adults. He watched as the computer continued to beep at him while it healed her injuries. Until the lid opened on its own, he wouldn't be able to see for himself just how grave her condition had truly been.

Movement to his right startled him from his silent contemplation. He'd been so focused on Eve, he didn't even realize others were in the room. Carelessness like that could get him killed.

A young girl, no more than nineteen if he remembered right, slowly approached him. She looked nervous. She probably thought he'd shoot the messenger, but he needed answers and she appeared to be the only one around who could give them to him. "What happened here?"

Several times she seemed to open her mouth to speak, but each time she shut it just as quickly. Finally, it looked as if she'd figured out what to tell him because she straightened her shoulders and walked right up to him. A *Lionese* woman, confident that she held all the power, now replaced the nervous teen. It was a remarkable transformation.

"Eve received several injuries in the Challenge Ring. Your computer showed us the way here and told me what to do to ensure all her wounds were healed properly."

"Why was she in the Challenge Ring to begin with?"

"Eve felt the only way she'd be heard and obeyed was if she took over leadership of the pride. Myra did not want to give up her place and issued a formal challenge. After Eve defeated Myra, the lioness attacked Eve, hence her current injuries."

"She attacked while Eve's back was turned?"

"Yes. I tried to warn Eve, but wasn't quick enough."

"Where is Myra now?"

"I had her sent to her chambers once the Medical Unit released her."

"What injuries did she sustain?"

"Eve took her left paw in the battle."

Taliff nodded, satisfied with the girl's answers. "By the way, what's your name?"

"Amy."

"Thank you for taking care of Eve for me, Amy." Taliff heard the tonal sequence that indicated the patient had been healed and bent over the unit just as the lid swung open. He watched as Eve's eyelids flickered, then finally opened.

He didn't even give her the opportunity to speak, just lifted her out of the bed and started toward the door. He looked down into his mate's face and said, "You and I have to talk."

"Oh, hell," Eve muttered and promptly closed her eyes as he carried her down the corridor to their rooms.

Chapter Six

Eve looked up at Taliff as he carried her down the hallway. Her heart lurched. A brief shiver rippled through her as she witnessed the tenderness and worry etched on his features. It must have terrified him to find her lying motionless inside the Medical Unit with no knowledge of the seriousness of her injuries.

Though his concern was evident, she didn't imagine it would prevent him from demanding answers from her. What could she say to him? How could she justify her actions? She had maimed another woman he was responsible for. How would he ever forgive her? Eve chewed her bottom lip with her teeth. What would happen now?

To Eve, it didn't take very long to get to their quarters. She couldn't tell if he rushed through the halls because he needed to vent his anger in private or because she'd scared him so badly that he needed to get her alone to see for himself that she had come out of the fight with just minor damage.

Taliff managed to open the lock to their door without so much as a jostle to her. She tilted her head back to peer at his face. Why hadn't he said anything since he lifted her into his arms and stalked off with her? If his intent was to make her nervous, his methods were quite effective.

Rather than put her down once they entered their quarters, he headed toward the sleeping chamber. Only once he stood at the foot of their bed, did he let her slide down the length of his body.

The rigid length of his cock brushed her belly as she slowly slid her feet to the floor. Her cunt clenched in response to his blatant arousal.

He tilted his head to the side and studied her for a moment. Then ever so slowly he lifted his hand and ran it through the length of her hair. The gentle movement brought tears to her eyes. "Are you all right,

Eve?"

Eve blinked back the tears that hovered on her lashes. His voice dripped with love and shook with worry. It moved her as nothing else had in a long time. How could his feelings, his concerns become important to her so quickly? She couldn't claim to be in love with him, but his opinion of her mattered and she would do just about anything to ensure his positive feelings never changed.

"I'm fine. I didn't mean to worry you, Taliff."

He continued to look down at her and, all the while, ran his fingers through her hair in soothing strokes. "What happened, Eve? You can't put yourself in danger this way." Raw hurt glimmered in his golden eyes.

Her gaze darted nervously back and forth. How to explain her actions so he'd understand? He stared back as he waited silently. She licked her lips, shuffled from foot to foot, before she finally looked into his patience-filled eyes. "I had no choice, Taliff. I needed to assert dominance and after she lost in the Challenge Ring, she attacked after I turned my back."

"So you took her paw?"

Afraid she'd see condemnation in his eyes, she lowered her gaze to the floor. "Yes, it was either her paw or her life. Maybe I should have killed her outright, but what lesson would that have taught the others?"

Taliff gently raised her chin with his finger. "You did the right thing, *moya*."

She wanted to sigh in relief, but something he'd just said caught her attention. She tilted her head in confusion. "What does *moya* mean?"

Taliff flushed. His golden brown skin took on a rosy hue. "It roughly translates into 'my love'."

Eve didn't know what to say in response to his endearment so she went back to the previous topic. "I really am fine, Taliff."

"I'd like to see that for myself, if you don't mind. Besides, we're in our quarters and you're supposed to remain naked until the next rising."

For a long moment she looked back at him before she reached for the buttons of her blood-soaked shirt. She'd be glad when she could toss the ruined garment in the trash. She wanted no reminders of what she'd done. And if she interpreted the heat in Taliff's gaze correctly, she'd be too busy to even think about the prior events of the day.

Once she tossed her ruined shirt and tiny scrap of a bra to the floor, she eased the zipper of her jeans down. She kicked off her sneakers and kicked off her sneakers and socks before letting her jeans fall to the carpet in a puddle. The entire time she stripped she never broke eye contact with Taliff. He had extraordinary golden eyes, flecked and ringed with amber. They entranced her. Hell, his animal magnetism, his charisma, and yes, his looks simply captivated her.

Taliff circled her slowly, turned her this way and that. His eyes scrutinized every inch of her skin. He paid careful attention to the still pink scar on her neck. He frowned his displeasure and looked as though he very much wanted to give in to his need to lecture her about the risks she had taken to gain control of the pride. She needed to do something to distract him before he upset himself again.

When it appeared that all he intended was to inspect her for injuries, Eve decided to take matters in her own hands. With as much grace as she could manage, she sauntered closer to Taliff, careful to leave just a hand's width between them.

With forced nonchalance, Eve trailed her hand down his chest, until she reached his jeans. She glanced up to see Taliff's reaction and was pleased to see a heated glitter to his gaze. He definitely approved of what she had on her mind. She'd have to remember to use seduction as a distraction in the future if his heated glances were anything to go by.

Eve slowly lowered the zipper, conscious of the fact he hadn't put on anything under his jeans when they'd dressed in a hurry earlier. His thick cock jutted from the opening of his pants as if begging for even the slightest touch.

She licked her lips in obvious appreciation. She doubted many men, human or *Lionese*, could boast of such a huge dick. She couldn't wait to find out just what he could do with it.

Unable to resist the delicious temptation in front of her, Eve slowly dropped to her knees, ran her fingernail down the length of his shaft and gazed up at him with as much mischievousness as she felt. Though she'd never given head before, she couldn't wait to try.

With deliberate slowness, she lowered her mouth to his throbbing dick. With confidence she didn't feel, she ran her tongue from the base of his shaft to the tip of his cock. She rimmed the head of his penis with her tongue, licking up the pre-cum that leaked from its tip, before she once again swirled her tongue down the length of his shaft.

Taliff groaned his pleasure. She felt his rumbling purr ripple through his shaft and gave an answering purr in acknowledgement. It made her insides quiver to know just how much he seemed to enjoy her ministrations.

Eve gripped the base of his cock with one hand and guided it to her mouth, taking his length deep into her throat. She slowly stroked up the length of his cock and down until she felt his hands tangle in her hair. His thrusts became more forceful as he held her head in place. "Goddess, Eve. You're killing me."

She smiled around the head of his cock. Not bad for an amateur. She could get quite used to this type of power. She had a grown *Lionese* warrior practically hers to command.

"I can't take anymore, Eve."

She could hear the desperation in his voice. With great reluctance, she took pity upon him and released his throbbing manhood from her mouth.

With shaky legs she made to stand, leaning more of her weight against him than she wanted. Who knew that giving a blowjob was as exciting as receiving one? With hands that still held a slight tremor, Taliff helped Eve to her feet and swung her up into his heavily-muscled arms. She couldn't stop herself from stroking his chest through the thin material of his t-shirt. There couldn't be an ounce of fat on his physique. All in all, he made an impressive figure. Power and strength radiated from him in waves.

In two long steps, Taliff reached the side of the bed where he tenderly placed her among the pillows. Eve tried to sit up, but Taliff placed his hand against her chest to urge her to lie back. She tried to reach for his shirt while he bent over her but he stepped away only to lift the shirt over his head and carelessly toss it across the room.

"I wanted to do that for you, dammit," Eve scolded.

Taliff just smiled and shook his head.

Eve gasped as she watched him lower his pants past his powerful thighs until he kicked them away, too. He stood before her, glorious in his nakedness. His red-gold hair gleamed in the light, swinging around his waist with every movement he made. His brilliant golden amber eyes glittered with passion as he once again closed the distance between them. With the ease of a feline comfortable with his strength and agility, Taliff gently lowered himself over her body.

"Now I have you exactly where I want you, Eve. And there is nothing you can do about it."

"Who said anything about getting away?"

Taliff chuckled. "Hmmm…" he whispered as his lips slowly grazed her ear, her neck until they finally slid down to the base of her throat. He gently nipped her at her pulse point, then swirled his tongue over the tiny wound. Goosebumps rippled across her skin as he continued to lave her with his rough tongue. She arched into his touch, desperate to feel his lips glide further down her body.

As though he could read her mind, Taliff's mouth drifted down past her neck until he reached the crests of her breasts. Eve couldn't hold back her moan as his tongue flicked over her rigid nipples. Again and again, he stroked her hardened peaks while gently rasping his teeth against them.

When she thought she could take no more, he eased away from her nipples and swirled his tongue on the underside of her breasts, his obvious intent to drive her mad. After taking each of her nipples into his mouth one last time, he released them with a pop before moving down her belly to her navel.

"Goddess, Tal. What are you trying to do to me?"

"Turnabout is fair play, *moya*."

Again she couldn't help but arch into his touch. She needed release and she needed it now. "Please, Tal. Stop torturing me already."

Goosebumps once again spread across her skin, her every nerve ending felt on fire and still he methodically trailed his lips past her naval, her cunt, until he finally reached the inner thigh of her left leg. He nipped her, leaving his mark on her pale skin, then eased the tiny ache with his tongue before he drifted lower down her body.

Eve screamed her displeasure when he skipped over her pussy. She was desperate to feel his tongue delving into her aching cunt. But no, he was bent on seduction and torture, she was sure of it.

His lips slowly trailed down her thigh, her calf and then to her ankle. All the time he ignored her pleas for mercy. After suckling on the toes on her left foot he moved to her right, kissing and nipping his way up her right leg. Tal clearly had learned love play from a master.

Eve thought she'd die if he didn't stop this slow act of seduction. Taliff looked up into Eve's passion glazed eyes and gave her an audacious wink before he carefully eased her thighs apart. With exaggerated slowness, Taliff bent his head and softly blew on her turgid clit.

When her clit started to drip with her passion's juices, he tenderly took it between his teeth and gave it a slight tug. Eve screamed her pleasure. Her body shook with pent up need. One more good tug on her clit and she'd explode. She couldn't stop the purr of contentment that rumbled from her chest. She was so close to climax. If she didn't get off soon, she might just kill him if he didn't kill her first. But damn, the wait just might be worth dying over.

"Taliff, let me come, please."

"Patience, Eve. The more drawn out the lovemaking is, the greater the pleasure you will feel."

"Ughhh... You can't expect me to last much longer, Taliff. I really can't take it."

Taliff smirked at her. Devilment lightened his eyes. "You'll take whatever I give you and love it, *moya*."

His touch gentle, Taliff spread her nether lips apart with his fingers, exposing her pussy to his gaze. "You have such a beautiful pink cunt, *moya*. I can't wait to taste your nectar. Cats do so love the sweet taste of cream."

He put his words to action and bent his head to her pussy. A deep purr rumbled from his chest as he stroked her pussy with his tongue. He swirled it around her erect clit and between her pussy lips as he drank her juices.

Oh, Goddess. The pleasure was so intense, unlike anything she had ever felt before in her life. Eve couldn't take much more and started to squirm. Apparently, Taliff would have none of that because he gripped her by her thighs and held her immobile as he continued to eat at her cunt.

He must have realized she could take no more, for he eased away, gave each of her thighs a tiny peck, then lifted her by her waist and flipped Eve to her stomach. He quickly replaced his lips with his throbbing cock. Slowly he stretched her tight pussy as he sank into her honeyed depths. He eased himself in and out ever so gently until he reached full penetration.

Once he was sure he was fully seated inside her, he moved her hair to drape over one shoulder, bent over her back and sank his teeth into the base of her neck. After what seemed an eternity but could have been no longer than a few seconds, Taliff released his fangs from her neck.

"Ouch, what was that?"

Taliff's voice dripped with satisfaction when he calmly stated, "I placed my mating mark upon you."

"Well, warn a person next time."

"There won't be a next time, *moya*. This mark is permanent and warns everyone that you've already been mated—mated to me."

He apparently reached his limit with speech, because without another word, he started to thrust with ever increasing force. She could feel every vein in his cock, every beat of his heart through their joining. Never had she thought to feel such exquisite sensations with another.

Eve met each stroke with one of her own, frantic to feel that connection, to feel his balls slap against her ass when they came together. And each thrust carried her closer and closer to climax.

She was so close to coming. If he didn't let loose the lion inside him soon, she'd die of frustration. It was time to take matters into her own hands. With deliberate intent, she clenched her inner muscles around his engorged shaft, making the fit just that much tighter. His thrusts became stronger, his purrs rumbled in his chest even louder. Within seconds, he drove her over the edge of the world. The pleasure was pure and explosive.

Her thoughts fragmented as his hands and lips continued their hungry search of her body even as his thrusts grew stronger, deeper. All she could do, all she wanted to do, was feel the bliss that pervaded every cell of her body. Lassitude began to seep in, but still Taliff forged through her pussy, striving to reach his own completion. All she could do was take it as all her nerve endings seemed to fire simultaneously. How could anyone survive such sensations?

Unable to hold back his release any longer, Eve felt Taliff stiffen, felt the ropes of his cum jet deep inside her cunt. The pleasure was unbearable and seemingly never-ending.

As though all the energy drained out of him when he shot his load, Taliff collapsed onto the bed, taking Eve in his arms as he rolled off her prone body.

While her heartbeat slowed and the silence spread over them like a warm blanket, Eve drank in the comfort of his nearness. She felt such pure trust and comfort as she lay safe in the security of Taliff's arms.

She buried her face against the corded muscles of his chest and just took the time to breathe in his scent. Right now, she imagined that anyone seeing her could see her inner glow and blazing passion. If only they could spend the rest of the journey to *Chantrea* in bed, all would be well.

"Are you okay, Eve?"

Taliff's voice sent another round of ripples through her. Her clit twitched in response. How could she still be horny after he so thoroughly ravaged her body?

"Hmm...never been better," she murmured.

"Good. I'm glad you feel that way because we need to talk."

Chapter Seven

She took a quick sharp breath and tried to pull away. Taliff would have none of that though and instead pulled her closer to his warm body. She stared wordlessly across at him. Her heart pounded. Would he condemn her for her earlier actions even after what they just shared?

A flicker of apprehension coursed through her as she waited for Taliff to tell her what he had on his mind. Panic like she'd never known before welled in her throat. The penalty for maiming another could be death on *Chantrea* for all she knew.

Taliff must have felt the fear twist inside her, because he began to rub her back with long even strokes. With his comforting touch, her mind quieted though it still held a crazy mixture of hope and fear.

When he still didn't say anything after several minutes had passed she finally gave into her nerves and asked what was uppermost on her mind. "You're not going to order my death or send me to a penal colony for my actions this morning, are you?"

Taliff chuckled. His eyes crinkled at the corners. "No, *moya*. I'm not going to order your death or have you imprisoned."

"Then what do you want to talk about?" Her voice sounded shakier than she would have liked. Fortunately, she didn't think he noticed the slight tremor. What would he do if he knew she feared him? Or, more to the point, feared her reaction to him?

"I want to talk about us, Eve. About why you and the other women are aboard the *Wanderer* and on your way to *Chantrea*." He didn't seem nervous, yet something about his manner made her nervous.

Eve remained motionless for a moment, then pulled the sheet up over her breasts and scooted up against the bed's headboard. Once she'd put a little distance between them, she looked into his eyes and nodded curtly. "Okay. I'm ready to hear what you have to say."

His expressive face changed and became almost somber as he seemed to collect his thoughts. After a second, a look of determination settled on his face. His voice was calm, his gaze steady as he started his tale.

"A few decades ago, our scientists began to notice a disturbing trend amongst the women giving birth. Or, I should say the trend has to do with the infants themselves. At first, it was barely noticeable, then as the years passed, it grew into the devastating problem that it is now."

"And what is the problem, Taliff?"

"Our women are no longer giving birth to girls. Once the last generation of females mature, there will be no one to give our people life."

"You mean there are no female children being born at all?"

When Taliff nodded, Eve closed her eyes and dropped her chin to her chest, now fully aware of just why they were abducted. "How long has it been?" Eve scooted closer to Taliff, laid her hand against his thigh to offer what comfort she could.

"It's been nearly ten years, Eve. Our people, our men, have given up hope for a future, for children and a mate of their own. We have begun to war amongst ourselves, something eradicated from our lives nearly a millennia ago." He turned bleak eyes her way. "How can we not fight amongst ourselves, striving to gain possession of the only females left?" He put his head in his hands. "Yet, even that is wrong — against our very nature. We know the women have mates and still we try to steal them from our brothers."

Eve tilted her head back and rested it against the headboard. Her thoughts ran in circles as she thought of possibilities and coincidences. "Taliff, the Earthbound *Lionese* are beginning to have the same problem, but in reverse. I just started noticing the extraordinary ratio of female to male children in the last couple of seasons."

"What exactly are you saying, Eve?"

"I'm saying that in the last couple of years, our women are birthing fewer and fewer males. I don't know about the other settlements of *Lionese* across the globe, but in my hometown, the ratio of females to males used to be pretty even. The last two years, however, females are born nearly seventy-five percent of the time. That's a twenty-five percent increase. At that rate, in another couple of years, Earth will find themselves in the same position as you find yourselves in now, but in reverse. All females and no males to carry on the line."

"Eve, it took decades for the decline to get to the level it is on *Chantrea*. What you're describing would mean that your people might reach extinction levels in one generation."

"I know, Taliff. If it took decades for this to happen to your world, why is it happening so quickly on Earth? And what could cause this?"

"I don't know, Eve. But if both our worlds are having similar problems, then they must have common factors contributing to them."

"What could they possibly have in common, Taliff?"

Taliff shook his head. "I don't know, Eve. As far as our records indicate, I'm the first to set foot on your world since your ancestors ship crashed nearly two thousand years ago."

"Is it possible that someone from your world has traveled to Earth undetected?"

"Possible, but highly unlikely. You must receive permission from the High King just to leave the planet. It took four of your Earth months to reach your world. Someone from *Chantrea* would be missed had they not reported in after so long a journey."

"Do you have visitors to *Chantrea*? Can they come and go as they please?"

Taliff closed his eyes, then nodded. "Yes. We have alliances with several planets and their people."

"So could someone have visited your world several decades ago and somehow poisoned your people, either the atmosphere or your food and water to cause this?"

"It's highly possible. We haven't been at war in many centuries, but there are always people who would see our world as a place to conquer."

"Why would they think that?"

"When you live in a peaceful society, many people believe that you won't fight, so they think you make an easy target and come after you with all their firepower. Yet others would rather take the easy way out if they could conquer a people without ever lifting a violent hand. Why use weapons when you can get rid of the population by slowly killing off its inhabitants with a poison or virus?"

"I don't like the way this looks, Taliff. We are talking total annihilation of our people. Genocide."

"Me either, *moya*. But we don't *know* anything. It's all supposition right now. There is no sense in jumping to conclusions."

"Well, how can we find out exactly who visited your world, who would have an interest in finding your missing colonists?"

"That's a good question—one that I'm sure *Shoshoni* will help us answer. But one best left for tomorrow."

"Why tomorrow?"

Taliff shifted closer to Eve, reached for her shoulders and pulled her beneath his body as he rolled them across the bed. "Because tonight's our mating night. Or have you forgotten that so quickly?"

"How could I possibly forget?" With a tiny smile, Eve lowered her head and pressed her lips against Taliff's, caressing his mouth more than kissing it. It was a kiss as tender and light as a midsummer night's breeze.

She felt transported on a soft and wispy cloud. Her thoughts spun and her emotions whirled. How could a simple kiss move her as this one had? Before she could think further, Taliff took control of the kiss, took control over her.

TALIFF HAD ENOUGH OF the teasing caress of her lips against his. He needed more from her. He needed it all. He wanted every bit of her passion, of her hunger to burn out of control. He wanted a raging inferno that only he could extinguish. And he would have it.

He wanted her completely submissive, even if it was only for this moment in time. He had to know, that at least for now, she was his to command, in body, heart and mind. He would settle for nothing less.

And he knew just how to do it too.

With steely determination, Taliff rolled away from his mate, stood up and faced the bed. If he was to make his *moya* submit, he needed to ensure she knew he meant business. He needed to shock her into compliance before she allowed her natural instincts for dominance to overwhelm the desire coursing through her.

Eve rolled over. Confusion laced her voice when she asked, "What is it, Taliff? What's the matter?"

"On your knees, Eve, and face the wall."

Her shoulders stiffened and her brows drew down into a frown. "What?"

"You heard me, Eve. I want you on your knees, in the center of the bed, your thighs spread shoulder width apart and your fingers laced behind your back." When she still didn't respond to his order, he scowled and firmed his voice. "Now," he barked.

Confusion, and perhaps even a little bit of hurt, raced across her features, but in the end, albeit reluctantly, she complied.

"What's this about, Taliff? What did I do wrong?"

"Oh, *moya*, you didn't do anything wrong. But I need to know that you trust me, that deep down, you will do as I ask because you know that I will never allow harm to befall you. I need to know that you have faith in me. This is for me as much as it is for you. Do you understand?"

Taliff watched as Eve seemed to come to some sort of decision. For just a moment he thought she would balk at his demands, but in the end, whether out of curiosity or the desire to be what he needed, she nodded her head in compliance and straightened her spine.

"Good girl, Eve. Now I want you to close your eyes and rest your weight on your heels for me. And don't move— no matter what you hear. Do you understand?"

Eve swallowed, then nodded her head in understanding.

"I said not to move, Eve, that means you can't even nod. If I ask you a direct question you may answer, otherwise you will not move and you will not speak. Say yes if you understand the rules."

Once again, Eve swallowed, obviously nervous about his demands. Was he taking this too far, too fast? When he'd begun to doubt himself, doubt the course of his action, he heard Eve's voice whisper, "Yes." But it was all the affirmation he needed that he was doing the right thing for the both of them. She needed to learn to trust in him unconditionally and for his own peace of mind he needed to know that her faith in him was absolute.

His heart leapt in his chest and his cock pulsed with need at the thought of what he was about to do, what he was about to demand. While Eve posed in the submissive position he'd placed her, Taliff made his way to the chest at the foot of his bed. What he needed to complete her submissive pose was nestled inside the chest, waiting for just the right person to use them on.

With nervous apprehension, Taliff bent over the chest and pulled out the package he never truly believed he'd have the opportunity to use. Nestled within several layers of *Chantrean* silk were the *Manruvian* Matebonds. Known through several galaxies as the one way to ensure the person you were contemplating to make your mate was indeed the one destined to complete your soul, the men of *Chantrea* carried them everywhere in hopes that one day they might have the opportunity to use them.

Taliff approached the bed, his footsteps sure, his gaze focused on the woman kneeling on the bed. Everything would come down to the next few minutes. His stomach tightened into a painful knot of anxiety as he climbed upon the bed behind her.

After a moment's pause, he bound her wrists with the ritual binding straps, hoping that she was truly the one. When the other end began to wrap itself around his own wrist, he breathed a sigh of relief. Several seconds later, it suddenly became thinner. It flattened against their skin, burrowing beneath the layers of flesh until it became one with them, blending its DNA with theirs, an invisible tether between them—and a marker to lead one to the other should they ever become separated. Now they were truly one, cleaving unto each other as nature had intended.

Eve's muscles tensed beneath his hands. He knew she had something to say, but she maintained the silence he demanded.

"You may speak now, *moya*. Ask your questions."

"What was that, Taliff? What just happened? I feel different somehow, like a part of me I didn't know was missing has somehow returned to me."

"What you feel is me, completing you, through the *Manruvian* Matebonds. I will always know where you are, what you're feeling, as you will always know my whereabouts and my mood. It is the way our people ensure safe and happy matings. If anything were to separate us now, I'll always be able to find you."

She shivered as his voice hardened. "And never fear, I would find you if anyone ever tried to take you from me."

Her eyes widened, whether in apprehension or arousal he didn't know. "Now, stay on your knees, but approach the edge of the bed and turn to face me. I want to feel those lush lips of yours wrapped around my cock. And you will take me, every inch. Do you understand?"

"Yes, Tal."

"Good. Now, do as I say."

Eve didn't hesitate even a second in following his instructions this time. Progress was definitely being made. The *Manruvian* Matebonds were beginning to affect his control, his sense of self. If she challenged his authority tonight, challenged his dominance, he couldn't guarantee that he wouldn't hurt her, albeit unintentionally.

He couldn't let that happen. "You have to do exactly as I say tonight, *moya*. No questioning my orders. The mating night is not always easy on the mate pair, but I am told it is unforgettable. I don't want to take the chance I could hurt you, even accidentally."

He paused to gauge her willingness before nodding to himself, satisfied that she was a willing participant.

"Now, open your mouth like a good girl."

Chapter Eight

Taliff knew the *Matebonds* had heightened Eve's natural desires as well. Her eyes shone with wicked amusement and deviltry. She may not have a submissive personality but it was clear that she liked acting submissively to him sexually. A man could get off on that knowledge if he were so inclined. And right now, he was definitely inclined. If his dick got any harder, he'd be able to drill holes through his ship's titanium armor plating.

His cock bobbed in front of her face, heavy with need. Eve moistened her lips with her tongue and a drop of pre-cum greeted her in response. He knew nirvana awaited him in the warmth of her mouth, if only she would get on with it already.

"Do it now, Eve. Take my cock in your mouth and suck it dry. I want you to take every drop of my cum when it spills."

Finally, after what seemed hours instead of just the few seconds that passed, Eve dragged her tongue over the head of his cock. His spine tingled from the pleasure as the rough texture of her tongue swept over nerves in his cockhead he didn't know existed.

More pre-cum spilled forth and Eve lapped it up again and again, never taking his shaft into the depths of her mouth, but always giving him just enough pleasure that he was too reluctant to forgo it in order to force her to take him deeper.

Before long, Taliff's legs began to quiver, a sure signal that he was close to coming. He couldn't let her have that control. Not yet, anyway.

With extreme disappointment, Taliff stepped back and away from Eve's oh-too-tempting mouth.

Eve mewled her disappointment, but he wasn't about to give in to her. Already his control hung in tatters. They had a long night ahead of him and he'd be damned if he wouldn't make them both work for their climaxes.

When the pleasure began to border on pain, then he would allow them the release they'd need. And only then. And in the meantime…let the naughty sex games begin.

Taliff let a few seconds pass and, when Eve started to fidget, approached the bed and her once again. Truth be told, he'd needed those few seconds just to get himself together.

When Eve went to reach for him, he shook his head. "No, keep your hands behind your back. Use your lips and tongue only."

Taliff watched as Eve lifted her gaze to his, expecting her to voice the question he could clearly see written across her face. But surprisingly, she wet her lips and leaned forward, taking the head of his cock between her lush, wet lips.

Ever so slowly, Eve took his shaft all the way to the base and, instead of stroking him with her mouth, began to growl. He could feel every nerve in his cock tingle. The vibrations zipped through his shaft and straight to his balls. Oh, Goddess. If she kept this form of torture up, he'd never last as long as he wanted.

Time to intervene. "Suck it, Eve. Don't make me tell you again."

With obvious reluctance, if her expression of aggravation was anything to go by, Eve relented and began to work his dick in earnest. In and out, he thrust in her mouth. The combination of wet heat and steady suction continued to push him closer and closer to the edge of sanity, of reason.

His hips began to jackhammer against her mouth. He knew he was being too rough, but he couldn't help himself. No way could he slow down. The mating rut was upon him and he would have his satisfaction.

Taliff felt Eve trying to swallow around the cock stuffing her mouth as saliva and pre-cum flooded her throat. Her breathing grew ragged and still he didn't slow down, didn't ease off the pressure or tempo. All he could do was hope to make it up to her later.

The pressure around his shaft increased and his balls drew taut against his body. Tingles raced up his spine and his hands began to shake and still he forced his cock even deeper, wedging it down her throat. Taliff groaned as he felt his cum rip out of his balls and down the length of his cock.

The only warning he gave her that he was about to come was a grunt of savage pleasure, then his roar of satisfaction. "Swallow it, Eve. Every drop."

To make sure she didn't pull away, or fight the forceful invasion of her mouth, Taliff clasped her head, wrapping her hair around his fingers just as hot jets of semen spilled down her throat. Over and over, ropes of cum shot out of his cock and still he didn't let up his grip. Eons, or perhaps only seconds later, he felt the last of his seed explode from his dick in one massive burst.

And still he needed to rut on her like a bull in heat. His climax had only lessened the pressure but not the need driving his actions.

So lost in the sensations of his release, Taliff almost missed the fact that Eve's fingers were digging holes in his ass where she'd at some point grabbed onto him during his climax. Had she been trying to pry him away from her or urging him closer? Either way, he'd wallowed in his own body's demands rather than see to hers, his motto of "ladies first" apparently forgotten.

Taliff frowned, worried that he might have hurt her with his mindless rutting. He wanted this night just as hot and memorable for her as it was already turning out to be for him.

Eve continued to suck on his cock, but with leisurely pleasure rather than rapturous need. She lovingly laved it, making sure she gathered every drop of his seed. She was turning out be just as sexually submissive as he'd always desired in a mate. Yet, outside the bedroom, she was just as dominant and forceful as he.

"Enough, Eve."

Eve ignored his order. Her purrs of contentment vibrated along the length of his shaft, sending new waves of desire shooting to his groin.

"I said, enough."

When she continued to disobey his command, Taliff stepped back, forcing her compliance. He didn't want to punish her for her disobedience, but he couldn't let this go unmentioned either. "That's your last warning, Eve. Next time you disobey, you'll learn about the way the *Chantrean Lionese* punish their mates firsthand."

Eve licked her lips that now glistened with the evidence of his release and smirked.

Obviously, she wasn't taking his warning seriously. Oh well, it wouldn't be long before she earned the punishment she doubted he'd deliver. Until then he'd enjoy the next few hours with his mate and, if she earned punishment in the meantime, so be it. Besides, he knew the punishment would soon become a pleasure for her. It always did. It was the way of their people.

Taliff could see the tension running through his mate's body. She quivered with need. It wouldn't take much to send her over the edge.

"Very good, Eve. Now, I want you to move to the center of the bed, position yourself on your hands and knees and face the headboard."

Eve's movements were wooden, her body protesting its need to change position, as she did as he ordered. A sheen of sweat glistened on her skin and he could smell her arousal as it perfumed the air. Thick cream coated the inside of her thighs, evidence of her desperate need for relief. Oh, he was so going to enjoy the next few minutes while he attempted to drive his mate out of her mind with ecstasy.

"Good girl. You're being so obedient now, *moya*. I'd much rather reward you tonight than punish you. Do you understand?"

Eve nodded, then dug her fingers into the silken coverings as the mattress dipped beneath his weight. He didn't want her to anticipate his actions, however, so he scooted back off the bed and once again rummaged through the chest at the foot of his sleeping platform.

The silence in the room was broken only by the sound of her rasping breaths and the slide of metal meeting metal as he latched the lid of the trunk closed.

"I don't want you to think right now, Eve. I only want you to feel the pleasure I'll be gifting you with. I'm going to cover your eyes so all your senses are narrowed to two—to hearing and touch."

She gasped when the cool satin band of uniform sash caressed her face. The red sash symbolized his place of honor in the king's personal guard, but tonight it would symbolize the honor Eve gave him by choosing him as mate. The honor and respect he wanted—no needed—to bestow upon her for her acceptance of who and what he was.

"Close your eyes, *moya*," he whispered into her ear, as he placed the cloth over her face. "Listen to my voice as I make love to you with words. Feel my heart beat against the silken skin of your back. Smell the heavy scent of your arousal as your cream spills down your thighs."

After a momentary pause, Taliff ran the tip of his index finger down the center of her back. Eve's body began to shake in earnest. An urgent moan of need echoed throughout the room and, when he knew the tension was at its most unbearable, he nipped her ear and slipped his fingers between her dripping wet pussy lips.

The evidence of her arousal coated his fingertips. He raised them to his mouth and licked them clean. He closed his eyes as he savored the flavor of her passion. He would never get enough of her, of her taste. Goddess, he was addicted to her already. "Oh, you are so wet for me, *moya*. Do you want to come, baby?"

When an inarticulate cry was her only response, Taliff knew it wouldn't take much to send her into oblivion. He couldn't wait to hear her scream in pleasure. He wanted to see her writhing in ecstasy atop their bedding, lost to everything but what he was doing to her.

And just as soon as she begged for her release he'd give it to her. Taliff gave a wicked chuckle and lowered his face toward her needy pussy.

Ahh...the smell of her passion was nature's own ambrosia. Who needed sexual stimulants when a woman's body produces such an enticing aphrodisiac without the cloying scent of drugs and herbs?

Her nether lips were plump and pink, the perfect combination as far as he was concerned. With infinite tenderness he spread her lips apart with his fingers and stoked her pussy from asshole to clit with a swipe of his tongue.

Eve groaned, her thighs flexed. "Please, Taliff."

Taliff turned his head and nipped her thigh. "Did I give you permission to speak, *moya*?"

After another frustrated groan, Eve shook her head. Her eyes were closed tight and a grimace spread across her face. He wouldn't be able to tease her much longer, before the intense pleasure his touch caused would turn to pain. With that in mind, Taliff decided to forgo a long drawn out session. She deserved to cum now, especially after she gave him such a wondrous blowjob just minutes ago. There would be plenty of time later for an extended bout of foreplay.

Straightening behind her, Taliff prepared to mount his mate. "Are you ready for me, *moya*?"

"Mmm…"

"Tell me, *moya*. Do you want my cock?"

"Yes, damn you."

"Say it, *moya*. Tell me exactly what you want."

"Fuck me, Taliff. Please, fuck me."

"Oh, *moya*. When you beg so nicely, how can I deny you anything?"

Taliff leaned over her back and gripped the base of her neck with his fangs, as he prepared to enter her. If he didn't sink his unruly cock into her wet heat soon, he might pass out since all the blood that normally sent oxygen to his brain had rushed to his groin in anticipation.

Several seconds passed while Taliff just inhaled the combined scents of their passion. After gaining control over his driving need to plunder, he wrapped his hand around the head of his shaft and placed it against her dripping sheath. With utmost care, Taliff began to enter the almost virgin hole, stretching her slowly so as not to abuse her tender opening.

"Please, Taliff. I need more. Please," Eve begged, wriggling her hips. Her voice cracked and her entire body vibrated with suppressed need. She pushed back against him in an obvious effort to force him deeper into her.

No more than an inch of his cock was inside her tight entrance and already he was close to exploding. Holy Goddess.

Taliff slowly withdrew, then after pausing long enough to make Eve rear back in frustration, began to enter her once again. Goddess, she felt so amazing. This moment was perfect. Nothing could mar what had become the single most erotic night of his life.

As though the fates were conspiring against them, the ship's proximity alarms chose that moment to shriek throughout the cabin.

The lights dimmed.

Eve screamed in frustration.

Taliff hung his head in dismay.

"Goddess, dammit," Eve bellowed. "This is so not fucking fair."

"Whoever set off those alarms is a dead man." With almost painful reluctance, Taliff slid from the wet haven of his mate's sheath.

"What are you complaining about? At least you got off. Me... I'm so desperate for relief, I might kill the first person who says a cross word to me."

Shoshoni interrupted Eve's tirade before he could respond to her well-deserved complaint. "Commander, I need you on the Command Deck."

"Understood, *Shoshoni*. Eve and I will be right there."

"Come on, *moya*. It seems our pleasure will have to wait. Let's go kick some ass."

Taliff was nearly to the door, when Eve called out to him. "Don't you think you should get dressed first, Commander?"

Chapter Nine

In just a few minutes, both Taliff and Eve were dressed and out the door of their cabin. Expecting to find the way to the lift clear, Eve was surprised to find the halls crowded with women in various states of disarray. From the looks of things, the shrill alarm must have woken most of them and they'd left their cabins to investigate.

Eve glanced over at Taliff, noticing the grimace on his face. A delay to get the women calmed and back in their cabins just wasn't acceptable.

Voices rang throughout the corridor, each vying to be heard above the other.

"What happened?"

"Are we under attack?"

"Are we in danger?"

"We're going to die, aren't we?"

"How can I sleep with all this racket?"

All right, now that last comment just pissed her the hell off. Eve tracked the owner to a woman leaning negligently against the wall, her arms crossed beneath her breasts and a sneer twisting her lips. Of course. She should have known. Eve didn't know her name, but recognized her as one of the women who had helped Myra after the challenge. That woman was going to be trouble. She would bear watching, but right now they had more pressing problems.

It was time Eve took control of the cacophony that had erupted the moment she and her mate had left their room. Eve tossed back her head, opened her mouth and roared. Her ears were met with blessed silence immediately.

When she glanced around the now quiet hall, she was happy to find that all eyes were on her and all mouths firmly shut. Ahh, that was so much better. "*Shoshoni?*"

"Yes, Eve?"

"I want all these women transported back to their rooms and the cabins sealed. No one is to go in or out until either Taliff or I have given the all clear. Is that understood?"

"Yes, Eve. Preparing for mass transport."

Before the women could argue at being summarily dismissed without an explanation, the hallway stood empty except for Taliff and herself. She sighed with satisfaction and turned toward her mate with a smirk.

A look of stupefied wonder graced his face. "What?" she asked.

"How the hell were you able to roar like that?"

Eve glanced away, tugged at the bottom of her sweater nervously. "What do you mean?"

"Eve, in your human form, you shouldn't have the same vocal abilities as you do while shifted to Lion."

"What do you mean?"

Then the implications of what he meant hit her. "You mean you can't?" she sputtered.

He shook his head. "Dammit, we need to talk about this, but now definitely isn't the time. Right now, we need to get to the Command Deck."

"Sorry, you're right. It would be quicker if we just have *Shoshoni* zap us there."

Taliff nodded in agreement. "*Shoshoni?*"

"Yes, Commander Shi'Lan?"

"Transport Eve and myself directly inside the control room on the command deck."

"Beginning transfer momentarily."

Before she could blink, Eve found herself standing next to the viewscreen, Taliff right in front of her. When she lifted her gaze from the sight of her mate's glorious amber eyes and looked over his shoulder to the view outside the ship, she gasped.

"You need to see this, Tal."

Taliff spun around and looked out the viewscreen. "Bugger. *Shoshoni*?"

"Yes, Commander Shi'Lan?"

"How close are those ships?"

"They'll reach us in less than three minutes, Commander."

"Have they attempted communication?"

"No, Sir. Their weapons are armed and shields are at full power."

"Do we have enough time to engage the light drive?"

"Negative."

"What are the viable options for escape, *Shoshoni*?"

"Our shields will not be effective in repelling an attack, Commander. Probables say outrunning the approaching ships will have only a four percent chance of success."

"What's your recommended course of action, *Shoshoni*?"

"Hide in plain sight, Commander. There is an asteroid field quite close, astronomically speaking. If we reach there safely, we can turn off all non-essential equipment, power up the experimental cloaking system King Shi'Lan had ordered installed and wait until they give up or pass us by."

If a computer could sound worried, this one did. Eve turned away from the viewscreen and glanced over at her man. His eyes were closed, his head tipped back. "If it's any help, I think we have a better chance if we follow her recommendations. At the very least, if we're forced to fight, they won't see us coming."

Taliff's gaze met hers and she could see the worry in his eyes. After a moment, he reached out and grabbed her hand, squeezing it gently before dropping it and turning back toward the viewport. "*Shoshoni*, implement your suggestion. I also want you to begin piping a sleeping agent into the cabins of all the women, starting now. If the worst happens and we're forced to scuttle the ship, I don't want them aware of what's happening."

"As ordered, Commander Shi'Lan. Ship's course adjusted. Sleeping agents now being administered. Engines at full sub-light power. Estimated arrival at the asteroid field is sixty seconds. Would you like me to keep an audio record of the countdown?"

"Give us an audio countdown until the approaching ships are within fifteen seconds of reaching us. After that I want absolute silence throughout the ship. When will the first of those five *Chantrean* Battleships reach us?"

"They will intercept us in less than ninety seconds."

Eve looked over at Taliff. Would he listen to her suggestion to buy them some time, or scoff at her? Guess there was only one way to find out and that was to just jump right in and see.

"Taliff?"

His distraction and worry were evident in the clipped tone of his voice. "What is it, Eve?"

"I know I'm not a strategist, or a computer able to weigh variables, but I might have a suggestion that might buy us a little time and ensure our escape."

He must have heard the hurt in her voice, because his voice softened when he said, "If you have any ideas that might help us, I would sure like to hear them."

He sounded sincere and there wasn't any time to try and psychoanalyze his feelings from his voice alone. "I know this is probably a cheesy and cliché thing to do, but what if we stage an explosion? Expel some supplies, set off a plasma burn just outside the ship, or whatever you use as fuel. And then cloak. If they hear our countdown, see the debris, they'll assume we self-destructed rather than chance capture. While they're searching the debris field, we can slide right past them without their knowledge or suspicion. By the time they figure it out, we should be able to use the Light Engines. Right?"

Taliff rolled his eyes.

Was that a good sign or not? He probably thought the idea was asinine. She waited for his response and cringed when he chuckled.

"*Shoshoni*, I want you to do exactly as Eve has suggested. Use whatever chemical compound mixture will get the job done, so long as it won't interfere with our mission to return to *Chantrea* in one piece. Expel the cargo we would have used for trade if the opportunity had presented itself. It will go toward saving our lives instead of filling our coffers. And make sure the explosion, expulsion of cargo and cloaking happen simultaneously. As soon as you're ready, make it happen."

Taliff grabbed Eve's hand again, smiled at her with joy twinkling in his eyes. "Hold on. This won't take long."

She was both relieved and stunned that he'd listened to her. He hadn't been scoffing at her after all, just laughing in relief. Eve's lips lifted in a small smile. She felt a small tremor of surprise that she could find something to smile about when their very lives were in danger.

"Fifty-nine..."

"Fifty-eight..."

"Fifty-seven..."

The computer's voice droned on and Eve moved closer to her mate. If this went badly she wanted to be holding onto him when it happened. After looping her arms around his neck and laying her head on his chest, she silently waited.

She felt Taliff's arms wrap around her waist and his chin rest atop her head, then waited as the computer continued the countdown.

"Forty-two..."

"Forty-one..."

"Forty..."

Before too long, Eve voiced the fear plaguing her. "Are we doing the right thing, Taliff?"

TALIFF LOOKED DOWN AT his mate, amazed that all his hopes and dreams were held firmly within his grasp inside this beautiful woman. He wouldn't lie to her, not even if it would make her feel better. "I don't know, Eve. I can't think of one positive reason that all these ships are out here and avoiding communications. And all the reasons I *can* come up with don't bode well for us, but especially for you and the other women."

He pulled her even closer against him. Not a millimeter of space separated them and yet, it was still too much distance for his peace of mind. If he could put her in his pocket and hide her there, he would. If he could absorb her through his skin to keep her safe, he'd do that too.

Eve tensed in his arms. "What do you mean?"

"They'd kill me Eve, but they'd capture you and the others. If they could breed females off of you, they'd have no reason to treat you as anything other than incubators for their future mates, whether they had to use rape to impregnate you or not."

"Oh..." She shivered against him, her body wracked with chills. All he could do was hold her tighter and pray to the Goddess Alana that they survive the next few minutes.

"Seventeen..."

"Sixteen..."

"Fifteen..."

The silence that followed was deafening. The ship shuddered beneath his feet as the engines engaged and the cargo was transported into space. A deafening explosion rocked the ship, before the stabilizing thrusters engaged. He could only hope the ship was cloaked and that their enemies were fooled—at least for now, anyway.

He'd worry about the rest of the trip home after they were clear of this latest complication. For ten minutes, neither he nor Eve moved. No one spoke. No one dared.

When Taliff thought his nerves were about to implode, *Shoshoni* beeped his wrist communicator. Hell, he'd forgotten he even wore the contraption. He never took it off, not even when retiring for the night. Thank the Goddess for lazy habits.

Taliff stepped away from Eve and brought the com unit to his mouth. "Go ahead," he whispered.

Until *Shoshoni* gave him the all clear, he didn't want to alert anyone who might be listening. There were some planets in his home star system that excelled at making listening devices that could be used to search for missing ships in deep space. He couldn't chance being discovered by their enemies.

"I am picking up several radio transmissions between the ships, Commander Shi'Lan. The ships are circling the debris field. I can plot a course around the debris field, but in order to avoid detection, the route will take us through the heart of the asteroid belt. We will not be able to use the Light Engines until we pass through the field. Do I go through the asteroid belt, Commander, or sit and wait until the ships depart?"

"What are the chances they know about the cloak my brother had installed?"

"There is insufficient data available to answer your query, Sir."

Taliff shook his head and glanced back at Eve to ask her opinion. So far, thanks to her wit, they were still alive. And he wanted to keep it that way. "What do you think we should do, *moya*?"

"I say we should take the chance and head for the asteroid belt. If we can get past there before they catch on, if they catch on, then by the time they figure out what we've done, hopefully we would have already warped out of there. Then it's just a matter of keeping ahead of whoever is trying to ensure you fail in your mission."

Taliff raised his eyebrows in consternation. Sometimes his mate said things he just didn't understand. "Warp?"

Eve shook her head. "It's not important. It's a phrase from a *Star Trek* show. It means use your Light Engines."

With a smile tipping up the corners of his mouth, Taliff approached Eve and pulled her into his arms. It was pure heaven to be able to hold her this way. "You are a delight, Eve. I don't think I'll ever figure out how your mind works, but I'm going to enjoy trying over the next couple of centuries."

"Centuries?" she screeched—well, as much as she could screech while keeping her voice below a whisper.

Taliff ignored Eve's outrage and pulled her into his arms. "Do as Eve suggests, *Shoshoni*. Head into the asteroid belt at a safe speed and distance to ensure we stay hidden. When we clear the belt, plot our course to *Chantrea* at 'Warp' speed."

Eve was still struggling in his arms, but instead of letting her go, he bent down and grabbed her beneath her knees, lifting her against his chest. "Yes, centuries, Eve."

Without a backward glance at the debris field slowly shrinking in the distance, Taliff carried Eve out of the Control room and headed back to the lift to finish their mating night. Perhaps, all that outrage she was feeling could be turned to passion. He couldn't wait to find out.

If Eve had looked up at that moment, she would have glimpsed the hunter he kept firmly leashed behind his carefree persona and known that she was about to become prey.

Chapter Ten

Eve didn't know whether to voice her outrage that he'd carried her off like a conquest or laugh at the outrageousness of his actions considering they could be attacked and killed at any moment. Either way, she knew it wouldn't change the outcome. He'd still ravage her and she'd love it. So why complain? Seriously, did she really want to waste what could be their last chance to make love?

With both her mind and heart in agreement, she relaxed and laid her head against his chest. The rapid pounding of his heart reassured her that she wasn't the only one feeling this way. He may not have told her he loved her, but there was more than just lust between them.

Come to think of it, she hadn't expressed her feelings to him either. She wasn't sure that what she felt was love, but then again, what was love really? She desired him. She cared about his thoughts and feelings. She definitely didn't want to see him harmed in any way. And, even as crazy as it sounded, she couldn't imagine ever feeling like this about another person again. So, was she in love? She didn't really know, but she sure hoped they lived long enough for her to figure it out.

"Stop thinking so hard. You'll give yourself a headache."

She shivered when the warmth of his breath brushed her temple. How could he always affect her this way? Just the sound of his voice or the smell of his skin had her creaming in seconds.

"How do you always know what I'm feeling? It's a bit disconcerting, to tell you the truth."

"The mating bonds united our souls. What you feel, so do I. When you're worried, I'll always know it. In that way, our people can strive to give each other what they need to remain happy." He wasn't sure if she was ready to hear that the mating bonds also tied their life forces together. If she died he would soon follow.

"How come I can't sense what you're feeling through these 'bonds' then?"

"Um...you are. All I'm feeling right now is an insane urge to press you against the walls and fuck you into oblivion. Why else do you think I can smell your pussy flowering even though you're worried?"

Eve could feel the heat in her cheeks as her blush spread like a match to tinder. She closed her eyes so she wouldn't see the smile she could hear in his voice. How embarrassing. Why did men, no matter what planet they were from, always say the one thing most likely to embarrass a woman? It must be some sort of genetic trait of the gender.

"Do you have to say stuff like that, Taliff?"

"Why wouldn't I? It's the truth. Why are you ashamed of your body's response to mine?"

"I'm not ashamed. I just don't want to hear that I stink."

Taliff chuckled. "I didn't say you stank, *moya*. I love the scent of your arousal. It's intoxicating."

"Still..."

She could feel his sigh as his breath teased her ear. "I will try my best not to embarrass you, Eve. But I can't help but tell you how much you turn me on."

"Ugh... Can we change the subject, please?"

"Anything for you, *moya*."

"Thank you." After a few seconds of blessed silence passed, Eve looked up. She didn't think it normally took this long to get to their quarters. Her brows lifted in surprise. "Ah, Taliff? Where are we?"

"You'll see."

"All I see is a door and it doesn't lead to our room."

His chest vibrated beneath her ear and she knew he was trying not to laugh at her again. "You're so impatient, Eve."

Before she could come up with a suitable reply, he pressed his security code into the keypad and the door whooshed open. She couldn't have contained the surprised gasp that flew passed her lips if she wanted to, but something this beautiful deserved any reaction it received.

"Do you like it?"

"It's stunning. But what is this place?"

"It's the conservatory. When ships are deployed for any length of time, our people have discovered that homesickness sets in, and with it, morale lowers. The scientists discovered that it was a chemical compound excreted by the plant's roots into the soil. It creates a sense of well being amongst our people. By putting an indoor garden on all our battleships and deep space explorers, our soldiers and scientists don't forget the paradise they left behind. Instead, they get to take a bit of home with them wherever they are sent."

"I really think I'm going to like *Chantrea*, Taliff. If your world looks anything like this, it must be very hard to leave home."

A feeling of well-being swept over her as she stared at the beautiful garden. No. It was more than that. It was a feeling of coming home. Flowers more exotic than she ever could have imagined hung from the ceiling and spread over the walls in a blanket of blossoms. Everywhere she looked colorful flora and vibrant green vines vied for her attention.

A flash of color caught her eye and she turned her head to look at the bloom. It looked like a cross between a tulip and a rose, but the deep purple hue of the petals was what captivated her. The purple was so dark, it was nearly black, but when the light hit it just right the richness and purity of the color amazed her.

"What kind of flower is this one, Tal?" she asked. Her fingers itched to pluck the flower from the hanging vine, but she'd rather the beauty of the bloom remained for her to see here, than to slowly wither and die in their cabin.

She tried to bend down to inhale the enchanting fragrance of the blossoms, but couldn't get close enough. "Put me down, Tal. Put me down." She probably sounded like a two year old asking for permission to run wild through a toy store, but she couldn't help it.

By the time he slowly lowered her to the floor, every inch of her skin was sensitized where he'd deliberately eased her down his length. Her stomach clenched. Her pussy spasmed. And her heart rate about quadrupled. She didn't know whether to jump him, or beg to be jumped. And all thoughts of smelling anything but his enticing scent evaporated from her mind.

"It's a Tupa."

"What?" What was he talking about?

"The flower you're reverently stroking with your fingertips. It's called a Tupa."

"Oh." She quickly stuck her hands in the pockets of her jeans. What the hell was happening to her? She was so horny she'd probably climax the second he breathed on her.

She didn't even realize she'd been stroking the flower's petals. She'd stood there and imagined using her tongue to stroke his cock, fingering the flower unconsciously, until he'd pointed it out to her.

When had these continuous thoughts of sex replaced all her common sense? After she met him, of course. Until Taliff, she'd thought of sex in an offhand manner, wondering when she'd finally find someone to screw that wouldn't leave a bad taste in her mouth the next morning, but she'd never obsessed about it before.

Goddess, just thoughts of licking his golden skin made her legs quiver and her pulse thump out a rhythm of desperate need.

She licked her lips, nervous at the sudden tension that radiated from him. As though he could read her mind and her thoughts were turning him on, Eve watched as his breathing escalated and his pupils dilated.

Oh Goddess, she was going to get ravished all right. And if the naughty twinkle in his eyes were any indication, he planned on screwing her right here. No way would they make it to their room from the looks of the massive bulge in his one-piece uniform. Which, come to think of it, was exactly what he'd probably planned all along.

Eve smiled up at her mate. She couldn't think of a more beautiful and inspiring place to make love. Her heart skipped a beat when she realized that although he hadn't spoken of his feelings, maybe he knew what they were to each other deserved to be recognized in a place so close to his people, so close to his heart.

And perhaps what she felt was love, because suddenly she couldn't think of any moment in her life she cherished more, or any person who she would ever want to repeat this experience with. And maybe, just maybe, she'd tell him of the feelings bubbling inside her. But not just yet. Right now, she wanted to enjoy the sensations and hold them close to her for a bit longer.

TALIFF'S COCK LENGTHENED BENEATH the confines of his pants, sending shards of frustrated pain to his groin. All he wanted to do was lie Eve down amidst the flowers of his home world and make love to her for hours. The combination of crushed petals and her womanly essence was sure to drive him mad with need, but what an experience it would be.

Although she stood less than a foot away, when she looked at him and smiled as she was doing now, he wanted to crush her to his length and absorb her through his pores until she filled all the empty places in his heart. Now that he'd found her, he'd do anything to keep her by his side for the rest of their very long lives.

He hungered for her. His soul had cried out to hers long before they ever laid eyes on each other. And tonight, he'd do his damnedest to ensure she never doubted what she meant to him.

With utmost reverence he lifted one of her golden tresses and placed it behind her left ear so that he could trail his fingers through the silky mass. Eve's eyes closed as his fingers caressed the side of her face and he could feel her pleasure through their bond. How had he lived so long without feeling her soul merged with his own? The answer was simple… he hadn't. He'd merely existed until he'd taken Eve from her home and mated her.

When she nuzzled the palm of his hand with her cheek, he was a goner. He just hoped he didn't disappoint her this night. The long, slow loving he'd planned would have to wait, because first, he needed her fast and hard. And he needed her now.

Thoughts of all the ways he wanted to love her, to touch her, rushed through his mind, but only one felt right for this moment, this place. He stepped back and held out his hand to her. It would be her choice whether or not she took it. Did she trust him enough to go where he led? "Come with me, Eve?"

Without hesitation, she placed her hand in his. "I'd follow you anywhere, Taliff."

He sighed in relief, unaware as he did so that he'd been holding his breath. With her fingers intertwined with his, Taliff led her deeper and deeper into the conservatory. By the time they reached the heart of the garden, the metal walls of the ship were impossible to see.

An oasis of beauty, the heart of the conservatory was Taliff's favorite part of the ship. He came here alone to think about his life, his duties, and he came here to dream. It was here where he'd often sit and hope his perfect match was out there somewhere just waiting for him to find her. So he thought it fitting that she be the only one he'd ever shared this place with. It was here he'd make love to her and here he'd pledge his undying love and devotion.

And love her he did. Her spirit invigorated him. Her trust enslaved him. And he hoped it was here that her love for him was spoken through the ritual mating promise. Only once she spoke the vows of mating could he respond in kind. But would the ritual words come to her as they did for all *Chantrean*-born *Lionese* women? Or would he never have that part of his dream fulfilled?

To have a female speak the words of love and devotion to her mate was the most important part of the mating night to every *Lionese* male. It proved beyond doubt that she pledged to honor and trust him, with not only her heart and her soul, but with her body and her mind as well.

All the items she needed for the ritual could be found here. The bathing pool was required to wash away the impurity in their hearts. The basin, filled with Alana's tears, the Mother Goddess of *Chantrea*, sat on a pedestal near the bathing pool. It was believed that to drink her tears purified the *Lionese* soul. The flowering garden where they'd lie represented their people's respect for nature and all living creatures. To make love here, to speak the vows in this clearing, would honor him, his people and their Goddess.

The next step was hers. The next few minutes would be the hardest of his life. Would she offer to bathe him in the pool, as was custom or would he have to forego the only chance he would ever have of having a true *Lionese* mating night?

With no small amount of hope and heaps of roiling uncertainty, Taliff released Eve's hand and stepped away from her. He prayed to the Goddess that whatever happened next, she'd know that for him, she was all he could ever want or need.

Chapter Eleven

"Oh, Tal. How can you stand to leave your home if it looks like this?" Everything about this indoor greenhouse amazed her. The farther they'd walked into the heart of this amazing garden, the more beautiful it seemed to become.

Her gaze darted around the foliage trying to take it all in at once. She didn't know what to look at first. If she didn't know better, she'd have thought they had stepped into an oasis.

A welcoming pool of glimmering water dominated the clearing. Flowering bushes and rose marble benches surrounded it and interspersed between them were statues of men and women in various poses, some sexual and some almost secular in design. The whole area shouted of the peace and serenity found here.

The benches would have tempted her any other day, just so she could sit by the water and contemplate life's daily trials, but it was the shimmering turquoise water of the wading pool that called to something deep within her soul.

"Taliff, can we go in the pool, or is that forbidden?"

"*Moya*, tonight, in this place, I want you to listen to your instincts. If there is something you desire, all you have to do is show me. If there is something you want to say, you say it. Tonight, you're in charge."

Eve nodded, but a hint of uneasiness crept into her thoughts. Why did that sound so ominous, so ritualistic? Was there something he wasn't telling her, something significant she should know? She hated feeling like something she should know was being kept from her, but in their short time together she'd learned to trust in him. If he was keeping something from her, it wasn't anything that would cause her harm. Of that, she had no doubt.

"Will you join me then?" she asked, as she slowly began to unbutton her top. By the time she managed to slip the second button from its hole, Taliff had unzipped his uniform and it hung precariously on his hips, held up only by an interesting part of his anatomy. Only luck kept it from pooling at his feet. Bad luck, that is.

She would have enjoyed seeing the shiny material fall to the ground in a heap, but she couldn't say the view of his chest wasn't just as mouth-watering as the rest of him. She had an insane urge to take him by the hand and lead him into the water. She wanted to bathe him with her own hands, to feel his muscles ripple as the water ran down his body in rivulets, to chase the running droplets with her tongue.

So, what was stopping her? He said to follow her instincts and that's exactly what she was going to do.

Although she may have only limited sexual experience, she wasn't about to let that stop her from seducing her man. She'd seen enough women with seduction on their minds to know that enthusiasm and passion were the most important ingredients to a successful seduction scene—those and a man willing to be seduced. And from the looks of the massive erection he was sporting, he was definitely willing.

By the time Eve shrugged out of her shirt and kicked off her pants, Taliff stood just in front of her gloriously nude. It only took a few steps for her to reach his side, and when she did, she took his hand in hers and led him to the water.

As she led him into the pool, her body creamed with excitement. She knew just what she wanted to do. First, she would lead him to the center of the pool and after she made sure to wet his skin thoroughly, she'd trace every droplet with her tongue. By the time she finished, she hoped his every nerve shrieked with intense sensation and he wouldn't notice any of the uncertainty and downright panic she'd no doubt feel.

Taliff couldn't believe this was really happening. Even though he hoped the *Chantrean* mating instincts would surface, he never truly believed they would. It seemed Alana really did answers the prayers of her people. What had he ever done to deserve such happiness?

She dropped his hand once they reached the side of the pool, but her body continued to press against his as they slowly walked down the steps and into the warm water.

Her scent wrapped around him like a blanket, beckoned him to sample her sweet nectar, to ride her into oblivion. And like a sailor answering a siren's call he had no choice but to follow wherever it led.

His thoughts scattered the moment he felt her hands brush against the sensitive head of his cock. Was it an accident or was she purposely trying to drive him out of his mind? Her eyes were focused on the tranquil turquoise water, so he couldn't read her intentions. Did it really matter?

With a resounding "No" echoing through his thoughts, he closed his eyes and let the water lap at his already sensitive skin. What would her hands feel like as she washed the impurities from his body? Would she be brisk and efficient, content just to share a bath? Or would she take her time and explore his body, creating an atmosphere of intimacy and caring? Taliff shivered in anticipation. He couldn't wait to find out.

Taliff continued to inhale her scent, to cherish her closeness as he followed her into the center of the pool. When he would have ventured into the deeper end of the pool, she grabbed his arm and pulled him to a stop.

When she peeked up at him beneath lowered lashes his breath hitched. Goddess, she was magnificent. When she took her lower lip and worried it beneath her teeth he thought he'd come right then and there. He couldn't get any harder. It just wasn't possible. She'd yet to touch him and he could already feel his seed spill from the head of his shaft. Slowly, she raised her hands and lightly pushed down on his shoulders. What did she have in mind now? It didn't take long to find out exactly what she had on her mind.

"Please, Taliff. Kneel down so that I can reach all of you. I need to wash you. Every inch of you."

How could he refuse such a request when uttered so sweetly?

Especially when at this point, she could ask him to plant citrus in the polar regions of his planet and he'd do so willingly, as long as she continued to touch him.

"Anything for you, *moya*. You've only to ask."

As he lowered himself into the pool of water and moved into the position she'd requested, Taliff thought of all the things he'd willingly do or sacrifice if it would only make his *moya* happy.

He'd leave his world and never return there if Eve demanded to be returned home. He wouldn't let her go and anticipated many problems once she realized a *Chantrean* woman's role on his planet. But in the end her happiness was paramount and, if that meant leaving his home and his family, then so be it. What he wouldn't do was ever give her up.

But thoughts like that had no business intruding on such a momentous night. There would be time enough later to worry about things that might not even come to pass. With a contented sigh, Taliff closed his eyes and rested his hands against his thighs. He didn't know if he could control himself if he reached out and touched her right now. It took all his immense self-control just to sit here passively and wait for her to make her move.

At the first touch of her hands as they caressed his biceps, he let out a stuttered gasp. Never had he felt anything so exquisite in all his life. His eyelids snapped open. He had to watch her face, see her expressions as she bathed him in the ritual way. This would only happen once in his very long lifetime and he didn't want to miss a single nuance.

Goosebumps pebbled along his skin as she lifted water between her cupped hands and let it cascade down his torso. He shivered in reaction and his unruly rod bobbed against the water as it begged for relief. Goddess, if just the water running down his body was this much a turn on, how would he handle the feel of her hands when they finally touched his skin?

Seconds passed and only the sounds of trickling water and his rasping breaths disturbed the stillness and intimacy of the moment. When he thought he could take no more of her torturous treatment, he learned the true torture had yet to begin.

As soft as a butterfly's wing, Eve's hands gently cupped his face. Her eyes shimmered with passion and ever so slowly she brought her lips to his in a fleeting kiss so soft, so full of sweetness and promise he wanted to weep in joy.

He hadn't realized his eyes had drifted closed until she stepped away and they opened in reaction to her withdrawal. Before he could utter a protest, her hands slid down his neck to caress his chest. It felt so heavenly to feel her whisper-soft touches he couldn't help but purr. Contentment and satisfaction filled him as he knelt at her feet and simply allowed himself this moment to enjoy her gentle touch.

Her hands slid over his biceps, his arms and finally trailed down to caress his hips as her tender touch followed the path the water had taken. More blood pooled in his groin and he groaned in frustration. He would never survive the night, not if she continued to torment him this way.

Minutes passed and, when she finally lifted her hands from his aching flesh, he thought the sweet agony was over only to have her circle him and begin the torment all over again. When his back had received the same tender treatment as his front, she leaned over his back and whispered into his ear, "Stand up and I'll wash the rest of you."

He groaned. How was he going to stand it when she finally touched the part of him that had spent the last thirty minutes desperate with need? And until the mating ritual was complete he couldn't spill his seed and this part of the mating night was all hers to control.

He'd heard it said by other males that their females could take hours to get through all the stages of mating seduction. How the hell did the men do it? He just hoped the Goddess Alana would grant him the patience he needed to make it through the night.

Eve must have known he was reaching his limit, because rather than draw out the rest of his bath, she washed his legs and feet with gentle efficiency. Only when the rest of him was clean did she reach out with her hands and cup his sex. Almost reverently her fingers stroked his turgid length, as though she found the feel of it fascinating. "I love your touch, *moya*. The feel of your hands caressing my shaft is almost more pleasure than I can take."

Her brows quirked and a mischievous smile flitted across her lips. "Is it?"

He swallowed in nervousness. He didn't need to read her mind to know that she was up to something.

"Only almost," she pouted before graciously dropping to her knees and taking his length into her mouth.

"Holy shit..." Argh. What new form of frustrated agony had his wayward tongue gotten him into?

After only a few strokes of her mouth down his shaft, she released him with a wet pop. "Poor, Taliff. Should you really be cursing in a place like this?"

He didn't know whether to whimper in relief or beg her to continue. Eve must have decided that she'd gotten him clean enough, for she scooted back and rested her ass on her heels and looked up at his face. Her gaze shot to his.

"I offer my life and love to you, to do with as you wish. I pledge to worship your body and offer up my own to you to worship and command. I in turn accept the same from you. Only to you do I offer my heart and my soul for you to protect or deny. I give all that I am and all that I will ever be to you. Do you accept me and all that I offer, my *moyo*, my mate?"

Chapter Twelve

Elation and relief swept over him as Taliff listened to the words he'd never thought to hear in his lifetime. The need to repeat the vows rippled through his soul. With as much grace as his trembling hands allowed, Taliff reached for Eve's hands and pulled her to her feet.

"I accept all that you are and all that you offer me, *moya*. I offer my life and love to you, to do with as you wish. I pledge to worship your body and offer up my own to you to worship and command. I in turn accept the same from you. Only to you do I offer my heart and my soul for you to protect or deny. I give all that I am and all that I will ever be to you. Do you accept me and all that I offer, my *moya*, my mate?"

Taliff waited for her answer. Fear ate at him until he saw Eve's nod. Her eyes were filled with unshed tears, and in that moment, he knew that whatever happened in the future they had this one night of perfect harmony.

Eve dropped her gaze, but didn't release his hands. After clearing her throat, she lifted her head and pulled on his hands. "Follow me," she whispered and began to lead him out of the water. He trailed behind her, one of his big hands intertwined with hers as she led him up the steps and over to one of the marble benches.

"Sit, please."

He nodded, aware of what was to come next and waited patiently. She might not fully understand what was happening and why she felt the need to do and say the things she was, but he wasn't about to interrupt the ritual because his conscience was screaming at him. Perhaps he'd catch hell later for not telling her, but he never said he wouldn't use her naiveté to keep her by his side if he had to.

EVE DIDN'T UNDERSTAND WHAT she was doing exactly, but it felt right, and for tonight, she wouldn't question her instincts. Maybe it wasn't the right decision and one she might well regret later, but this need driving her actions felt too important to ignore.

There was something else she needed to do, something vital, but what the hell was it? As her eyes scanned the clearing, her gaze darted over the various sculptures until it reached the one of a woman holding a golden chalice between her alabaster hands. The sculpture beckoned her to accept the offering as water flowed from the cup and pooled in a basin at the woman's feet in a continuous stream. Yes... That's what she needed.

She approached the statue silently, as though she was approaching Taliff's Goddess rather than her likeness. Even though she shouldn't know whom this woman represented, she could hear the musical sound of a woman's voice whisper through her mind and knew it to be Alana, the *Chantrean* Mother Goddess. The tinkling of her words vibrated along Eve's spine, as though a thousand harps should accompany the sound of her voice. *Drink my tears and purify your hearts. Share my tears and purify your souls.*

What did that mean exactly? Drink her tears she could pretty much understand. But how could she share the tears? Well, she'd figure it out when the time came, she guessed.

Reaching up, she pulled the chalice from the Goddess' hands and backed up a pace, before turning her back and carrying the golden cup to Taliff.

When Eve reached her mate's side, she knelt between his outstretched legs and slowly lifted the cup to his lips. "I beseech you to drink of the Goddess' golden chalice. Let her tears cleanse your heart and heal all your inner wounds."

Without hesitation, Taliff wrapped his hands around hers and tilted his head back, allowing the refreshing fluid to slide down his throat. Eve sighed in relief. Until her muscles suddenly relaxed, she hadn't known how tense she'd become while waiting to see if he'd accept her offering.

Once he quenched his thirst, he held the cup against her lips. This seemed too ritualistic to her. What was she doing? Why couldn't she stop herself?

Goddess, it was too late to think about that now. She needed to make love to him, but she needed to finish this first. She had no choice in the matter.

"I beseech you to drink of the Goddess' golden chalice. Let her tears cleanse your heart and heal all your inner wounds," he whispered. And like he, she tilted her head back and let the cool, clear liquid pour down her throat.

The moment the blessed water passed her lips a rush of feelings and sensations bombarded her. Joy, love, lust, hunger, need, desire, fear, worry and so many others she couldn't catalogue them all. But they weren't her emotions, or they weren't only hers. And after the rush of emotions settled into steady warmth, thoughts began to intrude. Her body began to shake as the emotional storm continued to rage.

Eve watched as Taliff's pupils dilated and his big frame shuddered.

Goddess, what a rush. There's so much...so much she feels. It's overwhelming. I can feel her fear as my own. How can I set her at ease with us, with our future?

Eve blinked in surprise. Is this what the Goddess meant about sharing her tears to purify their souls? She didn't know what to feel about this new turn of events. Would she not have privacy again? Immediately, she recoiled.

Pain and rejection slammed into her and she realized what she'd done by denying the connection they shared. She'd hurt her mate because of her own fear and she couldn't let that stand. She could already feel the distance between them and it terrified her that she might have destroyed their relationship before it even began.

How could she make this up to him? What could she do, say to make this right? Her anguish rippled through her and then she knew. She needed to share her tears by sharing her fears. She needed to embrace the bond developing between them.

After taking a deep breath, Eve closed her eyes and collected all her fears, her worries, and even her needs and desires, and tried to channel them through the bond.

She didn't know if she was doing it right, didn't really even know if it would matter to him now, but he needed to know it wasn't him she was rejecting. She worried he'd not only learn how cowardly she was when it came to loving another, but how terrified she was that she'd not be good enough at it to keep him with her. She'd always shied away from others, always more content to be alone than worry about another's wants and needs. If she couldn't make a go of it with him, someone she couldn't imagine being without, how would she survive?

"Oh, *moya*. Your worries can be seen to. Don't fret about something that will never come to pass."

Strong arms wrapped around her waist and pulled her against his solid frame. Eve closed her eyes in relief and tucked her head beneath his chin to rest her ear against his pounding heart.

A sigh of contentment escaped her parted lips. Relaxing further into his arms, she let the tension and nerves flow from her while she basked in the warmth of his emotions, which once again surged vibrantly strong through their newly formed bond.

"I'm so sorry, *moyo*. I didn't mean to hurt you," she mumbled against his chest. Tears of pain and regret trailed from her eyes and soaked his chest, but she couldn't seem to stop them.

"Ssshh, *moya*...ssshh."

"I can't, Taliff. What will I do if you leave me? Dammit, I'm not someone who acts this way. I'm strong. I don't know how to handle everything you make me feel."

"Baby, do you think you're the only one who worries that you're going to do something to screw things up? I'm terrified that you'll be taken away from me, that the men tracking us will succeed in capturing you, because I know the only way they'll get you is if I'm dead. Then who will be there for you? Who will save you then? It's not cowardly to be afraid. True courage is facing your fears, not avoiding them."

Silence descended between them while they let his words sink in, but it wasn't an uncomfortable moment, and after a few minutes, new sensations began to bombard her. The weight of his chin on her head and the feel of his hands on her waist no longer felt relaxing. Her heart rate soared and her palms began to sweat as she inhaled his musky scent.

She could feel his excitement through their bond and that only managed to ratchet up her own. Before long her tummy was jittery and her legs began to quiver. She knew he'd be able to smell her arousal, but she wouldn't let that bother her. Not tonight, anyway.

Goddess, she wanted to lead him to the nearest bed of blossoms and make love to him amongst his native flora. It seemed appropriate somehow that after tonight's events they consummate their mating night here where he felt closest to his home.

Well, what was stopping her? She was a mature adult. She could initiate lovemaking too. Eve took a deep breath to settle her nerves, then raised her head and looked into his glittering amber gaze. "Make love to me, Taliff. Here, where you're closest to your world and your Goddess. Let her bless our union."

Taliff groaned. "I thought you'd never ask, *moya*."

Taliff eased her out of his embrace and stood, careful to keep her at arm's length until he could lay her down and love her like she deserved. When she'd rejected him earlier he thought his heart would break. But it wasn't him she was rejecting and once he knew that, he realized that he would have to be patient and teach her that they could make their relationship work if only they tried. And he would start the instruction tonight, right here, right now.

Taking her hand in his, he led her to the far side of the clearing, pulled her to a stop and into his arms. "Close your eyes, *moya*. I want you to concentrate on my touch, on my voice. Just feel."

He planned on seducing her so thoroughly she'd not be thinking about anything other than the pleasure he could give her and the love and passion that blazed between them. After tonight, she'd never doubt what they were to each other again, or her own ability to be everything he'd ever need and want.

Taliff watched her eyelids flutter closed, heard her sigh of agitated frustration and grinned. She really didn't like to follow anyone's orders, so he couldn't wait to find out how far he could push her before she let loose that temper he knew simmered just below the surface. It was sure to be an experience he wouldn't want to miss or likely one soon forgotten either.

His blood pounded through his body at the thought of the intimate punishments he could deliver when she disobeyed his commands. But not tonight. He wasn't about to push her into the kinkier aspects of their intimacy until he knew she could handle it.

For now, their lovemaking excited him almost beyond bearing and he wouldn't do or say anything that might make her question that. With that in mind, he bent his head and gently pressed his lips against her temple, trailed down to the corner of her mouth and then finally, when her breath hitched, he kissed her full pouty mouth.

Lips and tongues met, breathy gasps and muffled moans echoed throughout the garden, but both were oblivious to anything but each other. Taliff knew the moment Eve let go and let the passion sweep her away, for he could feel her desperation and her acceptance of his passion through their telepathic bond.

He thought he could keep his control, lead them into a night of slow loving, but when her hands dug into his scalp and her fingers tightened around his hair, he knew that would be impossible.

When her knees began to shake and only her grip on his hair kept her standing, he bent down, swept her into his arms and slowly lowered her to the soft green grass. The sweet scent of the Tupas combined with the musky perfume of her arousal was indeed a heady and intoxicating blend.

His need was all encompassing and he knew that if he didn't fuck her soon, he just might release his seed in the grass instead of inside his mate. That just wouldn't do.

When her fingers reached up and brushed across his lips, his body shuddered. When she trailed her hands down his neck and over his pecs, he gasped. And when she took both his nipples between her nimble fingers and tweaked them, sweat beaded across his brow.

Was it her goal to totally shred his good intentions? Did she want to be ravaged?

Yes, Taliff. Ravage me. Hell, fuck me raw if you want. But do it now for Goddess' sake. I want it hard and fast, deep and rough. Don't hold back, moyo. *I need this.*

The sound of her voice brushing against his mind shattered what little control he had left. How the hell could he fight her when she wanted exactly what he wanted to give her? And why was he even trying?

"You want it rough, *moya*. That's what you're going to get. But one of these days, I'm going to give you the slow loving you deserve."

Thoughts of long kisses and extended foreplay disappeared from his mind the moment she grabbed him by his ears and pulled his body on top of hers. He groaned when his hard flesh met her soft curves. There would be no slow and easy now, just fast, hard fucking.

With more eagerness than finesse, Taliff positioned himself between her thighs, forcing her legs further apart. She lifted her legs and with a powerful lunge he seated himself fully within her gripping sheath. She was so incredibly wet. And tight, Goddess, she was so tight he thought she might lock him inside her.

She groaned loud and low and the huskiness of the sound rippled through him like an electric current.

He knew he hadn't hurt her despite his forceful entry, but he had to ask. "Are you okay, baby?"

"Shit, Tal. If you don't fucking move right this damn minute, you'll be the one hurting."

He chuckled. She sounded so fierce and intense. He could hear the growls rumbling in her chest and it turned him on even more. He could feel his shaft growing thicker and longer inside her and thought his heart would beat right out of his chest, the pleasure was so intense. He had to move and he had to move now.

He tried to ease out of her gently, but she wasn't having any of that and wrapped her legs around his waist to keep him lodged inside her clinging pussy. "Deeper, Taliff."

"*Moya*, baby, hold on."

His lungs labored and his pulse raced as he pounded in and out of her cunt. His pace was quick and hard and if the moans and whimpers coming from Eve were any indication, she loved the hell out of it.

Before long, they were heaving and sweating, writhing and grunting. The force of his thrusts grew stronger, the penetration deeper and still they fucked. Seconds later, he heard her scream out her climax through their bond and it nearly sent him over the edge with her. And when her clenching pussy tightened around his cock, it milked him of rope after rope of scalding hot and sticky cum.

"Fuck me, that was good."

"Unhh…"

He could hear her panting beneath him and knew he should move off of her. He had to be crushing the life out of her but he just didn't have the energy to move.

Eons passed, or maybe just moments, before he had the vigor to roll off of her and pull her into his arms. They lay like that, content, until she sighed. Uh oh, he knew he wasn't going to like whatever was about to come out of that lush mouth of hers.

"Um, Taliff. I hate to break the mood we have going here and everything, but I was wondering something."

She leaned down and kissed his chest, lapping at his nipple. He groaned, his cock stirring in anticipation of another round of lovemaking.

He waited for the hammer to fall and, when she remained silent, he turned his head toward hers. "What is it, *moya*?"

"When are all the woman supposed to wake up from their forced naps?"

"Oh, fuck…" He bounded to his feet, grabbed her hand and started to run toward their jumbled pile of clothes, dragging her behind him. "Get dressed, Eve. We don't want a mutiny on our hands."

Within moments, they were dressed and racing out the door. He just hoped all hell hadn't broken loose while they'd been incommunicado for the last few hours.

Chapter Thirteen

As they approached the corridor that housed the women, they heard the muted sounds of metal clanking and glass shattering inside the cabins. But the roar of hoarse voices, pleading whispers and angry shrieking that echoed up and down the corridor was loud enough to not only drown out their own thoughts but to announce to any ship nearby they were still alive. If the women didn't calm down soon, the chances of being ensnared by their enemies increased dramatically.

"What the hell do they have in their rooms to throw, Tal?"

He grimaced in distaste and looked toward his mate. "My guess, *moya*, is they're throwing their breakfast all over their quarters like rebellious children."

"Breakfast?"

"You don't think I'd allow them to starve, do you?"

"Well, you haven't fed me anything."

Goddess, she epitomized sexiness even when pouting. But he couldn't allow her to believe he'd neglect her by not seeing to her needs, while he made arrangements for the care of the others.

"*Moya*, have you even been hungry?" When she responded with a confused shake of her head, he decided to give her a break and explain. "During the 'Mating Rut' as we call it, it isn't uncommon for the pair to go days without sleep or even nourishment. It is believed that the building of the psychic bond provides energy for the pair. Once the rut diminishes, then both food and rest are needed almost immediately."

"Oh, I see."

A loud shriek and a muffled curse, followed by a damn ferocious growl had both of them looking down the hall in dismay, effectively ending any further conversation. "We better take care of this, Eve." With a shake of his head and fists clenched at his sides, he added, "Before we have more trouble than just a few dozen pissed off women to contend with."

"Well, then… What's your suggestion, Tal?"

"Let's gather them in one place and let them know exactly what's going on. They have a right to know how things stand."

"Fine with me. Why don't you have *Shoshoni* transport them to one location rather than letting them pour out into the halls and inundate us with questions and insults?"

Taliff thought it over for a second, then reached for Eve's hand and gave it a quick squeeze. "What did I ever do before you came along?"

"*Shoshoni?*"

"Yes, Commander Shi'Lan?"

"I want you to transport all the women to the Recreation Room on deck three once Eve and I arrive there."

"Understood, Sir." He tried to turn around and head back to the lift, but Eve seemed determined to stay right there in the middle of the corridor.

"What is it, Eve?"

"Oh, I just had a thought."

"Well, can you think and walk at the same time? We need to get those felines quieted down."

"Oh, hush, you smart ass. That's what I was thinking about if you must know."

"What do you mean?" He tried not to sound inpatient. He really did, but it must not have worked because she rewarded him with a scathing look and tried to tug her hand from his. "I'm sorry, Eve. I'm just worried, but that's no reason to talk to you as I did."

She must not have liked his apology because she ignored him and spoke to the computer instead.

"*Shoshoni?*"

"Yes, Eve?"

"Is there a way to put up some sort of barrier that would prevent anyone from hearing what's going on inside this ship? We'd really like to avoid being captured by whoever is after us if it's at all possible."

"If I divert power from unoccupied decks, I can create a containment field to surround that area as well as augment the shields surrounding the ship itself. It should muffle the noise. Had we had time to install all the software upgrades available, we might have been able to eliminate the voices completely."

"Is there a way to receive these upgrades through email or something?"

Taliff was getting pretty tired of being ignored and this was the perfect opportunity to interrupt. "Email?"

"It's a messaging system through the internet."

He must have looked confused because she sighed and pursed her lips. Before she could come up with a reasonable explanation, *Shoshoni* interrupted. "According to the information we gathered while hovering over Earth, it's a transmission of information through their computer networks."

"Well, that's close enough as explanations go. So, is there a way for you to receive the information without someone actually uploading the software manually, *Shoshoni*?"

"If I can send a transmission to King Shi'Lan and he's able to retrieve the data, it should be possible. Such a thing has not been done in millennia as most of our programming is learned."

"You mean you have AI?"

"What's AI, Eve?" She sounded so horrified he was almost afraid to ask.

"Artificial Intelligence."

"Of course. Once computers are programmed, most of their knowledge is learned from experience and their own observations. Is this not the way it is on your home world?"

"Of course not, Tal. There has been some success in the field, but humans are very wary of the possible consequences."

"You don't believe that computers should learn?"

"Tal, I haven't thought about it either way, but is now the right time to debate the pros and cons of your technology?"

Taliff stopped in front of the lift and, once the portal slid open, pulled her inside. "Deck three."

"You're right, Eve. But we will talk about this and your people's prejudices. We can't allow the women to fear what is natural to my planet and most of our allies."

"Fine, Taliff. But *not* now."

He chuckled. Goddess, he loved to irritate her. It made her eyes sparkle and her cheeks pinken. Blood rushed to his groin and he groaned, knowing he wouldn't be able to fuck his mate anytime soon.

"What?"

"Huh?"

"You groaned. What's wrong?"

He looked down at Eve's upturned face and smirked. What to tell her? Well, he hadn't lied to her yet. He wasn't about to start now. "I'm just thinking about the fact that I want you again and it's been less than fifteen of your Earth minutes since I was inside your luscious body." When her face turned a bright red, he just chuckled, swinging her hand in his while they walked out of the lift and down the corridor toward the recreation room.

"Stop it, Taliff. I have to face a room full of angry women in a minute and don't want to be flushed when I do so."

"I'm sorry, *moya*." He must not have sounded quite as contrite as he hoped because she cut him a nasty sideways glare. Time to change the subject. "The recreation room on this deck also doubles as a war room, so there will be plenty of seating for everyone."

"Good."

They'd almost reached their destination when he noticed her steps falter and her free hand go to the back of her neck. "What's wrong, Eve?"

"I don't know. I just had the oddest feeling like someone evil was watching me. It must be my imagination though."

Taliff narrowed his eyes and glanced around the corridor. He didn't see anything, but it was better to be sure than take unnecessary risks. "*Shoshoni?*"

"Yes, Commander Shi'Lan?"

"Have there been any transports on or off this ship since our prisoner escaped?"

"No, Commander."

"And all the women are accounted for? No women have left their rooms to roam the ship, have they?"

"Processing..."

"How can she know where everyone is, Tal?"

"Besides the fact she can detect heat signatures through the thermal sensors, everyone was tagged with tracking devices as soon as they were brought aboard the ship."

"You mean, we were *operated* on? While unconscious and without our permission?"

He could hear the anger and even disillusionment in her voice, but he didn't know what to say to set her at ease. "*Moya*, it was for your own protection. There's no reason for this outrage."

"So you say, but we *are* going to have a serious talk, and soon, Taliff. There are a lot of things about your people and your customs that I find very upsetting."

"Well, I can at least put you at ease a little. You weren't operated on. You were given an injection. The tracker moves through your bloodstream and attaches to your brain stem."

"Dammit, Tal. I don't want to know the hows and whys of it. That just makes it sound worse."

Okay, now her obstinacy was beginning to frustrate him. Did she just want to provoke him or was she really upset by what she'd heard? He could use their bond to find out but that somehow felt like an intrusion. He wanted her to tell him, felt she should tell him. And was that stupid or what? Goddess, he didn't have time right now to sort this out. It, and all the other things they really needed to discuss, would have to wait.

He shrugged and pulled her to a stop in front of the only door on this end of the deck. He hadn't lied when he told her it was large enough to double as a war room. "We're here."

She looked up and gave him a crooked smile. "I guess that means we have to go in then, huh?"

He grunted, then smiled himself as he watched her nervously wipe her hands on her thighs. "Yes, *moya*. We have to go in."

"All right. If we have to."

He could hear both resignation and a tinge of fear in her voice and wondered at it, but when she didn't say anything else and began to tap her foot somewhat impatiently, he figured he better stop procrastinating and get on with it.

As soon as they entered the dark room, Taliff knew something was wrong. If the absence of light hadn't told him the room's sensors had been tampered with, then the fact that a stranger's growl reverberated throughout a supposedly empty room would have.

Taliff pulled his mate behind him and faced the corner of the room where he knew someone lay in wait. As inconspicuously as possible, he reached for the communicator on his wrist and pressed the silent alarm. Now it was up to *Shoshoni* to get them out of this mess.

"Who's here?"

"Why, Taliff, don't you recognize me?"

The voice, although female, wasn't the least bit familiar to him. He could feel unease slither through his mate, but needed to focus on the stranger. "I can't say that I do. Should I?"

"Tsk...tsk...tsk..."

"Enough of the games and show yourself," he demanded. He wasn't about to let anyone distract him, because he doubted this female, whoever she was, acted alone.

When she stepped out into the light, Taliff gasped and pain the likes of which he'd never known whipped through him. "They told me you were dead."

Uncertainty and disillusionment blasted through his matebond. "Who is she, Taliff?"

"Yes, Taliff, tell her who I am. Or who I am to you anyway."

Chapter Fourteen

"It's not what you're thinking, *Moya*. This is Haeda, my sister."

"So, you *do* remember me. When no one bothered to pay the ransom, I figured you'd all decided to finally rid yourself of me. After all, I was only a lowly female, wasn't I?"

"What are you talking about, Haeda? There was no demand for ransom. Even though you were being held until your trial and more than likely would have died at Hunter's command, we would have rescued you from slavers had we known where to look. No one deserves such a fate. Not even someone who arranged for the murder of her parents."

Taliff heard Eve stifle a gasp behind him, but he was too worried about Haeda's presence here and the possible implications. Where had she been for the last fifteen years? How had she escaped the slavers witnesses had seen abduct her and the others?

Oh, Goddess, don't let what he was thinking be the answer. Could she really be the one they had been searching for? The elusive leader of the black-market broodslave ring Hunter and his council had searching so relentlessly for?

But somehow, it all made a perverse kind of sense. Shortly after he took the crown, word reached Hunter that women were being abducted. Rumor had it they'd been sold to breeding farms to produce female children who would in turn be later sold as mates.

Within weeks of their parents' suspicious deaths, he'd discovered his sister had plotted the 'accidental' drowning of their parents. He'd been forced to arrest Haeda and hold her for trial. The night before the tribunal, Haeda and three other women were kidnapped from their cells and never seen again. The only clue left behind was a black rose, the supposed signature of the Breeders.

Taliff cleared his throat. He had to hear her say she was the Black Rose, had to see her form the words with her own traitorous lips. "How long have you led the Breeders, Black Rose?"

Her sneering lips and vicious snarl marred her perfect *Lionese* features. Had she not radiated hatred and evil, you'd never believe she could be anything other than a typical *Lionese* female.

Thick hair hung well past her waist in various shades of blond and brown. Her amber eyes were slanted in the corners, giving her an exotic and very feline appearance. Tall and willowy for a *Chantrean* woman, at nearly six feet, she had always epitomized beauty and grace despite her height. So, how had they let her looks blind them to what she was inside? How had they never noticed her venomous core?

"I've been the Black Rose since I reached twenty cycles, Brother."

"You didn't disappear until after your twenty-fourth cycle."

"Yes, I know. And no one was the wiser. Four years I got away with my sideline and no one knew until Father overheard a conversation with my contact. Then of course, he had to die."

"Why? Why would you do such a thing?"

She laughed, an evil burst of sound that sent shivers down his spine. Why answer his questions? She had to be stalling for time, but what for?

"Because I can. I make a very nice living and no man can tell me what to do, where I can and cannot go and all the rest of the decisions our parents and now, Hunter, have taken away from *Chantrean* women."

Eve's muscles tensed beneath his hand. He could feel her anger build and build, flaring through their bond. Was she angry at what Haeda was saying about their society or was it something else? *What is it, Eve?*

Something is coming, or someone.

How do you know?

I'm not sure. Remember out in the hall? I felt evil watching, waiting.

Well, that feeling is emanating from your sister. And there are several more all over the ship. Somehow, I can feel them.

Thank you, moya. *Now we know why she's standing here answering questions.*

Taliff, what's taking Shoshoni *so long to transport her out of here? Something isn't right.*

You're right. Maybe Haeda will tell us herself, especially if she believes we're unaware others are aboard the ship.

Right. I'll play along for now, but that bitch makes one wrong move, even if she is your sister, her ass is mine.

My sister died the moment she ordered my parents' death.

Taliff could feel her subtle nod and knew only concern for his safety and that of the other women on the ship kept her from attacking Haeda. Man, he loved the woman. She was so fierce and protective of him and the others already. He couldn't wait until he got her with child. Mothering would come naturally to her. Their children would be the most protected children on the planet.

"Why are you here, Haeda? Why follow us and board our ship?"

"Why, brother dear, you're cutting into my business."

"What?" He couldn't believe it. Was she working with the other ships that had cornered them earlier, or was she just savvier and when they managed to escape, she decided to swoop in and make the kill herself?

"If you manage to bring a ship full of women to *Chantrea*, then eventually my 'services' will no longer be needed. And I just can't have that, now can I?"

Apparently, Eve had heard enough, because she yanked her hand free of his grasp, shoved him to the side and started to charge Haeda. "You bitch."

Taliff just managed to snag her wrist before she lunged for his sister.

"Oh, the little kitty has fangs after all. The way you were standing there behind Taliff, I assumed you were the perfect little submissive, just like every other *Chantrean* woman without a mind of her own."

Eve laughed. It was not a humorous sound. "Don't hand me that shit. Tal might buy your excuses, but I know them for the bullshit they are. If you didn't like the way women were treated you could have done something to try and change things. You're evil through and through and that's the only reason you do what you do."

"Give the little kitty a gold star." She shrugged her shoulders. "It was worth a try anyway."

"Why the games, then, Haeda?"

"It kept you busy, enough. Now, my crew should have managed to do enough damage to your ship to keep you here. You'll be trapped inside the asteroid belt until you crash into a floating rock and destroy yourselves."

Before Taliff realized what Haeda planned, her arm came up from her side and she fired a stun blast at him from a hand-stunner she'd hidden in her sleeve. He should have expected this. Unable to sound out a warning to Eve, Taliff crumpled to the floor.

With eyes he could barely keep open, Taliff watched in amazement as Eve launched herself at Haeda before she could fire off another blast. With a flying kick he'd actually only seen some of their greatest warriors manage, she knocked the weapon out of his sister's hand.

Her skills must have shocked Haeda, because she quickly backed up, tripping over his prone body before landing on the floor with a thud. Before he or Eve could reach her, she pressed a button on her own wrist communicator and disappeared from the room.

"Shit..." he heard Eve mutter.

Unable to speak due to the paralysis caused by the stun blast, Taliff voiced his agreement through their bond. *Yes. Shit about sums it up, moya.*

"What do I need to do, Taliff? How long are you going to be incapacitated?"

It shouldn't be long. My feet and fingers are already starting to tingle. Ten minutes and I should be up and around.

"Yeah, but a hell of a lot can happen in ten minutes."

What could he say to that? It was true and he knew it. *Before I left* orbit, I made arrangements for extra equipment. I loaded it myself and hid it in a secret compartment beneath the common room floor. A compartment that I designed and no one other than myself knows about. Not even the king and his advisors.*

"And that's going to help us how, Taliff? You can bet the reason we haven't heard from *Shoshoni* is that she's been taken offline and I know squat about computers. Especially computers that think and make decisions for themselves."

I'm already ahead of you, Eve. I had Shoshoni *back up all her essential programming inside a second 'brain'. Even if they destroyed the circuitry in her main console, all I have to do is slide the replacement in and connect a few wires.*

"You cloned, *Shoshoni*?"

In essence, yes. I tried to think of everything that could go wrong and made sure I had the parts necessary to make repairs myself. This mission is just too damn important to not take precautions. Our entire existence rests on this.

"Well, thank your Goddess Alana you thought ahead. But Taliff, what are the odds they've left this ship without taking some, if not all the women with them."

I don't know, Eve. I really don't know.

As the minutes ticked off, Taliff and Eve waited in silence for feeling to return to his extremities. He knew she wanted to rush out and check on the women. But she wouldn't leave him and he hated that she had to choose between them. He couldn't deny though, it left him feeling quite happy, despite their current circumstances, that she felt her place was by his side. And wasn't that incredibly selfish of him?

When the tightness in his throat began to loosen, he knew within seconds an agonizing wave of pain would boil through his bloodstream. So, when the pain hit he was prepared, or at least not surprised by it. He should have warned Eve though, was his last conscious thought before the convulsions started.

Only once the pain eased away and his body stopped seizing, did he hear Eve's frantic cries as she crouched over his prone body.

He tried to speak through swollen lips, but only a groan emerged. He licked his lips and tried again. Finally, he managed to whisper her name. "Eve..."

He tried again when she didn't seem to hear him, his voice much stronger than just seconds before. "Eve, I'm fine. Eve..." he hollered.

"Oh, shit, Tal? Don't you ever fucking do that to me again."

"So—" he croaked, then tried again. "Sorry, *moya*."

"Dammit, I'm going to be a nervous freaking wreck before this nightmare is over."

Taliff watched as Eve dropped her head to her chest and drew in a heaving breath. She shuddered once, collected herself, then raised her gaze to his. "Can you walk?"

"I think so. Give me a hand up. Although I know we need to account for all the women, as much as I don't like the delay in doing so, we need to make sure *Shoshoni* is operational first. If we crash into an asteroid while seeing to the women, all out efforts would be for nothing."

Eve nodded, but he could see the shadows in her eyes and feel the fear in her heart. "What is hurting you so, *moya*?"

"It's Amy, Tal. She's gone. I can feel it. That bitch sister of yours took Amy."

"If she has, we'll get her back."

"She has."

"Then let's get this ship fixed and find your Beta."

As Eve lifted him to his feet and wrapped her arm around his waist, Taliff prayed he would be able to make good on his promise. What would Eve do if she lost the only other person she trusted? Would she insist on leaving him to search for Amy on her own and risk her own capture? Haeda knew of her now, knew of their relationship. Until Haeda was captured, she would always represent a danger to Eve.

It didn't bear thinking of.

Without a backward glance, Taliff and Eve hobbled out of the room, both praying that they'd survive long enough to help their people.

Chapter Fifteen

Taliff and Eve took in the devastation in the Control Room on the Command Deck and winced at what was left of *Shoshoni's* mainframe. If he hadn't had the foresight to create a clone of his sentient computer's processing unit, they'd be without any hope of survival.

As it was, chances were slim they'd be able to return to *Chantrea* in one piece. Until *Shoshoni* could regain control of the ship, they were adrift in a sea of asteroids. If even one managed to punch through the outer Titanium hull, the ship would be destroyed along with everyone on board. And there were millions of potential projectiles out there.

Eve glanced down at the cart full of computer parts they'd wheeled out of the common room and grimaced. She didn't see how they'd ever be able to repair all the damage the Black Rose and her cohorts caused. "Do you know what you're doing?" she asked, looking over Tal's shoulder at the jumble of wires his hands were tangled in.

"Every battleship officer is trained to repair all areas of his ship. It might look like a mess, but it isn't so difficult to sort out once you learn what all the different colored wires represent and where they should attach."

"If you say so."

She must have sounded dubious, because he just shrugged his shoulders and grinned. "Trust me. I'll have *Shoshoni* up and running again in less than one of your Earth hours."

Eve decided to take him at his word and wandered over to where the viewscreen was usually visible. "I take it we won't be able to see outside the ship until you have her up and running again?"

"No, and truthfully, I'd rather not see how close we're going to get to some of the asteroids out there if it's all the same to you."

Eve shuddered as a chill swept up her back. He had a good point. "Yes, I can see how that might be just a tad bit stressful."

As Taliff worked to put his ship back together, Eve paced the Control Room, her arms crossed against the sudden chill. Hadn't she read somewhere that it was cold in space? Though her mate hadn't gone into details as to what happens to captured women, Eve knew that right now her Beta, and whoever else was missing, were suffering. Goddess, she could only imagine the atrocities they were experiencing at the hands of the Black Rose and her crew.

Amy was so young and so sweet. What would this do to her? After today, Amy wouldn't be the same woman who'd stood at her back just a day ago. She'd be forever changed, altered in ways no one could predict...if she survived at all.

Eve swallowed the lump in her throat and hastily wiped the tears from her eyes. She would not mourn her yet. If Amy was out there, she'd make sure she was found and nothing and no one would ever again take away someone she considered hers.

The Black Rose was dead. She just didn't know it yet. Eve smiled grimly and wondered what it felt like to be a walking, talking, dead woman.

"That should do it."

So caught up in her murderous thoughts, Eve hadn't realized that Taliff managed to finish putting all the wires back in place and sealed the panels closed. Nor had she noticed when the cart previously loaded neatly, became a jumbled mess of electronics and wiring.

"You're finished then?"

When he nodded and quickly moved the cart out of the way in order to reach the control console, Eve heaved a sigh of relief. "That's good news."

He turned to her, a half smile on his face, "It will be if I've done everything correctly, anyway."

"Okay, my fingers are crossed," and suited actions to words.

With a quirk of his lips, he turned back to his terminal and started pressing buttons. She had no clue what he was doing, but so long as it got them up and running, she didn't care. If they ever got out of this mess, she might want to learn to fly this metal monster, but right now her thoughts were on more important things.

"Intruder Alert! Intruder Alert! Intruder Alert!"

Eve snorted. "Better late than never, huh."

Taliff shook his head, twisted a few more dials, punched a few more buttons, then stepped back from the terminal.

"What was all that about?"

Taliff looked confused for a moment, then shook his head and looked her way. "Hmmm... I manually turned off *Shoshoni's* alarms."

"Okay, then why did you look lost there for a second?"

"Well, I replaced the entire memory unit of the computer. *Shoshoni* should only have the files and memories from before we left *Chantrea*, so how did she just remember the intruders?"

"Um, Tal, how do we know there isn't another intruder on board?"

Taliff closed his eyes and hung his head. "*Shoshoni?*"

"Yes, Commander Shi'Lan?"

"Where is the intruder?"

"A transport signal was detected on level three."

"Do you know how many people boarded the ship?"

"Insufficient data, Commander."

Taliff grunted. Eve grimaced. That was not particularly welcoming news.

TALIFF COULDN'T BELIEVE THE dramatic events of the last forty-eight hours. He'd found his mate, been attacked by a friend, fucked his mate gloriously, employed the *Manruvian* Mating bonds, completed all but the last stage of the mating ritual, discovered his sister was alive and learned the identity of the broodslave ring's leader.

And now, after all that and narrowly escaping death by asteroid, someone else had managed to board his ship. Could things possibly get any worse for them?

"What are we going to do now, Tal? We don't even know how many women were taken, and without that knowledge, we can't determine how many just arrived."

Taliff snorted. Like she wasn't telling him something he didn't already know. "*Shoshoni*, all the women originally transported on board this ship had DNA extracted and trackers in place. Can you take a sample of Eve's blood and determine the tracking marker frequency from that?"

"Yes, Commander. May I make a suggestion, Sir?"

"If you have any ideas that might keep us alive, I'm ready to hear them."

"Are you the only male who should be aboard the *Wanderer*?"

"Yes, *Shoshoni*. Besides myself and Eve Roberts, there should be forty-five other Earth *Lionese* women and no one else."

"I detect thirty-seven women aboard the *Wanderer*, each transmitting a low-range frequency similar to the female standing near you. There are eight *Manruvian* Mermen and three male *Chantrean* on board including you."

Eve gasped. "Mermen?"

Taliff nodded and smiled. Even with the news that eight of their women disappeared from the ship, things were definitely looking up. The *Manruvians* were staunch allies of his brother, Hunter, and would never be party to the assassination of one of his family members. "Who are the male *Chantreans*, *Shoshoni*?"

"Taliff Shi'Lan, Hunter Shi'Lan and Tanner Dav'Ren."

"Dav'Ren... Isn't that the name of the guy who planted that bomb on here yesterday?" Eve asked.

"It sure is. What the hell is Hunter doing here and with an apparent rescue team along?"

"I don't know, but if they're here to help, I don't care what prompted this unexpected visit."

"Good point, Eve. *Shoshoni*?"

"Yes, Commander Shi'Lan?"

"Transport all the members of the *Manruvian* delegation as well as the other two male *Chantreans* to this location."

"Yes, Sir. Transport lock enabled. Working. Transport complete."

Taliff couldn't help but roll his eyes. By the time *Shoshoni* finished speaking, ten men surrounded him and Eve, all aiming stun blasters at their chests. "This seems to be getting to be a habit for you, Tal," Eve murmured.

Taliff snickered, then stepped forward and pulled his brother into a hug. "Not that I'm unhappy you're here, brother—far from it, in fact—but why are you not on *Chantrea* right now?"

"I received an urgent message from *Shoshoni* on my wrist com while in talks with the *Manruvian* delegates here. When we realized the danger you were in, the *Manruvians* offered the use of their technology to reach you."

Taliff's head snapped up in surprise. "I thought that was strictly forbidden."

"It used to be," said one of the mermen. "This is the first step in forming a more permanent alliance with your world."

Taliff swallowed convulsively and reached for Eve's hand. "My mate and I thank you for your help. If you or yours are ever in need, call upon us immediately."

The blonde merman smiled and lowered his head in acknowledgement of the debt owed. "It will be as you say."

Eve tugged on her hand and tried to step away from his side, but he wasn't about to have any of that. "Eve, I'd like you to meet my brother, Hunter Shi'Lan, the High King of *Chantrea*."

Eve stopped squirming immediately. In fact, she looked a little green and panicked. "King?"

Taliff winced as her voice crackled with outrage. Now wasn't exactly a good time to introduce her to the way women behaved in front of *Chantrean* males, but what choice did he have? "You will not raise your voice above a whisper in the presence of others. Is that understood, Eve?"

She gasped and all the color in her cheeks blanched out of her face. He wanted to swear to the heavens. He'd known she would react this way. It's why he'd never discussed what was to be expected of her once he reached *Chantrea*. Perhaps he should have told her right away and trained her in the proper submissive behavior, but he hadn't wanted to tarnish their budding relationship.

The usually confident light in Eve's dimmed, her fingers grew slack in his and the bond, which had been burning with intensity between them for hours, winked out of existence. "I see," she whispered, then turned her gaze downward, too heartsick to even hold up her head. Tears splattered the decking beneath her feet, yet she didn't utter a sound, just let the tears silently fall where they would, a silent and poignant testimony to the depth of her pain.

What had he done?

Taliff swallowed past the lump in his throat and looked away from his mate. Pity gleamed in his brother's eyes and he prayed the others couldn't tell just how much he wanted to allow his own tears to fall.

He would fix this thing between them. There were no other acceptable options. But first, he had to get them and the remaining women to *Chantrea*.

"So, tell me, oh king of mine, how in the hell are we to get home without suffering yet another attack?"

Hunter's eyes sparkled with mischief. "Oh, let me take care of that."

Taliff shook his head, hard pressed not to laugh. Once, Hunter was well known for his devilish, and oft times, depraved humor. He couldn't wait to see what he had up his sleeves.

Chapter Sixteen

Eve watched the proceedings from a distance. In fact, everything felt distanced to her. Where before joy had filled her heart, now despair dwelled. A black cloud of depression had extinguished her hope for a happy future among the *Chantrean* people.

She lost Amy to the Black Rose and Taliff to his customs. Only the women who'd been aboard the *Wanderer* were hers to care for now, and even that seemed too much responsibility for her to bear.

She had no idea where Taliff had gone after he deposited her on board the *Manruvian* Ship, *Victory*, several hours earlier. All she'd been told was that all of the women would be transferred to the Merman's ship and escorted into *Chantrean* air space.

Eve was thankful that she'd be alone for the journey. She didn't know what to say to Taliff, or hell, what to feel. The hurt and pain were so deep, so debilitating she could only assume she did indeed love the ass. Too bad she'd figured it out too late to do anything about it.

The longer she stared out the viewport of her quarters, the larger the pink and purple world of *Chantrea* grew. Soon, they'd arrive and instead of excitement and anticipation, Eve felt nothing but dread. How was she to lead the women, to make them see the positives of the situation, when she couldn't see them herself?

It seemed an impossible situation, but there was nothing else to do but get through it one day at a time. And if those days were now something to dread rather than anticipate, it was her problem, not that of the others.

She'd ensure they knew about all the rules of *Chantrean* society, so they wouldn't be blindsided as she had been. Perhaps then they at least would have a chance at finding happiness with their future mates. Her happiness died nearly a day ago.

A lone tear trailed down her cheek and she absently flicked it away. Would the heartrending pain never end?

TALIFF SWALLOWED THE BILE that threatened to spill from his throat. The pain on Eve's face and the total absence of spark in her eyes nearly destroyed him. Somehow he had to make this right. But how?

What if he'd damaged their relationship beyond repair? Didn't she realize he didn't want her to be submissive all the time, just in public? And how insane was that? Other than in the bedroom, Eve didn't have a submissive bone in her body. She was alpha through and through.

His thoughts should have been on her needs, not on saving face in front of the other men. If he could reach around and kick his own ass, he would. But that would only serve to make him feel better, not fix the mess he had made.

Perhaps he and his people needed to change, rather than their Earthen counterparts. What had his people really gained by having the men make all the decisions? Hadn't he repeatedly insisted, at least to himself, that Eve was just as strong and dominant as he? Why would the *Chantrean* females be any different? And why in Goddess Alana's name hadn't he realized this earlier, before destroying whatever faith and love Eve had begun to feel.

"For what it's worth, Eve, I am sorry. I was wrong. Wrong about so much."

He watched as Eve's shoulders stiffened, but she refused to turn and look at him. He couldn't blame her, he'd treated her abominably, and he knew it. Somehow, he'd earn her respect back and maybe one day her love, though he didn't hold much hope for that.

Shit, what was he talking about? What nonsense was his subconscious spouting? He snorted. He was just as Alpha as she, her match in every way. He would find his way back into her heart. No other alternative was acceptable. And it was about damn time he remembered that, too. "I can't change the way all the women on our planet are treated, *moya*. But I can treat you the way you deserve. I won't be placing you in the women's wing at the palace, but moving you into my personal ones."

"You think that makes everything better, Commander Shi'Lan?"

Tal winced at Eve's use of his station rather than his name. Things could be better, but at least she'd finally spoken. "No, *moya*, but perhaps you and your pride will have the influence over their mates to change the way things are. One day, we might be worthy of your respect, but until then, we can only take one day at a time and do our best to become the men you all deserve."

Eve shook her head in denial as she continued to look out into space. "Pretty words, Tal. That's just a bunch of pretty words."

He didn't know what else he could say to her, and maybe words weren't enough anyway. He'd prove to her he respected her opinions, her strength and even her independence.

"You're right, Eve. Until you see that I'm speaking the truth, that's all they are. Pretty words." He straightened from the doorway and moved across the room to stand behind her. He ached to pull her into his arms, to promise her he'd make things right. But no matter how much it would ease his despair, it wouldn't make her believe him, or make things better between them.

"Please, Eve. I can't stand this distance between us. Maybe that's selfish of me, but the pain is too much."

When she still didn't turn to face him, he did the only thing he could think of to prove that he didn't need to always be in charge. He dropped to his knees, lowered his head to the floor and placed his hands behind his back. "I submit to you, *moya*. All that I am, all that I will ever be, is yours to do with as you please."

He heard her suck in a startled gasp and prayed he'd done the one thing that showed his sincerity.

As the seconds passed and Eve made no move to accept his submission, the last of Taliff's hope vanished. His heart, which he thought could hold no more pain, overflowed with it. Tears flowed from his bowed head in rivers and he made no move to wipe them away.

"Oh, Tal," Eve sighed. "I don't want your submission. I only want to share my life with you—to be your equal, not your doormat."

His voice thickened with tears. "Forgive me, *moya*."

He heard the rustle of her ankle-length skirt as she moved to kneel in front of him. The whisper soft touch of her trembling fingers beneath his chin sent a shiver of longing through his frame. When she finally raised his face to look into hers, he could see the light in her eyes he thought to never see again.

He wanted to hold her so bad, but would she welcome his touch?

You won't know if you don't try, Tal.

Eve?

Who else speaks to you this way?

Only you, moya. *There is only you.* And he knew she realized exactly what he was saying. From now on, her thoughts, feelings and needs, took priority over all else.

Taliff felt Eve's tentative psychic probe as she attempted to reestablish their mate bond. He mentally grabbed hold of the flickering connection and poured all his emotions, all his fears and worries, through their bond, until the link between them was as solid and strong as titanium forged over the fires of Gangi.

With infinite tenderness, he pulled Eve into his quivering arms, doing his best not to crush her with his strength. When she nestled her face into the curve of his neck, he breathed a sigh of relief and laid his head atop hers. He'd allow nothing to come between them again, especially not his own stupidity.

Minutes passed as Taliff held on to his mate, aware only a few minutes remained of their time alone. Soon they would approach the space dock and be expected to immediately transport to the planet below. He wanted to show Eve all his planet's delights, but until their plan was implemented, he'd need to forego the grand tour.

Her safety and the safety of her pride demanded extreme precautions, but he'd do his best to ensure Eve never felt a prisoner in her own home. If he had to bring the wonders of *Chantrea* to her, she'd never feel as though he kept her only to serve as his broodmare.

Enough of their women had suffered that fate over the generations and he'd perpetuate the custom of isolationism and servitude no longer. Now, if only he could somehow convince the rest of *Chantrea's* males to change their ways. Ah well, that was something to think about another day.

The intercom chimed and Taliff reluctantly let loose his grasp on his mate. "It's time, *moya*."

Eve nodded, then glanced away, but not before he saw the worry skitter across her face. He sighed, understanding the difficulty she'd face. As strong and independent as she was, it would be very hard for her to see how the others were to live. Her compassion for others was just one thing he so loved about her.

After getting to his feet, he pulled Eve into his arms, gave her a quick squeeze, then with her hand in his walked to the intercom panel. "Go ahead, Computer."

"Your presence is needed at the demarcation point."

"Understood, Computer. Wait thirty seconds, then transport Eve Roberts and myself there."

"Understood."

"Are you ready, Eve?"

She gave him a fleeting smile that didn't reach her eyes, before nodding. "I'll make things right for you and the others, Eve... somehow."

"I know you'll try, Tal, and that's all you can do."

He could hear the resignation and doubt in her words and vowed to do his best to make his words reality.

Seconds later, Taliff and Eve stood amongst the others transporting down to the surface. Not only were the rest of the Earth women transporting down as well as Tanner and Hunter, a contingent of armored *Manruvians* would accompany them. They were taking no chances of losing the women to a surprise attack upon their arrival on the planet.

Hunter Shi'Lan, High King of *Chantrea*, looked over those gathered in front of him and sighed wistfully. His gaze landed on his brother Taliff, who held the hand of his mate securely. He was happy for his brother, truly he was. But he wished that his match had been found among this batch of *Lionese*. He hadn't given up hope that he'd find her, but the wait for her disheartened him.

Pasting on a smile he knew didn't reach his eyes, he addressed those gathered in front of him. "*Chantrea* is a land of prosperity and peace, but a land suffering for lack of women. That is where you all come in. Our people need you. Our men need you."

Muttered voices and darting glances met his unflinchingly honest statement. Better to lay out all the facts now than to withhold information. He'd seen the results of that just yesterday between Taliff and his mate.

"However, *Chantrea* is also a land of subservient women." Startled gasps and heartrending moans filtered through the crowded room. He hadn't expected anything less after witnessing Eve's reaction. Hopefully, what he said next would ease their hearts and fears some.

"I have witnessed with my own eyes the deep pain this type of treatment causes, so I can promise this...I will share this information with my council and will urge my advisors to make changes. Change won't be complete overnight, but as High King of *Chantrea*, I vow that women will have greater opportunities afforded them."

The women wore various expressions on their faces, from disbelief and outrage, to resignation and hope. His advisors were a stubborn lot as were most men of *Chantrea*, but the felines of Earth were their last hope. If they were to survive, their customs and traditions would no longer serve them.

Hunter smiled in anticipation at the battle to come. He'd always loved a challenge and trying to convince *Chantrean* men they didn't need to do all the thinking for their mates was a worthy one. "I hope you all find happiness on your new home. *Chantrea* and all her bounties await you below."

Hunter glanced at the contingent of *Manruvians*, looking for the familiar golden hair of their commander. When his gaze met Mikel's, his long time friend and ally, he nodded. Once he heard his friend issue the order to stand ready, he turned his head toward the Merman operating the transportation station. "Transport us directly to the coordinates I gave you, Captain."

"As ordered, Sir. And good luck."

With a tingling in his extremities, the steel gray of the ship disappeared in a blink and he found himself and the other men locked behind titanium bars, in the dungeon of his palace.

"Goddess, dammit," Taliff shouted.

What else was there to say? The women were gone and their supposed protectors were trapped in an impenetrable prison unable to come to their rescue. Hell, they couldn't even rescue themselves. And somewhere, the Black Rose and all her followers were crowing their triumph.

Chapter Seventeen

Though she shouldn't have been, Eve was surprised to find herself and the other women locked behind the gilded doors of a harem, or what she'd always associated as 'harem-esque' anyway. Was that even a word? And why did inane thoughts always flutter through her mind when she should be thinking of more important things? It made her feel stupid.

"Well, isn't this an interesting turn of events?" Eve looked over the group of gaping and flustered women and knew it was time they showed the *Chantreans* that women were useful for more than procreation and servitude.

"All right, ladies, let's kick some ass. From what I've learned about *Chantrean* males, the women here are kept submissive and so the men aren't used to strong women. That's to our advantage."

The women smiled and nodded amongst themselves. Until the *Chantrean* men were shown that women could take care of themselves—and others— they'd never be considered equals.

Every woman in the garishly decorated red and golden room was aware that this was their opportunity to prove their worth and their usefulness. Female lions on Earth were more than decorative, skillfully providing food and protection to their prides. The *Chantreans* were about to discover just how capable these *Lionese* were.

"Any suggestion on how to get out of here, ladies?"

A petite brunette in the back of the cluster held up her hand. "I've an idea."

"What's your name?"

"Liana Peterson."

"Okay, Liana, if you have an idea that might get us out of this room, I'm all ears."

Liana swallowed and looked to the other women surrounding her. Eve could feel her nervousness. This omega obviously was unused to speaking her mind. The fact that she'd chosen to do so now, when the others were all watching, said strong things about her true character. Once this was over, Eve would take Liana under her wing and teach her some assertiveness.

"If anyone managed to leave Earth with some bobby pins, I think I'll be able to pick the lock. It appears to be of the same variety we used on the bathroom doors at my house growing up. My little brother was forever locking himself in there and needing rescued."

"That's a great idea. Do any of you have a bobby pin lodged somewhere in your hair?" After feeling around in her own tresses fruitlessly, she shrugged. "I lost mine during my capture."

Finally, after several minutes of groping and prodding through their tangled tresses, someone shouted. "Ah ha. I found one."

"Thank God," someone muttered from the back of the room. Eve agreed wholeheartedly with that sentiment. But she couldn't help but interject a bit of knowledge while they were trapped here. "The *Chantreans* believe a Mother Goddess protects and shelters them. The Mother Goddess Alana."

"Well, at least they got one thing right on this backward planet. Earth women have always known that God had to be a woman."

Chortles and snorts erupted from the women as they let the witty comment wash over them and lift their spirits. Seconds later, they really had something to laugh over. Liana stood in the doorway, the view of the empty hallway apparent to them all. "You're a gem among women, Liana."

Liana's blush spread as the women surrounded her and began to hug her in appreciation. No matter how much she'd like to hang around and bullshit with the women, they had men to rescue and the Black Rose to capture. For she had no doubt, the Black Rose had something to do with the treachery that put them in this situation to begin with.

"Liana, I want you to close the door for now, but make sure it stays unlocked. When we leave here I want you to lock the door as though we're still trapped inside." When she nodded in understanding, Eve turned to the rest of the ladies waiting for their orders.

"I need to try to reach Tal. Maybe he'll know where he is and where in the hell we are. After that, we can figure out how to rescue them and figure out what in the hell is going on in the palace."

Eve closed her eyes, blocking about the muted whispers of her pride. *Tal?*

Moya?

What the fuck is going on, Tal?

I really wish I knew. We're locked in the damn dungeon of the palace. We're still trying to figure out how to get free. There are quite a few pissed off Manruvians *in here with malfunctioning weaponry.*

Well, if you can tell us how to get to you, consider yourself rescued. We've already managed to pick the lock of our hideously decorated prison.

She could feel his laughter through their bond and knew her inane comments amused him.

What does the room look like, moya? *Perhaps you're somewhere in the palace.*

Hell, I could have told you that. They put us in a red room full of pillows and gold trim. Looks like a harem crossbred with a whorehouse.

Taliff snorted. *You're in the Easers apartments. The sex workers use them to ease our warriors.*

I so do not want to know that, Taliff. She huffed in exasperation. *Just tell us how to get to you, will ya?*

Take the hallway to the left until you reach an intersection that splits in five directions. Take the hallway farthest to the right and follow it down to the end. It will look like a dead end, but if you face the wall and press the right bottom brick it should release the hidden latch. The dungeons are at the bottom of the stairway.

Hang tight. We'll be there shortly.

Be careful, moya. *There will be opposition. You can count on it.*

I'm looking forward to it.

After blowing him a mental kiss, Eve's eyes snapped open. "Okay, ladies. I know where the men are. Now let's go save their asses."

With enthusiastic nods, the woman all fell behind Eve as they silently left their prison.

The halls were empty and eerily silent as they made their way to the five-way intersection Taliff spoke of. Where the hell was everyone? Shouldn't the palace be overrun with people? Where were the maids, the advisors? Hell, even the sex workers were missing.

"Keep your ears open, ladies. I don't like the feel of this. All this quiet is making my senses shriek in warning," she whispered to those next to her, indicating they should pass the word.

If someone had told her that thirty-seven women could move together in absolute silence, she would have thought they were stoned, because everyone knows that you put two women together in a room and silence was impossible. But Eve was impressed with the stealth these women used when the situation called for it.

They were nearly to the end of the corridor where the hidden door waited when they were spotted by a group of *Chantrean* men dressed in unrelenting black. "Spread out, ladies. Go for the kill, for now. Let's rescue the men before we take prisoners."

As though they'd hunted and fought together as a unit for years, the women spread out. The betas paired up with the gammas and omegas…the strong protecting the weak.

And she, she faced off with the apparent leader of this particular bunch. It wasn't the Black Rose, but the conceited sneer and leering glances clearly revealed his sense of self-importance. She didn't need a bit of her psychic abilities to know he and his men planned on raping them as soon as he had them hidden away from prying eyes.

Like hell.

Eve's lips curled in distaste. He wouldn't get one of his grimy paws on her or any of her pride.

"Why is it evil souls usually wear pretty faces?"

"Are you talking to me, woman? Get on your knees where you belong."

Eve laughed. She just couldn't help it. When Taliff said those words, her panties became soaked with need. This creep didn't even warrant so much as a quirked eyebrow in response. He might be a sexual deviant, but he wasn't sexually dominant.

"You couldn't get me to kneel at your feet, even if you had help holding me down."

She could hear the growl of pure meanness erupt from his throat and knew any second he would try to take her down. He'd never get the chance. "Now," she hollered.

The men, expecting the women to put up little or no fight, were unprepared for the roars of rage that shattered the eerie silence. While the men were distracted, the women went for the kill, ripping the throats out of the rebels with unsheathed claws. Only the leader still lived, though from the amount of blood pooled beneath his body he wouldn't last but a minute or two.

She squatted next to the dying leader and looked upon him with disdain. "Where is everyone being held? You have to be keeping them somewhere."

"Go... hell...bitch." Blood gurgled from his gaping wound until he breathed his last. Less than a minute had passed since she ordered her pride to attack.

"What do you want us to do with the bodies, Eve?" asked Lily, one of the eldest of the women.

"Leave them here. Let the others see for themselves what will happen if they don't surrender."

The women quickly backed away from their prey, surreptitiously wiping blood from their clothes and hair. Eve almost snorted. Even when in battle, a woman tried to keep her appearance presentable.

Eve quickly led the women to the end of the hall and pressed the appropriate brick. Once the hidden door swung open, she waited until the last of them entered the unlit stairway before letting it swing shut, sealing them in to the musty darkness.

"Okay, ladies. The dungeon is supposed to be at the bottom of this staircase. I imagine it will be heavily guarded. If you have the chance to get the cells open, go for it. It will be easier to defeat the opposition if the men are fighting with us."

Whispered murmurs of agreement drifted up the stairs, then all went silent as they descended deeper and deeper into the bowels of the fortress. It wouldn't surprise her to find that all of the *Chantrean* males who usually roamed the castle were being held in the cells. It was the location of all the missing women they needed to discover. But first things first.

Once they reached the bottom of the steps, Eve squeezed past the others. She pulled on the metal door, praying it would open silently. Nothing happened. Dammit. It, too, appeared locked and this lock looked nothing like that of their earlier prison. In fact, it didn't look like a working lock at all. Maybe some sort of decoration. Shit...

"Liana?"

"Yes, Mistress?"

"Oh, please. Just call me Eve. Come here and take a look at this lock. How can we get through here?"

The others spread out a bit to let the petite woman through. Seconds passed as Liana inspected the lock. "I don't know. I doubt a bobby pin will work on this. It looks like an electronic key of some sort is needed. See?" she said, pointing at the panel mounted on the wall near the door.

"Hmm... that gives me an idea. Did any of you happen to hear where our ship was taken?"

"I did," Lily piped up. "They attached some sort of tow beam to it and dragged it behind them."

"So, theoretically, *Shoshoni* should be above us somewhere."

At Lily's nod, Eve reached for her link with her mate. *Tal?*

Moya, what is it? Is all well?

Just a slight delay. Are you still wearing your communicator?

Yes, though I'm not sure it works since no one has responded to our numerous calls for help.

Try Shoshoni's *frequency. I need her to send a signal that will unlock all the electronic locks in this place.*

Minutes passed before they finally heard the nearly silent beep of the lock being disengaged.

Thanks, moyo. *We're on our way.*

"Let's go, ladies. Try to leave two or three guards alive if possible. We need all the information we can get."

Eve eased the door open and crept into the dimly lit corridor. The others entered the hallway just as silently. She could see several hallways that branched out from this main one. A lot of people could be held down here. They needed to search them all.

"Split up," she whispered. "Stay in groups of three or more, if possible, and take no unnecessary chances."

Like shadows, the women disappeared down the different corridors, careful to move with absolute silence and always on their guard.

Eve, with Lily and Liana, made her way down the main hallway. She could feel the tug of her mate and followed the tenuous link down the darkened corridor. Just before they reached the end, Eve spotted another door. She crouched down to peer at the nearly rusted through lock. This one at least appeared similar to one that used skeleton keys back home. "Liana, can you pick this one?"

Liana looked over Eve's shoulder and whispered into her ear, "I should be able to. Give me a sec."

It took longer than a second, but in the end this lock gave just as easily as the one upstairs in the bordello. Liana nodded at Eve and stepped back, fully aware as Alpha, Eve would enter first.

"If you're in there, Tal, I'm coming in."

Slowly, Eve turned the handle and made to step into the darkened cell. Too late she remembered that Taliff said that their cell had bars. Perhaps if she remembered sooner, she would have been prepared for the sight that greeted her. But in all honesty, after what Taliff told her yesterday, nothing could have readied her for this discovery.

Chapter Eighteen

Tal?

Yes, Eve?

Has someone released you yet?

Not yet, but by the sounds coming from the head of this corridor it won't be much longer. Why, Eve? What's wrong?

I wouldn't say wrong, exactly, but definitely unexpected.

What is it, Eve?

What do your parents look like, Tal? Because I swear I'm looking at your brother's mirror image, or what he'd look like if he were in his sixties.

That's impossible, Eve.

Well, tell that to the man asleep on this well-worn cot. And he isn't alone.

Eve approached the sleeping man and his female companion as cautiously as she could. If she had been trapped beneath her home for fifteen years without anyone's knowledge, she'd attack her rescuer if it meant freedom.

She could feel Lily and Liana at her back and hoped they'd continue to watch the door. She really didn't want them to be discovered by the enemy right now.

Eve reached out to lightly shake the man's shoulder. Before she could react, he reached out and snagged her hand, pulling her onto the bed. His other hand quickly wrapped around her throat. "Who are you?" he demanded.

When it looked like Lily and Liana would intervene, she held up her hand to stop them. "My name is Eve Roberts. I am Taliff's mate."

"Impossible. Taliff and Hunter died fifteen years ago."

"No," she croaked. His fingers squeezed her throat tighter at her denial. She needed to speak fast before he killed her. "Are you their father?" She knew the answer, but she had to have confirmation.

"Yes, I'm Brantiff Shi'Lan. And this," he said, dragging his unresponsive mate onto his lap, "is their mother, Luma."

Well, now she had verified their identities, but how were Taliff and Hunter going to handle the news? "To them, *you* drowned fifteen years ago."

"Haeda didn't kill them then?"

"No. But they think she managed to kill you." His fingers eased up a little and Eve took a gasping breath. "Somehow, she escaped her cell here when you disappeared at sea and took on the role of Black Rose fulltime."

She must have said something that struck him as honest, because he dropped his hand from around her swollen throat. She didn't waste any time jumping up from the bed and out of arm's reach.

"Where are my sons?"

"They're being held in one of the cells down here. We were trying to find them as well as everyone else who's gone missing around here."

"It's been nearly a week since we've eaten. All we'll do is hold you up. Find my sons."

"Don't be ridiculous," she scoffed. First she'd assess Luma, then they'd figure out how to get the two out of here unseen. "How long has she been in this state?"

"She hasn't woken in two risings. I fear her life on this realm is drawing to a close."

"I'm a healer. Let me see what I can do for her."

Seconds passed and finally he relented, waving her forward with a regal sweep of his hand. Even filthy and near starved this man oozed power and authority, his nobility shining through.

Eve approached the unconscious woman and gently rested her palms on Luma's torso. With eyes closed, Eve tapped into her inner self, the place where her healer's warmth flowed strong and sure. She gathered her power, built it up until she thought she'd lose control if she tried to collect any more and eased it through her body and out through her hands.

A golden light bathed Luma as Eve's powers seeped into her pores. Minutes passed silently while she willed all her strength into Tal's mother. She couldn't allow Luma to die. This family had suffered enough tragedy at the hands of Haeda and she'd be damned if Tal would lose his mother all over again.

Just as her strength began to wane, she felt Tal merge with her, driving his healing powers through the bond. Thank the Goddess. She didn't know Taliff could heal, but it just might be enough to mend the internal injuries his mother suffered. Some of the organs had deteriorated due to continual starvation, while others look like they'd been the result of beatings. The energy she was infusing should go a long way toward giving Luma the energy to eat on her own.

Finally, the golden light thinned and eventually disappeared. Eve had done all she could. It was up to Luma now.

Eve staggered back and dropped to her knees. She barely had the strength to hold herself upright. If Lily and Liana hadn't jumped forward and caught her as she slumped down, she'd be laid out flat on the dirt-covered floor.

She didn't know where Tal was, but he was moving closer. The flickering signal she'd followed earlier was gaining strength every second. And it wasn't a second too soon. If a large contingency attacked now, they wouldn't stand a chance. She was just too whipped to help.

TALIFF STOOD IN THE open doorway and gaped in wonder. How could something like this be kept secret for fifteen years? How could their king be kept prisoner in his own home? Taliff turned tear-filled eyes to his brother. "How?"

"I don't know, Taliff. But we'll find out and all those involved will die."

"Boys?"

The crackling voice that drifted from the bed sounded nothing like the man they'd once known. But there was no denying his identity. "Father? Mother?"

The bedraggled *Chantrean* nodded and a crooked smile spread across his face. "Took you long enough to find us, don't you think, sons?"

Eve, still slumped on the floor, chuckled. "I found you, not him."

"And so you did. And saved my wife in the process. How can we ever thank you?"

Eve smiled and Taliff knew exactly what thoughts were running around in her mind.

"I have a few ideas."

He snorted at the understatement. His father had no idea just how much Eve would change given the chance.

Even though he wanted to rush to his parents and pull them into a hug, his mate and her needs came first. While Hunter moved toward the bed and the couple there, Taliff went to Eve's side and scooped her up into his arms.

After brushing a fleeting kiss against her temple, he turned toward his brother and parents. "I say it's past time we get the hell out of here."

Hunter nodded and walked out into the hall. Seconds later, he returned with Tanner and three of the *Manruvians* in tow. "Tanner, take my mother. I'll help the king. The rest of you, keep your eyes and ears open. We aren't free yet."

Once the group reached the relative safety of the open hall, where their chances at being trapped were lower, Taliff reached for his wrist com. "*Shoshoni?*"

"Yes, Commander?"

"Lock on to my location and transport the eleven of us directly to the infirmary aboard the *Wanderer*."

"Understood."

Eve raised her head from where it rested on his shoulder.

"Where..." she licked her lips and tried again. "Where is the rest of the pride?"

"*Shoshoni* transported them to safety the moment we were released."

Three days later...

Taliff looked down at his sleeping mate and couldn't help but smile. With her flushed cheeks, lush red lips and sexily tousled hair, Eve looked well and truly loved. Too bad she'd been unconscious for days and the closest they'd come to loving had been when he chastely pecked her forehead before he crawled into bed beside her.

The healer who'd supervised both Eve and his mother's care assured him that she'd wake today. He hoped so, or she'd miss the ceremony being held this evening in her honor.

"Eve?" he whispered, laying fluttery soft kisses against her temple, her cheek. "*Moya*, it's time to wake, beloved."

Taliff knew she was awake and playing possum when Eve's mouth twitched. Let her play for a few more minutes. He enjoyed this playful side of her.

He skimmed his lips down her neck and over her pulse. He could feel its rhythm increase and smiled against her skin. She always responded so magnificently to his touch. If only he had time to love her now, but alas, duty beckoned and they needed to prepare.

It had taken many hours of planning and restructuring to come up with an answer to many of Eve's worries. Hopefully, it all met with her approval.

"It's time to rise, Eve."

"Do we have to? I've been having the most marvelous dream."

From the sweet smell of her arousal, she must have been truly enjoying it, too. Best not to mention that though, not if they were to arrive in the Grand Ballroom on time, because she was bound to say something that would earn a sensual punishment.

His cock lengthened beneath the thick leather of his trews and it took all his control not to reach down and adjust himself. He muttered beneath his breath and pushed himself away from her luscious curves.

Once he was far enough away from her scent to once again think clearly, he cleared his throat. "Eve. There is a ceremony to be held tonight returning the rightful king to power. Would you attend with me?"

Eve sat up and was no longer intent on seduction by the serious expression she wore. "Of course. What's to happen to your brother?"

"He never wished to rule. At least, not for a very long time and until he secured a mate of his own. He's decided to search for the other women that were taken from the *Wanderer* in repayment to you for returning our parents to us."

Eve's eyes glistened with unshed tears. "He's going after Amy?"

"Yes. He's to leave immediately after the ceremony tonight."

"But, Tal, he just got his parents back. He shouldn't leave them so soon."

"He wants to do this, *moya*. He says something is driving him to. All we can do is support his decision."

Eve nodded, a worried look on her face. "He won't be alone, will he?"

"No. Tanner and Hunter's *Manruvian* ally, Mikel, will be traveling with several of Mikel's most loyal soldiers."

Eve's shoulders relaxed and a small smile lifted the corners of her lips. "Wouldn't it be strange if he found his own mate during his search?"

"We can hope and I think, deep down, Hunter believes, he needs to find her. That's she waiting out there for him. Maybe he'll find his own cure for loneliness as I have found mine in you.

"Now, that's enough stalling. I've laid out a change of clothes for you in the bathing chamber, which is just through that door," he said pointing toward the only other door in the room. "I expect to find you ready when I return."

When Taliff returned to his chambers an hour later, he found Eve sitting atop the window seat, her gaze drawn to the activity below. "Are you ready to go downstairs, Eve?"

"In a minute. Can I ask you something, Tal?"

"You can ask me anything, *moya*. There will be no more secrets between us."

Eve nodded, then began to fiddle with her clothes. "How were your parents kept prisoner without anyone's knowledge?"

Taliff sighed and ran his fingers through his hair in frustration. "We may never know how it all came about. But nearly a hundred guards and advisors were found dead in one of the cells. We can only assume the Black Rose was cleaning house. She's still out there, Eve, and still a danger to us all." When she didn't appear to have any more questions for him, he reached for her hand.

"So, are you ready now?"

She turned to meet his gaze and smiled a little shyly. "I suppose. I thought women were expected to dress femininely here. I expected to find a sarong or something and instead found this."

He wasn't surprised that Eve was confused. Instead of laying out typical *Chantrean* woman's wear, he'd left her the smallest utility uniform he could find. It would be only the first of many pleasant surprises for her this evening.

"I promised to show you equal respect and honor, *moya*. This is but a first step."

Tears gathered in the corners of her eyes, but she didn't let them fall and he could only be thankful. If she lost her composure over this, what would she do later when the rest of the evening's events came to pass?

"We must be going now, Eve."

Without further hesitation, Eve stood and made her way to his side. Taliff pulled her into his arms and slowly lowered his head to hers. There was no way he could get through the next few hours without at least tasting her luscious mouth. The kiss started out gently, but before long, his tongue swept over her parted lips and they each became lost in the heat of their passion.

Minutes passed and neither cared. Only when his wrist communicator began to buzz insistently did Taliff break the kiss. He laid his forehead against hers and tried to reign in his hunger. If he didn't make love to her soon, he'd spontaneously combust.

"Let's go, before we hold up the celebration even longer."

Eve giggled as he dragged her out of the room. He didn't see a damn thing funny about the situation and if the pain in his groin was any indication, his cock was in definite agreement.

Decorated in white and gold, the Grand Ballroom glittered with wealth and majesty. Honeysuckle scented candles were suspended from the ceilings with wire and their flickering flames cast gentle shadows along the walls.

The crowd parted for them as they made their way toward the raised dais where High King Brantiff and his mate awaited them. Eve's palms began to sweat as all eyes followed their progress through the room.

Only once they reached the foot of the dais did Taliff pull them to a stop. When Eve would have curtsied as a sign of respect, he shook his head. *What's going on, Tal?*

You'll see, moya. *Be patient.*

Neither Brantiff nor Luma showed signs of their fifteen-year ordeal and Eve hoped that she in some small part helped in their transformation.

When High King Shi'Lan raised his hand, the room grew silent in anticipation. For many long years, most had thought him dead. The return of their beloved king must be a welcome surprise.

"For fifteen years, my mate and I were held prisoner on these very grounds, believing that our sons had been killed by one of their own blood. And for fifteen years, they believed the same. But because of thirty-six brave women and their Alpha, we have been reunited.

"During the course of our incarceration, I took the time to get to know my mate. To learn her strengths and her weaknesses, her beliefs and her desires. I am ashamed to say, it took nearly a year into our imprisonment to learn what it took Eve Roberts three very long days to teach my son.

"Males may be physically stronger than the females, but they are not superior to them. It is my honor to award Eve Roberts to the position of Chief Advisor in my new cabinet."

Shocked and a bit petrified, Eve looked to Taliff for help. "Go on, *moya*. Step upon the Dais and stand behind the king."

"But...but..." When Taliff just continued to look at her with love and patience, she swallowed thickly and forced one foot in front of the other, until she'd done as he directed and positioned herself behind and to the right of the king.

While Eve tried to process what had happened, High King Shi'Lan began to once again speak, this time addressing Taliff.

"The floor is now yours, son."

At the sound of her mate's name being spoken, Eve dragged herself back to the here and now. She watched as he pulled at the collar of his uniform and fidgeted with his wrist com. *What's going on now?*

He may have looked nervous, but when his voice rang out strong and clear, reaching even the farthest corner of the room, all sense of nervousness disappeared. "It has always been tradition that in order for a mated pair to be formally recognized, the female demonstrated the ultimate in submission toward her mate in front of witnesses. That tradition is retired here and now." With grace and dignity, Taliff lowered himself to his knees and bowed his head.

"I offer my life and love to you, to do with as you wish. I pledge to worship your body and offer up my own to you to worship and command. I, in turn, accept the same from you. Only to you do I offer my heart and my soul for you to protect or deny. I give all that I am and all that I will ever be to you. Do you accept me and all that I offer, my *moya*, my mate?"

Eve swallowed the lump in her throat and drifted down the stairs and to his side. "Never kneel before me again, my *moyo*. Stand as my equal for I accept all that you are or ever will be."

Whistles and cheers erupted throughout the room, but the pair was intent on only each other. The world disappeared as the lovers embraced.

IN THE FARTHEST CORNER of the room, away from the surging crowd, Hunter sighed. His mate was out there somewhere. It was only a matter of time before he brought her home.

HUNTER'S REVENGE

Prologue

Brantiff Shi'Lan, High King of *Chantrea*, sat at his throne holding his mate's hand as he watched the festivities going on around him. His younger son, Taliff danced with his new Earther-*Lionese* mate, Eve. What a strong, proud woman this Eve was. So courageous. She would be a strong mate to his son and would not only be good for Taliff personally, but would be good for *Chantrea*.

He turned to his mate, Luma, and smiled at her as he raised their entwined hands to his lips and kissed her knuckles. It had taken their kidnapping for him to see what a strong woman his mate was. For so long, he'd taken her for granted, ignored her strengths and used her only as a vessel for his seed. Only during their captivity did he finally come to know and love his mate. That was a damn crime, in his opinion.

Now if only Hunter could find someone who would make him as happy as Eve had made Taliff and his own mate, Luma, made him. Where was Hunter anyway?

He searched the crowd until he finally spotted him, leaning against the wall, watching his brother and Eve dance. Brantiff put his hand to his chin and watched his elder son thoughtfully. What thoughts could possibly be responsible for the desolate expression on his face?

In the farthest corner of the room, away from the surging crowd, Hunter sighed wistfully as he watched his brother and Eve dance. His mate was out there somewhere. It was only a matter of time before he brought her home. Easing away from the wall, Hunter left the others behind and made his way to his suite. He had packing to do.

Chapter One

Above the ice planet, Visara...

Hunter Shi'lan, former High King and now, once again, Crown Prince and heir to the throne of *Chantrea*, stared down at the barren planet below him. Tension ran through his body, causing the beast within to stir and stretch. If he didn't get a grip on his emotions soon, he would end up shifting into his *Lionese* form right here in the middle of the command deck of the *Manruvian* Warship, *Victory*.

He could feel her—feel his mate. He didn't know her. He didn't know her name or what she looked like, but somewhere below, on a planet of ice and snow, his lady mate awaited him.

He shuddered, imagining all the horrors she could even now be suffering. He had no doubt that the rebels had raped her, probably repeatedly over the course of her imprisonment. Such was the fate of every one of the unfortunate females kidnapped by the infamous Black Rose and her demented followers—those who were unlucky enough to survive their capture, anyway. At least six of the women from his brother's ship were below, according to the microscopic tracking devices Taliff had inserted into their bloodstreams when they'd left Earth.

Once he freed the women held captive within the subterranean caverns, he would finally meet the *one* woman whose injured spirit had called to him across the vast emptiness of space. Even now, he could feel her body's intense suffering, sense her waning spirit, feel her tears of grief and rage in his mind—as he had for the last three lunar cycles.

Three moon rotations of her suffering had about driven him mad, enraging the lion within who roared his anger, his thirst for vengeance. How had she survived such torment for so long? Even now, he knew of the insidious whispers in her mind, telling her it was best to end her life. She felt she would be better off dead—than in the hands of the vicious Black Rose, it was true. But soon, he would have her, hold her in his arms and somehow he would find a way to make her world right again. He had to.

"Excuse me, Prince Shi'Lan?"

Startled out of his dark thoughts, he growled, then turned toward the *Manruvian* warrior standing behind him. "Yes, Sander?"

"Prince Logann is requesting your presence in his private quarters."

Hunter nodded, then turned his gaze back toward the viewport. "Tell him I'll be there momentarily."

"Yes, your Highness."

Braced against the viewport with one arm, Hunter lifted his free hand to run his fingers down the *transomani*—the translucent and indestructible material the *Manruvians* developed to mimic windows. Close. He was so close to being able to touch her with his hands.

His gut twisted. What was he thinking? She'd be traumatized and no matter how much he would want to hold her, to explore her body, he'd have to proceed with restraint. No doubt she would fear him. She would fear any male. He'd die before he purposely inflicted harm upon her.

Straightening away from the portal, Hunter tucked his hands in the pockets of his uniform pants. "Soon, my mate. Soon, I'll bring you home where you belong." With one last glance at the icy planet below, he turned and walked away.

AMY MORGAN LIFTED HER bruised and battered head when she heard the groaning creak of the opening door. Not another man. Not again. She couldn't take another one so soon after the last. Already she felt as though she would never heal from the numerous injuries she'd suffered during these animals' attempts at impregnating her. How did they ever expect a woman to survive, to carry a child to term? If she *were* to become pregnant here, her child would never draw its first breath. She was certain of it. And, if it were a female, would she have the heart, the strength, to smother her in her sleep to spare her this fate?

"Please, Goddess, just let me die," she sobbed into the dirty mattress as she felt the bed dip beneath yet another man's weight. She tried to shift away from the new arrival, helpless to stop the agonized moan when even the slightest movement of the mattress sent shards of burning pain through her abdomen.

A tender hand pushed the hair from her face and she cried for she knew she must be dreaming. No man residing in this forsaken outpost they all called the 'land of promise' had such capacity for gentleness.

"Please, please don't touch me," she sobbed onto the stained mattress. "If you ever loved your mother, your sister, take pity and kill me when you're through with me."

The large hand splayed over her back, gently rubbed soft circles on her bruised flesh. It wasn't the first time one of them tried to trick her with the illusion of kindness. She wouldn't fall for it this time. Not again—never again would they trick her into believing they cared for her welfare. It had taken a while, but now she understood that these animals didn't know the meaning of true gentleness. She wondered if any man truly did. The men here didn't have an ounce of compassion between them. They liked to hear her beg them to help her escape, to return her to her home world, Earth, or simply for mercy. Even hell would surely be a better place than this.

She'd been tortured, abused, raped several times a day since they had kidnapped her from the ship that stole her from her home. She longed to hear her mother's voice again. Wished she could be home, held in her father's arms. He may have been strict, but he'd loved her and would certainly have protected her from animals such as these.

Her body ached, sometimes bled from each encounter. One day ran into the next and she just wanted to rest. To die would be a welcome alternative to the countless men raping her day in and day out.

The hand stopped its soothing motion and she knew her nightmare would begin again. She clamped her mouth shut, determined not to scream. They always liked it when she screamed.

"Ssshh...*moya*, do not cry so. Your ordeal is over. It's time to take you home."

She shuddered. She couldn't bear to listen to the soothing rasp of his voice, wouldn't dare to believe he had come to help her escape. Thoughts like those led to madness.

She felt the air stir beside her, felt the bed rise once the male behind her stood. The air whooshed out of her lungs when she realized she might actually get a reprieve. Why wasn't he groping her, ripping the sheet from her body, shoving her legs open and rutting on her? Or was this just a way to catch her off guard?

Minutes passed and the silence lengthened. The tension in her shoulders, her spine, began to ease. He must have left. Why would he leave before he got what he wanted? Wasn't impregnating her to breed females the entire reason they'd kept her locked behind iron doors?

Only when she was sure he'd left did she relax enough to ease away from the rough cavern wall. Despite the excruciating pain moving caused her, she rolled to her back and forced open her swollen and bruised eyes.

"There you are, *moya*. What is your name, little one?"

Oh, God. Why hadn't she realized he'd never left? Were her senses now failing her just as her body had? "Why?"

Through heavily swollen eyes, she watched the large man make his way toward her. She gasped, in fear, in confusion. His face...his face looked so familiar. Yet she couldn't quite place him in her memories. He looked wrong somehow.

Why couldn't she remember him? Had the continued beatings affected her memory? Did she even know him or had she finally cracked? Perhaps she had a concussion. With as many times as they'd beat her, she wouldn't be surprised if she had suffered brain damage.

There was no time to figure it out as he moved closer and closer. Her heart stuttered in her chest. She tasted the fear in her throat. Even now, knowing he couldn't possibly do anything worse than the others had, she feared his touch. Why couldn't she just lose herself and grow used to it as she'd been told so many of the others had? She'd been told some of the captives actually welcomed the men to their beds. She shuddered at the thought. Before she could prepare to defend herself, he leaned over her, reaching out with his large hands—hands that were scarred, calloused, rough looking. They were hands that could crush her with a single blow. How had she ever thought he would be gentle?

She inwardly cringed, swallowed past the lump that suddenly lodged in her throat. She couldn't take her gaze off those large hands, knowing they could tear her to pieces with barely any effort, especially considering the shape she was in.

She whimpered when he touched her, ran his fingers through her greasy, limp hair. Tears poured from her eyes when she knew it would come as it always had. How many weeks, months had she spent here, dreading the arrival of the next male? How much time had passed while she'd been held here in her stone prison as nothing but a vessel for her tormentors' seed? How long had she spent in stasis as her kidnappers transported her to this frozen wasteland? She felt so much older. When she'd woken inside the stasis chamber, her body didn't quite feel like it used to and then the first of many men had come to her and used her. Nothing had mattered since.

She couldn't even starve herself. If she didn't eat the slop they provided, they injected her with something that replaced the nourishment she refused herself and the beatings would begin anew. She wasn't supposed to fight or rebel. They expected her to simply submit, to just spread her legs and take it. In the beginning, she couldn't do that. Just as she could never seem to find the courage to end her own life.

She shuddered as his hands smoothed over her flesh. His lingering touch passed over her arms, her legs before he pulled away. When she thought she'd get a slight reprieve, he once again touched her, this time sliding his hands beneath her bottom.

She groaned. Grief and pain warred within her. She was a coward.

No. She was worse than a coward. She deserved everything she got because, although she'd fought at first, after countless males violated her, she resigned herself to the fact that no one would come. No one knew where she was, no one cared enough to come for her and she was lost.

For the last several weeks, she'd lain on her semen-stained cot and waited, dreading the inevitable visit of the next man. One after another, they visited her—sometimes as many as six or seven in a day. Those days she tried to leave her body, lose herself in her mind. There she was free, they couldn't touch her and she lost count of the men who visited. She no longer fought them, no longer even acknowledged them, just let them use her body for their cause.

One after the other, they came to her. They came inside her with brutal disregard for her well-being. She didn't have the heart—or the courage—to bring her life to an end. What kind of worthless piece of shit did that make her?

He lifted her against his chest, then stood, cradling her against his torso. "No, please. Please. Don't take me to them. No, please. You can fuck me, do what you want with my body, but don't take me to those butchers, the ones who call themselves healers."

With what little energy that remained in her body, she jackknifed against him, desperate to get out of his arms. She'd do anything to avoid another internal exam while the doctors stuck their dirty instruments in all her private areas and her captors looked on with maniacal glee.

"Hush, *moya*. It will all be over before you know it."

Before she realized just what he'd planned, everything went dark. She could feel herself slip into darkness and thanked all that was holy that they'd finally decided to end her worthless life.

AS HIS MATE SUCCUMBED to unconsciousness, Hunter dropped the tiny syringe on the dirt floor, crushing it beneath his feet. He hadn't wanted to give the sedative to her, especially since he didn't know what other drugs they'd pumped into her during her captivity, but she'd given him no choice. He wouldn't take a chance with her life. If she inadvertently raised the alarm and the enemy captured them while they tried escaping, her life would become even harder, if such a thing were possible.

When he'd first entered her cell, his inner lion roared in denial. It took all his control to prevent himself from shifting and ripping her bedding to shreds with his claws. The smell of other males in the room and the scent of their semen mixed with his mate's essence had nearly driven him over the edge to madness.

Seeing her lying there, battered and bruised, her spirit nearly broken, was all that kept his beast leashed. Her needs, her welfare came first. Tears of frustration and rage burned his eyes when she begged him to kill her. That his mate felt so alone, could feel such hopelessness, nearly brought him to his knees.

Pushing down his anger and despair, he vowed before all that was holy—on the feet of the Goddess Alana herself—he would avenge his mate. He'd hunt down every man whose scent still hung in the air. Every vile creature that soiled her would die. Slowly. Painfully. When he finally found their ringleader, the Black Rose, she would wish she'd stayed dead to him, his sister or not.

Pulling his mate closer, Hunter trembled with the effort of containing his rage. No matter what he had to do, he'd see that she healed. She'd never want for anything again, be it emotionally or physically. First, he had to get her out of these seemingly endless subterranean caverns.

It had taken hours to locate her and the others—hours of slipping unseen through the tunnels while they searched for as many prisoners as they could. He needed to get her and the others aboard the *Victory* for immediate medical treatment. That, however, might not be so easy.

This far below the ice planet's surface, they couldn't use the ship's transporting technology to transfer themselves directly aboard the warship. Instead, they'd need to travel on foot through the tunnels until they reached the surface, each carrying an injured or traumatized woman. The task ahead was daunting, but not impossible with the right amount of determination. He and the men who'd accompanied him were *very* determined, indeed.

Careful not to jostle his mate, Hunter made his way to the thick iron-ore door and slowly eased it open. As he expected, his ally and closest friend, Mikel Logann, High Prince of *Manruvia*, stood guard, watching his back even now, when danger literally surrounded them.

Nodding at Mikel, Hunter silently moved behind his friend and into the narrow, low-slung, rock-carved tunnel.

"You had to sedate her then." It wasn't a question so Hunter didn't bother to answer. He could only be thankful his brother's mate, Eve, had commissioned their planet's healers to make a large enough supply of the powerful sedative. With it, those in pain and suffering from their injuries would be more comfortable for the trip home to *Chantrea*.

While sedated, their bodies would have a chance to heal and they would be blessedly free from the pain they had lived with over these last months. Their minds, however, were another matter. It could take years for their psyches to recover and even then, the women would forever carry mental and emotional scars.

"Let's go. All teams have reported in and are on the move back to the pickup point," Mikel whispered through his com unit, a tiny black matte microphone clipped to his collar. It was an ingenious design. If one didn't know where to look for it, it would appear as simply part of the uniform. His gaze constantly roved the dark tunnel, searching for any potential danger. They'd been lucky to get this far without raising an alarm. Tarrying only made the risk of discovery that much greater.

They'd gone no more than a meter down the length of the tunnel when all hell broke loose...almost literally. Alarms blared. The tunnel shuddered. The ground quaked. Rocks fell out of the tunnel walls, the ceiling. Hidden lights flashed, temporarily blinding them. With his arms filled with his precious burden, Hunter could do naught but run, staying a step behind Mikel as they raced toward the surface—or so they hoped.

One meter closer.

Five.

Twenty.

For what seemed like hours, they ran. Hunter carried his beloved mate, refusing to hand her over to Mikel even for a brief respite as they dodged falling debris and evaded the enemy patrols.

Finally, they could see the opening to the hidden cave entrance up ahead. Almost there. Five more meters. Almost there. *Come on, almost there.* Hunter pumped his burning legs harder, held his mate tighter against his chest. One more meter to go. By the Lady Goddess Alana, they were going to make it. Thank the Goddess. They were going to make it.

"Stop, or I'll shoot."

Chapter Two

"Stop or I *will* shoot you in the back. Don't expect me to say it again."

Hunter stopped and turned. Mikel shifted behind him, preparing to fight if he knew his friend as well as he thought he did. With his mate clutched to his chest, Hunter eyed the rebel warily. Beneath the layers of filth, Hunter could see that this follower of the Black Rose enjoyed what he did. It was in the maniacal light in his eyes, the leer twisting his lips, the steady aim of the laser gun aimed at them. And, of course, his scent.

This man's scent was all over the woman Hunter held in his arms—Hunter's own mate. The fact that at the moment, he could do naught but ensure she wasn't injured in the coming confrontation made the lion inside him snarl his fury. And there would be a confrontation. This man would rather die than let them go. Right now, with his lion roaring for vengeance, he would rather rip her assailant to shreds than leave. But he had his mate to think about. Her life was more important than his need for revenge.

Through his com unit, Hunter heard static, then Mikel's voice whisper, "Drop." He didn't hesitate. Following his friend's instruction, he dropped instantly to his knees, then rolled with his precious burden out of the line of fire. He knew Mikel would do whatever he needed to get them out of there alive, even sacrifice himself. He hoped it wouldn't come to that. He would not want to be the one to tell the *Manruvian* people that the heir to their throne had passed over to the other side because he'd chosen to save his life.

He covered his mate as best as he could and watched as laser fire lit up the tunnel walls. The hiss of the guns, the smell of burning flesh and the startled gasp of the fanatic rebel as he died, were all memories that would forever stay with him, though only seconds had passed since the rebel announced himself.

Hunter turned his head, expecting to see Mikel waiting for him at the entrance to the tunnels, a cocky grin on his face. Instead, Mikel lay on the cavern floor, his chest covered in his own blood. His golden skin was now pasty white. Strain lines bracketed his mouth. Hunter could hear the *Manruvian's* lungs rattle. Mikel's lips were already turning blue and his eyes glassy as the fight to remain conscious got the better of him.

Shit. Shit. Shit. If he didn't get help for Mikel immediately, his closest friend would die. Nevertheless, he couldn't carry both his mate and Mikel. He'd have to leave one behind.

Unless...

Seeing no other choice, Hunter reached inside his vest, pulled a marked hypodermic needle out of the hidden pocket, and without wasting any more time wrestling with his decision, injected his mate. *By the Lady Goddess, please, please let her understand what I'll ask of her.*

Hunter waited as the counteractive agent went to work on waking his mate. The only way all three could get to the rendezvous point on time was if his mate could walk with his assistance while he carried Mikel over his shoulder.

AMY OPENED HER EYES and looked around her. Instead of the walls of the grimy cell she'd occupied since her kidnappers brought her here, she was in a cave. Light came from behind the man she recognized from her cell.

Her heart stuttered. Her stomach clenched. Her vision blurred. *No, no, no.* She scurried backward, out of his reach, unable to bear for him to touch her. Still, things didn't seem quite right. What was going on? Where was she? Why was she here? She shook her head, confused and frightened. Nothing made sense.

"It's okay, *moya*. Everything is going to be okay. I need your help or my friend is going to die."

Ha! Like she'd never heard that before. She continued to move back, her eyes never straying from the stranger's gaze until she bumped into something, something softer than the rock wall. It was warm. She raised her hand, saw the fresh blood and screamed. She gasped, shuddered, closed her eyes momentarily and then warily looked behind her.

She stared down at the man she had hated most. His glassy, lifeless eyes gazed unblinkingly at the roof of the cave. His life had completely gone from him. No breath moved his chest and no evil leer marred his features. How many days and nights had she wished, dreamed, of seeing him this way? Of all the animals here, he'd been one of the cruelest.

She looked back at the man who had carried her from her cell and licked her lips. What if he had truly come to help her? Looking beyond him, she noticed another man who lay dying on the floor. His chest barely moved. She could hear his raspy breaths as he struggled to draw the frozen air into his lungs. Blood coated his front, yet even so gravely wounded, he still clutched his weapon in his hands. It didn't take long to realize this man had sacrificed himself for her and for the man standing before her. At least now, the beast would never harm another woman.

Wiping her hands on the stained sheet the stranger had carefully wrapped around her like a toga, she stood and kicked the dead body, unable to keep herself from showing her anger, her despair. If her rescuer used it against her in the future, so be it. At least she'd had that one momentary pleasure.

Amy looked beyond the two men to the light. A cold breeze touched her face and fresh air brushed the greasy hair at her temple. Could that really be the entrance to the cave? Was she really that close to freedom?

Even with the excruciating pain crippling her body, the thought that freedom was just feet away gave her the motivation to do whatever she needed to escape this freaking cold-ass barren planet and its vile inhabitants. "What kind of help do you need?"

It seemed to be relief she saw crossing his features as he leaned down to lift the downed man into his arms. "I need you to trust me, *moya*. We are so close to freedom. Just a few more yards, but I can't carry you both. He risked his life to save ours. Now I ask you to trust me. To follow me from this hellhole and do your best to keep up." His gaze traveled from the top of her head to her bare feet and his expression gentled. "I know you're in pain and unprepared for the bitter conditions and I will help you all that I can. Will you do this?"

She knew she wasted precious time, but she had to know. The question plagued her. The last thing she wanted was to jump from the frying pan and into the fire.

"Where do I know you from?" She tilted her head with a frown. "I know I have seen you before. You're too familiar to me."

He smiled. The action made him seem even more familiar. Still, she couldn't think of where she'd seen him before.

"We have never met before this day, *moya*. But you *have* met my brother."

"Your brother?" *Oh no, oh no, oh no.* She backed away. *Goddess, please don't tell me his brother is one of these animals.*

"Yes, my brother. I am Hunter Shi'Lan. You met my brother Taliff, Eve's mate, just before you were stolen from his ship."

Memories came flooding back. Eve, with her kind ways, keeping that bitch Myra from queening over everyone. Taliff, who had kidnapped them all, promising them a better life...she barely stopped a bitter laugh at that memory. Then the ship had gone dark, there was gunfire, women screaming and then darkness.

"Will you trust me and follow me to your freedom, *moya*? Even now, Mikel dies in my arms."

She nodded as she remembered that his brother had called Eve, *moya*. Something about that memory, something elusive, made her realize that she could at least trust this man to get her out of this hellhole.

"Hunter? You did say that was your name, right?" She frowned, trying to remember what it was that his brother had said about him. It seemed important... She shook her head. It didn't matter now. All that mattered was getting the hell out of here and getting his friend the medical attention he needed. It was the least she could do for what he was suffering on her behalf.

"Yes, *moya?*"

"Lead the way. If you hand me the weapon, I'll do my best to cover you, though I don't know how much help I'll be."

Hunter nodded and handed her his friend's weapon. "Any help is better than none. Follow me."

He led the way toward the light, his friend cradled in his arms. The closer they got to the entrance to the tunnel, the more excited she got. *Freedom.* She could practically smell it. The fresh air caressed her skin and though it was cold, freezing even, for the first time in months hope filled her heart. Hope and the first stirrings of rage. She would have her revenge somehow, someday. The Black Rose and all her followers hadn't seen the last of Amy Morgan. Not by a long shot.

Clutching the borrowed weapon in her hand, she took her first step into sunlight in weeks, months—hell, it could even have been years. She just didn't know. As far as the eye could see, there was nothing but snow and ice. The light from the sun glistened everywhere. It would have been beautiful had it not been for the fact that she'd been held captive here. The glittering world before her only served to remind her that she'd been kept prisoner underground, forced to live in the bleak artificial light her captors chose to provide or withhold as they saw fit. The only things distinctive about their surroundings were the mountain peaks around them and the small, barely noticeable valley below.

She looked down at the trail she'd have to follow and glanced at her feet. She shook her head, knowing the only way she could get down this trail was if she shifted to her lioness form. She could just as easily defend the men in that form.

Hell, she didn't even know if she could shift. The few times she tried to shift below the surface, blinding pain had incapacitated her for hours, leaving her at the mercy of her jailers. But she wouldn't know if she didn't try, and standing here wasting time as Hunter's friend lay dying in his arms, was unacceptable. Besides, if she were in her other form, the pain she felt now wouldn't be as debilitating. These injuries were next to nothing for a lioness. Without giving herself any more time to worry, Amy closed her eyes and called upon the shifter magic inside her.

Searing heat blasted through her body, truly warming her for the first time in months. Even behind her closed eyelids, she could see the light coalescing around her body as she shifted in an instant. She felt her face turn into a muzzle, felt the fur warming her body for the first time in ages. She dropped to the ground on four large paws. The lioness roared its joy at finally having the freedom to run, to hunt. She shook her body, luxuriating in the feeling of being in her hunter form after so long a slumber. Why hadn't she been able to shift in the caves? Had they used some form of technology to keep them from shifting, some sort of medication in their food? She hadn't eaten last night as she'd been too sick. She'd flushed the so-called food down their version of a toilet to avoid the beating she knew she'd get for refusing to eat. She turned in a circle, sniffing the air.

There. She could scent the path Hunter had followed on his way to rescue her. Skirting past the gaping man, she led the way down the trail. She'd have time later to think about why he'd looked at her so strangely later. Right now, all she wanted was to get off this planet, heal, then get her revenge.

Behind her, Hunter followed, carrying his burden gently in his arms. They were nearly halfway down the mountain when the scent of fear hit her. The sounds of whimpering and flesh striking flesh soon followed. Then that voice—the voice she'd never wanted to hear again echoed across the frozen tundra.

Hunter also stopped, turning his head toward the newcomers. He started to put his friend down to go help whomever had been recaptured. Amy couldn't let him sacrifice his friend. She'd take care of this herself. Amy padded over to Hunter, grabbed his pants in her teeth and started pulling him back toward the trail.

His gaze was uncertain, guilt and responsibility warring on his face, but he finally nodded and continued down the trail. Once certain he wouldn't turn back, she darted off the trail and headed toward the downed rescue team. The voice of the betrayer grew louder as she approached.

"Too bad her rescuers had to die. I would have liked to ride them. Grab the woman and take her back to her cell. The more women here when the Black Rose hears about today's rescue attempt, the better for all of us."

"Yes, Lady Myra. It will be as you say."

Everything in Amy, both the human and the lioness, demanded revenge. She wanted to rip the woman apart. Eve had done no favors for the women when she had spared Myra's life on Taliff's ship. Amy didn't blame Eve for what had happened to her and the others at Myra's hands—didn't blame her for sparing the bitch's life—but that didn't mean she'd follow Eve's example and show the traitor mercy. No, if it was the last thing she did before she died, she would make sure Myra paid for all the pain and suffering she'd caused.

Amy slowed as she neared Myra and the others, lowering her body until she was creeping just above the snow-packed ground. She did her best to stay upwind to lower the chances of Myra catching her scent. No sense in making herself a target before she pounced, or so her ma back home had taught her when she'd taken her on her first hunt as a child. The men would be no protection for Myra in their human form. They were little more than brainless brawn.

These people hadn't learned it yet. Centuries on Earth had taught the Earth *Lionese* that the female was truly the stealthier of the species. The male was stronger, but only with the strength of numbers and if the female lacked the element of surprise. Both luck and circumstances were on her side this night.

As physically weak and exhausted as she was, she needed as much of an advantage as she could get if she hoped to rescue the woman they'd recaptured. During their captivity, the rebels had gone out of their way to ensure that bitch Myra stayed happy and healthy. *Compensation for her role in procuring the Black Rose females, most likely.* Crawling forward on her belly, she watched, hoping to find an opening that would give her the advantage over her enemy.

"No. Please. I can't go back. Just let me go, I beg you. Just let me go." Amy knew that voice. A female from the cell next to her—Maryann. How had she gotten here, anyway? Taliff hadn't taken her from Earth aboard his ship. Had they sent more ships to Earth to procure more females? She shook her head. Now wasn't the time to ask those questions. They would have to wait.

Another slap, another pitiful whimper. Fury and rage rode Amy hard. That was the last time Myra or the others would raise a hand to the once exuberant girl. The next person to raise a hand to her would die.

Amy stopped, plastering herself against the cold snow to see the horrifying scene in front of her unfold. Myra stood with her back to Any, a laser whip fisted in her hands as she towered over the sprawled unarmed girl. Though, she wasn't really a girl now either. She looked to be in her early twenties as least. How long had they kept her in stasis—forcing her body into a slowly aging hibernation—before bringing them all to this planet? How many years had they lost?

As Myra lifted the whip, Amy crept forward, shoving her worries to the back of her mind. Time enough to contemplate her miserable life later. Besides, she was in no hurry to see herself in a mirror. Right now, Maryann needed her and for once, she wasn't helpless. This she could do something about.

Just as the bitch began her down swing, Amy lost what little control she possessed and pounced. Quickly losing her element of surprise, she tackled Myra from behind, pinning the woman to the ground. Before she could move to tear out the traitor's throat, she felt the sting of the whip rip across her back. Dammit! How could she have forgotten the men? *Such a stupid, stupid, mistake, you idiot*, she berated herself. She knew better than that. She'd just made a foolish mistake that may have just cost both her and Maryann their lives.

Another man stepped into view. With one jailor at her front and the other at her back, wielding the whip, they had her at a disadvantage. She recognized her mistake. It was her mother's first rule of the hunt. *Never let your emotions rule your actions.* A clear head meant a clear target and an easy kill. This had just become anything but easy.

"Back off," the man gestured with his phase pistol, "or I'll rape the girl in front of you. Would you like that, you feline bitch? Like to hear your friend beg me for mercy before I strangle the life out of her?"

Maryann whimpered. Amy's hackles rose and she cursed her own stupidity. Fuck, what was she going to do now?

Chapter Three

AGITATED BEYOND BELIEF, HUNTER WATCHED AS THE TRANSPORTER took his friend to the ship where med-techs were on standby, awaiting their prince. He hoped he wasn't too late. The last thing he wanted to do was let Mikel go up to the ship alone. He felt as though he should be there. Mikel had risked his life for Hunter and his mate and going with him to ensure his injuries received proper care seemed such a small thing to do in return.

He hated to leave him alone with the healers. No one deserved to wake injured and alone, but Hunter needed to go back for his mate. As much as he hated to admit that his bond with his oldest friend was changing, his mate needed his help now more than Mikel did. Mikel was their prince and his people would do everything in their power to ensure he lived.

Turning back to the path that would lead him to where he'd last seen his mate, Hunter inhaled deeply and followed her scent. Pride filled him at her inner strength. She would be no submissive to follow his lead. This woman was strong enough to rule by his side and as his father had just decreed, that was as it should be. Even while injured and struggling with pain, she'd managed to overcome her own inner turmoil to help when needed.

Hunter longed to bond with her—to truly be one. Yet, he knew he must wait a while longer. He knew she wasn't ready for a mate bond. Hell, she might never be ready for it, but it would come, no matter how hard she resisted. She might not realize it, but the emotional tie between them was strong and soon, like it or not, their bodies would demand the formal binding of the *Manruvian Matebonds*. It was strange how for months he and his mate had shared a connection, both mental and spiritual, and yet he still didn't know her name.

He heard a woman's scream, and though he knew it wasn't his mate's cry, quickly shed his clothes and changed to his other form on the run. He would stop any threat to his mate, no matter the cost. Their tie was already strong enough that he knew he would die for her—heir to his father's rule or not. His life would be worth nothing without her in it.

When he rounded the corner, he saw a man using a laser whip on his mate. Cold rage ripped through him. A fury as icy as the planet they now found themselves on roared through his body when he saw the wide gash in his mate's fur. Blood welled up from the wound, dripped down her side and stained the snow red. His anger intensified and he seethed as he watched her precious life's blood flow onto the once pristine snow. For spilling her blood, the man would die.

Another male loomed over a trembling female, no doubt the one he'd heard scream no doubt. The young woman cowered, wounds covering her arms and hands where she'd already attempted to deflect the blows from the deranged fanatical follower of the Black Rose. She scurried backward, terror on her face as the large man stalked her. He gripped a laser whip gripped in one hand and a phase pistol in the other as he looked on her horrified gaze with maniacal glee. Pinned beneath his mate's weight, a lone female struggled, doing her best to escape her fate. Obviously, this one had lost a challenge in the past if her lack of left hand was any indication.

He'd seen enough. It was time this ended. With little regard for his own safety, and before anyone could react, he pounced on the one holding the whip, ripped his throat out and was landing on the other male roaring out his outrage before the stunned enemy could so much as utter a sound.

Behind him, he heard a terrified whimper. Knowing there was no time to waste, he made quick work of the trembling male beneath him, tearing out his throat as quickly as he could. He ignored the inevitable death twitch and whipped around, scenting for danger, ready to defend his mate against anyone who dared harm her or those she protected.

His mate, though injured, was in fine form. She made quick work of the traitorous female, swiping a paw across her throat, leaving her to bleed out on the ground. Though he wanted nothing more than to comfort his mate, Hunter padded over to the still trembling woman instead. As gently as he could, he nudged her with his muzzle, indicating she should climb onto his back.

Rather than taking his hint, she scurried away, curling into a tight ball and began to rock back and forth, whimpering into her chest. Realizing that his nearness only caused her more anxiety, Hunter retreated a short distance and lowered himself to the ground. Laying his head on his front paws, Hunter waited for the woman to relax, though he knew before long they'd have no choice but to leave. The last thing he wanted to do was force either of these two women to do anything. Up until now, others had forced their choices on them, giving them no say in what would happen. He refused to begin his relationship with his mate in the same way, if he could help it. Within seconds of his lying down, his mate nudged the other woman. When she didn't respond, his mate nipped the woman's thigh, then gave a low growl.

His mate nudged her again and this time the woman pushed herself to her wobbling elbows before sitting up. She reached a shaking hand out to the lioness, rubbing her behind the ear as if she were a pet. "Thank you," she whispered.

The frail woman turned toward him, lowered her gaze. She swallowed once. Twice. He could tell the thought of speaking to him directly terrified her. "Thank you, too. If you two hadn't shown up when you did, they would have taken me back down there." She shuddered, whether from cold or fear, Hunter didn't know. "I couldn't have survived down there much longer." Tears ran down her cheeks, glistening on her face as they froze in the icy cold of the elements.

Hunter grunted, the only acknowledgement he could give her while still in lion form. Again, his mate nudged the woman, this time none too gently as she grabbed the woman by the bottom of her thread-bare tunic. She had to be freezing, but at least she had some form of covering. His mate had naught but a filthy sheet to wrap around herself.

His brave lioness pushed the woman closer until she slipped up onto his back. Burying her face in his thick mane, she sighed. "You're so warm. I haven't been warm in weeks—maybe months." She turned to look at his female. "Oh Goddess, I can't thank you enough for rescuing me. I should have known, should have been stronger, should have fought harder."

The woman continued to babble as Hunter began the long trek down the mountain, evidently soothed by the droning sound of her own voice. It was fine with him as long as his mate kept at his heels. He refused to leave her on the mountain this time. If there were others to rescue, he would send more men down after. His mate needed medical care and she needed it now. She would also need the help of the female healers—those who healed the mind as well as the body. Both of these women would soon need to seek their counsel.

They rounded a bend he knew led to the clearing where his ship sat below. He would have simply had them transported aboard, but it was more difficult for the *Manruvian* transporters to lock onto their life signs while they were in their *Lionese* form. And now, with their weapons and clothing left behind, their human forms were not only more vulnerable to the weather, they were also more vulnerable to attack.

A cold feeling clenched his gut and he rolled onto the ground, throwing Maryann into a nearby snow bank. His mate, too, felt the threat with her heightened *Lionese* senses. She ran to the girl, pushed her toward the ship and snarled. The girl, not needing another warning, turned and ran toward the relative safety of the ship until she reached the entry and several males rushed out. His bodyguards and Mikel's rushed toward them as he and his mate turned to face their enemy. When would these poor, demented souls realize they worked for a lost cause? When would they give up and quit trying to stop their escape?

Hunter barely had the time to wonder exactly how many women they'd actually rescued from this hellhole before his mate growled a warning. With a speed that astounded him, she threw herself at the lion easily twice her size that seemed to appear out of nowhere to ambush them.

By the Goddess Alana, he'd never seen a lioness move that fast. Before he could aide his mate, more than a dozen lions rushed the small clearing, surrounding them and keeping them from the ship and their avenue of escape. With a roar, he charged into the fray, taking down every lion shifter between him and his mate. He'd fight by her side, in this, as in all things.

By the time he reached her side, the frozen ground was littered with the dead and dying. Some were his allies, but most were the enemy. Back to back, Hunter and his mate stood, their bodies quivering, their lungs billowing as they tried to absorb the frozen air.

Energy coursed through his body. He knew that as soon as they reached safety, he'd want only one thing, especially with his mate finally within touching distance. He'd want to mount her. He knew that he wouldn't be able to take his mate, wouldn't be able to sate the desire that would bombard him, and knowing that, he wanted to destroy the rebels that intercepted their departure all over again.

Through their bond, Hunter could feel his mate weakening. Her body swayed and their connection dimmed. Sensing her coming collapse, he shifted back to his human form and moved to her side.

"It's okay, *moya*. I have you. Shift and I'll get you to safety."

A few seconds passed while Hunter waited, holding his breath to see what her decision would be. Would she trust him in this? He hoped she'd rely on him, at least in this. If not, he'd do whatever he needed to earn her trust. He wouldn't give up on her—on them.

As though the Goddess Alana herself heard his prayers, his mate shifted, collapsing into his arms in an unconscious heap. With great care, Hunter lifted his mate into his arms. Heedless of the cold or his nudity, he carefully navigated the clearing. "Gather up the living, have their wounds treated and then move them to a holding cell. I want to know everything we can about the Black Rose's activities."

"And the dead?" Beran, one of Mikel's bodyguards, asked.

"Leave them for their compatriots to deal with. I'll be in the medical bay if anyone needs me."

"Understood, Prince Shi'Lan, and may I be the first to congratulate you on finding your mate."

Hunter nodded, then moved into the transport beam. Only after the medical personnel could assure him she'd live would he finally be able to rejoice. Until then, all he could do was pray.

FOR THE FIRST TIME in Goddess knew how long, Amy felt well rested and ready to take on the day. She slowly stretched, luxuriating in the feel of the soft mattress beneath her, the sweet scent of lilies in the air and the blessed warmth of the bedding around her. She smiled, enjoying this lovely dream. All too soon, she'd wake and she'd be back in her dank cell waiting for the next male to rut on her unwilling body.

She shoved her bleak thoughts aside, doing her best to enjoy this short respite. She rolled onto her side, smiled into her feather soft pillow and inhaled the clean scent. Minutes passed and still she didn't wake. Her brows furrowed in confusion. The scents were all wrong. The warmth, the comfort, the feeling of safety—all wrong. Everything felt too real, too substantial to be a dream. And, if she wasn't dreaming, that meant this was all real... The bed, the warmth, everything. How?

Afraid to open her eyes, Amy just lay there, allowing her mind to work through the problem. Questions circled in her mind, questions she had no answers to. Where was she? How had she gotten there? Who had her and what did they want? In the time that she'd been held captive, she had learned one thing—favors were never given for free. Her only question was how high was their price?

Her heart thumped madly against her chest. Panic threatened to overwhelm her. She continued to lie still and feign sleep while she tried to calm her racing heart. It wouldn't do to alert whoever guarded her that she'd regained consciousness.

Before she could come up with any answers, she heard the unmistakable hiss of a door opening, then muffled footsteps approaching. That answered one question, then she was on a ship. The sliding of the doors wasn't a sound she'd likely ever forget. Her body tensed as she sensed the newcomer approaching. This might be her only chance to flee and she wouldn't waste the opportunity to escape if it presented itself.

The footsteps grew closer, then stopped altogether. Someone cleared her throat—a woman, if she had to guess. "Why don't you get some sleep, Hunter? You haven't left her side in three days."

Amy's breath hitched. Her heart stuttered, then galloped in her chest. She knew that voice, had prayed for months she'd hear it again one day.

"I can't, Eve. Could you leave the room if it were Taliff lying in that bed, unconscious and unresponsive?"

Amy heard Eve sigh. "You have a valid point. I wouldn't want to leave his side either, Hunter, but collapsing from both exhaustion and starvation won't help either of you in the long run. You should at least eat something. You haven't eaten since we brought her aboard."

"I can't just leave my mate, Eve. I need to be here when she wakes. She needs to know that I'll be by her side—that I will always be there when she needs me."

Amy could hear the male's worry, could feel it in her mind. She barely kept herself from shuddering. She didn't want to be connected with a male. Any male. After the horrors she'd been through, she didn't think she could ever let a man touch her again. Not willingly.

"Amy isn't going anywhere, Hunter. And you were right there when the healer who treated her insisted she only needed sleep."

"But it's been three days."

"Yes, Hunter, and it may be three more. Look, go eat, and while you're at it, bathe. By the Goddess Alana, you stink. You don't want your mate's first glimpse of you when she wakes to be of you with your hair sticking up every which way, three day's worth of hair growth on your face and bloodshot red-rimmed eyes."

"But…"

"No buts, Hunter. I'll call you on the communications system the second she shows signs of waking."

"Fine," the man agreed. She could hear both reluctance and resignation in his voice, could almost feel it. But that was impossible. Wasn't it? Nothing about this situation made sense, especially nothing they said. And what was all this mate business anyway?

She felt the lightest touch as someone smoothed a hand down her hair. Calloused fingers trailed down her cheek, the column of her throat. Then the hand retreated and so did some of the warmth surrounding her. Goddess, she'd lost her mind. It was the only logical answer to the strange connection she sometimes sensed between her and the male—if you could call insanity logical. She couldn't be connected to him. She refused to admit to any connection with him. He was a man. That alone was enough to keep her from wanting anything to do with him.

"Already I can't live without her, Eve. What if she won't accept me? Won't accept the bond between us?"

Amy sensed Eve move closer. "Just give her time, Hunter. She needs time to adjust—adjust to her new surroundings, even to the freedom she'll have aboard your ship. Hell, Hunter, nothing is going to be easy on her once she wakes. Let her take this time to sleep so that at least her body is rested and strong when it's time for her to face the everyday things we take for granted."

Amy heard Hunter's sigh and relaxed a bit, knowing he'd soon leave the room. How could she tell Eve she would never be comfortable here? She could never be comfortable with a man, ever again.

"You're right, Eve. No wonder my father made you his advisor. You are wise beyond your years. I'll be back shortly. Take care of her while I'm gone and if..."

"Yeah, yeah. I know. I'll call the second she so much as twitches."

Even with her eyes closed, she sensed Hunter's hesitant nod, could visualize it in her mind's eye. Within seconds, she heard the door whoosh open, then close. She felt it the instant he left the room. Some insane loneliness crept over her when he left. Just knowing he was gone left her feeling strange, bereft, insane. She would *not* feel anything for the man. She would *not!*

"It's okay, Amy. He's gone. You can open your eyes now."

At first Amy stiffened, then she relaxed, opening her eyes for the first time since she regained consciousness. She should have known that Eve would realize she was awake. She squinted, holding her hand above her eyes, the muted light of the room nearly blinding her. It took a moment for her eyes to adjust, even with the lighting dimmed as it was. Only half the bulbs of the recessed lamps were lit and she still felt pain when she opened her eyes. How long had she been kept in the dark tunnels? How many months had they kept her there, trying to impregnate her and the others?

When her eyes finally grew accustomed to the light, the first thing she noticed was the beautiful woman sitting across from her. Oh, Goddess. She was real. Eve. So many days she had woken in hell, wishing, praying that Eve would come for her. Days had become weeks, weeks had become months and, eventually, all hope for rescue had withered and died. "It's you. It's really you." Tears slid down her cheeks as she stared at the woman she'd yearned to see for so long.

Eve smiled, tucking a long strand of her blonde hair behind her ear as she leaned forward. "Yes, it's me."

Amy watched as tears filled Eve's eyes. She turned her head away and quickly wiped them away before turning back. "We never gave up hope of one day finding you." Eve cleared her throat. "You and the others," she added. "Hunter wouldn't give up. He knew you were out there. After a few years of searching, he said he finally felt you. He said he felt your pain, your humiliation. He wouldn't rest—hasn't truly rested—since he connected with you several months ago."

"Connected?" What connection was she talking about? She wondered, but her heart knew. She'd felt him there from time to time. Felt him giving her comfort. Whispering unbelievable promises of rescue. She'd never believed him. How could she? He was a male, after all. What man would ever be that caring, that compassionate?

One question ran through Amy's mind repeatedly. She needed to know. "How I—"

Her voice cracked so she tried again. "How long?"

Eve winced, lowering her gaze to the floor. Amy stiffened and tried to sit up. Eve stood and quickly pushed her back against the pillows. "Just lie down and rest. Your body still needs to recover. I'll answer your questions." With a sigh, Eve returned to her seat, rubbed her back yet again. That's when Amy finally noticed the curve of Eve's belly.

"You're pregnant," she said, though how she hadn't noticed it at first she'd never know.

Eve chuckled. "Yes, and not for the first time either." Eve's smile disappeared and her gaze grew somber as she reached for Amy's hand. After lacing their fingers together, Eve looked her straight in the eye. "Nearly six years, Amy. The Black Rose attacked Taliff's ship, kidnapping you and the others nearly six years ago."

Amy swallowed, looked away. She fisted her hands in the sheets as rage boiled up inside her. Six years of her life stolen with no way to ever get them back. Six fucking years. When she got her hands on the Black Rose, nothing and no one would stop her from hacking the woman into bits with her claws.

She licked her lips, then turned back to Eve, letting her see all her hatred and rage. "How many women were rescued besides me?"

Eve stood, running her palms over her belly as she did. "Counting you, we brought nearly three dozen women on board."

Amy heard the sadness in the woman's voice and knew whatever Eve said next would not be pleasant. "One woman died before she could get to the medical bay for help. Several more are in critical condition."

"And those sent down to the surface? How did they fare?"

Eve grimaced, rubbed her belly before returning to her seat. "Two, as you know, died protecting Maryann. There was nothing we could do for them, but—"

Amy pushed herself to her elbows before slowly sitting up. Gripping the sheet beneath her arms, she scooted back until she rested against the headboard. Even that much movement wore her out. She didn't have time for weakness, not now, maybe not ever.

"What aren't you telling me?"

Eve stood again, paced from one end of the small room to the other and back again, rubbing her lower back the entire time.

"What, Eve?" she asked again. "Don't stall. I'm obviously not the girl I once was." She cast her gaze around the room thinking. God, how old was she now? Twenty-five, Twenty-six? Shaking her head, she turned her thoughts back to what was important. Her age didn't matter anymore. "I can handle whatever you have to say."

Eve winced, then nodded before turning to face her once again. "Myra wasn't with the others. Somehow she managed to crawl away before we sent the guards to retrieve the fallen men."

Amy snarled, not even bothering to control the furious lioness that raged within. She should have made sure the treacherous bitch was dead before they headed to the rendezvous point.

Eve nodded. "I had the same reaction when I heard that piece of information. The good news is we have one of the Black Rose's followers in a cell for questioning. Perhaps we can finally learn where she keeps her headquarters."

"I want to be there. When you question the rebel, I want to be there."

"I figured you'd feel that way." She stood and made her way to the door, then stopped and turned back, a thoughtful look on her face. "You're right, you know. You're not the same girl I knew. Now you're a strong, courageous woman. You've grown. You've become stronger and more sure of yourself and you've become a woman who has and *can* face anything and don't you forget it." Eve stepped forward as the door slid open, then paused on the threshold. "I imagine Hunter will be here shortly. I suggest you take this time to shore up your defenses. It's never wise to let a man—any man—see you at your most vulnerable. It always has a way of coming back to bite you on the ass when they do." She turned to go, then stopped herself once again. "He's a good man, Amy. He deserves a chance. At least give him that."

"I'll remember that," Amy whispered, but Eve was already gone leaving her alone with her thoughts.

Chapter Four

By the time Hunter managed to clean up in the public bathing pool and grab a quick meal in the ship's refectory, more than one standard hour had passed. He hated leaving Amy, even for that long, no matter the reason. He couldn't fault Eve's wisdom though. He *did* feel better, rejuvenated, after the small respite. But he'd been gone long enough and needed to return to his mate.

He wondered how much longer would she sleep. If she slept much longer, he'd contact his father's personal physician on *Chantrea*. Perhaps he'd have some advice, something to suggest that the *Manruvian* healer may have missed because of the differences between the *Lionese* and *Manruvian* physiologies. Briefly he wondered if she would be upset or relieved by the news she had yet to hear.

As he moved closer to their quarters, Hunter's connection with his mate intensified. He knew before he reached their suite that she was awake. Awake and agitated. When he reached their cabin, he braced himself before entering the security code that would allow him access to the suite. He just prayed that whatever his mate needed to heal, to move forward in her life, he had the power or the resources to give it to her.

He closed his eyes and prayed to the Goddess Alana that he would also have the patience. His body raged at him, his inner beast demanding he claim his mate, but he knew she needed time. He just hoped he had the strength to give her the time she needed. The last thing he wanted was to become the kind of monster she now thought every male to be. Taking a deep breath, he forced his raging libido under control and waited for the door to open.

Tucking his fear and nervousness into the farthest corner of his mind, Hunter stepped into his quarters. He immediately looked toward the bed, expecting to find his mate huddled beneath the covers. Instead, he found her bent over one of his storage chests, rummaging through its contents. Pride surged through him as he realized just how strong his mate was. She was one to take action when the situation warranted it. She stepped up and took charge of her life, instead of sitting back and waiting for things to happen. Those were wonderful and welcome qualities vital in a queen.

His cock jerked, pulsing with need as he glimpsed the pale cheeks of her rounded bottom as she bent over. She hadn't heard his approach yet, so for just this moment he could watch her while her guard was down. She had managed to locate one of his tunics to cover herself in his absence, but that didn't prevent him from remembering exactly how she had looked unclothed while in the healing chamber.

Her skin had been as soft as a dream, her complexion creamy and flawless. Her golden-red hair hung long and thick, nearly to her waist. Her breasts—her breasts were perfect, high and firm and would completely fill his hands. He closed his eyes for a moment and swallowed thickly at the memory. Her waist was narrow, her hips and bottom curvy. His breath hitched when he glanced at her legs. They seemed to go on forever. Her entire body had a lushness to it that absolutely fascinated him.

The healers had thought him out of his mind when he demanded that every cut, every bruise be healed before she awoke. It was bad enough she would have her memories of her time with those animals. She didn't need the visual reminders of her abuse.

He'd give anything to have the right to touch her right now, to bind her to him using the *Manruvian Matebonds* stored in the trunk she was busy ransacking. He wanted to sink his cock into her wet heat, to merge their bodies as the *Matebonds* bound their souls together. But no matter what his body wanted or his soul craved, her needs came first and would always come first. He would not take away her choices, would not force such a bond on her. She'd suffered enough at the hands of others. He refused to act like all those other men, taking away her choices for the sake of his own selfish needs.

Knowing she'd hate being caught unawares, Hunter silently stepped back out into the hallway. He pressed the button for the suite's intercom system. He hoped that by announcing himself to her before she saw him face to face, she might feel more of a sense of control, thus feel more comfortable in his presence. That was the plan anyway.

"Yes?"

Hunter shook his head when Amy's voice cut through his thoughts, feeling surprised to be caught daydreaming. *I wonder how many times she responded just now?* He cleared his throat, then spoke as gently as he could. "Good morrow, Amy. My name is Hunter Shi'Lan. May I come inside and speak with you for a few minutes? I'm sure you have many questions you'd like answered."

Several moments passed without an answer. Just as he began to wonder if she'd deny him entry, he heard a breathy sigh through the intercom.

"Are you alone?" she asked, her voice sounding both wary and resigned.

"Yes, *moya*. I'm alone. If you'd like to have Eve or another woman here with you, I can arrange that. I live only to please you, *moya*."

Another pause, this one shorter. "No. No, you can come in."

Hunter shrugged his shoulders and rolled his neck, trying to ease the tension that had gathered while he'd awaited her answer. After once again entering his access code into the security keypad, Hunter slowly entered their quarters, keeping his hands by his sides and in full view. He would do nothing to alarm her if he could help it. However, by the confident way she held his sword in front of her, maybe he should be worried about his own safety. Both pride and humor swept through him at the thought of his very strong-willed mate brandishing his own sword at him in his own quarters. It struck him as very ironic.

"Is there a reason that you feel the need to have a sword in your hands, *moya*?" he asked, trying to keep the smile from his face. If she only knew how incredibly enticing she looked standing there, her hair still in wild disarray, as she held his sword pointed at his chest.

"I hear you have a prisoner aboard this ship."

She kept looking at the door behind him as though she expected an army to follow him through it. Hunter reached back and pressed the button to close the door, hoping that would settle her nerves a bit. Then again, perhaps not.

"Yes, *moya*, we have a prisoner onboard. We are waiting for the healers to determine that the rebel is well enough for interrogation." He frowned, wondering what her interest was. He wouldn't blame her if she wanted the rebel dead, but they needed information. With luck, they would find at least one more of the Black Rose's outposts.

"I want to talk to the prisoner." She licked her lips, her gaze darting around the room. "I need to talk to the prisoner." Tears began to trickle down her face. "I have to see him. I have to know why they're doing this." Her breath hitched on a sob and the sword wavered in her hands. It no doubt grew heavy, weakened as she still was from her injuries and malnutrition.

Hunter glanced over at the tray of food next to the bed. It was untouched. Even the glass of water was still full.

"Is there a reason you haven't eaten, *moya*?"

She stiffened as though his words made her wary. "What does it matter? Will you beat me if I don't eat? Will you force your drugs on me, your potions, to ensure I'll want to do as you say?"

Hunter moved over to the tray. The disappointment he felt was sharp. He'd hoped that Eve's visit would have assured her that they had no intention of harming her.

Picking up a slice of the meat on her tray, he took a bite and drank down a good portion of the water. "See? Nothing in there that will harm you." Turning back, he gave her a sad smile. "I'm sorry for what you suffered, *moya*. I cannot change what they did to you. I can only show you that you will never be treated that way here. I wish there was some way to prove to you that you can trust us."

She thinned her lips. "Then take me to your prisoner. I want to talk to the rebel. I *need* to talk to the rebel."

He thought it was more likely that she needed to take the sword she held and run the rebel through with it, but he kept that thought to himself.

"If that is what it takes to begin your healing, *moya*, I will gladly take you to the rebel we captured. But be forewarned. You will not find any satisfaction in revenge upon this one. This prisoner is merely a pawn—one who when healed, will likely see and regret the harm caused."

"You'll take me now? Before I eat? Before I do anything you wish of me?"

"If that is your wish, *moya*. I only want your happiness."

"Then take me to the rebel scum. I can't wait to show him my wrath."

THE ONLY THING THAT could have surprised Amy more when they walked into the prisoner's cell was if the prisoner standing before her were her own father.

"Why?" she asked, her heart breaking as she watched the woman pace the cell they'd put her in. Tears streamed down Amy's face as she stared at her best friend. Or at least, the woman she'd thought to be her best friend. "You told them when I didn't eat, Chrissie. You told them when I cycled so they would better know when to come to me." She slammed her fists against the nearest wall. "Only you knew I could mask the scent of my cycle. I should have known when they allowed you to visit those first few weeks after I woke up in that frozen hellhole."

Amy stared coldly at the woman she once called friend. Chrissie's betrayal devastated her. How would she ever know who spoke the truth and who didn't? If she couldn't trust her best friend, someone from her own pride back home on Earth, whom could she trust? No matter the circumstances, she would never have sold herself out for another. She'd die before putting another woman through what she'd endured—the physical agony, the humiliation, the shame.

She continued to stare at the woman with hate-filled eyes, rage filling her mind as the need for revenge filled her heart. Behind her, she could feel Hunter's surprise, then his anger as she'd spelled out Chrissie's crimes against her.

Tired of waiting for Chrissie's answer, Amy turned toward Hunter. "If she refuses to answer your questions, terminate her. I have no desire to waste my time or anyone else's on someone who refuses to answer for her crimes."

Hunter nodded. "If that's your wish, *moya*, I'll see it done."

Amy forced herself to walk away from her one-time friend and toward the cell door. She put one foot in front of the other, praying she wouldn't collapse until after she'd made it off this level of the ship. She wanted no one to witness her breakdown. As Hunter stepped away from the door to let her pass, Chrissie's shaky voice halted her. "Please," she whispered. "Please, wait."

Amy stopped, keeping her back toward the woman. She couldn't bear to look her in the eye, knowing how she'd betrayed her to her captors. Fisting her hands by her sides, Amy kept her voice even as she said, "Answer my question, Chrissie. Why would you betray me this way? Why?"

Behind her, Chrissie sobbed and Amy stiffened her back in reaction. "I had no choice. They have my baby brother. Unless I do as they say, report to them, they'll kill Donny."

Amy whipped around, needing to see Chrissie's face, gauge her truthfulness. "They have Donny? How long ago did they take him? How did they get him? Get you? I just assumed Taliff took you and I just never ran into you on the ship before we were attacked."

Chrissie shook her head, then dropped onto the metal bunk. With head down and shoulders sagging, she whispered, "No, I guess about a year ago, two women showed up at the Pride. One called herself Myra."

Hunter eased away from the wall and headed toward the rebel. "And the other?" he asked. He remembered Taliff telling him that his sister had taken Myra when she took Amy and the others. His brother had been happy when that troublemaker disappeared.

"Haeda. At the time, she went by Haeda. They said they'd been banished by their pride and needed sanctuary."

Hunter gasped and turned away, leaving Amy to finish questioning the traitor. When Chrissie didn't say anything more, Amy walked over toward her, stopping directly in front of her. "And the Elders gave them sanctuary?" Amy prodded.

Nodding, Chrissie lifted her head, finally meeting Amy's gaze. "Yes," she whispered. "We took Myra into our home, while Haeda spent the night with your parents. The next morning, the village was overrun with men. Several of the women were taken while they slept. Any villagers who fought back were killed. When we refused to cooperate, they rounded up all the children and told us they'd kill them if we didn't come willingly."

With tears trailing down her cheeks and her shoulders slumped in defeat, Chrissie looked completely broken. She didn't look anything like the carefree girl Amy had grown up with any longer. What could Amy say? That it was all right? It wasn't. That she forgave her? Right now, when the memories of her captivity were so fresh, she couldn't. That she understood? Maybe.

Then something the other woman had said caught her attention. "Did you just say the other woman spent the night with my parents?"

Chrissie bit her lip, then lowered her head, nodding. "Yes, she stayed with your family."

Amy's gut tightened. Her hands started to shake and her legs began to quiver. Oh, Goddess. Amy shook her head. She couldn't take any more bad news.

Hunter must have sensed her unease because he moved behind her, placing his hand against her back. Terrified of what Chrissie might say, she didn't have the strength to worry about the fact that a male had his hand on her. "What happened to my family, Chrissie? What happened to my parents, my siblings?"

With head still bowed, Chrissie lifted her knees to her chest and wrapped her arms around her legs as she began to rock back and forth atop the bunk. "They took them. They took them all. They took them all," she repeated.

"Where, Chrissie? Where did they take them?" So worried was she about her family, she barely noticed when the hand on her back started to move in soothing circles, warming her there, when the cold fear slipped past her defenses and gripped her heart.

"It was so dark there. Always dark there."

Amy's heart pounded. Her stomach clenched in fear. Part of her wanted to shake the information out of the other woman.

Chrissie snapped her head up, finally met her gaze. "To the Black Rose's home base, of course. Where else could she keep an eye on them?" She looked away, staring at the far wall. "She knew that's where she needed to keep anyone who was of importance to her cause. She wanted leverage against the House of *Chantrea*. That's *all* I know."

"You know where the Black Rose calls home? You know where her base is?"

Hunter moved closer behind Amy, wrapped his arms around her waist as he pulled her against his chest. So caught up was she in her fear and rage for her family, Amy didn't protest when he brought her body up against his in silent support. Her energy and concern were focused on her family. What were those beasts doing to her mother, her sisters, her baby brother?

She knew that Hunter had just as much a need for revenge against the Black Rose as she did. Through their physical contact—his large hand splayed over her stomach, his strength at her back—she could clearly feel his anger at the Black Rose and his utter horror that his sister was capable of such evil acts. Because she could feel the tension running through his frame as he waited for Chrissie's answer, she didn't try to evade his touch even though being so close to him set her nerves jangling and sent a strange feeling into the pit of her tummy.

"Tell us, Chrissie, please," Hunter added. "Help us find the others she's taken. The others she's tormented as she has you and Amy. Where does she call home?"

Amy held her breath and waited for Chrissie's answer. Knowing her family needed her, she'd do everything necessary to save them from whatever fate the Black Rose planned for them.

She watched as the other woman sat on her cot, her knees to her chest and rocked back and forth. Her anger at Chrissie faded a bit as she wondered—what sort of bargains would she have made had she known her parents and her siblings were in the clutches of the same animals who had abused her?

Chapter Five

WITH HIS MATE HELD SECURELY IN HIS ARMS, HUNTER WAITED impatiently for the woman's answer. Did she know where Haeda based her slaving operation or didn't she? He'd much rather be spending this close time with his mate convincing her she could trust him than standing here knowing the only reason she allowed his touch was because of the shattering news she'd received.

Once they learned the location of the planet where his sister hid, where Amy's people were hostages, he could tell Mikel. Then he could focus on his mate while they traveled to their destination. Did he wish he could order Amy to stay out of the coming battle? Of course he did. But as he held Amy's trembling body in his arms and understood her fear through their growing connection, he knew that no matter the danger involved, his mate needed closure. He wanted her to heal emotionally, and to do that, she needed to feel useful and in control. And, that was something he *could* give her, even if the mere thought of what could happen to her made his heart squeeze in terror. Besides, the followers of the Black Rose would never believe that a *true Chantrean* woman could be the warrior he knew his mate to be.

Finally, Chrissie lifted her head, her eyes pleading for understanding. "I know some details—nearby planets, stars in the sky above the prison itself, but I don't know the name of the planet. The rebels called it The Black Abyss, but I doubt that will help you figure out the planet's true name."

Hunter sighed, then flexed his shoulders. Amy tensed at his sudden movement, then slowly relaxed against him. He couldn't help but smile.

She might not want to trust him, might even actively fight trusting him when she felt stronger, but her body and her subconscious mind already trusted him on some level. He could work with that. This seed of trust would give him something to hold on to during those times when she was sure to object to his pursuit of her.

"You do know we can't just let you go, don't you?" Amy asked.

Hunter could hear the cynicism in his mate's voice. Did she suspect that Chrissie had lied so they'd let her go? Or did she suspect a trap of some kind? "If this is a trap, Chrissie, you will not escape punishment," Hunter added. He watched as Chrissie swallowed convulsively, then nodded.

"If you get my brother out of there, my parents, then no matter what happens to me, it's worth it."

"Fine. But we need more details about the planet you were on if we're to have any hope of locating it." Amy remained silent and unnaturally still in his arms. What was going through her mind, he wondered.

As Chrissie closed her eyes, Hunter let his hands slowly run up and down Amy's sides, her hips. Perhaps if she got used to his touch gradually, her fear of him would slowly dissipate. He could hope anyway. Amy stiffened in his arms at first, but when he made no move to touch her anywhere else, the tension in her body seemed to ease a bit. The sound of Chrissie's low voice in the small cell jerked him from his thoughts.

"There was a small window high up on one of the walls in my chamber. Sometimes, when the men came to me, I would stare out that window and try to imagine myself somewhere else. Some place where I was free and didn't have to submit to—" Her voice caught, she swallowed and seemingly shook off the horrifying memory. "A small planet seemed to hover in the distance, a beacon, I guess. Something beautiful." She sighed, a somewhat wistful sound, then continued speaking. "The beauty of it always struck me as ironic. Here I was, a prisoner, raped daily by my guards but the view from that tiny window captivated me, drew me. I wanted to be able to free my soul from my body and fly to that place where no one would ever be able to touch me again."

Chrissie shook her head and grimaced. "Anyway, the planet itself looked sea-foam green. It had rings around it. Three of them. Pink, then silver, then a deep, dark purple outer ring. The planet always looked like it was shrouded in mist, no matter the time of day." She shrugged. "It was probably planetary gasses but looking up at it, at the mystical beauty of it, gave me a focal point, a place for my mind to escape to while the guards used my body." She swallowed, then wiped away the tears trailing down her cheeks. "Anyway, I did overhear one of the guards say that while half the planet was filled with light and life, the Black Rose chose to make her home on the dark side."

When Chrissie shuddered and began to rock back and forth once more, Hunter decided to halt the questioning. She couldn't escape her cell, so he didn't see any harm in letting her compose herself. They knew where to find her when they needed more answers.

As though Amy could read his mind, his mate slowly stepped out of his arms and placed her hand on Chrissie's bowed head. That simple act of compassion stunned him. He'd doubted he'd be able to offer even that small comfort if he were in her position. "Get your rest, Chrissie. I'm sure we'll have more questions soon."

With that said, Amy turned away from the prisoner and made her way toward the cell door. As Hunter turned to follow her, Chrissie lay on her side and drew her knees up against her chest. He watched her for a minute, filled with pity. She looked so lost and alone, lying there knowing that her future was in another's hands. Again. She'd gone from one prison to another, but at least now she had a chance of coming out of this nightmare alive. And no one would abuse her here. Perhaps, in time, she would heal and find that she herself had a mate.

By the time he left the prisoner and sealed her cell, Amy had disappeared. Rather than chase her down as the lion inside him demanded, Hunter let her go. He didn't want her to feel trapped or hunted, but letting her go freely had to be among the hardest decisions he'd ever made. However, just because he wouldn't chase her down didn't mean he had to stay ignorant of her location.

Knowing the *Manruvian* ship had a sentient computer running its systems, Hunter spoke aloud. "Computer?"

"Yes, Prince Shi'Lan?"

"What is the current location of Amy Morgan?"

"Amy Morgan is in the transportation tube on level twenty-three."

"What is her final destination?"

"Final destination is the private quarters of Princess Eve Shi'Lan and Prince Taliff Shi'Lan."

"Thank you, computer. Open a communication channel to Prince Taliff Shi'Lan's private quarters, please."

"Working. Communication channel open."

The sound of Taliff's voice came through the speakers overhead. "This is Taliff Shi'Lan."

"Hello, brother. I wanted to inform you that my mate is en route to your quarters. The prisoner delivered some disturbing news to Amy and I think she may feel the need to speak with another woman, someone she considers a friend."

"Understood. Is there anything I should know?"

"Maybe. I want to speak with Mikel's navigation officer first. Once I know something definitive, I'll let you know."

"Sounds good."

In the background, Hunter heard a series of chimes, then his brother calling out for someone to hold on.

"I must go, Hunter. It seems your mate has arrived."

"Thank you, Taliff. If Amy needs me, I'll be in our quarters."

"Of course. I'll let her know."

Knowing that what Amy needed more than anything else right now was to feel safe to speak with Eve freely more than anything else right now, Hunter sighed, then made his way to their quarters.

AMY STOOD OUTSIDE EVE'S cabin, unsure whether coming here was the right thing to do. Could she walk through that door, knowing the man who took her from her family, from the only life she'd known, was in there. What choice did she have though? She needed to talk to someone she trusted and though she wanted to trust Hunter, she knew Eve would never betray her. That was about the only thing she could be certain of, especially after what she'd just learned.

"Well, I can't stay out here all day," she muttered. Shaking off her nervousness, Amy finally pressed the door chime and waited for someone to answer. By the time the door finally slid open, she'd managed to calm her frayed nerves. Just because Taliff was a man, it didn't mean that he'd harm her. *Maybe if I tell myself that often enough, I'll start to believe it.*

"Come in, Amy. Little Delilah and I were about to read a story. Eve's in the bathing chamber overseeing Elijah's bath, but she'll be out shortly."

Stunned, Amy shook her head as she slowly made her way farther into the main sitting room of Eve and Taliff's quarters. "Delilah? Elijah?" she asked, though it was obvious who Delilah was the moment she spotted Taliff sitting on the sofa with a little girl on his lap. She couldn't be more than two. Tiny and delicate, the child seemed almost ethereal, especially in comparison to her well-built father. Her strawberry blonde hair hung past her shoulders in waves and her amber eyes sparkled with mischief. The boys were going to be all over her when she reached puberty, if not before.

"Our children. Delilah here will be two in just over one of your Earth months and our son, Elijah, just celebrated his fifth birthday."

"You're going to have your hands full when she gets older. You know that, don't you?"

Taliff threw back his head and laughed. "What do you mean, when she gets older? She already causes more mischief than her brother ever did."

Dragging her gaze from the child, Amy finally looked at Taliff. Really looked at him. No wonder Hunter had seemed familiar to her when she had first seen him. Taliff and Hunter were nearly identical in looks and build. Taliff's hair was a lighter shade than Hunter's and a good six inches shorter. And, while Taliff's eye color was the same shade of amber as his mate's, Hunter's were green. Other than those, and the aura of power that seemed to surround Hunter, they'd be impossible to tell apart.

As Amy moved closer to the father and daughter, she looked around the room, surprised to see how homey the cabin looked. Taliff sat on a plush brown sofa. It looked like leather but not quite. Several matching chairs were scattered around the room, so she made her way to the one farthest from Taliff. She sat down on the edge of the seat and continued to scan the room. Two end tables flanked the sofa, each covered with plush toys, baby blankets and children's storybooks. There was a small nook off to the right, which held a small table and chair set. Pictures of the children hung upon the walls along with prints of several beautiful planetary scenes. Finally, she noticed several closed doors that seemed to branch off the main room.

"You can relax, Amy. Nothing and no one here will harm you, though I don't expect you to take my word for that."

Amy stiffened. Deep inside she knew Taliff wouldn't harm her, especially with a child in the room, but she couldn't seem to help her reactions. "Oh, I'm fine." She prayed he had no idea she wanted to run from the room and find some place to hide from everyone, including Eve. Licking her lips, Amy tried to think of some conversational tidbit to distract her. "How long will Eve be, did you say?"

Taliff chuckled softly and his eyes twinkled in mirth. "She should be walking through the door behind you any second.'

Amy nodded, then looked down at her lap. A smile twisted her lips when she noticed she had her hands fisted in her tunic. "Oh, I wanted to thank you and Eve for arranging the clothing. It was very generous of her to give me something out of her own wardrobe."

"Those aren't Eve's clothes, Amy. Hunter had her work with a tailor before we left *Chantrea* to make those for you. As soon as he felt the connection with you, he'd started making the arrangements. He insisted Eve not overlook even the tiniest detail."

"Oh." What else could she say? Confused and uncertain, she once again glanced around the room. What was taking Eve so long?

Taliff nodded, seeming perhaps to understand her confusion, because he added, "Do you know what a mate bond is, Amy?"

This she could at least answer truthfully. "No, not really."

"Maybe if I explain it, it will help you understand just how safe you are on this ship."

She nodded, knowing that learning all she could about her new situation would only help her in the end. Knowledge was power after all, or so the saying went. "Okay. What exactly is the mate bond?"

"Let me ask you something. When you're near Hunter, can you feel his emotions, sometimes catch a quick glimpse of his thoughts at times?"

Amy nodded. At first, she'd thought herself crazy but after a while, she hardly seemed to notice it. "Sometimes," she agreed.

"Well, imagine that a hundred, a thousand times over. Right now, you and Hunter share a connection. A mate connection. Hunter can feel some of what you feel, hear some of your thoughts, just as you can feel his, but right now you're mostly closed off to each other. But once you actually bond with him, you'll know his every thought, feel everything he feels. One mate cannot lie to the other once they bond."

"You mean, if I bond with him, however that's done, he can't betray me?"

Taliff winced. "Not exactly. What I mean to say is, you'll know if he's going to betray you the moment he thinks it." Shaking his head, Taliff laid his now sleeping daughter next to him on the sofa and, after tucking a blanket around her, leaned forward. "I'm not explaining this well. The thing is, Amy, once a *Chantrean* male feels that initial connection with his mate, he has two choices—complete the bond with her or not. If he completes the mate bond, all his thoughts, all his needs, center on her. She becomes his everything, tied to him in life and death."

He raised his hand when she started to object. "Yes, some men cheat, but that happens with every species, be they human, *Chantrean* or *Manruvian*. But those who complete their bonding using the

Matebonds do not. It's impossible. Your souls bind together. Your hearts and minds become one. He will never be able to betray you and you him once you bond. Because you share emotions, betraying you would become as abhorrent a thought to him as it would be to you and vice versa."

Taking a deep breath, Amy tried to digest everything Taliff said and not said in his brief summation. She had a lot to think about. Getting to her feet, Amy quickly glanced over at the sleeping child. She looked so peaceful lying there. If only Amy could find such peace in her own dreams. Shaking herself out of her thoughts, Amy looked to Taliff. "Tell Eve I shall return later. I have much to think about."

"Of course. Any time you need to talk—to either of us—we'll be here. Finding you has eased something inside Eve's heart, and thus mine, as well. It's very good to have you back."

Amy looked away, swallowed past the lump that seemed lodged in her throat, then nodded. She needed to get out of here before she did something stupid. Like cry.

When she turned to walk away, Taliff called her name.

"Yes?" she asked, her voice just above a whisper in deference to the sleeping child.

"Just so you know, Hunter called earlier to say he was returning to your quarters."

Amy nodded, then headed for the door. Yes, she had a lot to think about.

Chapter Six

As Amy wandered aimlessly through the corridors of the *Manruvian* ship, her mind kept running over everything Taliff said. She just didn't know what to do or what to believe. What would it be like to know absolutely that you could trust another? To know that you'd never have to fear that person's betrayal…to know that, above all, there was one person in existence whom you could trust implicitly. What a relief it would be to know beyond a shadow of a doubt that the person you spoke with told you the truth. Could such security really exist? If it did, would she have the courage to face it, to try it?

She had to admit, the idea appealed to her, especially considering the most recent betrayal she'd had to face. But no matter how appealing the idea, it definitely included one major drawback—Hunter himself. If she agreed to the bonding and it worked, she would be tied to a male. A very strong and, by the looks of it, very virile male. Did she have the courage to agree to try such a thing?

How could she ever give herself over to another man? She shuddered. Her stomach clenched and bile began to rise in her throat. Just the thought of being intimate with a man—even Hunter, who'd been nothing but kind—nauseated her.

Do not fear so, my child. I would never pair you with a man who'd do you harm. He is a strong man. A man of great honor and personal integrity.

Amy stumbled to a halt and reached out for the nearest wall as a wave of dizziness washed over her. What the hell? Now she'd begun to hear voices. Well, one anyway.

Tinkling laughter rippled through her mind. *Don't you know who I am, child?*

Closing her eyes, Amy braced herself against the wall and rubbed her forehead. "Should I?" she whispered. She quickly glanced down the hall. Her eyes scanned the corridor in both directions. Thank the Goddess no one stood nearby or they'd hear her talking to herself.

Why would I allow others to witness what passes between us?

"You mean—"

Just think your thoughts and I shall hear them. And yes, I am Alana, the Mother Goddess of the Chantrean—*and others.*

Amy hung her head and slid down the wall, unable to continue standing on wobbling legs. *Why? Why speak to me now? Do you know how many times I called out to you, begged you to help me, to let me die?*

Great sadness poured through her. She could feel the Goddess's tears as though they were her own. *Each time you shed a tear, child, I shed one, too. Each time a male violated you, they violated me. Each time you begged for help, I listened. I answered.*

Why? Why couldn't you save me, save us all before they raped us, defiled us? You're a Goddess.

Even I must follow certain rules, Amy. So, I did what I could. I found the one person who could help you when I could not. I found your life mate, the other half of your soul. I found Hunter.

Why him? Why must I need any man?

My child, you and Hunter were always meant to be together. Only with him by your side will you become the woman you were destined to be.

I'm scared, she confessed. That was the gut-wrenching truth. She was scared—scared to the depths of her soul.

Of course you are, child. Only a fool does not fear the unknown. And you are not a fool. All I ask is that you listen to what Hunter has to say. Listen with your heart, not just your mind. It will not lead you astray. Not in this. Now, enough talking. If you continue down this corridor, you'll find the Manruvian *people's favorite part of this ship. Let your worries go for now, my child, and enjoy the pleasure found in the home away from home.*

Knowing the Goddess spoke true and her worries and fear would still be there later, Amy reluctantly nodded. Pushing herself to her feet, she looked down the hallway to her right. At the very end of the corridor, a single door faced her. A sign hung above it, written in a language she couldn't read.

Oh well. What did she have to lose but a little time?

Exactly, my child.

Just before she reached for the door release, Amy closed her eyes. She had one last thing she needed to say to the Mother Goddess. Concentrating on the Goddess, Amy initiated contact with her. *Thank you for saving me, no matter how you chose to do so.*

I only wish I could have protected you from all that you suffered. As quickly as the connection began, it ended.

Shoving all thoughts and worries from her mind, Amy pressed her palm against the identification pad. She shook her head, still amazed at the technology the *Manruvians* and *Chantrean Lionese* had at their disposal. The pad grew warm beneath her hand as it identified her and in seconds the door slid open.

She'd only set one foot in the door when she stopped, too stunned to walk any farther into the room. One minute she stood in a spaceship heading toward a new planet she'd call home, the next she'd been transported to a seaside getaway.

Turquoise water crested in waves as far as the eye could see. Strange creatures she'd originally thought only fodder for children's bedtime stories sat sunning themselves on huge rocks and boulders. The scent of salt water wafted past her, the breeze ruffling her hair. Cream-colored sea foam washed against the white sandy beach as the waves thrust forward and receded. One of the mermen looked her way, smiled and dove into the water only to jump back out, his entire body rising at least twenty feet over the water. With a twist of his glistening rainbow-colored glistening tail, he dove straight back down into a cresting wave.

So real, she thought. "It looks so real."

"It's as real as you want it to be."

She whipped her head around, surprised to see Mikel standing behind her. She looked back toward the ocean, shaking her head in wonder. "How?"

"Our technology is very advanced, even more so than that of the *Chantreans*. To tell you the truth, I'm not quite sure how the scientists are able to do most of what they do."

"The mermen, mermaids," she said, pointing out toward the water, "they're real?"

Behind her, Mikel chuckled. "You could say that. I, too, can shift into what you see out there. Our people love the water, though as you can see, it's not necessary for us to live in it."

Amy nodded, then turned back toward Mikel, too stunned to say anything more about the fantastical reality of mer-people. "I want to thank you for saving me, for saving all the others. Without you, I never would have gotten out of there—not alive, anyway."

Mikel shook his head. "That's not true. Hunter would have come for you, crawling on his stomach if he had to. Nothing would have stopped him. For five years he hunted for those his sister had abducted, determined to find you all. But once you woke, once he connected to you, nothing mattered but getting to you, rescuing you."

Amy swallowed, feeling self-conscious. What exactly could she say to that? "Well, thank you for accompanying him. I am just sorry you were harmed in the rescue."

"I know a way you can make it up to me."

Though nervous about what favor he'd ask, Amy owed him. "What can I do?"

"When Hunter asks you to wear the *Matebonds*, agree. If you are not truly his mate, nothing will happen. If you were meant to be with him, what more could you want than a male who would do anything for you, including die for you?"

"When you put it that way, but I don't know —"

He raised his hand, halting the excuse she already had waiting on the tip of her tongue. "I dream of one day finding my mate. I know what it's like to fantasize about the day I'd finally meet her and know that I'd never be alone again. I know what it's like to wonder if she's even out there. But now he knows and, though he'd never push you for more than you could give, I don't think I'd have the willpower to do the same." His mouth twisted into a sad smile. "Anyway, I am long overdue for a good swim and the water is calling my name."

Amy nodded and watched as he skirted around her and headed down the beach. Yes, she definitely had a lot to think about and what better place to think than at the beach?

After toeing off her sneakers and rolling up the pant legs on her jeans as high as they would go, Amy headed toward the shoreline, in the opposite direction she'd seen Mikel take. She imagined a lot of people would want to reassure themselves that Mikel was fine, so being anywhere near him would not be conducive to quiet introspection.

Only when she looked behind her and could barely make out the others in the distance did she stop and look out into the ocean. It amazed her, this technology the *Manruvians* possessed. She truly felt as though she were walking along a beach on Earth. Seeing no one nearby, Amy sat down in the surf, letting the waves gently wash over her feet, her calves.

She tilted her head back. Leaning back on her elbows, she closed her eyes and let the heat of the sun wash over her skin as the water caressed her flesh. It felt so good, so real.

"And what has put such a beautiful smile on your face?"

Amy yelped, unable to stop herself. She hadn't realized she was no longer alone. Her eyelids snapped open and she found herself looking into Hunter's twinkling green eyes. His long golden-red hair hung past his shoulders in loose waves. The muscles in his thighs and chest flexed as he squatted beside her. As her gaze roamed over his body, she gasped. Her eyes grew wide.

Hunter didn't have a stitch of clothes on. And he was huge. Everywhere huge.

She turned away, her mind whirling at the fact that she wasn't afraid of him. In fact, her cheeks burned with mortification because, for once, she wondered if a man truly could bring a woman to pleasure as she'd heard.

Reaching out, he tucked a strand of her own red hair behind her ear. "Do you mind if I join you?"

"You want to sit here? With me?" Why the idea surprised her, she had no idea. Unable to think of anything to say, Amy simply nodded. Now what had she gotten herself into?

"THE *MANRUVIANS* LOVE THIS place. Their home world is mostly water. It's quite a bit like your world, actually." He leaned back, resting on his elbows in quite the same way as she was. "This is their way of relaxing. They don't mind if we join them. In fact, they enjoy our company." He grinned. "Personally, I think they enjoy showing off to other species." He shrugged. "Who wouldn't want to be able to launch themselves into the air like that?" He pointed out another merman who had jumped high into the air, doing a summersault on the way down.

"I suppose you're right. I would show off if I could do that too, I imagine."

She kept her gaze out over the water. He figured it was much easier than looking at him and facing the strange feelings he invoked in her. He felt her attraction through their bond, if only he could convince her that's what it was.

He rolled onto his side. Just a small movement would put his most private part in contact with her hand. She didn't move, merely stayed stiffly by his side as if to show she hadn't even noticed what he'd done. Their connection was strong—he just wondered if it was strong enough.

"I have something to ask of you."

She turned, careful to keep her gaze above his neck. "Yes?"

"Don't think that I want to force you into anything. I'm asking and it's all right for you to say no. It is your right to refuse me."

"Refuse you what?"

He ran his hands through his hair, nervous. "Before I make my request, there is something you must know." By the Goddess, he didn't know how she would take the news he needed to impart.

"What is it, Hunter?"

"When we took you to the medical bay for healing, the doctors discovered something."

Hunter watched as Amy shuddered and her face paled. "What? What did they find?"

"You were with child when we rescued you, but because of the blood loss during the attack afterward they were unable to save the child."

Amy stilled, then slowly sat up. "How far along was I?"

"The healers say that sometime within the last week you ovulated. The embryo was too small to handle your blood loss."

Amy swallowed, then turned her head away. "I don't know what I'm supposed to think, supposed to feel. This was my child, but instead of grief over its loss, I feel relieved that I will not bear my rapist's child. And I feel guilty that I feel this way."

"You have no reason to feel guilty. I would think all the things you are feeling are normal under the circumstances." Amy nodded, but he could tell that she didn't believe him. He could feel her doubt through their connection, yet he had no idea how to reassure her.

"So, what is it you'd like to ask?"

He knew she'd likely talk about anything other than the child and he wouldn't push her now. If she ever wanted to discuss it in the future, he'd be there for her. He understood that she'd have much to process before she'd possibly be really ready to face it. At least, that's what Eve had said and he was going to take his sister-by-marriage's word on it.

When he noticed Amy's patient gaze, Hunter realized he'd been silent far too long. It was now or never. "I know you've noticed the connection between us. Sometimes...most times, when a couple has such a bond they know they are meant to be together, or at least they hope they are. The *Manruvians* have a thing called *Matebonds*. If two people who were meant to be together wear them, they are tied to one another for life and beyond. I would ask you to accompany me to the

Chantrean garden aboard this ship and agree to wear the *Matebonds*. This way we can know if we were meant to be together or not. If you are not my mate I will leave you alone. I will still care for you, but as a sister, not a mate. If you are my mate, we shall work things out from there."

"What if I'm not your mate? What of my people?"

"I shall still help your people, *moya*. No one deserves the treatment the Black Rose dishes out."

"And if I agree to wear these bonds? What then?"

"Then we will go on as we have. Only when you are ready to consummate our mating will we do so. I respect you and care for you far too much to ever force myself on you."

Amy sighed, then turned her gaze toward the water. They sat that way for several minutes as they silently watched the water, each lost in thought. What would he do if she refused? Did he have the strength to let her go if that's what she wanted? Yes, it might kill him to see her leave, but if it helped in Amy's healing, he'd see her on a ship to Earth himself. He loved her too much already to ever cause her misery by keeping her with him when she'd rather be elsewhere.

When Amy finally broke the silence, he thought he must have misheard her. "What was that?"

"I said okay. I'll let you use the *Matebonds*, but for right now that's all I'm agreeing to."

Hunter nodded. He could hear the fear in her voice, see the fright in her eyes. Did she fear him or what lay ahead? He just didn't know.

Reaching behind him, Hunter grabbed the uniform he'd been carrying when he'd spotted her. As he dressed, he watched Amy's reaction to his nakedness. She seemed both enthralled with his body and terrified of it. Until he proved to her he'd never harm her, he had to expect this reaction. He just had to remember not to push her for more than she could give and to step away immediately if she asked it of him.

By the time he'd dressed, Amy had already dusted the sand from her pants, rolled her pant legs down and donned her shoes. He could feel Amy's tension. Her nervousness seemed almost a living thing, choking her.

"If you don't want to do this, I understand.'

Amy shook her head, "No. We both need to know."

The fact that his mate would use the *Matebonds* even though her fear nearly consumed her showed him again just how courageous and strong she was—a fitting mate for the next ruler of *Chantrea*.

Reaching down for her hand, Hunter gave it a quick squeeze. "Remember, all you have to say is *stop* and I'll walk away."

Knowing only once they used the *Matebonds* would she truly understand what he was asking of her, he wasn't about to waste time. With her hand in his, Hunter led her out of the recreation deck. Within minutes, they'd traveled the length of the ship and reached their destination. Before entering his security code, Hunter needed to be sure this is what she wanted. "Are you sure, *moya*? There is still time to say no."

"Have you changed your mind about bonding with me? I'm not whole. I may never be what you want or need."

Hunter shook his head. "That isn't possible, *moya*. After we bond, you'll understand. I promise."

He watched her nervously. What would she do?

"All right. I'm ready if you are."

"I've been ready my entire life, Amy." Knowing that only showing her the truth of his words would convince her, Hunter entered his security code and led her into the *Chantrean* Mating Garden.

"Sit here, *moya*. There is something I must retrieve first." With nervous apprehension, Hunter went to the base of one of the nearby statues where a secret compartment was located. Earlier today, he'd placed what he'd need there for the bonding, hoping, praying he'd have use for them. Nestled within several layers of *Chantrean* silk for protection were the *Manruvian Matebonds*. The use of the *Matebonds* ensured the person you wanted to make your mate was indeed the one destined to complete your soul. The men of *Chantrea* traveled with them in hopes that one day they might come across their mate and have the opportunity to use them.

He quickly made his way back to the stone bench where Amy waited. Hunter paused. He refused to do anything she didn't want, even if it was what he wanted more than anything. When she gave him a slow nod, he took her hands in his and bound her wrists together with the ritual binding straps, hoping that she was truly the one, the one who could complete him.

When the other end began to seek his own wrist and wrapped itself around him, he breathed a sigh of relief. Several seconds later, it suddenly became thinner. It flattened against their skin, burrowing beneath the layers of flesh until it became one with them. Its DNA now blended with theirs, forming an invisible tether between them. Nothing could separate them now, in heart, mind or body. If they were ever separated again, for whatever reason, she'd not be alone. Never again would either of them be alone.

Chapter Seven

"What just happened, Hunter?" Amy asked, her eyes widening with fear. She felt something new inside her, something crawling through her system, tying her to this man. She turned away, rubbing her wrists, trying to remove the thing that had just burrowed into her flesh.

"I feel different." She looked at him, nervously licking her lips. "Why do I feel so different?" She fought the urge to try to dig the bonds from under her skin. The way they burrowed beneath her flesh like a living thing was the most remarkable and frightening thing she'd ever seen—ever felt—in her life.

Amy couldn't blame him for the results. He'd warned her. She turned, ready to bolt from the room. He'd told her, yet a part of her hadn't believed him. That they could be permanently bound, by living cords was unbelievable, preposterous, yet it seemed as though what he said was true.

She felt him within her. She felt his fear of her rejection, his desire to be what she wanted, his determination to help her overcome her fears and the overwhelming love he already felt for her. Could she trust what she felt through the bond? Should she trust it?

The cord had come to life, wrapping itself around them before dissolving beneath their skin all on its own. The one small part that remained between them seemed to simply disappear into oblivion.

Warmth and love filled her at his look. His expressive eyes told her what he felt. She know now, even without the bonds, that he would die for her. Why was this happening? She didn't want this. Her body screamed out for him. Even the atrocities she'd been forced to endure didn't detract from the attraction she felt when he was near.

Through their newly intense connection, she knew he was a good man. She knew that he'd never intentionally harmed a woman or child and that he loved his family almost as much as he loved her.

Her gaze darted around the room. How could he love her when he didn't even know her? Not really. How could she feel these impossible feelings so soon after her ordeal? What kind of woman was she that she could just accept her heartbreaking past and move on as though nothing had happened? Her skin should crawl at the thought that he wanted to touch her in the way those other men had. But something told her it would not be the same with him.

Hunter moved closer and she shrank away, pressing her back against the wall. "It is the bonds, *moya*. Since we are *true* mates, we can feel each other's emotions." He moved closer still, his breath brushing the side of her face. "If you open your mind, you can even read my memories, my hopes and my dreams."

She closed her eyes. Her feelings, her senses frightened her. His very nearness brought her nipples to hard points, heat moving through her. She couldn't read him as thoroughly as he said she would. But she could still feel his need to comfort her, even as his body raged at him to make her his.

"Why do I feel so different?" She couldn't understand it. It was almost as though there had always been a part of her gone—a part of her missing, and when he wrapped the strange band around her wrist, she felt somehow complete. She'd never felt lacking before now, but with the bonds uniting them together, she noticed the difference.

"The sensation you feel is the bonds tying us together, uniting us in the way that only the *Manruvian Matebonds* can. The longer we are bound to each other, the more of this connection will feel. The closer we will get."

He pressed even closer and she fought the sense of panic that rose at his nearness. A centimeter closer and his body would be pressed against hers. He wouldn't hurt her. Intellectually, she knew he would rather die than harm her. She could feel his need to comfort her through their bond, but she'd suffered so many cruelties it was hard to consider making herself vulnerable in such a way.

"Our connection through the bonds completes us. Makes us one. That is why I said it would be a useful tool when we reach the Black Rose's home base. If we complete the mating ritual, we would even be able to communicate telepathically through the bond, even over long distances."

He reached up and brushed a stray hair from her cheek. She closed her eyes and shivered. Not from fear or disgust, but from arousal, and that shocked her.

"What if I were taken again? If someone stole me away, would that mean you would know where I was?"

Hunter moved that last centimeter closer and pressed his body lightly against hers. "I would be able to find you before they could secret you away. I would like to say I could find you before they could violate you again, but I will not have lies between us. However, I would get there in enough time for you to watch them die."

He leaned down and inhaled deeply. "Have I ever told you how much I love the way you smell?" His body pressed closer and she felt herself stiffen. "All you need to do is tell me to back away, *moya*. If anything I say or do hurts or frightens you, just tell me and I will stop immediately."

He didn't frighten her. She frightened herself. How could she feel such want, such desire, when only a few days ago she'd been brutally handled by the Black Rose's men? She'd learned the woman was his sister, by his own admission. How could one be so good and the other so evil? It was almost as if every moment she spent in his presence, she were waiting for the other shoe to drop.

"Now that you have seen who I am, will you consent to the mating? Only the true mating will tie us together, bind us to one another in such a way that no one will ever be able to separate us."

His breath fanned her ear and heat rushed though her blood to pool in her middle. Her panties grew moist, a sure sign that her body was willing to mate with him, whatever her thoughts and feelings were on the matter.

She licked her lips, watching as his eyes darkened to a deep jade, so dark they were almost black.

"Will you mate with me, *moya*?" His hands slid down her arms, his fingers tangling with hers. "Will you take this chance and accept my love?"

She gazed down. His erection was so large it threatened to burst the seams of his pants. Yet he still asked her. He kept his touch gentle as his fingers trailed lightly over her skin. She knew he wanted her. She even knew how much. She felt his inner lion raging at him to take her despite her feelings and still he held back, waiting for her acquiescence.

She looked around the garden he'd taken her to. It was like an indoor greenhouse. It amazed her that the farther they strolled into it, the more beautiful it became. She looked up at the towering trees over their heads, barely realizing that their hands were clasped. Their fingers intertwined and she inhaled at the rightness of it. This was right. He was right. If only she could overcome her fears and allow him to do what he wanted.

"I would never hurt you, Amy. I would stop if you said to stop. I swear it."

Tears slid down her cheeks and she wondered if she really could have the happiness Eve seemed to have found with Taliff. She glanced over at Hunter, felt his need to have her, his even stronger need to protect her and led him further into the lush green garden.

They'd gone what seemed a long distance when she led him to a clearing dominated by a pool of glimmering turquoise water so clear, she could see the bottom. Surrounding the pool were marble benches that invited her to sit while she basked in the tranquil setting. Scattered around in an almost haphazard fashion were flowering bushes with pink and orange blossoms. Between the benches were statues of men and women, all undressed, in various sexual poses.

Even though the whole clearing seemed designed for sex, for mating, a sense of peace and tranquility washed over her. It was as though she belonged here and someone, something, was welcoming her home.

Something about the turquoise water of the shimmering pool called to part of her deep within. She had the overwhelming urge to strip and walk into its soothing depths.

She turned to look at Hunter. "Can I wade into the pool? Something within me needs to wade, to swim in these waters. Can I?"

He took her hands in his, bending to kiss them. "Tonight, *moya*, listen to your instincts in all things. If you wish to bathe, by all means, bathe. If you wish me to join you, you need only to voice your request."

He turned around, facing the other direction. "I shall even look the other way as you undress if it makes you more comfortable. Remove your clothing and let the waters of the Goddess wash your tensions away. This night in the pool is your night. If you wish to complete the bond, you merely need to direct me to your wishes. If there is something you wish do to, do it. If there is something you wish to say, say it. In this pool, you are the one in charge."

Amy nodded, though he couldn't see her with his back turned. Quickly, she stripped off her clothing and waded into the pool until the water covered her breasts. Something about being in the pool both relaxed and rejuvenated her. Still, something didn't feel quite right. It was as though a part of her was missing.

Invite him into the pool, Amy. It is your destiny—and his. He will not harm you. In fact, he loves you so much already that to harm you would be to harm himself. Invite him into the pool and welcome your destiny.

Amy licked her lips, nervous. *What if he hurts me? With the others it always hurt.* Fear gripped her at what she was about to do, about to allow. Yet how do you ignore an instruction from the Goddess herself?

He will not. The Matebonds *make it easy to know your fears, your feelings. As soon as you complete the ritual, he will know exactly what to do to please you. Show him he is mated to a strong woman who will face her fears rather than run from them. Reach out to him and offer to wash him, comfort him.*

Amy looked away to make her offer, unable to watch as he undressed. "Will you join me in the pool, Hunter?"

It didn't take long to receive his answer. She heard the unmistakable whisper of his zipper as he shrugged out of his uniform and the rustle of the material landing at his feet.

She turned back to face him when she felt sure that he was in the water deep enough to cover the part of him that frightened her, then realized she hadn't waited quite long enough.

He was so tall his hips were still above the water. That part of him she'd hoped to miss jutted up from a nest of red-gold hair, a drop of clear fluid at its tip. She felt his need to be inside her, to feel her lips wrapped around his shaft. Her face burned at the thought. For now, she'd do as the Goddess suggested and offer to wash him.

Strangely, she wanted to bathe him with her own hands, feel his flesh beneath her fingers. She could almost feel the rippling of his muscles beneath her fingertips already.

He moved deeper into the pool, covering that part of him that made her so nervous. For a fleeting moment, she wondered if the waters were drugged some how, but the slight shake of his head told her no. What was happening to her? She actually wanted to seduce this man, to feel his hands and lips on her skin. Why him when so many others had made her shudder with revulsion?

Remembering the TV shows she'd watched on Earth and how the other women seduced their mates, she used that knowledge to bring Hunter closer.

She had no sexual experience barring what she'd endured during her captivity. She couldn't draw from that. According to Eve, that had been an abomination. Sex between two people who loved each other was a beautiful thing, or so she said.

Amy moved closer, just close enough to take his hand and lead him into the center of the pool. After reaching the center, she circled him. Stopping behind him, she splashed water on his back, watching as the silver droplets ran down his muscles in rivulets.

She massaged the water into his shoulders, growing bolder by the minute as he stood and accepted her ministrations. Pulling on his shoulders, she dunked his head beneath the water, rubbing his scalp, massaging his head and rinsing the day's perspiration from his hair.

When he turned around, his hair slicked back from his face and the muscles of his chest rippling, she almost panicked, almost ran from the pool. But as the Goddess said, she was a strong woman, willing to face what she feared.

She could barely believe she was really standing here in this pool with a naked man and not running for her life. Hunter stood so still, he could have been one of the statues surrounding the pool. She wondered at what kept him from grabbing her and sinking his cock into her, willing or not. She knew she was young, relatively pretty and standing quite naked in front of him. She had never witnessed any restraint like his before. Either the man had extraordinary self-control or he truly cared about her. Perhaps even both.

She washed his chest and stomach, moving lower and lower, stopping just short of his jerking cock. She stared at it for a moment, wondering how much control it took for a man like him to keep his hands to himself. She stole a glance beneath the clear water at his clenched fists. His tightly clenched hands and his heavy breathing were the only indication she even affected him in any way.

She wasn't sure what to do next. She'd washed him, like the Goddess suggested—what was next?

He washes you, Amy. The Goddess had spoken again, giving her instruction and Amy nodded imperceptibly.

Turning her back to him, she lowered her head under the water. When she surfaced, his hands gently massaged her scalp, her shoulders, moving down to her back as he washed every inch of her. During his ministrations, he pressed a quick kiss to her shoulder, before moving away. Another quick kiss pressed to the side of her neck, just behind her ear, sent her pulses racing, but not with fear.

His thumbs found and pressed into the dimples just above her rear, holding her hips in place.

Fear speared through her. She was certain he would impale her now with no other thought to her pleasure—no other thought to her wants or needs. When instead he bent his head and pressed another kiss to her neck, she allowed herself to relax slightly in his arms. It was all she could do to keep herself from raising her arm and burying her fingers in his hair. His hands moved from her hips to rove over her stomach, spreading tendrils of desire and warmth in their wake. His hands moved up, gently cupping her breasts, and she arched her back, leaning into his gentle kneading. Nothing she'd ever experienced compared to this. Nothing. Hunter may have rough, calloused hands, but those hands smoothed gently over her skin as he bathed her.

"Turn around, *moya*." Reluctantly, she turned in his arms, part of her waiting for him to laugh at her, another waiting for a rough slap to her face, her breasts. Instead, he surprised her again, by pressing his lips gently to hers, sipping from her mouth as though she were the most fragile of creatures and would break in his arms. "Open for me," he said, pulling his lips from her mouth, then sinking his tongue into her moist depth with a groan when she complied.

Nothing prepared her for this. Nothing prepared her for the utter worship Hunter bestowed upon her. He kissed every inch of her flesh, caressed every fading bruise, then laved them with his tongue. Then finally, when she thought it couldn't get any better, he stroked her nipple with his tongue, pulling the turgid tip into the warmth of his mouth and she cried out. One after the other, he licked, laved and suckled her breasts. His mouth moved between them until she twisted restlessly against him, instinctively knowing there was something more, something other than pain and degradation, and she suddenly wanted Hunter to show her what it was. His mouth moved to hers once again for a long, drugging kiss.

"Please," she begged against his lips, not quite knowing what she asked for. "Please, Hunter." He pressed one last kiss to her lips. It was so full of his love for her, so full of promise that she nearly fell to her knees.

"I offer up my life and love to you, to do with as you wish. I pledge to worship your body and offer up my own to you to worship and command. I in turn accept the same from you. Only to you do I offer my heart and my soul for you to protect or deny. I give all that I am and all that I will ever be to you. Do you accept me and all that I offer, my *moyo*, my mate?" When the words spilled from her lips she almost fainted with fright. Where had those words come from? What had she just done? What had she said? Had she just tied herself to this man forever?

"I accept your offer and extend one of my own." Hunter reached for her hands and pulled her to the edge of the pool. He looked so happy, how could she even consider trying to take those words back when merely saying them had put such a look on his face? She felt his elation and relief that she'd chosen to say the words. Yet, she didn't remember a choice. Not really.

He sat her at the edge of the pool and knelt between her knees. She knew what a vulnerable position she was in. She also knew fighting would get her nothing but another beating. So she sat and waited for him to assault her.

"You really have no trust for me in your heart, do you, *moya?*" He really looked hurt and Amy almost felt bad for her thoughts.

He took her hands in his larger ones and repeated his part of the vow, "I accept all that you are and all that you offer me, *moya*. I offer my life and love to you, to do with as you wish. I pledge to worship your body and offer up my own to you to worship and command. I in turn accept the same from you. Only to you do I offer my heart and my soul for you to protect or deny. I give all that I am and all that I will ever be to you. Do you accept me and all that I offer, my *moya*, my mate?"

Amy waited silently, blinding fear keeping her from responding to his words. She simply waited for him to drive his hard shaft into her, to hurt her as so many others had. When instead he lowered his gaze away, she knew—she could trust him to never behave the way the others had. She laid a trembling hand on his shoulder to stop him from leaving. With a small nod, she accepted his offer and he pulled her into her arms with a groan.

Soon he was kissing her again, his mouth on hers, sipping gently from her lips. Then he moved lower to her breasts. He laid her gently back on the grassy bank at the edge of the pool and caressed her belly button with his tongue, making her squirm.

"I know you were taken against your will, *moya*. I know they never saw to your pleasure. I want you to see that love can make all the difference in the world. I do love you with everything in me, and I would prove it to you tonight and every night for the rest of our lives."

Then he grabbed her hips, tipped them forward and buried his head between her legs. Amy let out a startled scream.

Her eyes widened at his sensual assault. Even that was the wrong word. Her pulse pounded, but no longer from fear as he brought her pleasure beyond belief as his tongue circled her clit. His teeth nibbled gently before he sucked it into his mouth and drew on it with alternating pressure. Thick fingers gently entered her vagina, moving in and out as he suckled her.

Tension built within her and her muscles tightened. Her hands found his head, her fingers tightening in his hair. Never, ever, had she felt anything like this. Her head thrashed in the grass, her body tightening even more before it shattered, splintering into a million shards of light as Hunter took her over the edge of her first orgasm. She called his name, breathlessly, shamelessly. She called his name needing him to give her more. She needed more.

Her face burned with mortification when she realized she'd begged. Amy had never felt such intense pleasure before in her life. Withdrawing his fingers from her channel, he smiled up at her, his understanding reflected on his face.

"You see, *moya,* it can feel good. Let me show you how good, how much better it can be." He kissed his way up her body at her nod. Stopping at her chest, he took the time to worship her breasts, before moving up to press his lips against hers and slipping his tongue into her mouth.

Nervously, she spread her legs again. For the first time in her life, she willingly let a naked man settle himself between her thighs. Fear swamped her for a moment as he positioned himself at her gate. What if it all changed from here? It was a bit late to worry about that now, wasn't it?

"Ssh...*moya*. What you felt before was only the beginning," Hunter whispered into her ear as he eased the head of his cock into her. "I'll go slowly, I promise. I'll be sure to give you your pleasure." He waited for her body to adjust to him, then withdrew and eased forward again, moving his shaft deeper. Reaching down, he pulled her legs up around him.

Knowing what he wanted, she wrapped her legs around his waist.

"No, *moya*. Let me show you." He loosened her legs from around his waist and brought them to her chest. "Don't be frightened, *moya*." He eased back into her, burying himself deep into her channel and she screamed with ecstasy.

He stopped immediately. "Did I hurt you?" he asked, still holding himself deep inside her, unmoving.

She shook her head. "No." She reached up and cupped his face. "For the first time in my life, I want this. I want...I want you, Hunter."

"Then you shall have me," he whispered. As though he had all the time in the world, he began to move again, slowly thrusting and retreating in long, smooth strokes. He filled her up. The fullness bordered on pain, but he wasn't hurting her, wasn't pounding into her as her rapists had. Never again would she compare him with her attackers.

She could feel the difference between those selfish acts and this. She could feel the care Hunter took with her, but it wasn't enough. "Please Hunter, I need more."

"I know exactly what you need and before this night ends you will know it too."

And with those cryptic remarks, Amy stopped thinking all together, allowing herself to feel the pleasure her mate was doing his best to give her.

Before long, an unfamiliar fire began to burn in her womb. Pleasure pain ripped through her as her body clenched and released, preparing for something, something powerful and all encompassing.

"Hunter, I...I..."

"I know, *moya*. Feel. Just let yourself go and feel."

She could feel his shaft growing thicker and longer inside her as his thrusts grew more urgent, more demanding. The pleasure grew so intense she was sure her heart would beat right out of her chest. Her lungs labored as she gasped for air and gifted him with a long groan of sensual gratification.

She clutched his hair, tightened her legs against her chest so he could get that much deeper. She arched her back, doing her best to raise her hips to meet his every thrust. That's when it happened. Every muscle in her body tightened, clenched. Her clit pulsed, throbbed every time his pelvis bumped against it. The muscles of her thighs clenched and the world was forgotten as she tumbled over the edge into oblivion.

As though he had only waited for her to reach her release, Hunter let go. Sweat dripped from his brow as he labored over her, his hips pistoning in and out in an ever-increasing pace. She came again, screaming his name, her nails scoring his back as he pounded into her once, twice, thrice. Then he, too, was coming. His cock pulsed inside her as his hot seed splashed against her womb. Her entire body quaked as he rested atop her. His arms braced him above her, even now protecting her from harm as he rested above her trying to catch his breath.

But even as her body felt deliciously replete she sensed that something was still missing, something been left undone. Did Hunter feel the same? Was she somehow lacking? Was he disgusted with her?

You must drink of the Goddess' Tears, Amy, and have Hunter do the same. Find the chalice and complete the binding ritual. Only then will you understand just what you are to each other. Once you drink of my tears and share your worries and concerns, will your healing be complete.

And to heal I must find the chalice and drink?

Yes, my child. I would not steer you wrong in this.

Above her, Hunter grunted. "I must be crushing you, love," he whispered against her temple. His warm breath against her skin sent another tremor of need racing through her.

"Hunter, there is still something I must do. Will you show me where the chalice is?"

Hunter lifted his head, searched her gaze. "Are you sure, *moya*?

Once you drink from the chalice, we will truly be one in heart, mind, body and soul. Even in death we will be tied together. If one of us should die, the other will follow."

She licked her lips, nervous at taking such a monumental step, even though it felt right to do so. After only a moment's more hesitation, she nodded. "Yes, I'm sure."

"Then so be it." Hunter eased himself out of her channel and stood, holding out his hand to her. "The Goddess' chalice is in the statuary. I shall take you to it."

When they reached the clustered statues, she scanned the clearing. Finally, she spotted the one. She knew exactly what she needed to do. With confidence, she approached the statue where a woman held a golden chalice between her alabaster hands. The sculpture beckoned her to accept the offering as water flowed from the cup and pooled in a basin at the woman's feet in a continuous stream. Yes... That's what she needed—exactly what she needed.

Reverently, she approached the statue. She moved silently, almost as though she were approaching the Goddess Alana herself. Once again, the Goddess whispered in her mind. *Drink my tears and purify your hearts. Share my tears and purify your souls.*

Reaching up, she pulled the chalice from the statues hands and stepped back a pace, before turning to carry the golden cup to Hunter who sat patiently on one of the marble benches inside the clearing.

When Amy reached her mate's side, she knelt between his outstretched legs and slowly lifted the cup to his lips. "I beseech you to drink of the Goddess' golden chalice. Let her tears cleanse your heart and heal all your inner wounds."

Hunter smiled sweetly at her, love and heat lighting his eyes, then wrapped his hands around hers and tilted his head back. Once he quenched his thirst, he held the cup to her lips.

With gentleness in his voice and love in his eyes, Hunter repeated her request. "I beseech you to drink of the Goddess' golden chalice. Let her tears cleanse your heart and heal all your inner wounds," he whispered. And like he, she tilted her head back and let the cool, clear liquid pour down her throat.

At once, a rush of emotions overwhelmed her. Joy, excitement, loneliness, sadness, worry, angst, anger. So many emotions and not all of them hers. Tears ran down her face unchecked. Hunter scooted off the bench and knelt in front of her. His strong arms wrapped around her waist before quickly tucking her head beneath his chin. *Sshh,* moya. *Let your tears flow, let your heart open and your wounds heal. I shall be here, holding you when the storm of emotion passes. Never fear, I will always be here for you.*

Amy closed her eyes, enjoying the sound of Hunter's voice in her mind. She let the beating of his heart against her cheek soothe her. For the first time in a long, long time, she actually believed in something, in someone. It was a nice feeling to have.

It is nice, isn't it? This is how we can communicate whether or not we are separated by choice. We will always know where the other is, what the other is feeling—fear, pain, joy...

She knew what he meant. She could feel his overwhelming joy at their binding. She heard the steady rhythm of his heart, knew that somehow her heartbeat matched his as well.

She reached out, put her hand on her chest and managed to look into his eyes. Placing her hand over his heart, she said, "I don't know what I feel here, other than somehow it's taken on the same steady beat of yours."

The high-pitched chime of the ship's intercom interrupted their conversation. "I apologize for interrupting, Your Highness, but you wanted to be informed if we found a planet matching the description given by our prisoner."

"Thank you, Mikel. Do a long-range scan and we'll take a rendering to our prisoner to identify. If it's the correct planet, how long will it take to reach it?"

"About two days at interstellar light speed, Hunter. Not too long, but still...long enough."

Chapter Eight

As the pair dressed, Amy reached for Hunter's hand. "Is there a way we can get a picture of this planet? I'd like to show it to both Chrissie and Maryann."

Hunter grinned, pleased beyond words she now felt comfortable enough with him to reach out and touch him. "That's a great idea. Besides, I know you've worried about Maryann since you woke from your healing sleep."

She blushed and turned away, obviously uncomfortable with his praise. He liked the way her skin pinked when he complimented her. He needed to remember to do it more often.

After clasping her hand in his, Hunter led Amy back through the lush garden and headed toward the exit. By the time they reached the door controls, she'd laced her fingers with his.

"I want to pick up a *compu-pad*. We can download planet images on it and take it to the women."

Amy licked her lips and gave him a tiny smile. "And where would they hide a computer here in this room?"

Smiling, Hunter approached the control pad. After he keyed in his access code, a recessed cabinet opened in the wall to the left of the door, revealing a tray bearing a handheld instrument. The matte silver instrument had a glowing green touch screen. He lifted the thin electronic pad upright, fastening it into the ridges in the tray. "Computer, download planetary images onto the *compu-pad* please."

"Working. Transfer complete."

Amy sidled closer to Hunter. He could feel her desperate desire to see the planet where her family and the others were held captive. He could even feel her confusion over what had happened between them, when she'd been so certain she would never willingly bear another male's touch again.

He shook his head. With Amy so close, his body couldn't help but respond. His cock, sated minutes before, began to grow hard and ready as her scent enveloped him.

"Wow. Chrissie is right. It does seem to have some sort of mystical veil covering it. And the sea-foam green color is shot with swirls of silver and pink. Definitely a good focal point if you need one. I wish..."

As Amy's voice drifted off, she looked away. He knew exactly what she wished. She wished she'd had this planet to focus on while her captors raped and tormented her. Hunter could feel her renewed pain and all he wanted to do was take it into himself where it could never torture her again.

Looking down, he noticed he held the device so tightly, only a miracle kept it from shattering in his hand. "Shall we go visit our prisoner and see if this is the planet she'd focused on so many times?" He needed to get her mind off what happened to her. He knew she would never forget her ordeal, but he wanted to help her move beyond it.

Hunter couldn't shake the idea that what she endured was at the root his fault. If he hadn't sent Taliff out looking for more women, if he hadn't ordered him to bring women home—especially *Lionese* women—the Black Rose wouldn't have had a ship full of females to steal. She would never have gotten hold of Myra and subsequently the coordinates of Amy's home planet, she would never have returned to steal even more women either.

His greatest fear was that when his mate finally decided to probe his mind, his memories, she would see what part he'd played in her abduction—what role he'd had in the endless abuse she'd suffered while in the clutches of the beasts who called themselves 'The New Hope'.

Beside him, Amy tensed. Maybe she sensed his inner turmoil, or maybe the prospect of seeing her former friend made her edgy. Either way, he wanted her at ease. "Yes, let's take this to Chrissie, but I'd like to check on Maryann first."

"The woman you helped rescue?"

"Yes, she's human. Her mother was human, a widow when a male from our pack met Maryann's mother and mated her. So she couldn't shift on the mountain even if she wanted to. She knows our ways, our customs and I treat her as I would my own sister, but others in the pack tormented her as she grew and didn't develop the same skills and abilities as her peers."

Hunter ran his hand down his mate's back in soothing strokes. "Then I can do no less than what you've done. She'll be under my protection and that of my family until she decides what she wants to do with her life."

Hunter hung his head as shame filled him. Since taking Amy to the medical bay after their rescue, all his thoughts, his entire being had focused on her. And since she's awakened, he hadn't even thought about the other women they'd rescued. What kind of man did that make him? What kind of leader?

As though she sensed his thoughts, and perhaps she did, Amy reached out and lightly ran her hand down his arm. Goose bumps rose in her wake and his body tightened once again in need. Goddess, he'd never get enough of her.

"Yes, Maryann first, then Chrissie." She hesitated, then after quickly licking her lips spoke again. "Afterward, would you mind if we spent some time alone getting to know each other better?" Amy worried her bottom lip and his cock twitched. He had to focus his attention back on what his mate was saying before he completely lost control of his wayward body and jumped her here and now. "I'd like to learn about the man I've taken to mate."

"Of course." How could he refuse such a simple request when he wanted exactly the same thing?

You can't, moyo.

His gaze snapped to her mouth where an impish smile tilted up the corners of her lips. His heart clenched as he realized she'd purposely used their new mate-bond to speak to him.

You honor me—honor us—by using our bond to speak your thoughts and to learn mine. I hope you feel you can trust me once you learn all that you do.

"What do you mean, Hunter?"

Hunter shook his head. "I will not influence you or what you'll see when you look into my memories. All I will say is that the decisions I made as High King were made to benefit *Chantrea* and our people. I only wish I could have foreseen the consequences my decisions would bring"—and he knew they hadn't seen all of them…yet.

After slowly stroking Amy's back one more time, he stepped away, tucking the compu-pad into the inner pocket of his uniform jacket. "Now how about we track down your friend Maryann and see how she's faring?"

Amy nodded, then cleared her throat. "Sounds good. I'm ready whenever you are."

"Computer?"

"Yes, Prince Shi'Lan?"

"Where would we find the rescued female called Maryann?"

"Maryann Wilson is in the botanical gardens on deck eighteen."

"Thank you, Computer. If anyone is looking for us, please direct them to that location."

"Understood, Prince Shi'Lan."

After giving his mate a short bow, Hunter held out his elbow, inviting her to take it. Instead, Amy blushed prettily and reached for his hand, twining their fingers together. "Together, let's talk to her together."

Giddier than he could ever remember feeling, Hunter squeezed Amy's hand and led her out of the *Chantrean* Mating Garden, praying the rest of his courtship with his mate continued to go this smoothly.

As they walked down the corridor hand in hand, Amy couldn't help but wonder just how Hunter managed to become so important to her. When she took the time to think about it, there should be no way that she'd allow his touch, much less welcome it. But after the bonding ceremony, she couldn't help but crave his touch, desire his closeness.

She felt like two different people—the frail tortured woman Hunter had rescued and the semi-confident woman that was now Hunter's mate. She could actually feel his confidence in her, feel his belief in her strength and courage, and that support empowered her. His belief in her made her want to prove him right and gave her the strength to fight her insecurities. She'd need all her courage and strength in the coming days if they were to rescue her people and defeat the Black Rose.

As they rounded the corner, Amy pulled Hunter to a stop. "What is that?" she asked, pointing toward the tiny creature cowering in one of the doorways.

Hunter shook his head and chuckled. "It seems that one of my niece's pets has gotten loose. That's a *Durling*. It's a cross between a cat and a fluff bunny. It's as round and fluffy as an Earth bunny without the long ears but purrs and pounces like a kitten though it has just a tiny nub for a tail."

"I assume it's harmless then?"

Chuckling, Hunter dropped to his knees and slowly crawled toward the frightened creature. *You can say that. The only harm he will do is to your clothes when he's upset. He tends to lose control of his bladder when stressed.*

Amy snorted but kept her gaze focused on Hunter's ass as he continued to crawl down the length of the corridor. His uniform pants pulled tight across his bottom, outlining his tight buttocks to perfection. She had to bite her lip to keep from saying something crude. She couldn't believe the change that had come over her in just one day. Could Hunter have put some sort of spell on her, or somehow drugged her into compliance? It must have something to do with the *Matebonds*. Perhaps the *Matebonds* made her feel that way.

She shook her head. No. No, he couldn't have. Besides, the *Matebonds* worked both ways. He knew what she was thinking, feeling, just as she knew what he was. She'd feel his duplicity, his sense of guilt, through the bond, and she sensed none of that. All she felt from him was his need for revenge on her behalf and his overwhelming feelings of love and compassion for her. How could she continue to hold herself back from him, knowing how he felt about her? It was impossible.

With that realization, something inside her eased. Instead of waiting for something bad to happen, she could be proactive. She'd dive into her own psyche. She'd build herself up both mentally and physically by speaking with the healers and working out in the exercise room. She wanted to come to Hunter, to her mate, as whole as she could.

With her decision made, Amy once again focused on Hunter and his determination to capture the runaway *Durling*. She couldn't help but smile as she watched him babbling to the black ball of fluff. After what seemed forever, the tiny creature slowly approached Hunter. She couldn't make out any of the *Durling's* features except for its bright orange eyes and tiny, white-tipped, pointed ears. As soon as Hunter cuddled it to his chest and rubbed its ears, it let out a rumbling purr. It sounded like a very contented feline.

Amy smiled, then cleared her throat. "Should we drop Delilah's pet off at her cabin? I'm sure your niece must be frantic looking for it."

Hunter grinned, then slowly stood. "That might be wise. You've not seen Delilah when she's upset about something." Hunter shuddered. "She has a roar that does the *Lionese* proud."

Within minutes they'd reached Eve and Taliff's quarters and dropped off the *Durling* to the precocious toddler who'd misplaced it. Eve and Taliff were seated on the sofa, amusement plastered across their faces.

"But Uncle Hunter, I only let Jazzy out of her cage for a minute so I could get her some water. I don't know how she got out of the cabin."

"Why didn't you wait until your father could help you, little one?"

With hips cocked to the side, Delilah stuck out her chin and crossed her arms. "I'm a big girl. I don't need Daddy to do everything for me."

Hunter shook his head. "Well, be more careful next time. You wouldn't want your pet to get lost and hurt aboard ship, would you?"

The little blonde bit her bottom lip and shook her head. "No, Uncle

Hunter. I promise that I'll be more careful."

Hunter shook his head again. "The better promise would be to make sure your parents are around when you let her out again."

Delilah pursed her lips and let out a gusty sigh. "All right. I won't let Jazzy out of the cage unless momma or daddy is there with me."

"Good." After nodding once toward Eve and Taliff, Hunter turned toward Amy. "Now, are you ready to speak with Maryann?"

"Yes. I want to make sure she's okay. She probably suffered much more than any of the others the Black Rose captured. Being Human, her body would take longer to heal, the damage inflicted on her nearly impossible to survive. The fact that she's still alive proves that her will to survive must have been tremendous."

Eve patted Taliff's knee, then stood and approached them. "If you'd like, I could accompany you."

Even though Amy would like nothing more than to fall back on Eve's strength, she couldn't do it. Amy shook her head, but reached out and squeezed Eve's hand. "That's okay, Eve. I can handle this. Maryann knows me, but she might not be willing to speak in front of strangers."

Eve nodded. "Of course. But if you need anything, you know where to find me."

Amy stepped forward and wrapped her arms around Eve, embracing the woman for the first time since her rescue. "I know you'll be there," she whispered. Her voice cracked as she continued to speak. "Even in the frozen hell where I was imprisoned, I knew you wouldn't give up looking for me. It's probably the only thing that kept me going all those months."

As they each wiped tears from their eyes, Hunter cleared his throat and turned to face his brother. "We will bring the image of the planet to Chrissie after our visit with Maryann."

"Sounds good. If you need help interrogating the prisoner, call me. I haven't forgotten what the Black Rose has done to our own family. I'd like a chance to learn exactly where that treacherous bitch calls home."

"Taliff," Eve scolded. "Watch your language in front of your daughter."

"Yes, dear."

As it was said playfully, with some humility and contriteness, Amy couldn't help but laugh. If felt good to laugh, to be a part of something good and healthy, something happy for a change.

"Well, on that note, we better get out of here. We've still got to see our prisoner and confirm the Black Rose's home base. Only then will I feel like I can relax. At least for a time," she murmured.

As Amy stepped toward the door, Hunter walked up behind her and placed a hand gently on her lower back. "Are you all right?" he asked, his voice just above a whisper so the others couldn't overhear. She could love him for that alone.

She stopped. Her heart stuttered. Love him? Could she love him? After only a few days and most of those spent unconscious? She just didn't know.

"What is it, *moya*?"

Amy shook her head. "Nothing. It's nothing." Pushing thoughts of love to the back of her mind, Amy left Eve and Taliff's quarters, Hunter right behind her. "Computer?"

"Yes, Amy Shi'Lan?" The computer's answer gave her pause. Amy Shi'Lan. It was her name now that she was mated. She supposed she should get used to it. She took a deep breath and shook off the strangeness of it.

"What are the current whereabouts of Maryann Wilson?"

"Maryann Wilson is still in the Botanical Gardens."

"Thank you, Computer."

Amy glanced over at Hunter and found him staring at her. "What? What are you staring at?"

"You, *moya*. I'm staring at you. In the last few days, the rate of your healing, both mental and physical, has been phenomenal."

"I just want to be what I should have been all along, strong and secure in my own abilities."

"Then I will do all that I can to help you."

Amy turned toward her mate, reached up and lightly ran her hand down his cheek. "I believe you. I believe you'll do whatever is needed to make me both happy and healthy. That's not something I could have even imagined a week ago."

Hunter caught her hand and held it against his cheek. "Well, perhaps after we talk with Maryann and Chrissie, we can spend more time getting to know each other."

Chuckling, Amy pulled her hand away and started walking toward the nearest transport tube. "Perhaps we can. If you think you can sweet talk me into it."

"I'll do my best to convince you."

"You do that." Inside, Amy felt light and carefree for the first time in ages. That in itself was a miracle. Once they stepped inside the transport tube, Hunter punched a few buttons on the control panel.

What did you just do?

Input our destination.

"Oh, I always just tell the computer aloud where I want to go and it takes me there."

Hunter shrugged. "Well, this way, if there are others around, they can't overhear where you're going. It's safer this way."

"Will you show me how to use the interface?"

"Sure. We'll practice tomorrow while we tour the ship."

Before she could thank him, the transport tube stopped and the doors silently slid open, directly inside the botanical gardens. Hanging plants and climbing vines were everywhere. Beautiful flowers of every hue spilled over in all directions. One plant, a cross between a tulip and a long stemmed rose was a vibrant shade of orange. "What is this one?" she asked Hunter, pointing toward the beautiful orange bloom.

"It's a *Tupa*. It comes in shades of blue, red, orange, purple, white and yellow. Our scientists are trying to create a pink one now through hybridization."

"Neat. Well, no matter how much I might want to look at the flowers, we're here to find Maryann."

Hunter reached for her hand, squeezing it gently. "You're right, *moya*. Let's find your friend and see how she's faring."

They found Maryann deep inside the garden, seated on a bench while she stared out into space through the large viewport opposite her. Amy made sure to shuffle her feet noisily as they approached so she didn't startle her friend. "Maryann?"

Even with the warning, her friend obviously tensed before slowly relaxing her posture after turning to see who stood behind her. "Hi, Amy," she whispered.

Stay here, will you, Hunter? I think you make her nervous.

Of course. I'll wait by the entrance. There is another bench just inside the door where I'll wait for you.

Thank you for understanding.

I'd do anything for you, moya. *I hope you know that.*

I'm beginning to. Amy turned away from her mate and made her way toward Maryann. After sitting on the bench beside Maryann, she decided to wait. She'd speak when she was ready to.

"They have your mom and dad, even your sisters. I thought you should know that."

Amy swallowed past the lump in her throat, battled the tears that threatened to fall. "Do you know if they are still alive? Still being held captive and where?"

"The night before we were all taken, your mother had found out through our healers that she was pregnant. She never got a chance to tell your father."

"My mother's pregnant?"

"Yes, and because of it, she was able to convince her captors early on that their job was done and they left her alone. Your father though, they've enjoyed tormenting your father with the knowledge that she's carrying another man's seed."

"And she has no way to tell him the truth."

"No, because the women and men are kept completely separate in opposite sides of the camp."

"How long ago were you all taken?"

"Not too long ago. Maybe a year, a little longer maybe. It's hard to keep track of the days, the weeks, the months, when you're a prisoner." Amy nodded, understanding Maryann completely.

Amy reached out, desperate for answers and squeezed Maryann's hand. "And you've seen the camp? Seen the planet they're held on?"

"Yes. I'd know that planet anywhere. You get me close enough to it and I can point it out."

"I can do one better." *Hunter, bring that compu-pad. Maryann knows what the planet looks like as well and would like a chance to identify it.* "Hunter will be here shortly with an image. Just let us know if it's the planet you remember."

Within moments, Hunter arrived, *compu-pad* in hand. "Is this the place where they kept my parents? Is this the place they're being held captive?"

Amy held her breath and waited. Finally, Maryann raised tear-filled eyes. "This isn't it. This isn't the place. We did stay here yes, for a time, but afterward we were moved again. I'm sorry, this isn't where your family is, but Taliff Shi'Lan's mate—her family is here, or was the last I heard."

"Then where is my family? Where are my parents, my siblings?"

As Hunter gathered Amy into his arms, she wondered if she'd ever see her parents again.

Chapter Nine

Hunter looked at Maryann. He could feel Amy's fear and the depth of her concern through their bond. "Do you know anything about the world you were held on?"

"I would know that planet anywhere. One side was light and the other dark. I was kept on the light side. Do you have any idea what it's like to never know when it's day or night, never to have any darkness to help you sleep, to block out the demons? I think I would rather have been kept on the dark side where in the darkness I could at least escape my nightmares and the monsters who kept entering my room."

"And where was Amy's brother kept?"

"I never saw Ryan once we left the ringed planet, so I can only assume he's still there. The sisters were separated. Tyra had a cell near mine and Brenna was sent to the dark side of the planet."

"Why wasn't Ryan moved?" Amy asked, her voice more subdued than he'd ever heard it. She feared for his life. He could feel it.

Maryann grimaced, then looked away. She was silent for a moment, her fingers twisting in the front of her gown. "They began force-feeding him some drug. They used his body, priming him so he'd fuck whoever or whatever they put in front of him. He had no free will, no will at all. It was as though he wasn't Ryan anymore. Like any human, caring tendencies were just gone. He became just a rutting animal."

"But why?" Amy cried out. "Why would they do such a thing?"

"They weren't sure if it was the females who would produce the females or the males' genes who produced them. They weren't taking any chances. They would use us all. It's like we were all a part of some sick experiment."

Amy tried to wrench herself out of his arms. He wouldn't have it. Right now she needed him, needed his comfort, his sense of control. With his arms sheltering Amy, Hunter began to plot aloud. "So, we need to plan a three-pronged attack, sending raiding teams to not only the camps on both the light and dark side of the moon, but the camp she has set up on the ringed planet as well."

Maryann frowned. "I don't understand why you would need to attack the other planet. Wouldn't attacking one planet at a time work better?"

Hunter nodded. "You'd be right, if they were farther apart. But all three of these planets are in the same system and only the element of surprise will have the effect we want." He tapped the pocket that held the picture on the pad. "This planet with the rings," he met Maryann's gaze. "It seems it's only visible from the dark side of the planet." He smiled, though it didn't reach his eyes. "Maryann, had you been on the dark side of the planet you would have seen this above you. But you would have been treated so much worse than you already were. Apparently, the dark side is where those the Black Rose wants brutalized and tortured without mercy to be taken. As a human, you would have never survived."

Hunter watched as Maryann swallowed convulsively and shuddered. Amy reached out and pulled the frail woman into her arms. "It's going to be all right. We got you out of there and you'll never suffer at her hands or the hands of her followers again."

With the woman distracted by Amy, Hunter moved to sit next to the traumatized Human. "And what happened to your parents, your family, Maryann?"

She shook her head, whimpering as she burrowed her face deeper into the crook of Amy's neck. "Dead. My parents are dead. They never even made it aboard the ship. They fought and fought to save me and in the end they died and I was still taken."

"Oh, sweetheart," Amy murmured.

"I'm alone. All alone," she cried.

"Never," Hunter and Amy vowed together. "You'll never be alone again."

After a few minutes, Maryann seemed to pull herself together and the three of them found themselves staring out into the blackness of space. It was Maryann who first broke the silence. "We were taken together and formed a close bond those first few weeks of our kidnapping."

What do you think, Amy?

I think she needs this. She needs to take back her life, to feel like she can contribute something to the coming battle. She has to know that as a Human she won't be able to do much physically against her captors. Let her help in this, at least.

You are very wise, moya. *It will be as you suggest.* "Good idea, Maryann. Let's head on over to her cell now. Afterward, I thought I'd take you lovely ladies to dinner."

Maryann gave him a shy smile and Amy blushed to the roots of her red blonde hair. Rather than read Amy's mind, he'd rather imagine just what thoughts were running around in there. Maybe, once they were alone, he could convince her to tell him just what she'd imagined that had her blushing so prettily.

She reached out and took his hand. "Let's all go see what she has to say."

Her face said she wasn't sure what she wanted to do, but her determination to find her family and the families of the others in her community shone through her eyes. His mate wanted retribution for the atrocities levied against her people. Hunter's only fear was what the retribution might be for the part he played in the nightmares she had suffered.

CHRISSIE SAT IN HER cell, rocking back and forth, her knees to her chest, her head buried in her arms. Amy tried to feel sorry for her. She wanted to understand the reasons Chrissie had done everything she had. For a moment, she tried to put herself in the other woman's situation. What would she have done to protect her family? Would she have given the information they required of her or would she have refused and watched her family die? Would their deaths have been preferable to the torment they found themselves enduring now? The woman before her had been her best friend. Could she ever forgive her for her duplicity? What would she have done? The questions kept dancing around inside her head, making her feel crazy. Did she have so many friends that she could allow herself to just throw them away like this? One thought led to another until she felt driven mad with unanswered questions.

Finally, with a decision made, Amy moved to sit on one end of the bed. She could say one thing for Hunter's people. The cell was clean. The food that sat untouched on the tray in the corner at least looked edible. And the cell smelled fresh—uncontaminated by the horrible scents of semen and sweat so much a part of their last prison. But Amy couldn't blame Chrissie for not trusting the food placed in front of her. From her viewpoint, she was a prisoner again, just with another set of captors.

Maryann moved to kneel in front of the bed at Chrissie's feet and Hunter stood guard at the door. They'd surrounded Chrissie and it would remain this way until all their questions were answered.

"Chrissie, do you know how many rebels follow the Black Rose? How many men make up..." she grimaced, "...The New Hope"? Maryann asked. Her voice was soft, soothing, as though they were simply chatting around the dinner table, not discussing life or death issues.

Chrissie shook her head, but she did scrunch her eyes closed and bite her bottom lip. After what seemed ages, she whispered, "Hundreds. Each planet had at least three dozen guards that rotated shifts.

"Plus, that didn't count the Black Rose's personal bodyguards or Myra's. There had to be at least two dozen between them. Then there are the ones who went off world and raided other planets of their women. There could be thousands. I'm sorry," she said, twisting the sheets between her fingers. "I haven't been much help to you."

"Where did she find so many *Lionese* men to join her army?"

Hunter asked.

Surprised, Chrissie jerked up her head. "She didn't. It's not only *Lionese* men, but *Manruvians*, Humans, even wolf shifters. This is so much bigger than you know. They use a drug on the unwilling that turns them into beasts. Once addicted to the substance, they'd do whatever they needed to keep getting the drug and even sell out their own family members to get it. Nice, polite men have become monsters right before our eyes."

Amy licked her lips, nervous now that the time had come for Chrissie to identify the planet she had been able to see from her window. Pulling out the compu-pad from her jacket, Amy handed it to Chrissie. "Is this the planet you saw? This planet is called *Drimada*. Is this what you could see from the window in your cell?"

Tears welled up in Chrissie's eyes, then spilled down her cheeks. She began to sob into her pillow. She nodded, then whimpered as her eyes rolled into the back of her head as she fainted dead away.

HUNTER KNEW GETTING ANY other information out of her would be nearly impossible in Chrissie's current state. Maybe after she calmed down some, she'd remember more details. For now at least, they had enough rough information to begin formulating a plan.

He walked over toward the women and reached for Amy's hand. "I think we've bothered Chrissie enough for now. How about we leave her alone for a little while? I'm sure she doesn't really want or need an audience right now.

Amy nodded but Maryann shook her head. "I'd like to stay here with her a while. I don't think she should be left alone with just her memories for company."

Hunter was torn. Chrissie was a prisoner, not an informant, but as he looked at her he couldn't help but feel compassion for her. If the situations were reversed, he wasn't sure what choice he would have made. Would he give up others to protect his family? He'd like to say he wouldn't but unless faced with that choice in real life all this speculation wouldn't get him anywhere.

You wouldn't have sacrificed others to protect your family. You would have found another way, Hunter.

I hope so.

I know so. Should we leave Maryann here?

I don't see any harm. Place a guard in here if you're worried about her safety. Let Maryann help Chrissie if she can.

Thank you. You are very wise.

Amy snorted, then spoke aloud to Maryann. "Go ahead and stay as long as you like, Maryann. We're going to give Mikel this new information, then go to our quarters. You can find us there if you need to talk later."

As Chrissie lay unconscious, Maryann nodded. After pulling Amy to her feet, Hunter guided her out of the room, his thoughts already fully focused on Amy and their night ahead. For the last standard hour, it had become increasingly difficult to concentrate on anything other than her and the lovemaking he planned on sharing with her this night. He had to get control of this need soon or he'd get naught done.

Answering his thoughts aloud, Amy said, "You aren't the only one. I feel like I'm about to crawl out of my skin. This isn't normal; especially considering a few days ago I couldn't stand the touch of a male, any male. Craving your touch this much, no matter how wonderful it feels, seems wrong somehow."

"It's the bonding. We've gone too many hours without intimacy. Usually, we celebrate the bonding over the course of an entire day and night—completely naked for the first twenty-four hours. This craving will grow worse until we give into it. After the first day, we'll still feel the need to touch, to be close to each other, but it won't control our rational thoughts as it does now."

Amy let out a gusty sigh. "Thank the Goddess. If felt wrong to have thoughts of running my tongue down your stomach while you questioned Chrissie."

"Not as wrong as wishing it was you kneeling at my feet sucking my cock when Maryann knelt down in front of Chrissie."

Amy snorted, then began to chuckle. He couldn't hold back his own laughter. Thank the Goddess Alana, Amy could find humor in this situation.

Before she could respond, Mikel approached them from the other end of the corridor. As they grew closer to him, Mikel stopped, tilted his head to the side, closed his eyes and inhaled.

"Where have you been recently?" His normally calm voice had grown husky, rough.

"Why?" Amy asked, though Hunter had seen this reaction from a *Manruvian* once before. That man had scented his mate on another and a brawl had ensued. Was Mikel's mate aboard this ship? One of the women maybe?

Hunter answered his question. He wanted nothing more than for Mikel to find his mate. Mikel had been lonely long enough as he hunted for a mate. "We spent some time in Eve's quarters, then visited with Maryann, the woman I carried on my back off the ice planet, *Visara*. Then we went—the three of us—to visit the prisoner, Chrissie."

"That's it?"

Hunter nodded and smiled. "That's it, my friend. Happy hunting."

Mikel gave them a distracted nod, then took off down the corridor, following their scent trail, Hunter imagined.

Amy just looked confused as she watched Mikel walk away. Her brows were furrowed and she was frowning. "What just happened here?"

Hunter chuckled. "He smells his mate, and since Eve is taken and Delilah is unlikely since he's been around her before, chances are that either Maryann or Chrissie will soon be the focus of a *Manruvian* mate-hunt."

"Oh, I see. I hope it's Maryann then. She deserves a family of her own and I'm not sure a *Lionese* woman and a *Manruvian* merman can reproduce. But there has to be a greater chance for a Human woman and a *Manruvian,* I would think."

As they continued to head toward the transport tunnel at the end of the corridor, Hunter grunted. "Probably, but the Goddess Alana chooses who our mates will be, genetics aside."

"Oh, I see."

"Now, how about we head to our quarters and order a meal before spending the evening getting to know each other better?"

"Getting to know each other, or making love?"

Laughing, Hunter shook his head. "Both, my love, both." With that said, and his intentions clear, they entered the transport tube. "Computer, take us to our quarters."

"Yes, High Prince Shi'Lan."

Chapter Ten

Within minutes, Amy and Hunter were safely ensconced once again in their quarters. This time she knew exactly how the night would end, and instead of feeling terrified, she was impatient to begin. She really did feel like she'd crawl out of her own skin if she didn't get to touch him soon, taste him. What had gotten into her?

Even before her capture, she'd never felt this need for one man, this overwhelming desire to make love to one man and only one man. Hell, she hadn't even played the field as a teenager when all of her other friends seem to have a new lover every other weekend.

She drummed her fingers on the table as she waited for their meal to arrive. She wasn't sure how long she would last, being this close to him and not yet touching him. "Where the hell is it?"

"Where is what?"

"Dinner. I'm starving."

Hunter grinned. "Liar. You just wanted something to do to take up the time. I can feel your need to jump my bones from here."

Amy put her hands to her burning face. "I'm going to take a bath. You wait here for dinner." She stomped from the room amidst his laughter.

She entered the bathroom and started the water running. She wished she had some bubble bath, but had no idea where to find anything like it. Besides, it was the hot water that relaxed her—bubbles were just a nice luxury. After stripping, she stepped into the steaming water and groaned. The water felt so wonderful, she leaned back against the edge of the tub and closed her eyes. Only a few minutes had passed when the water splashed and her eyes flew open.

Covering herself with her hands, her face burned as Hunter settled next to her and pulled her into his lap. "I'm sorry if I frightened you. Do you wish me to leave?"

Forgetting about their mind link, she shook her head, mortified that she wanted him to stay, yet wasn't sure what she should do. Should she be the one to initiate sex, or leave it up to him?

"Just relax, *moya*." He wrapped his arms around her, letting them rest just under her breasts.

Leaning her head back against his shoulder, she allowed him to pour the warm water over her shoulders, relaxing her even more. He pressed a kiss to her shoulder, moving his mouth to her neck and she groaned.

"This is your night, *moya*. You need only relax and allow me to please you or you may take the lead. Your wish is my command."

Amy sat up, pulling away from him. She felt his disappointment as he watched the water sluice down her skin as she stood and moved away. He watched her hungrily, filled both with disappointment and hope.

Grinning, she moved closer and sat back on his lap, facing him. He wrapped his arms around her and lowered his mouth to hers. He sucked her bottom lip into his mouth, ravenous for a taste of her. She felt his arousal, could hear his thoughts. He could smell her excitement, even taste it on her skin and he would never get enough of her.

Her hands moved up over his shoulders and fisted in his hair, pulling him more tightly against her. If she could have crawled inside him she would have. She groaned when his hands slid down over her sides to cup her rear, gently kneading the full globes. His fingers brushed over her plump labia and she groaned into his mouth, grinding herself down onto his lap. She needed this. She needed more, so much more, and she wasn't sure how to tell him.

She nearly screamed her pleasure when his fingers slipped though her wetness and found her clit, circling it with his fingers as his thumb found the entrance to her channel. His hard cock pressed against her gate and she groaned, moving against him. She didn't know how she could need a man so much and so quickly, but she knew there would be no rest, no comfort for either of them if they didn't finish this soon.

Taking the lead, she sucked his tongue into her mouth. He tasted of a hint of the wine he'd ordered for their dinner. "Started dinner without me, did you?" she said against his lips before sliding her tongue back into his mouth. Their tongues moved together as she ground herself onto his lap, waiting for his inevitable penetration.

The head of his cock moved past her gate and she arched back in an attempt to take him deeper inside her. Breaking their kiss, his lips traveled down to her neck, suckling her shoulder before his mouth closed over her nipple. Tunneling her fingers through his hair, she cried out her pleasure as his tongue circled the light pink bud he stroked into pebbled readiness.

Lifting herself from his lap, she dropped down on his cock, driving him deep, all the way inside deep. His hands molded her rear. The thumb of his right hand moved over her thigh to between her legs. He unerringly found her clit, circling it, taking her over the edge of a massive climax. Arching her back, she pressed her chest harder against him, rubbing her breasts against the stubble of his face as he continued to suckle her breast.

Grabbing his hair, she continued to ride him and couldn't believe what she was about to say. "Fuck me. Please, Hunter, I can't go slowly now. Now I need you pounding deep inside me. Fuck me, please!"

THE DELIGHT OF HEARING the words he never thought to hear her say nearly made him lose control as he brought her down onto him and raised his hips to deepen his thrust.

"Yes!" she screamed as he wrapped her legs around his waist and stood. The water sluiced down over his legs as he continued to raise and lower her over his hard cock. It had grown impossibly larger when she begged him to fuck her, more immense than he'd even thought possible. His size had grown to that of a *Lionese* male mating with his lioness. She screamed again, her nails digging into his shoulders and he stopped. Sweat poured from his brow, droplets of water and sweat ran down his shoulders and legs. His chest heaved with the effort of halting and he forced out a vital question.

"Have I hurt you, *moya*?" He gritted his teeth, trying to regain control over his raging hormones. "I'll stop if I'm hurting you. I swear it."

"Only you stopping could possibly hurt me now."

"That's not going to happen, Amy. There is no way I'd stop now unless you asked, not after such a bold request, nay, demand, for me to fuck you."

"Then stop talking and start moving already."

Hunter grinned. How could he not? She couldn't be more perfect. Even after the tremendous emotional and physical trauma she suffered at the hands of her rapists, she was growing, changing into the woman he knew her to be inside. And he couldn't be more proud of her.

When her woman's cream began to slide down the length of his cock, he tenderly took her clit between his fingers and pressed. Amy screamed her pleasure, wrapping her legs around him even tighter. Her body shook with pent-up need. One more good tug on her clit and she'd explode. Hunter held back, waiting…waiting.

When she almost pulled a clump of his hair from his head and screamed, '*NOW*', at the top of her lungs, he couldn't make her wait any longer. With one sharp pull on her turgid clit and one hard deep thrust into her channel, Amy exploded. He could feel her channel clasping his cock, tightening around it until he had no choice but to spill his seed. With one last thrust, he lodged his cock deep within her and bathed the entrance to her womb with his life-giving fluid. With the Lady Goddess' blessing, a cub would be born of this union—a cub made in love and raised in love.

He placed a tender kiss against her temple and held her as the trembling in her body subsided. Before he could gently raise her and pull out of her well-sexed channel, the ship's breach alarms began to blast through every nook and cranny of the ship, from personal quarters to transport tubes. Everyone had been given notice than there was a hull breach.

"Hunter, Hunter, what's going on?" She tried to unwrap her arms and legs so he'd let her down but there was no time. No time at all.

"Trust me, Amy. When the hidden compartment opens—and there is one in every room on every ship in the *Manruvian* Fleet—find a gray bodysuit that seems closest to your size and put it on. We may only have seconds before we lose all air pressure and environmental controls onboard."

Amy nodded. Fear replaced the hazy afterglow of lovemaking they'd just enjoyed. Hunter quickly eased out of his mate, and without even putting her down, raced toward their closets. He stopped halfway between the "his and hers" closets, not approaching either of them but the empty wall space between them.

After he pressed a hidden release switch in one of the seams along the wall, a huge double hanging rack of uniforms and *Manruvian* pressure suits came sliding out. The pressure suits needed to be donned immediately in case of a loss of atmosphere or air contamination.

After selecting a suit for himself, he looked over at his mate. A look of grim determination was all he could see as she slipped her legs into the form fitting material. The material was the same as that of the *Matebonds*.

Hunter snorted.

What's so funny?

I'm just thankful we completed the mating before this happened.

Why's that?

Because once Manruvians *scent their future mate, they go into mating heat. If this happens while they are wearing the suit, it becomes a part of them and can't be taken off. The suits begin to affect the two mates and their libidos. It also works on other shifters.* His gaze became thoughtful. *I don't know about full humans though.*

What do you mean?

If one or both fights the union, the suits will make any unmated pair sexually frustrated to the point of pain before allowing the suits to dissolve just enough that intercourse can happen. And that can only happen if there is no danger to their bodies and both people are mentally accepting of the mating. Until then, The suits intensify an extreme case of sexual need with no release in site—for either of them. Only once the male is lodged in the female's channel does the mating heat begins to subside and only when all danger has passed in the atmosphere will the suits completely dissolve into the mates' skin as with the Matebonds.

Amy's eyes widened. *Oh crap, I sure hope Mikel either has already started bonding with whoever his mate is, or doesn't fully catch her scent until the danger is past then.*

Hunter nodded. He couldn't agree more.

They were both pulling the fitted masks over their faces when Mikel burst through the door of his cabin. He'd already donned his pressurized suit.

Fully adorned in the *Manruvian* pressure suit, Mikel looked like he was about to go diving in an ocean. The only thing missing was an air tank and those were unnecessary as the material itself converted the external air into breathable, oxygenated air.

"We've got to secure the decks. We're putting all the non-warriors and children in one central location so they'll be easier to protect. All men and women with warrior training will be searching the ship, one level at a time, until we find the ones is causing trouble on this ship,"

Amy looked from Hunter to Mikel, then lifted her head proudly. "Do you have an Empath on board? It would be helpful to have several who could catch someone lying about why they are where they are."

"I have about half a dozen, Amy Shi'Lan. What do you suggest?"

"Then I suggest placing an Empath with each team or level who can question stragglers on the levels, those who don't seem in any hurry to be somewhere."

Hunter nodded. "That is a very wise idea."

"And I'll be on one of the teams. I've always hidden my abilities." She paused. "Among humans on Earth, I would have been considered a freak so I've always suppressed them, but I think it's time I used them how they were meant to be used," Amy added.

How could Hunter refuse her? Not only was it a sound idea, but his mate needed to be needed, to discover her own worth.

Decision reached, Hunter nodded. "Fine, let's go. Taliff will guard Eve as well as all the women and children along with his security team. You and I, along with Mikel and his warriors will search the ship." He turned to Mikel. "How does that sound?"

Mikel smiled. "It's more of a plan than I had. Let me organize the teams. Meet me outside the Recreation Room. It's the area of the ship closest to where the damage was done."

Hunter didn't want to ask Mikel this, but somebody had to say it. "Sabotage?"

Mikel grimaced. "Looks like it. The fuel cell was tampered with. The environmental and gravitational systems are going haywire. And worst of all, the ship's shielding has been completely disabled."

"Well," Hunter said, "let's not waste any more time finding the culprit or culprits. You can never be too careful."

Mikel clasped Hunter's forearm in a warrior's embrace. "Agreed."

Amy adjusted her facemask one last time, then said, "I suggest we check the prisoner level first. The Black Rose has a habit of killing her compatriots when they've outgrown their usefulness."

Grimacing, Hunter placed the palm of his hand against her lower back. "If it's all right with Mikel, we'll check there on our way to the Recreation Room."

"No, that's fine and it saves us from wasting time. You and Amy and your royal bodyguards head down to the prison level. When it's all clear there, head to the rendezvous location."

Hunter and Amy, and his two bodyguards, Andre and Meric, made quick time getting to the prison level. Unfortunately, it was clear someone else had gotten to it first. Laser scorches pit marked the walls. Cell doors had been blasted off their hinges. And when they reached Chrissie's cell it looked like a small battle had occurred there. Blood splattered the walls and bedding was shredded. Furniture and clothes had been tossed every which way. Even the metal ledge that was her bed looked partially melted.

Beside him, Amy trembled. "Where's Chrissie? Where the hell is

Chrissie?"

His guards searched the room. Finally, after nearly five minutes of searching the tiny cell, Meric approached Hunter, a piece of paper in his hand.

"What is it? Hunter, what is it?" Amy cried.

Hunter turned toward his mate, knowing she could see the pain in his eyes. "It's a letter from the Black Rose."

"What does it say? Please, what does it say?"

Chapter Eleven

"*Which of my prisoners do I kill, dear brother? Those who only help my cause because I hold their families? Or should I kill their families themselves? I hear you have found your mate. Did you know that her brother is the only male born to her pride in the last nineteen years?*

Should we kill him or should we continue to torture him with the drugs that make him the animal he is now? You choose, dear brother—who shall live and who shall die? You will never find us. The Black Rose will forever be out of your reach."

Amy fell to her knees. "Nineteen? He's nineteen now?" Somehow she hadn't connected the passage of years to her brother's growing up. He'd remained the loveable teenager he'd always been in her mind. "How can so many years be lost? How does one woman feel that she has the right to do this?" She fisted her hands, her anger finally showing in the changing color of her skintight pressure suit. "What gives her the right? What makes her think she has the right to interfere, to torture and dictate other's lives the way she does?"

Hunter took her by the arm and practically dragged her from the area to the rendezvous point. On their way, they found a severely injured Chrissie. Her arms were bent at odd angles. Her face was battered and bruised, barely recognizable. Cuts, some minor, some inches deep, ran up and down her entire body.

Amy searched her mind ruthlessly to see if she'd been left as a spy or for dead. Apparently it was the latter as the woman knew nothing and was near death. They quickly transported her into medical stasis and headed toward the recreation room. As soon as they reached it, they found Mikel directing his people.

"Did you find any traitors on board?"

He nodded. "A few. Some were influenced by drugs. Others were just fanatics, following the Black Rose. But your mate's suggestion of taking Empaths along was a wonderful idea. There were several spies. It was a good thing they weren't in areas where they were privy to any sensitive information. She still knows nothing of our plan. This was just another raid to gather single females. By the looks of it, she has no idea about our impending raid."

"Hull breach now repaired, recommend removal of environmental suits," the computer announced as Maryann walked into the room tugging on the facemask.

"Why the hell can't I take this thing off and what the hell is that I feel crawling up my...aiieee!"

"Uh oh," Amy muttered as she slid her own face mask off.

Behind her, she heard a muttered, "By the Goddess, not now."

She whipped her head around to find Mikel on his knees, quaking. His gray pressure suit was quickly changing colors and, within seconds, had turned vibrantly red.

Amy turned her head and looked back at Maryann. Her suit had changed colors, too, and now matched Mikel's. Maryann had her eyes squeezed tight as she panted.

"Well, Hunter, it seems these two need a few minutes alone. Why don't we go back to the medical bay and check on Chrissie while the computer counts personnel and finds out just how many people the Black Rose seized this time."

Hunter smiled at Mikel who had begun to groan. Beneath his facemask, sweat pooled and heated hunger filled Mikel's gaze. "I think that's an excellent idea, Amy. I think these two have some serious talking to do."

Amy watched Hunter's shoulders shake as they made their way out of the Recreation Room. Although he liked Mikel, he was certainly finding this situation humorous. *You think Mikel's situation is funny, do you?*

Well, yes, actually, I do. Mikel has been searching for his mate as long as I have. The fact that the suit won't free him until she commits to him, I find incredibly ironic.

Well how do you think Maryann is going to feel? Her body is being used against her again, but this time she has nothing and no one to fight but her own fears. She's going to feel helpless, then angry that her body is betraying her. I don't think anything about this is funny.

Hunter shook his head and sighed. *Put that way, I must agree.*

Amy smiled, then elbowed him in the ribs. *Tell you what, when all the danger has passed, let's see who can withstand the pressure in the suit better, you or me? Can they be programmed to work like that on a mated couple?*

It would work if we abstain long enough before putting them on—especially if you're in heat. Hunter quirked an eyebrow and smiled as though the bet had already been won. *I'll have to take you up on that when we have the time. But right now, we need to question Chrissie, then head to our targets. We aren't going to let this latest attack change our plans, no matter what my sister thinks.*

Amy squeezed his hand in comfort, then went silent. She couldn't imagine what Hunter feel must knowing his sister was the Black Rose and was responsible for the horrendous acts of slavery and sexual torture of others. When she opened herself to their bond, she could feel his profound sense of guilt. It was eating him alive.

She stopped dead in her tracks. Faced her mate. "Hunter," she said, lifting her hand to caress his cheek, "what your sister has done as the Black Rose is not your fault. The fact that she's still free is not your fault. Eventually, she will get caught. She will pay for her crimes. And in the meantime, we're going to continue doing just what we are—rescuing those she's captured."

Hunter smiled faintly and closed his eyes as he leaned into her hand, savoring her touch. "You are too good for me, love. I don't think I'll ever deserve you. I'll pray to the Goddess every day, thanking her for blessing me with you for a mate."

Amy could feel the heat flooding her cheeks, could feel Hunter's sincerity blasting through their bond. He truly felt she was the greatest blessing of his life and she couldn't quite believe it. Her life, her psyche, were so messed up that she might never be whole, yet he still thought she was a blessing.

And you are, my mate. I will never, ever regret that you are mine. The Goddess blessed me and that's all there is to it. Get used to it. You're mine and I'm never letting you get away from me.

Amy licked her lips nervously, then searched his gaze. Was it the right time to tell him what she was feeling? What if something happened to her during the coming battle? And that thought was all it took for her to make her decision. After taking a deep breath, she laid her other hand against his heart and once again caressed his cheek as she looked deep into his eyes. *I think I love you, Hunter. I'm not sure I could live my life without you. Not anymore. You're my blessing.*

Amy's heart clenched when she noticed the tears filling her mate's eyes. He didn't even try to hide them from her. When he let them flow freely down his cheeks even though they stood in the middle of a busy corridor, she knew she loved this man. If it was the last thing she did, she'd show him just how much his love for her, his faith in her strengths and his belief in her courage meant to her.

Wrapping her hand around the nape of his neck, she slowly pulled his head down. She stood on her tiptoes, leaned in and lightly skimmed his lips with her tongue. When he gasped, surprised by her boldness, she took full advantage. She kissed him, tangling her tongue with his, lingering and savoring his taste. Only when her knees began to quake and threaten to buckle did she slowly draw the kiss to an end.

She turned her face into his neck, doing her best to control her wildly beating heart. She heard Hunter clear his throat just before he tipped her face up to his. This time he searched her gaze, seeming to look for something.

"What was that all about, *moya*?"

She met his gaze without flinching and spoke from the heart. "I don't think I love you. I know I do. It felt like the right time to tell you, that's all."

"Oh, *moya*, the gift of your love will be treasured all the days of my life and beyond."

Now tears filled her eyes and she, too, let them fall. She didn't care what the others in the corridor thought. All that mattered to her was that Hunter loved her and she loved him. That's all that mattered.

Amy looked around the crowded corridor and smiled. "Haven't you all seen a mated pair in love before?" she said, shaking her head in amusement. She turned back to Hunter. "I think we better get to Chrissie. She should awaken soon from the healing chamber."

Hunter dropped a kiss on the tip of her nose, then stepped back. "You're right. Let's get things figured out, speak to the navigator on this ship and see about destroying the Black Rose and rescuing all her prisoners. After that, you and I are going to spend some time exploring just how much we love each other," he whispered, following that brazen statement with a wink.

Amy couldn't help but chuckle as she reached for Hunter's hand. "Sounds like a plan to me." Taking her at her word apparently, Hunter made no stops on his way to the medical bay.

Tears filled Amy's eyes as they entered the medical bay. Chrissie still lay beneath a healing force field, one that kept her vital signs at normal levels while she stayed within its protective barrier. Amy swiped her hand over her face. How could anyone be so cruel as to leave Chrissie for dead? How could they do that to her? Her rage and hatred for the Black Rose grew as she watched the last of the bruises heal and Chrissie opened her eyes.

The golden field around her lowered and she turned to Amy. "Why didn't you just let me die? Dead I can no longer be used as a weapon against you. Against my family."

"That wouldn't have been fair to your mate, Chrissie," Amy said, gently helping the woman from the table.

"I don't want a mate! I—I couldn't bear to have another man touch me the way these men have."

Amy looked to Hunter, then toward the door. *Do you mind leaving us for a moment? I don't mind that you hear what is said, but I'm sure that Chrissie isn't comfortable with you here.*

I agree, moya. She looks rather lost and alone. Aloud he said, "I'll just be outside in the corridor, *moya*. I think perhaps you two need some time alone together."

HUNTER MOVED OUT INTO the corridor and paced while trying not to listen to the women's whispers. Chrissie had her right to her privacy and he would not do his mate any favors by listening in on her fears and proving that males couldn't be trusted.

He strode to the nearest console and punched a series of buttons. "Taliff Shi'Lan's quarters, please."

After a moment's pause, what sounded like sheer chaos spilled from the intercom. After a bout of laughter and a few girlish squeals, Eve answered, "Yes? This is Eve."

Hunter leaned against the wall, wondering if he would ever have a home life like his brother's. Although he was the crown prince of their people, he would gladly give up the privilege for a life like his brother's—one filled with the comfort and laughter of his own children.

"Eve, this is Hunter. Chrissie has just woken and Amy is with her. I thought you might like to join them. Chrissie is having a crisis."

"I'll be right there." Silence from the other end told him she'd ended their transmission. Now there was nothing to do but stand with his hands in his pockets and wait. Perhaps he should hunt down Mikel and see how he fared in his new predicament. It surely couldn't be a good thing to be stuck in a pressure suit with one's unwilling mate wandering about. Maybe he could help take his mind off matters for a bit.

With that in mind, Hunter called out, "Computer, send me to Mikel's location, please."

"Working."

"By the way, what do they call you?" he asked as he found himself watching Mikel beating the crap out of a training bot.

"I am *Skalldari*."

"Thank you, *Skalldari*. I see you brought me straight to Prince Logann as I asked." And not a moment too soon, he thought to himself. "I should be fine. If Amy Shi'Lan requests my presence, please notify me at once."

"Yes, High Prince Shi'Lan."

Hunter continued to watch Mikel pound the robotic sparring partner for a few more minutes. It always amazed Hunter how the *Manruvians* had created a training bot that looked perfectly humanoid. If one didn't know it was an AI training bot, one could never guess by looking at it.

When it looked like his friend had finally started to slow down, he cleared his throat to announce his presence.

Mikel grunted. "Stop training program." As the training bot headed back toward its storage room, Mikel walked over toward one of the benches scattered throughout the gym. After sitting down, he finally looked up and met Hunter's gaze. "I heard you come in. I'm surprised you didn't just jump in. It wouldn't be the first time we sparred."

Hunter walked up to his friend and sat down beside him, then snickered. "No thanks. I'm not in the mood to get bruised and battered. I'd bet, in the mood you're in, you'd beat the crap out of me. I figured, maybe you needed to talk with someone more."

He looked at Mikel, saw the strain on his face. His pressure suit had turned a lighter shade of red so at least his libido had calmed a bit. Unfortunately, one whiff of his mate's scent and he'd be right back where he was before his impromptu workout. "How are you? Really? It's difficult to know your mate fears your touch, your presence, through no fault of your own. Believe me. I know. It's hard to look at her and know that she was out there, unprotected while countless others forced themselves on her when you would have cherished the very ground where she walks."

Mikel hung his head and let his shoulders droop. "You're right. And now, knowing that my mate is on the same ship, that all I have to do is ask *Skalldari* her location and be transported to her side, makes it difficult, if not impossible, to resist doing just that. Yet I must. It is her right to come to me, her choice. I just hope she does it soon. You know how long I've hunted for my mate—decades, Hunter. It's been decades since I've started my search."

Hunter nodded, knowing full well how much his long-time confidant had wanted to find his mate, to have a companion and life partner to come home to, to build a family with.

"How do I make myself stay away from her?" He punched the bulkhead to his left. "How long must I stay away from her? How much time will she need?"

"You will stay away from her as long as it takes because you know that right now it's what she needs. Until this battle is fought, getting anywhere near Maryann will endanger you. As the mating heat takes over, it will distract you both. You must stay away from her to protect her. When it's safe, then you can gently pursue her, help her deal with her fears." He smiled. "Send her small gifts while you must keep your distance. Your scent will not affect her as much. Since she is human you can communicate with her from a distance—court her from a distance."

Mikel nodded, but Hunter wasn't through giving his friend advice. "Amy pointed something out to me that I thought you should know. Maryann is going to be frightened at first, which is normal, but Amy thinks that eventually, Maryann will become angry, enraged that her body seems to be betraying her, making the choices for her that her mind does not want to accept, taking her sense of control. My advice, when it happens—and it will—don't take it personally. She will probably feel that the pressure suit is forcing her to accept a mate, to be intimate with a virtual stranger. Get to know her and let her get to know you, even if it's from a distance. It may help her to feel she has some power over what is happening."

Sighing, Mikel looked off toward the viewport to his right. "I know you're right and your words make sense, but that isn't going to make this any easier to deal with."

"Do you really want easy?'

Mikel shook his head, chuckling. "No, I've never taken the easy path. You know that. So, what brings you here besides worrying about my well-being?"

"I think it's time that we head toward *Drimada*. My sister knows I'm not going to just give up, but Chrissie didn't tell her that we know where she's based her operations, though she and Myra did their best to torture the information out of her. If we hurry, we might be able to get the *Chantrean* and *Manruvian* fleets in position before she even becomes aware that we are there."

"Then what are we waiting for? *Skalldari*?"

"Yes, Prince Logann?"

"Transport the two of us to the command deck and plot our course to *Drimada*. Also, contact the rest of the *Manruvian* fleet, giving them the coordinates of *Drimada*. They should head there immediately, keeping their ships cloaked. Then send a coded transmission to King Shi'Lan on *Chantrea* to ask for their assistance. Let him know where our ships will be and tell him to meet us there as soon as possible." He turned to Hunter, his gaze intent now that he had something to focus on. "Anything else?"

"Not that I can think of. I contacted my father while Amy was still unconscious. He's had all our ships readied for battle and is just awaiting our target location."

"Good."

"You have your orders, *Skalldari*."

"Working."

In less than a second, Hunter and Mikel stood on the command deck. Already he could feel the slight tremble beneath his feet, as the ship made its course corrections, changing directions as it headed toward *Drimada*, toward the upcoming battle. He could only hope and pray that Amy's family still lived. He didn't want her hurt anymore. Losing her family was more than anyone should have to bear.

Knowing you'll be by my side no matter the outcome of the upcoming battle will be all the support I'll need. I, too, hope that my family still lives, that my father doesn't turn away from my mother because of her pregnancy and that my brother can be saved from your sister and can live with the guilt of what he has done to helpless women because of the drugs he was fed."

I don't know about your brother and what he can live with when it comes to the acts he's committed, but as for your parents, the Manruvian Matebonds *will bond your parents as we've bonded. Your father will know beyond a doubt that the child she carries is his.*

He felt her sigh of relief through their bond and was thankful he could offer her that small comfort. *Is all well with the three of you?*

Yes, we're still in the medical bay, but Eve was just about to leave to be with Taliff and her children.

And you? Will you be heading to our quarters soon?

I'll be leaving momentarily. I'm just waiting until I know that Chrissie has fallen into a healing sleep. Oh, and Maryann stopped by. She was agitated so I sent her to the Recreation Room. I thought spending some time on the beach might calm her.

Good idea. We just need to keep them separated until after the battle is over. I'll make sure Mikel stays away from Maryann's quarters and the Recreation Room until all this is over.

Thank you.

Hunter felt Amy close their connection, then focused once again on Mikel. His friend seemed to have returned to staring out into space. Knowing that he'd prefer his privacy while he worried over his mate, Hunter said his goodbyes and headed back toward his and Amy's quarters. He wanted to spend as much time with her as he could before they reached *Drimada*. Once there, time alone would be impossible to come by in the battle to come

Chapter Twelve

Three days later... Above Drimada, *aboard the cloaked* Chantrean *Warship* Vengeance

AMY STARED DOWN AT THE RINGED PLANET BELOW, AWED BY ITS beauty, so at odds with the ugliness of the activities she knew took place there. Soon, they'd move the *Chantrean* fleet into position. Their ship, the *Vengeance* would move to *Drimada's* moon, *Vinusa*, where they were set to raid the dark side. Mikel's fleet was already positioned to target the Black Rose's camp on the light side of *Vinusa*. Brantiff, Taliff and Hunter's father, and Taliff himself would remain above *Drimada* and attack the Black Rose's base of operations there.

If all went as planned, within days, possibly hours, most of the Black Rose's captives would be free and the Black Rose and all her followers would find themselves locked inside the prison levels of the *Manruvian* and *Chantrean* ships. She could only pray to Hunter's Goddess that all went as planned and that their injuries would be few.

I am your Goddess as well, little one. Have faith in yourself and your man. You have a good plan. Just remember if you get into trouble to use the Matebonds *to call out to Hunter and encourage him to do the same. Good Luck, my child.*

Amy swallowed hard and sighed. *Thank you, my Goddess for your well wishes. We'll need them, I fear.* Even now, Hunter was making last minute plans with his father and brother. Both Mikel and Hunter's fathers insisted that Hunter take *Chantrean* and *Manruvian* guards with him into battle to help protect him. Only when Amy also pressed him to accept their offer did Hunter finally relent and give permission for the teams of bodyguards to accompany him when the time came.

As though her thoughts had conjured the man himself, she knew the moment he entered their quarters. She didn't leave her post at the viewport, instead, took the last few seconds to prepare herself for what lay ahead.

Do not worry so, moya. *We'll protect each other in the coming battle, and no matter what happens in the coming hours, you need to know that I won't leave your side.*

Amy turned and faced Hunter as he quickly closed the distance between them. When he reached out to pull her into his arms, she didn't resist, laying her head on his chest just over his steadily beating heart. "I know you won't leave me, but I have this horrible sense of doom that I can't shake. I don't even know if it has to do with the mission itself or what we'll find on the dark side of *Drimada's* moon, on *Vinusa.*"

Hunter ran his hands through her hair, gently stroking its silken length until she began to purr against his chest. His rumbling laughter didn't even faze her. As far as she was concerned, these might be the last peaceful moments they'd have together for the foreseeable future and she would enjoy them while she could.

After a few more moments passed, she felt Hunter's sigh. "It's time to put on your fighting leathers, *moya*. I'll have your back and all those guards you insisted on will have mine. The three-pronged attack is scheduled to commence in less than an hour."

Amy nodded and with one last gusty breath, pulled out of her mate's arms. "Okay. Give me a few minutes to suit up and I'll be ready to accompany you to the debarkation chamber."

Matching actions to words, in less than five minutes, she was dressed for battle in the tan and brown fighting leathers Hunter presented her this morning. As she turned to tell Hunter she was ready, she found him holding a woman's sword—not just any sword, but one identical to his own, perfectly sized to suit her.

Nothing else Hunter could have done would have made her happier. He truly wasn't going to keep her in a safe place as he fought her battles for her but was instead going to let her stand up to her rapists, her tormenters. Not only that, but he was giving her the means to truly fight by his side.

She didn't even have the words to thank him properly. Nothing she could say would be enough, would mean enough.

Words are unnecessary, moya. *I know you can wield this with as much skill as you showed when you held me off with my own sword.* "Happy hunting, mate," he said as he handed her the weapon he had crafted for her.

Amy nodded, took the weapon from her mate, then repeated the warrior's phrase. "Happy hunting."

Together, Amy and Hunter left their quarters and headed toward the debarkation chamber. They had a battle to fight and to win. She'd allow no other thoughts or worries to intrude. There would be time enough to worry later.

TEAM ONE, CHECK IN, Hunter demanded. He was ready to kick some rebel ass. He just hoped he ran into his sister at this base. Sister or not, she'd die by his sword or at the hand of one of his compatriots. He'd never allow her to continue her utterly abhorrent crimes against women. Transporting her to *Chantrea* for trial would just give her another chance at escape. That he couldn't allow.

Team One, in place, Taliff answered, speaking telepathically using their blood-bond. Hunter sighed in relief, knowing that right now, Taliff, their father and three squadrons of warriors were positioned to attack the Black Rose's supposed main base of operations on the ringed-planet of *Drimada*.

Pressing the mini-microphone button embedded in the sleeve of his leathers, Hunter spoke to Team Two. "Team Two, report."

The gruff voice of Mikel whispered through Hunter's nearly invisible earpiece. "Team Two, in place. There is some movement. It looks like they are preparing to take off. Since out arrival an hour ago, I've seen several male prisoners in chains being dragged toward a transport ship."

"Then we're out of time. On my mark, all teams attack."

Amy, who sat crouched beside him behind one of the large black monoliths scattered across the dark side of *Vinusa*, reached out and gripped his arm, then nodded, a fierce expression on her face.

After giving her cheek one last caress, Hunter returned her nod. It was time to take back what was theirs.

"Three."

"Two."

"One."

"All teams converge on targets. Converge on targets."

As the sounds of battle began to transmit through his headset, Hunter's own adrenaline started to rise. He could even feel Amy's impatience to begin. Using their night vision goggles, Hunter, Amy and their team quickly and soundlessly approached the base camp the Black Rose had built inside of a mountain. First they crossed a murky lake, then climbed a set of steps carved into the mountain itself. Only at the top of the steps did they finally discover access to the hidden tunnels where the captives were stashed.

This whole side of the moon felt spooky to Hunter. He could only imagine the apprehension his mate was feeling, knowing that she might run into her rapists and tormentors. He couldn't forget about Chrissie who had to relive her torment while giving them the general layout of the tunnels within the mountain. Without her painful sacrifice, they wouldn't have a plan to put into action. Even Maryann reviewed every detail of her horrendous captivity so that Mikel's team was armed with enough knowledge to rescue anyone still held there on the light side of the moon. These Earth women had more courage and strength than any race of people he'd seen to date. They continually impressed him and his comrades.

With one last glance at his mate to reassure himself that she still remained by his side, Hunter led the squad into the belly of the mountain. He'd gone no more than three meters when he began to hear static through his communications unit. "Say again, Mikel. Say again."

"Shit. My woman transported down here when she recognized one of the men being dragged to the transport. She's threatening to hijack one of our ships to follow it if I don't let her go willingly."

"Why that ship? Who's on it?" Hunter asked, fully aware everyone around him was listening in on their conversation.

"She just spotted Amy's brother and the Black Rose get onboard so she had *Skalldari* send her down here to plead her case."

Hunter didn't need to think about it. He reached out and squeezed his mate's hand in reassurance. "You and your mate go after that ship. Take your warship, *Victory,* with you. Leave the rest of your team to continue the raid. We'll make sure they all have quarters."

"But the prisoners, the rebels, what if—"

"You have your orders, Mikel. My sister must be stopped. And recovering my mate's brother would be appreciated. I trust you to carry out those directives where I'd trust few others."

"Understood. *Skalldari*? Two to transport up to the command deck of *Victory*." Hunter heard a little bit of a scuffle, then nothing as Mikel and Maryann were transported to Mikel's ship.

Amy closed her eyes, then sighed. "Be careful, my friends," she whispered. "Be careful."

Before they could resume moving down the darkened tunnels, Hunter stopped as he received a telepathic message from Taliff.

What is it, Tal?

There's nothing here. Nothing at all. This place looks completely abandoned. Eve's parents aren't here and neither are Amy's. There is no sign of life here at all though it looks like this place was just abandoned, maybe only hours ago. I suspect she's deserting all three of these bases so be on the lookout.

Understood. Return to the Adventurer *and await word. We may need you down here before this is through. And while you're up there, see what kind of scans* Shoshoni *can perform on* Drimada *and* Vinusa. *Perhaps the rebels are gone, but some of the prisoners could be trapped somewhere we can't see.*

Understood.

Hunter raised his sword as he and his team continued down the tunnels, following the directions Chrissie had given him for the locations of the cells. He hoped to find at least some survivors, but if any rebels got in the way, he and his team wouldn't hesitate to cut their way through them. They would not be stopped. Not by fear of the unknown. And not by the rebels.

THE DEEPER THEY MOVED into the tunnels, the more Amy's stomach began to cramp up. Something was going to happen, something bad. Before she could even shove that thought away, a feline growl ripped through the tunnels.

A shiver ran down her spine. She'd recognize that particular growl anywhere. Apparently, this was the hellhole Myra had chosen to heal in. Well, it would be the last mistake she ever made.

The feline shriek sounded eerily close in the enclosed darkness. Back to back, she and Hunter searched the tunnels, while the others spread out, looking for Myra's hiding place.

But Amy knew Myra, remembered her treachery. She wouldn't fall for her tricks again. She'd go after the Alphas on this mission, meaning Amy and Hunter, Hunter. For now, everyone else would be safe.

Be on your toes, Hunter. It's you or me she'll go after, not the others. Eve bested her once and I nearly killed her the last time we met. She'll be after blood.

I remember. I've got your back and you've got mine. The others can take care of themselves.

Amy grinned, even knowing that in just a few moments she'd have to kill another being. She could give Myra no mercy.

Amy didn't have long to wait. Without any warning, the huge lioness jumped out of a corridor and straight for Hunter. *Hunter! Duck!*

As Hunter rolled out of the way, Amy drew up her sword. The cat was just getting to her feet, a task made more difficult by her missing paw, courtesy of Eve's swift retribution during the challenge aboard Taliff's ship.

As Myra made to attack, Amy stood her ground, raising her sword. Just as the lioness' gaping jaws began to descend toward Amy's neck, she twisted out of its way, making sure to swipe the blade across its neck. In one smooth motion, she severed its head from its body.

Hunter rushed to her side, grabbed the sword from her and handed it to one of the bodyguards he'd assigned. "Thank the Goddess Alana that you're all right." Hunter roughly pulled Amy into his arms but she wasn't about to complain. Already her knees were beginning to quake.

As she rested against Hunter, the ear bud in her own ear began to pick up static before Eve's voice filtered through the noise. "Amy, good news. *Shoshoni* has been hard at work over here on the *Adventurer*. She managed to pick up scattered life signs on both *Drimada* and *Vinusa*. The life signs were weak, but she was able to transport all captives off both surfaces. Both your parents are on your ship, *Vengeance,* with a lovely baby boy of perhaps six months, and your sisters were sent here to the *Adventurer*. They've also recovered nearly everyone from my own pride. Your brother is among the missing and there are still several women from your pride unaccounted for, according to your parents."

"What about the two women they took from *Skalldari* the other day?"

"They were found, too, injured, but alive."

"That is very good news indeed. It could have been so much worse. And we'll continue to search for the others. I'd like to spend a few days with my family before Hunter and I head out to follow Mikel. He's got a lead on the Black Rose and my brother."

"Eve," Hunter interrupted. "Please have Taliff assure Amy's family that we'll be together as we search for their son and any others that my sister may have taken with her. We'll spend the next couple of days with them to give them some private time together, but then we must follow Mikel who is on the Black Rose's trail."

"Understood. Standby for transport to your ship. Amy's family is already healing in the medical bay."

Amy laughed in pure joy. They might be scarred, but they were alive. That was all that mattered, and after she had a chance to hold them in her arms and assure herself that they were truly going to be okay, she and her mate would search for her brother, Ryan. Deep in the pit of her belly, she knew—just knew—that when the time came, they'd find him alive as well.

Epilogue

Five days later... Aboard the Chantrean *Warship,* Vengeance, *trailing the* Manruvian *Warship* Victory *by two days*

"Ready to give up yet?" Amy asked, rubbing herself sinuously over Hunter. If he didn't give up soon, she would. This suit was driving her mad. She went for the big guns, literally. Reaching down, she grabbed his hard cock and squeezed.

"You only need say the word," he said with a grin, pressing her hand tighter against his cock. "Can you not stand the pressure anymore?"

"The suit I can stand," she said with a grin. "It's the underhanded pressure you're using, you big jerk," she said with a giggle as he slipped his hand between her legs. Their suits turned from orange to crimson and Hunter cupped the cheek of her ass, drawing her closer against him.

"Give up?" He breathed against her ear. "Have you given much thought to how all this anticipation is going to affect us when we do finally remove these suits? What it's going to feel like with my cock pressed into your tight pussy? How will it feel, *moya*? Think about it." He pulled her closer, moved them until her back was pressed against the wall and her front against him. All of him. The bulge of his shaft pressed against the lower half of her stomach and she almost gave in. Almost.

"No," she nearly panted. "You give in. Tell me how much you want me. Tell me how long you've already waited for me. Tell me you need to bury yourself inside me or you'll die."

"I will die, *moya*. I can't wait to bury my cock deep in your tight little cunt. I need to feel the cream slide from your channel and coat my shaft as I slide into you." He pressed his face tight against the mask. "Wrap your legs around me and we'll give in at the same time, *moya*. It will end both our suffering. The suits will disappear and we'll soon be allowed to wallow in each other's touch."

As soon as Amy wrapped her legs around his waist, the suits melded into their bodies. Hunter slid his cock into her already streaming channel and their mouths couldn't find each other fast enough. They both groaned when he pulled out and slammed into her. His cock teased her to the point of pain. Their need had grown beyond that of the usual mating heat. If she wasn't already pregnant, she would become so this night. His seed, especially potent from the waiting, would quickly find her ripened ovum and her belly would soon grow round with his cub.

She screamed her first orgasm, surprised at the speed and strength in which she'd reached her peak. Pulling his mouth from hers, he laved her nipples, suckling and biting, causing the pleasure pain of a true *Chantrean* mating as he thrust her against the wall with each stroke. Finally, he sank his teeth into her shoulder, marking her as his mate.

Her incisors elongated and she did the same. Sinking her teeth into the strong muscles of his shoulder, she held him to her. He climaxed, emptying his essence into her tight channel and bathing her womb with his powerful seed.

Exhausted, Hunter carried her back to their bed and laid them both on the soft covering, too tired to even pull the blankets up. Wrapped in each other's arms, they fell into a deep, exhausted slumber with the words, "I love you," on both their lips.

.

Mikel's Wrath

Prologue

Mari, the Mother Goddess of the Sea, contemplated the many paths of the future spread out before her. So many different paths. So many different futures. One mistake, one wrong choice, and disaster awaited the *Manruvians*...among others. Hidden from all but her most faithful priestesses, she stared into the *Crystal Lake of Ikaria*— the lake of foretelling. Swirling the vision waters with her hand, she broke apart the images, having seen what she needed to make her decision.

The time had come for change. Some would die, fated to pass over to a higher plain. Some would battle with all their hearts and succeed. Others would fall. War would soon reach the peaceful *Manruvians*. How she wanted to step in, to stop events before they even began. Yet even a Goddess must follow certain rules—and thwarting the three sisters of fate was the rule she must not outright break.

If the *Manruvian* Merfolk were to endure the coming trials, they'd have to use all their resources, all their allies. Many challenges were coming, many changes, and only the strong of heart and pure of soul had a chance at survival.

The time had come for her to whisper in some ears, to plant some ideas, even if it did bend the rules a wee bit. She had to be careful what she said or she might do more harm than good, creating the very disaster she wanted to avoid. Even Goddesses had their limitations.

With that firmly in mind, Mari closed her eyes and thought of whom she'd speak to first. Her lips tilted into a smile. Yes, Brantiff Shi'Lan, King of the *Chantrean Lionese* would be the best person to approach first. He would be especially sympathetic to what was coming, given his years of imprisonment by his own daughter, the Black Rose — a *Lionese* infamous for enslaving people of all taces and forcing them to perform in her vicious in her breeding experiments. His counsel to his sons, Hunter and Taliff Shi'Lan and to their friend and ally, Mikel Logann, would be invaluable in the battle to come. He'd be their strongest ally, their fiercest protector.

Visualizing the *Chantrean* Palace, Mari let her powers loose. They coalesced around her body, wrapping her in a ball of brilliant white light. With just the narest thought, Mari, Goddess of the Sea, found herself on *Chantrea*, invisible to all, even her most powerful *Chantrean* Priestesses. Now to assume the persona that the *Chantreans* recognized—Alana, the Mother Goddess of *Chantrea*.

While transforming, her flaming red curls to golden corkscrews and her long, aqua gown to one of diaphanous white silk, Mari, aka Alana, passed through the halls of the palace completely unnoticed. Carried on the wind, the only sign of her passing was the fresh scent of sea that followed in her wake.

Time grew short with much still to accomplish and she'd yet to find her quarry. Only when certain she'd have a few moments alone with King Shi'Lan would she reveal herself to him. For now, few—if any—could know of her presence here or all could be lost. Even amongst his own people, there were traitors in his court and tipping them off too soon could have disastrous results—for everyone.

Chapter One

MIKEL LOGANN, HIGH PRINCE AND HEIR TO THE THRONE OF *Manruvia*, glanced through the *transomani* at the planet below, his hands fisted at his sides.

Maryann could feel the anger coming off him in turbulent waves, so for now, she kept silent.

"The planet is devoid of life. Either the Black Rose has left no survivors or she and her followers have removed everyone to another planet. Do we waste our time on the surface below looking for the bodies of the dead, or worry about locating the living?"

His anger kept her firmly rooted in place, unable to answer him. Did he expect her to run from him in fear, or perhaps he wanted a different reaction all together? Either way she chose not to say anything at all, knowing her silence would goad him into facing her rather than looking out toward the vastness of space.

As she expected, he turned around, facing her for the first time since she entered the room. "I will leave this room once again, Maryann, because I know you think it is my fault we are in this situation and you are angry your body is seeming to make choices for you that you cannot consciously fathom. But I warn you... One. Last. Time." He turned to face the door. "If you follow me again, I will not be held responsible for my actions. If you follow me from this room and into my quarters, I will take it as your consent to start my seduction. And if you think your suit is painful now, wait until I begin to touch you."

Shame filled Maryann Wilson as she watched Mikel storm off. She purposely provoked the *Manruvian* prince, hoping he'd do exactly what he accused her of just a few moments ago—take the decision out of her hands and seduce her. She didn't want to take responsibility for either her emotions or her actions. She actually didn't want to feel at all because it was easier to seal off those emotions that hane them spark memories of pain and torture, rape and abuse, betrayal and starvation—memories she'd prefer to bury forever.

Now, her body had betrayed her, choosing Mikel as her mate when she'd not been looking for a man—not now anyway. She didn't blame all men for the actions of her rapists. In fact, she wanted a healthy, normal relationship—someday. What she objected to was that her body—and the symbiotic suit she was wearing—could choose someone for her without so much as one word passing between them, not even an introduction. It seemed ludicrously arbitrary.

If the Black Rose hadn't attacked, hadn't forced them to take refuge in the symbiotic *Manruvian* pressure suits that conformed to the body like a wet suit, she would have at least had time to meet Mikel, find out his name. Instead, once she donned the suit to protect her from possible air contamination, it had taken over monitoring and controlling all her bodily functions.

Then, within seconds of being cleared to remove their facemasks, she'd inhaled Mikel's scent. Apparently since mikel was supposedly her mate, the symbiotic suit immediately bonded with her skin, making it impossible to remove until she accepted a mate-bond with Mikel, both emotionally and mentally.

She couldn't trick her suit off either, couldn't pretend to want to become his mate—she'd tried that already and failed. A sentient, symbiotic being, it knew her every emotion and thought, fed off them in fact. Until she truly accepted him as mate, the suit would continue to stimulate her sexually, feeding off her frustration and need.

Every few minutes it sent waves of heat pulsing into her pussy, zipping her clit with energy when she least expected it. She swore the suit even tightened around the areolas of her nipples, tweaking them, pulling them into tight buds even in her sleep.

After nearly a week of nonstop arousal, she was about ready to give in, but she couldn't see tying herself for a lifetime to a virtual stranger just for an orgasm. In truth, her clit was so hard and throbbing, one good tug would probably get her off, but she couldn't get her fingers near it. Of course, that just pissed her off even more.

It wanted Mikel or no one, would settle for nothing less. Whatever happened to getting to know someone first? Dating? Finding out if you even like each other before deciding to do the horizontal mambo? No, her body liked the smell of his and that was that. It wanted no other for the rest of its life. And from what little she'd learned this past week from the ship's sentient computer, *Skalldari*, once his super semen made its way inside her and started her conversion—whatever that meant—she'd live for a very long time.

Goddess... Why couldn't her life be simple, like any normal human? But no—she'd gotten mixed up in a shifter breeding-sex slave ring when the Black Rose kidnapped her from Earth, was rescued and was now on the verge of war with said slaver, which is why they were searching the galaxy for her and the bases she'd stashed her other victims. To top it all off, she was about to be forced to become the mate to a merman Prince, if she ever wanted control over her own body again. Life couldn't get any more complicated than that.

Well, the time had arrived to strap on her big girl boots and take an enormous leap of faith that the *Manruvian's* symbiotic suit—and she really needed to find out the proper name of the sentient material—knew best when it had chosen Mikel as her mate. She knew she was being stubborn and yes, childish, by not speaking to him in kindness. She'd yet to give him a chance—she knew that, too. It didn't mean she wasn't scared shitless at the idea of getting in bed with the guy—any guy at this point, even one she knew wouldn't ever hurt her, not intentionally anyway.

She couldn't run or hide from her future though, no matter how frightened she felt. They were mates. She needed to face that head on. If she continued merely to provoke him, she'd never get to know the real man, which would totally defeat the purpose behind her decision to delay mating with him this long.

Knowing that it wouldn't be any easier to take this step by waiting until morning, Maryann headed toward Mikel's quarters, fully aware of just where this move would lead. Except, instead of his seducing her, he'd be the one seduced. He'd damned well like it, too. Then in the morning, she planned to get to know the man behind the crown.

Finally, feeling more confident for having made plans, Maryann walked faster, wanting to run a brush through her hair before stopping by his room. She also wanted to pick up some supplies she had *Skalldari* transport to her room throughout the week. She'd give Mikel such a show, he'd be begging her to take him before the night ended and, for once in Goddess knows how long, she'd be in control of things.

Maryann transported to her room, then decided to walk to Mikel's cabin to give her nerves time to settle down. The ship was so big. The hallways were huge, the walls, floors and ceilings were cylindrical in shape, and yet her feet were always firmly rooted to the ground. That was some form of artificial gravity at work, according to the sentient computer, *Skalldari*. So even if they were tumbling through space and the transporters were down, as long as their feet were on one of the walls, they would be able to walk anywhere they needed to go within the ship. Otherwise, with just a verbal command to *Skalldari*, they could be whisked wherever they wanted.

Ten minutes later, Maryann stood outside Mikel's quarters, her bag of supplies draped over one shoulder, ready to take her man. Taking a deep breath, she raised her hand and, after only a small hesitation, placed it on the control pad, allowing *Skalldari* to confirm her permission to enter—at least Mikel had basically implied that permission earlier.

After scanning her palm print, the lock beeped twice before the door slid silently open. She froze, her hand still resting against the security pad when she caught her first glimpse of her mate. Mikel stood just inside the doorway, lounging against the wall as though expecting her arrival—and maybe he had. She swallowed hard and really looked at him, trying to take in every detail of this moment—the moment she'd finally take control over her life—her future.

"I've been waiting for you, Maryann."

She tilted her head back, looking up into his blue-green eyes. She could feel the heat of arousal burning in his veins. She sensed his edgy need as though she were inside his thoughts, his skin. She had to step away from him before she did something completely foolish—like beg him to fuck her. She wanted, no needed, him to end the agony the suit had put her through for the last week. She had a plan for tonight and in it, the only one who'd lose control stood in front of her. She just had to stick to her plan.

Skirting around him, she sauntered into his private quarters as though she didn't have a care in the world and had every right to be there. She looked around, fascinated by the wide range of styles he'd chosen to decorate his cabin. Oversized furniture, colorful artwork, luxurious floor coverings and various types and styles of tables were scattered around the room.

Her gaze rested on an overstuffed leather-like chair that looked more comfortable than anything she'd ever seen back home on Earth. It faced the rest of the room, allowing any occupant to see everything at once, so she headed toward it, confident that at this point Mikel had no idea just how much she wanted to turn tail and run, leaving his seduction for some other time.

Acting with nonchalance she didn't feel, Maryann settled back into the chair, sinking into its comfy depths before slowly crossing her legs. When that didn't get her the reaction she craved, she lightly bit her bottom lip as she casually stroked her leg from knee to thigh, drawing heart-shaped patterns along her skin-tight suit until her hand was just a hair's breadth away from her pussy.

She wanted his complete attention on her. Though he remained by the door, she swore she heard him draw in a sharp breath. She smiled, enjoying her growing sense of control. A feeling of power washed over her, something so new and precious she didn't know what to do with it. So for now, she just enjoyed it and continued to lightly caress her skin through her suit, watching him watch her.

Since the moment they met, he continually caught her attention with his looks and mannerisms, but now, wearing only the body-conforming silvery grey pressure suit he usually covered with his uniform, she couldn't help but stare. The man was gorgeous.

With his face bronzed by wind and sun, Mikel epitomized the phrase *ruggedly handsome*. He had a small bump on the bridge of his nose from an obvious break, proving he'd not lived a pampered life. His lips were full and sensual and she'd bet money he could kiss her unconscious if he chose to. His hair hung to his shoulders and gleamed gold in the low light. By the Goddess Alana, she couldn't wait to run her fingers through it and see if it felt as soft as it looked.

More often than not, he held his head high with pride, aware of his station in life, his destiny, but every once in a while she caught a glimpse of his loneliness in his eyes. There were age lines around his eyes and mouth that muted his youthful appearance, though he could be anywhere from mid-thirties to much, much older.

Skalldari had not skimped in the information Maryann had asked her for and it didn't take long to realize that once the *Manruvians* reached their mid-thirties, then the aging process practically stopped. After they reached that peak reproductive stage in their maturity, they aged only one year for every twenty or so human years.

She continued to stare at him, inspecting him as she would a new stud she wanted to purchase. Until she gained control over her own arousal, she needed to keep the upper hand, however she could.

Mikel towered over most men by a good four inches and stood at least a foot taller than her own five foot five inch height. With broad shoulders, muscular arms and a narrow waist, he had the perfect swimmer's body—strong, powerful and agile. His torso practically rippled as he moved. She couldn't wait to see if her imagination rivaled the real thing when he revealed his body to her the first time. She licked her lips and watched, amazed as his cock grew and grew and grew beneath his taut suit. Goddess, that had to hurt.

Maryann bit back a moan of need as her clothing took that moment to stimulate her clit, sending pulsing waves of warmth through the small bud. She gripped the arms of her chair, then took a deep breath before returning her focus to Mikel and his reactions to her subtle movements.

Even without considering her body's desperate need, she had to admit, at least to herself, that she couldn't wait to get her hands on him, to feel his controlled power quiver beneath her touch. He exuded masculinity and leashed power with every breath and, no matter how much she wanted to jump him, she wouldn't. Not yet, anyway.

As the seconds passed with nothing but tense silence building between them, she could feel the control she craved slipping away and that was something she couldn't—wouldn't—allow.

After taking a deep breath, Maryann looked him directly in the eye, needing him to understand and agree to her terms. "I'm willing to become your mate tonight—in fact I'm looking forward to it, but on one condition."

He looked at her intently, then waved his hand for her to continue. "And what's that?"

"I get to do this my way, to be in control of tonight's...festivities." She forced herself to spit out the rest of her condition. "And... I want to tie you down when we mate for the first time."

Chapter Two

When he first heard the tiny chime beep twice announcing that someone stood outside his door, Mikel tensed. He hadn't been sure when he issued his challenge up on the observation deck that Maryann would follow through.

For the last week, he'd watched her watch him. He had discovered more than a week ago that she was his mate, but wanted to give her time to get to know him before telling her about the bond between them. Then the Black Rose had attacked his vessel and forced them into the *Abacine* pressure suits. Now her body demanded sexual release and wouldn't give it to her unless in the presence of her mate.

He hated that she felt no choice but to mate with him and would have preferred to court her as she deserved. But with their mission in jeopardy because of their desperate arousal, he couldn't help but feel relieved that she'd come to him, even as a last resort. And considering how he'd searched, prayed and finally given up on finding his mate, her presence was no less than a miracle.

Seconds had passed that felt like hours before he released the door lock, allowing her entrance to his private quarters. He sucked in a deep breath when he saw her, amazed and awed yet again by her gentle beauty.

She had a full mouth, lips glossy with moisture. Her rich brown eyes glowed with a fierce inner fire. Her cheeks were flushed a dusky rose. She had a wealth of rich, glowing auburn hair that hung in tousled disarray more often than not, as it did now. Wispy curls fell across her forehead, framing her lovely face. She looked both scared and determined as she stood frozen in his doorway and damned if that didn't make him want her even more.

He let his gaze wander over her body, imagining what she'd look like beneath the *Abacine*—the living material of her body-conforming pressure suit. Even completely covered in the smoky grey material from neck to toes, he could see the fullness of her high-perched breasts, her slim waist, gently rounded hips and the magnificent length of her long, shapely legs. She'd fit him just right—of that, he had no doubt. She was breathtaking and, as of right now, completely his.

By the time she walked passed him and got comfortable in his favorite chair, he had to take a deep breath and rein in his desires. It wouldn't do to trip her to the floor and mount her. She'd come here with a purpose in mind and, as long as she agreed to mate with him in the end, he'd let her tell him in her own way what that was. He never expected her to say what she did though. "Can you say that again?"

Maryann stood and fisted her hands by her sides before nodding. "I need to feel in control, especially the first time we're intimate. I've not been with anyone—ever—except my rapists and I need this. For tonight, I need to feel comfortable knowing that you can't hurt me, even accidentally, and tying you to the bed will do that for me."

Mikel hesitated, but knew he'd do whatever she needed him to if it would help put her at ease with him, including allowing her to restrain him. Dipping his head slightly, he said, "If that's what you need, then yes, I agree to your terms."

When Maryann's shoulders lost some of their rigid tension, he knew he'd made the right decision. Besides, she only said she wanted him restrained the first time they mated. That left the rest of the night for his brand of seduction. That fact she feared their mating night fueled his determination to make this an unforgettable memory for her, one that she'd look back on with a heated smile of remembrance in the years to come.

With that thought in mind, he held out his hands. "I'll never do anything to hurt you, but you don't know that yet." He nodded toward the small black bag she'd dropped next to the chair. "Am I right to assume you brought what you need with you?"

A charming blush spread across her cheeks and, when she bit her bottom lip, then straightened her spine as if daring him to say something negative, he wanted to enfold her in his arms. He hadn't meant to embarrass her, just find out if he had to use his own *Manruvian Matebonds*, bindings he carried with him everywhere since he's reached his maturity and began his mate-hunt. The *Matebonds* were sacred to his people and the fact that she thought to use them tonight, even just to assure her safety, meant she thought about his beliefs and what he'd need to make this night special.

It pleased him as well that, even when embarrassed, she didn't back down from him. It proved to him, at least on *some* level, she did trust him not to hurt her. By the time this night ended, he vowed she'd know it to the depths of her soul.

Maryann swung around, turning her back to him as she bent over to pick up the small bag she dropped. His cock grew impossibly harder as the *Abacine* lovingly displayed her luscious ass to his gaze. They couldn't wear the thin, indestructible material over clothing of any type, so it flaunted her curves to perfection.

Mikel turned his head away as she rummaged through her bag. His self-control had worn thin since they started on their mission to track down the Black Rose and rescue her captives. Their continued presence in each other's company, combined with the *Abacine* heightening his arousal, made it nearly impossible to keep his primitive instincts in check. He wanted to mark her, needed to bind her to him as his forever-mate. Not doing so over the course of the past week had been nearly impossible.

"Where would you like me?" Mikel watched, fascinated as Maryann's skin flushed crimson. Even the tips of her ears turned pink. Shy one minute, bold the next, she intrigued him as no other ever had. Even though they'd yet to bond formally, he knew he'd never give this woman up. He'd do whatever he had to, to keep her by his side.

Maryann gazed around his quarters slowly, thoroughly, then glanced back down at his chair before shaking her head. "Your chair won't do.

Neither will your sofa. Take me to your bedroom."

Surprise at the command in her voice and the rigidity of her spine had him nodding and leading the way before he realized how quickly he'd jumped to do her bidding. Damn! He never expected her to slip into the dominant role quite that easily. He'd have to be on his toes if he wanted a chance to control even the slightest thing this evening. But even as he led her to his sleeping chamber, he couldn't contain the excitement building inside him.

His imagination took flight as he opened the door. "Illumination, thirty percent, *Skalldari.*" Would she ride him, taking what she wanted from him without concern for his needs, or would she draw it out, try to seduce his seed from him? His cock hardened further as he pictured her mounting him while he lay helpless to stop her, her breasts swaying freely in front of his face, teasing him with their nearness while he lay powerless to touch them.

Knowing that reality often surpassed the imaginary, he headed straight for the bed, since no other piece of furniture in here would suffice for what she planned. He probably should let her dictate his every action, but at this point the anticipation of finally taking a mate—taking Maryann to mate—left him in a hurry to see things progress. Besides, he sensed she didn't find the role of dominant female to his submissive male comfortable and he didn't want her shying away from him or her feelings tonight.

Only after he settled back against the headboard in the center of the bed, did he notice the longs strips of shiny black material in her hands.

He smiled, unable not to once he realized she came prepared, not just to ensure her safety, but to follow the mating ritual as the *Manruvians* had for hundreds of generations. Using the *Manruvian Matebonds* as restraints told him more than her words that she fully intended to mate with him this evening.

She stopped running—from him and her future. Her willingness to face life head on rather than run from it filled him with pride. She'd be the perfect queen to the *Manruvian* people once the Trident of Ascension passed to him, of that he had no doubt.

When she stopped at the foot of the bed and didn't say or do anything more, Mikel crossed his arms and lifted one brow in question. "Now what?"

MARYANN KNEW MIKEL WONDERED at her silence, but now that the moment had come to mate with him, she wasn't sure how to proceed. Should she tie his hands together above his head or have him spread his arms and legs and tie them to the bedposts? Though she wanted to maintain control, she didn't want him to feel used either. She shuddered, remembering exactly what it felt like to be helpless as someone used her body without care or compassion. She'd not inflict those same sensations on another being, especially not her mate.

Nervously, she licked her dry lips. She had to stand firm on her decision to restrain him, but she could give him a choice in how she accomplished it. "Would you prefer your hands tied together and secured to the headboard or would you be more comfortable with your limbs tied to the four bedposts?"

As she waited for his answer, she quickly glanced around Mikel's bedchamber. Spartanly furnished, she only spied two low-slung tables that flanked the oversized bed and a deep burgundy chair similar in design and size to the one out in the main room. Without doubt, the bed in this room had been built solely for the prince's comfort. Bigger than any bed she'd ever seen, it took up at least three-quarters of the floor space. It wouldn't surprise her if half a dozen men could sleep in it comfortably and still have room to spare.

Maryann tipped her head to one side. Come to think of it, she wasn't sure the bindings she brought would even be long enough to reach the bedposts, never mind leave him enough slack so that his joints weren't injured during their mating.

Mikel clasped his hands above his head and smiled gently. "I would suggest you tie them above my head, love. It will ensure I'm unable to touch you, but won't overtax my joints."

Relieved that he'd spoken up, Maryann sighed. This taking charge was a lot more difficult than she thought it would be. "Thank you for your suggestion." She bit her bottom lip, needing to explain herself to him, explain her hesitancy and yet her need to follow through with restraining him. "I'm not exactly comfortable ordering you about and I know this can't be easy for you either. I can't quite explain why I need to do this, just that I do." With the *Manruvian Matebonds* in her hand, she didn't wait for him to respond to her, just climbed atop the bed and made her way to his side.

Seconds passed as she looked over Mikel's still body. He didn't try to touch her, didn't tell her to hurry up, just let her look her fill. It would be a lot easier to explore him if she could figure out how to remove their pressure suits though. Then again, seeing his body in all its glory just might make seducing him even harder. He looked so big and muscular covered, how would he look naked? Would his size intimidate or excite her? She didn't know, but sooner or later, she'd have to find out.

Turning her head, she met Mikel's patient gaze. His blue-green eyes were completely serene, showing none of the discomfort she was positive his forced submissiveness caused him. Mikel epitomized the term *Alpha Male*, and allowing her to have her way with him had to go against his natural, instinctive impulses. Not sure just what to say or how to proceed, yet knowing she couldn't continue to just sit and stare at him, she pinched the fabric of his silver suit between her fingers. "How do I remove this? We can't mate with our clothes on."

He smiled up at her. "The suits don't come off until we're both truly committed to mating with one another, Maryann. Even then, we can't remove them. They will simply be absorbed into our bodies. They're made of sentient material and will not release us until we are both positive mating is what we want. You still have doubts. The suit knows it."

She looped the bonds loosely around his wrists and then around the center columns of the headboard. They were still loose when she released them. She didn't know how tight to tie them and didn't want to hurt Mikel. The bonds shocked her by tightening up on their own, tugging his arms over his head until they looked close to discomfort and she squealed, reaching for the ties.

"Don't worry, love. They aren't hurting me. The bonds are also sentient. They know just when to stop to keep me bound without pain."

His soothing voice stopped her from removing the bonds and throwing them to the floor in a fit of guilt. She looked at his bound body and wondered how she would ever be able to go through with this. She shifted and looked down toward his feet. Should she tie his legs or not? It wasn't as though he could do much with his hands tied. She wasn't sure what to do. Looking back at his face, she bit her lip, undecided.

"Bind my feet together and tie them to the foot of the bed, Maryann. If you attach them to each post separately, it will be too difficult for you to mount me, if that is your desire."

His voice was husky. It was almost as though he liked this, though she was sure he couldn't. He was a very dominant, very alpha male. She was afraid she might make him feel less than he was by doing this, the way her captors had made her feel. Goddess, she didn't want that.

"I don't have anything else to tie you with." She hadn't come fully prepared. She should have thought about binding his feet. Darn it. She looked away, tears of frustration stinging her eyes.

"I have a restraint on the table."

He shifted his gaze to the left and she spotted the restraint. Had he planned to do this to her or had he known she would want to do this? She swallowed, refusing to let her fears stop her now. This needed to be done. She flicked her gaze back to Mikel. He looked up at her, expressionless. There was no prodding coming from him. This was her decision. She smiled grimly.

Sliding from the bed, she retrieved the *Matebond* laid out and wrapped it around his feet and then the posts of the footboard. The material again tightened up, securing his feet firmly. Her eyes widened when he groaned in response. Was he in pain? Too uncomfortable in this position?

She looked up the length of his body and gasped when she saw his massive erection straining against the material of his suit, which shimmered strangely in the dull light. She couldn't help but wonder if they were beginning to absorb into their bodies as he'd promised or if it was simply a figment of her imagination.

As she climbed up onto the bed, her suit sent another shaft of sensation through her pussy, making her moan in frustrated need. Another sensation spiraled through her, something she never felt before. It felt as though something was burrowing underneath her skin. "What's happening, Mikel?" she asked, aware her voice betrayed her fear and not caring in the least.

"It is the *Abacine*, the sentient material of your suit, absorbing into your body. Touch me, Maryann."

She heard the command in his voice and obeyed, not even stopping to think about her actions. Following an instinct she didn't understand, she straddled his waist and placed her hands flat against his chest. Within seconds, the suits shimmered again, before they both slowly grew thinner and thinner until they seemed to disappear completely.

She shivered, not from the cold, but the feeling of *otherness*, as though someone else, someone powerful, resided in her skin, in her soul.

"You're feeling me, Maryann, my essence."

"How did you know?"

Mikel chuckled beneath her.

She gripped his waist with her thighs to keep her body steady while he laughed. Why was he laughing at her? Before she'd even finished that thought, she felt a stirring in her mind, like a gentle breeze, and somehow she knew he wasn't laughing in cruelty, but because he truly felt happy about the fact she had gone through with the first step of their mating.

I know because I can feel what you feel. I hear your thoughts as though they are my own. Just as you can know mine—if that's what you wish.

"Really?" She didn't know if he'd hear her, but she had to try to answer him in the same way. She'd never backed down from a challenge before and she wasn't about to start now. *Really?*

Mikel chuckled again and then replied directly into her mind, *Really.*

Again, she shivered. Cool air caressed her bare breasts just as a wave of heat washed through her. She scooted closer to the headboard to double-check that his bindings were still secure. When he leaned forward and kissed her thighs, then paused to inhale the scent of her before touching his lips to the top of her mound, she froze, shocked and somewhat surprised by his actions. She shivered with pleasure, his and hers.

Mikel hadn't lied to her. She could feel what he felt, could even smell her own musky arousal. Their minds truly were connected, bound together as one. With her reservations finally gone—because she had to admit to herself at least that there wasn't any way for him to hide his thoughts or feelings from her—she gave into her own desires and moved away from his mouth, no matter how much he tempted her to stay right where she was.

Once she had returned to her original position of straddling his waist, she met Mikel's gaze, then quickly lowered her head to his chest and lapped at his nipple, swirling her tongue around the hard nub.

His breathing grew harsh and she could feel his desire, the urgency raging through his body to finish their mating, to join physically as their minds already had. Having never been in control in such a way, the sense of freedom that blossomed inside her soul eased away her remaining fear and apprehension as though they never existed.

As he shuddered beneath her, Mikel groaned. He pulled on his bonds and flexed his hips, rubbing his hard cock against her pussy. "Please, Maryann, let me taste you."

She lifted her head, met his heated gaze. "What?" Had he asked, no begged, for what she thought he had?

"Scoot closer to me so I can reach your pussy, love. I want to taste your cream. I've imagined doing so since the moment I caught your scent aboard my ship that first time."

Surprised, she couldn't help but ask, "You have?" Mikel chuckled, once again forcing her to grip his waist with her thighs so she didn't tumble off him.

"Have you already forgotten that it was your scent—and mine—that trapped us in the *Abacine* suits to begin with?"

She had forgotten that. But why did he want to do that? The thought of his mouth caressing her down there was as exciting as it was embarrassing. She bit her lip, nervous, but secretly titillated at the idea.

"What have you to be frightened of, love? I'm tied up and at your mercy. I can do nothing but what you allow. I merely ask you to allow me to pleasure you with my mouth."

Maryann bit her lip, undecided. What would he think of her if she agreed? She knew he believed he could give her the ultimate in pleasure. Still, she wasn't sure. Could she overcome her hesitance, her self-consciousness and let him kiss her pussy? Did she want him to?

Sighing, she looked at him. He was so handsome, so strong. He had such presence. Even with his hands tied over his head, he had an air of authority and command about him, integrity and honor. Her face burned at the thought of straddling his shoulders, her mound over his face.

Moving slowly, she crawled up his body, laving and licking, waiting for him to make demands. But the demands never came. He merely watched her, a loving expression on his face, in his eyes. She searched his mind and found only his desire to pleasure her, to show her that intimacy wasn't about taking control or causing pain.

It was his resolve to show her she could receive pleasure from intercourse that gave her the courage to straddle his shoulders. Slowly, she lowered her pussy over his mouth.

Chapter Three

Mikel started, amazed she followed his instructions. His mate might still be unsure, but she didn't lack courage. Pride and awe filled his chest when she moved into position. "Grip the headboard, Maryann."

He watched her eyes widen before she swallowed and gripped the ornate titanium rings fastened to the headboard for just that purpose. He had every intention of leading this mating dance, even if it appeared he were the submissive just now. "Now, lower yourself just a little bit more."

Goddess, her scent captivated him. It wrapped around his balls and squeezed. His cock throbbed and his pulse hammered as the smell of her arousal triggered his mating instincts—an instinct that would grow increasingly more difficult to control until his flesh joined with hers and released his seed into her fertile womb.

Only once his child grew safely inside her would the fierce need to mate with her lessen enough that thoughts of lovemaking wouldn't override his common sense. Until then, until they conceived their child, his judgment remained compromised. And considering the enemy they were hunting, the potential danger involved in the Black Rose's capture, that couldn't continue.

But what would Maryann say if she knew that his every instinct would demand he impregnate her immediately, before they had time to get used to being together? Envisioning her heavy with his child, sent another surge of white-hot lust raging through his body, forcing more blood into his already enlarged shaft. He couldn't remember ever being this hard, this desperate for a woman in his many long, long years.

He'd soon reach his nine hundredth birthday, and though still young compared to others of his people, he'd long ago passed the age most of his kind took mates and began their families. No wonder just the thought of her carrying his child made his instincts rage. He'd been waiting his entire life for his Forever Mate—the one woman meant to be his above all others—to come along.

His breath whispered over her flesh, rebounding back with her scent. He could smell her excitement, could even hear her pulse pounding in the otherwise silent room. Through their new bond, he could sense her unease and her willingness to trust him to keep his word, to bring her pleasure.

Something in his heart eased just a bit, calming the need to take her immediately, to rip his bonds and roll her over until she lay beneath him, submissive to his every desire. With that sense of calm, he'd be able to do this for her—give her the gift of pleasure—knowing that, in the end, it would give him so much more. Doing this for her would give him her trust and that was a gift he'd not throw away.

He turned his head to the left, placing a kiss on her inner thigh, then did the same to the right. When her body tensed, then relaxed, he knew going slowly with Maryann and gently leading her where he wanted would net him far better results than rushing onward as his warrior's soul cried out to do.

He continued to press nibbling kisses to her inner-thighs, until her body grew fluid, arching and shivering beneath his touch. Her arousal grew brighter, her scent sweeter as her need rose inside her. When she began to pant and moan, he knew it was time to take this loving further than he had. Finally, he'd get to taste her, to drink of her body.

After drawing in one deep breath, he exhaled, letting the heated puff of air waft over her pussy. The little, red curls on her mound quivered, then grew wetter as a drop of her woman's cream spilled from her channel. This close to her pussy, he could see her clit peeking out and growing redder with pent-up need. Soon, soon, he'd suckle it, until her nectar flowed, bathing him with her essence.

Maryann gasped, then groaned. Her body trembled above his and he could feel her clawing hunger as if it were his own. The sensations multiplied, surging through him and back to her again—loop of pleasure, desire, need and hunger the likes of which neither had ever experienced.

"Please, Mikel. Do something. Please," she sobbed.

Finally, finally she was ready for what he wanted to give her. Thank the Mother Goddess, Mari, that the time to claim a mate and be claimed in return had arrived. How much longer, he wondered, would he have wandered the known galaxies looking for her before going quietly insane, sinking into the madness the absence of a mate inspires?

Now, thanks in part to his friends, Hunter and Amy Shi'Lan, that wasn't to be his fate. Somehow he'd have to thank the *Lionese* couple for putting his mate in his path. But...he'd think on that later. He had much more pleasurable pursuits in mind, for the moment.

Mikel felt her surrender and his heart stuttered, then galloped in his chest in response. He lifted his head away from her mound and stared up at her. Even though her eyes had grown hazy with desire, he knew she could still read his dominance, his possession in his gaze. He wanted her to see, to know and ultimately to trust the male beneath her. Lifting his head, he once again nuzzled her woman's mound. His breath caressed her folds. Her body trembled.

"Mikel," she moaned.

He could hear her desperation, feel it through their new bond—a bond growing stronger every moment. At last. The time to claim her and be claimed in return had arrived. His tongue flicked over her turgid clit, once, twice, three times, then swirled around the nub before delving in her channel.

He explored her with his tongue, wanting—no, needing—to taste her completely, to taste her essence and mark her with his own. Soon, he told himself. Soon.

When Maryann began to arch away from his intimate touch, he nipped her thigh, careful not to break her skin. "Stay still, Maryann. You'll get what you need, love." With a rumbling growl, Mikel went back to feasting on her pussy, licking her from perineum to her clit. He lapped up every drop of her cream as it spilled from her. Her curls were wet with her arousal, her clit rigid and pulsing with need for release.

Please, please, Mikel. I need... I, I, need...

I know just what you need, love. Joy poured into his soul. He hadn't expected Maryann to initiate a telepathic conversation with him—not yet anyway. Taking care not to hurt her, his lips latched on to her clit and suckled it, first gently, then relentlessly, until she exploded, bathing him with her essence. Her keening cries and gasping breaths were music to his ears.

Her body heaved as her muscles jerked. Her thighs flexed, trapping his head between her spread legs as he continued to lap up her woman's cream with slow, lazy strokes. Pride and happiness filled him when Maryann collapsed and cuddled into his chest, nuzzling his neck. Her warm breath caressed his ear, sending shards of erotic sensation through him.

It was time to find out if she truly trusted him enough to release the bonds holding him to the bed. Girding himself for rejection, Mikel took a deep breath, then gently nipped her ear. *What are your plans now? Do you wish to make love with my hands bound or do you want to release me so you can feel the touch of my hands upon your skin?*

Mikel waited to see what would happen next. Her heartbeat sped up until he could feel it pounding against his chest. This wouldn't be easy for her, but if they were to become one, heart and soul, then they must learn to trust one another, completely. Her muscles tensed as though she were going to retreat from him, then she exhaled, relaxing her body against his once again.

Again she nuzzled her nose into his neck and exhaled. His lungs hitched, then stuttered back to life. Would she release his bonds? Did she trust him enough to know he'd rather die a thousand deaths than hurt her?

When she sat up and looked down into his eyes, he thought for sure she'd tell him no. Instead, she leaned forward, her breast swaying in front of his face, teasing him with their nearness. Grabbing one swollen nipple between his lips, he suckled it with strong, hard pulls. When she began to fumble with his bonds, his heartbeat galloped in his chest. She was going to release him.

Releasing her nipple with a smacking pop, he moved to the other swaying breast, desperate to mark her, to place his scent everywhere on her body. She was his and soon she'd be his in every way.

Maryann groaned, then shuddered, but she didn't stop what she was doing. Her arousal scented the air, making it nearly impossible for him to remain still while she completed her task. His cock had long ago starting leaking pre-cum and now, knowing that he'd finally get to sink into her welcoming sheath, he battled his instincts, forcing himself to stifle his dominance. But that wouldn't last long.

He had waited centuries to find his Forever Mate, and knowing the time had come, made it nearly impossible to remain passive. For her, for now, he could. But once those bonds came off, it would take every scrap of his self-control not to attack her as his warrior's soul demanded.

Maryann needed care and consideration during their mating, not a ruthless ravishment. And he was going to do his best to see that she received all she needed—even if he had to use his magick to ease the pressure in his cock. He would do nothing to harm her. Nothing.

MARYANN WRESTLED WITH THE binding strap. By the Goddess, was she doing the right thing by letting him go? She didn't know. But something powerful inside her infused her with a sense of strength she'd never experienced before and gave her the courage to listen to her instincts when it came to this male—this mate of hers. And those same instincts insisted he be free for what happened next so that's what she'd do...if she could get the damn strap off.

When Mikel latched onto her breast and suckled, a flash of heat raced through her from her nipple straight to her clit. *Ah, Gods... Too much, Mikel. It's too much.*

He chuckled in her mind, a sexy rumbling that had goose bumps rippling along her skin. Heat and need, desire and hunger—she felt them all. There were too many sensations raging through her, threatening her composure. The passion he built in her would erupt any moment and it terrified her. Never had she felt this way before—confused, needy, wanting, hungry, animalistic. What had he done to her? What was she supposed to do now?

Just finish what you are doing and then enjoy yourself. I'll never harm you, especially not in love play. I know that we won't always agree and things are sometimes said in the heat of the moment that we later regret for the harm they've caused, but I'd never take out my anger on you. Believe that, love, if nothing else. Trust is built over time and I understand that. Besides, after we finish our mating, time will be something we'll have plenty of.

Maryann froze. *What?*

Once my seed enters you, you'll begin to change on a cellular level. Within weeks, sometimes days, depending on the inner strength of the woman, you'll become like us. You'll be Manruvian.

Dropping her arms, Maryann stared down at her mate. "And you're just now telling me this? Don't you think I should have been told that after we mated I wouldn't be human anymore?" She knew he could hear the hysteria in her voice, but she didn't care. This wasn't a minor detail he'd neglected to tell her. This was life altering.

Not even bothering to stop and think about her actions and what he might do in retaliation, Maryann reached down and pinched both his nipples. "Dammit, how could you forget to tell me something like this?"

"Unghh..."

Mikel moaned, though she could feel his pleasure whipping through her. By the Goddess, he liked the small pain she'd given him. She'd have to remember that for later—when she wasn't so pissed off at him. Her arousal had disappeared the moment he'd made his proclamation. "I might be an ordinary human amongst galaxies full of shifters, but that doesn't mean I'm weak, that you can just do this to me without my permission."

"Calm, love. Without the ceremony, you'll continue to age, and after your passing, I will forever grieve over my loss. Without the transformation, you can't live with me beneath the pink waters of *Manruvia*. Without the transformation, neither of us would feel completely happy with our bonding."

Maryann wanted to scream at his presumption. Why even bother telling her if he hadn't intended on giving her a choice? Pissed beyond belief, she jerked away from Mikel's sprawled body and literally jumped off the bed. She wanted to just get away from him, but she sure as hell wasn't going to leave his rooms naked and give the rest of the crew on his ship a free show. How had tonight gone so wrong?

About to lambast him, her eyes widened when his bonds magically untied from his hands and feet. Her spine stiffened and her hands fisted at her sides. Why that son of a bitch. "You could have just loosened your bonds at any time, couldn't you?" she accused.

She watched as he scooted up the bed and crossed his arms over his chest, doing her best to ignore his cock, standing at attention. It looked too long and thick to fit inside her comfortably. Maryann swallowed before giving herself a mental slap. She had things to say and she wasn't about to be distracted by Mikel's body.

"Yes, doesn't that tell you something?"

"Yeah, it tells me that you played me from the start. You're a liar."

Mikel scowled, sat up, then swung his legs over the side of the bed and began to rise.

Wary, Maryann retreated just a step, but it was enough to get his attention and kept him seated at the edge of the bed. "Why, Mikel? Why didn't you tell me what mating entailed? Did you think I'd let you get away with taking my choices away from me? I won't. Never again will I allow someone to tell me how it's going to be. I may be human, but by the Goddess, I'm not a wimp."

Mikel sucked in a deep breath and raised his eyebrows, seemingly surprised by her tirade.

Good. She wouldn't be anyone's doormat. She may have had bad things happen to her, but she wouldn't allow them to control her life. Nothing and no one would make decisions about her life without consulting her first—not ever again.

Running his hand through his hair, Mikel sighed. "Honestly, it never crossed my mind that you wouldn't realize that the mating would change you, Maryann."

"And I'm just supposed to believe that?" How stupid did he think she was? A wave of hurt washed through her and it took a moment for her to realize it was Mikel's. The brilliance in his blue-green eyes dimmed and his lips turned down in a grimace.

"Yes, Maryann. If you bothered to listen with more than your ears, if you used the bond between us, you'd know I'm telling you the truth."

After searching his gaze for a moment, Maryann moved back toward the bed, toward Mikel. Her shoulders sagged, knowing she'd hurt him by accusing him of lying to her. Perhaps she overreacted, but it was so hard to trust, even knowing he couldn't lie to her without her knowing. The bond between them was new, but she couldn't use that as an excuse. By the Goddess, she could be such an insensitive bitch sometimes.

Knowing it was up to her to set things right, she closed the distance between them and knelt on the floor between his legs. Her eyes of course zeroed right in on his cock. What red-blooded human woman wouldn't? When Mikel cleared his throat, Maryann snapped her gaze up, embarrassed that he caught her gaping at his erection.

Not sure what to do with her hands, she kept them folded on her lap. "I'm sorry I blew up at you the way I did. It was uncalled for and, though it's not a good excuse, I'm not used to being near a man who's honorable. I shouldn't have compared you to others in my past, even subconsciously."

Mikel framed her face with his hands, a small smile tilting up the corners of his lips. His thumb lightly caressed her bottom lip, sending shards of pleasure zipping through her body. "It's all right, love. I shouldn't have assumed you knew what mating entailed. That was my mistake."

Sagging with relief, Maryann reached up and held Mikel's hands against her cheeks. "Do you think we could get back to what we were doing before I had my meltdown?" She prayed he'd say yes. Though she was new to lovemaking, she knew without a doubt that it would be wonderful between them if they ever got around to actually having sex.

Rather than answer her directly, he picked her up by the waist as if she weighed nothing and pulled her onto his lap. "Wrap your legs around my waist, love."

Her eyes widened, knowing full well that once she did so, his cock would be nestled against her naked pussy. Nothing would prevent them from joining now.

"High Prince Logann, there is a high priority message coming through for you from *Manruvia* on the secured frequency," the intercom broke in, slicing through the sexual tension developing between them.

Maryann dropped her head against Mikel's chest. Nothing but an urgent message from *Skalldari* could prevent their joining apparently.

Chuckling, Mikel sat alongside her on the bed. *I'm sure it's just a message from my father asking about our progress. Why don't you slide under the covers so you don't catch a chill while I talk with him, okay?"*

Sure, she replied, though a sense of doom invaded her consciousness. Whatever the incoming message was, it carried nothing but bad news. As she watched Mikel head toward his private communication terminal, Maryann prayed that whatever the message, she'd be strong enough to help Mikel get through it.

Chapter Four

As soon as *Skalldari* interrupted them with a message from home, Mikel knew something catastrophic must have happened on *Manruvia*. Only something dire would compel the sentient ship to go against orders not to disturb them. After quickly donning lounge pants and a tunic, he pressed his security code into the communication terminal and waited for the transmission to begin.

He could feel his mate's concern through their bond and knew that however disastrous the news, having her by his side would make it bearable. But that didn't stop his gut from clenching in dread or his mind racing with questions.

When his mother's tear ravaged face filled the screen, his heart stuttered in his chest. Sweat broke out on his brow and his knees shook. "Mother... What is it?"

"Your father, Lortan, is in a coma. We need you here."

His voice cracked, "What happened?"

"Your father's personal physician believes he's succumbed to poisoning."

Behind him, Mikel heard the rustling of bedclothes. Seconds later, his mate took his hand in hers. He looked down in her concerned eyes, then squeezed her hand in thanks. Looking back toward his mother, Vandora, the current *Manruvian* queen, he cleared his throat. "We'll be there in two days, Mother."

More tears trailed down his mother's cheeks, but he didn't take it as a sign of weakness, just proof of the deep love she felt for his father. "Thank you, my son. You and I both know that with your father unable to lead, you must assume the throne quickly to avoid a coup."

"I understand, Mother. We'll be there as soon as possible."

His mother's gaze strayed toward Maryann. "I'm sorry we must first meet under such difficult circumstances. Mikel has long awaited his mate, and as his parents, we've looked forward to the day he would bring you home to us."

"Please, you don't have anything to apologize for. If there is anything I can do for you when I get there to make things easier on you, anything at all, please, don't hesitate to ask, Queen Logann."

"We shall take your words to heart, Maryann. Now, I must go, my son. Much unrest has overtaken our cities since word of your father's illness has spread."

"I understand. Please, take your rest while you can. We shall be there soon, Mother." As the communication panel grew dark, Maryann's steady presence at his back did more to soothe his nerves in that moment than anything thing she could have possibly said.

After a few minutes of companionable silence, Maryann drew back. "I'll go to my rooms. I'm sure you'll have some calls you'll need to make to your allies—to the Shi'Lans—to Hunter, Taliff and to Brantiff. He'll want to know that his closest in rank has fallen to poison. I imagine he'll have good advice to impart if you'll listen to him."

Mikel reached out for Maryann's wrist as she passed. "Wait, Maryann. Thank you. I know none of this has been easy for you. You didn't ask for anything that's happened to you and now I'm asking for you to handle even more. Are you're sure you're up to this?"

"Do you doubt me, think that because I'm human, I'm any less capable of handling the duties that are going to be thrust on me the moment I step foot on your planet? Get real. Right now, I have to go to my room and learn protocol from *Skalldari* because you certainly are in no shape to teach me and I don't think you would be the one to normally do so anyway. So…" As Maryann gently pried her wrist from his grasp, she continued toward the door. "You do your thing and I'll do mine."

By the time Maryann escaped, and she'd definitely escaped, Mikel didn't know what to think of the woman she'd become the last few minutes in his presence. She definitely had taken charge and he had liked it.

AS THE DOORS CLOSED behind Maryann, she shook her head, surprised at her own outburst. "*Skalldari*, take me to the Archives room. I need to know what to expect when we land on *Manruvia*. If they've poisoned the king, I can only assume there is some kind of coup underway and I need to know how we can thwart such an attempt."

"As you command, Maryann." Between one heartbeat and the next, Maryann found herself inside what she could only surmise was the Archives room. Not only were there two walls of bookshelves overflowing with texts of every size, but computer equipment covered several long conference style tables. The room itself looked like a library on Earth and immediately she felt at ease. Now if only she could read the language in the books, they might get somewhere.

Skalldari's voice echoed in the small room, drawing her attention away from the rows of texts she longed to investigate. "If someone poisoned the king, then right now, High Prince Logann is the Presumptive King and you, the Queen in Waiting. The Trident of Accession must be passed from mother to son and then you and he will officially be in power. But before that can happen, you two must be mated first."

"Mated first… You mean we have to finish having sex first and then he changes me, like he explained tonight before his mother's call interrupted us?"

"Yes, Maryann. Once his people sense his DNA mingling with yours, once the mating mark appears, they'll know you've officially mated and then they'll accept his right to take up the Trident of Accession and rule in his father's stead. No one other than his parents knows he's found his mate. No one could have predicted this, which is to your advantage. This mating might be the only thing that can save Prince Logann's world from whatever someone has planned for it."

Maryann snorted. "You and I know exactly who has done this *Skalldari*. Mikel has stood by the Shi'Lans against the Black Rose throughout the years, fighting her slavers, hunting her breeding camps and freeing her slaves. She'll do whatever she can to destroy Mikel and his people as an act of revenge. Besides, with the king incapacitated, Mikel has no choice but to return home, leaving the hunt for the Black Rose and her followers to others."

Looking around the small chamber, her gaze once again locked onto the bookshelves loaded down with books. Some looked ancient while others looked fairly modern. She couldn't wait to get lost amidst the history of the *Manruvians*. Back on Earth, before her kidnapping, she had spent hours every day reading books—everything from ancient history about Earth's early civilizations to modern day romances, thrillers and fantasies.

Escaping into the worlds created by others helped her cope with her differences. As the only human among shifters, her life had not been easy and she found early on that books were her salvation when things grew too hard to handle amidst her stepfather's people, the *Lionese*.

As though her feet had a mind of their own, she found herself standing in front of one wall of shelves, contemplating the many titles on the spines. Most she couldn't translate, but she was determined that one day she'd read everything in here. For now, she looked for something—anything—written in a language she did know. Perhaps the *Manruvians* had some sort of technology that would help her learn their language.

As Mikel's mate and the queen of the *Manruvian* people, she'd need to communicate with those around her. Depending on others to translate for her would only emphasize the fact that she was different, a Human reliant on others to see to her needs. She'd not embarrass Mikel that way.

"*Skalldari*, do you have some sort of technology on this ship that will teach me *Manruvian* quickly? If I'm to be helpful to Mikel, I'm going to need to understand what's going on around me."

"There are several options available. However, the most expedient and least invasive option is to allow Mikel to finish the mating. Once you've been exposed to the *Manruvian* genome, you'll find that speaking the language comes naturally."

Maryann sighed and crossed her arms over her breasts. "Well that figures, doesn't it? Everything about these people revolves around sex and mating. It makes me wonder what my life is going to be like with the man. Boring definitely does *not* come to mind." She gave a half grin. "*Skalldari,* would you be so kind as to send me to see my mate? I need to speak with him."

Boy did she need to speak with him. Not only did everything on his planet revolve around their finishing their bond, even her own ability to read every one of those delicious-looking books in that huge library depended on it. She grinned, a plan forming in her mind. She was hunting and nothing was going to keep her from her mate this time.

"Of course, Maryann."

Almost as soon as the computer spoke, Maryann found herself not in Mikel's quarters as she expected, but on a sandy white beach that seemed to stretch out for miles. Turquoise water crashed on the shore, its white-capped waves foaming in the distance. Rocks and boulders jutted out of the water and she imagined Merfolk sunning themselves atop of them.

Maryann could hear seagulls flying overhead and immediately searched the skies for them. Lifting her hand to cover her eyes, she wasn't surprised to see three suns overhead, rather than the one that she was used to seeing on Earth. A warm breeze lifted her hair from around her neck. She closed her eyes and smiled. Taking a deep breath, she inhaled the scent of the ocean and wished nothing more than to strip down to her skin and take a dip.

Where am I? "*Skalldari*, where am I?"

"You are in the recreation suite. This is as close to Prince Logann's home world as he can get without actually being there. When a *Manruvian* is worried, he tends to spend time in the water here, allowing it to free his mind, to think and to plot."

"And you're sure Mikel is in here?" Why she doubted the sentient computer, she didn't know. The sand, the water—it was beautiful. How could he stand to be elsewhere on the ship when this was here to tempt him?

"He's beneath the waters, but he should surface soon if you want to wait for him."

"Thank you, *Skalldari*. You've been a huge help during the last few days. I think I'll go to the water's edge and let the waves tickle my toes while Mikel finishes his swim."

"Of course. If you need anything else, just call my name. I'll hear you."

Chapter Five

MIKEL LAY AT THE BOTTOM OF THE OCEAN AND ALLOWED THE WATER to surround him in its comforting caress. Closing his eyes, he let his worries and fears drift away with the current. Here, in the waters so similar to those of *Manruvia*, he could embrace the other half of his soul. It'd been too long since he had last swum, allowing his body to shift into its other form—that of a *Manruvian* Merman.

As his tail swayed back and forth in the cool water, his thoughts turned to the conversation he had with Brantiff Shi'Lan just before he sought the sanctuary of the *Manruvian* waters.

"Mikel, during any time of political unrest, you must always search for answers other than what is obvious. Those you thought of as friends could now be enemies. Look beyond the facts in front of you for the reasons behind this attack against your people."

"And if it proves to be more than just a coup for my father's throne?"

Brantiff stood straight, raised his fist to his heart before saying. "Then know that the *Chantreans* will be by your side to rout your enemy as soon as you call for reinforcements. We *will* be there."

Mikel nodded at the screen, both relieved and thankful for the staunch support of his allies. "Between us, hopefully we can get to the bottom of this while my father heals. I never expected to become king of my people this soon, but I will strive to make you and my people proud."

Brantiff smiled. "I have no doubts in your ability to lead your people well. You have a good heart and strong character, and keep the safety of your people as your priority."

With one last wave, the communication terminal went dark. Mikel's thoughts automatically turned to Maryann, wondering what she had discovered about the proper protocol of his people when ascending to the throne. His cock hardened at the thought. Soon, she'd learn that everything hinged on their mating. Would she come to him once she made that discovery or would he have to go to her? Thoughts like that would get him nowhere fast except sexually frustrated. Instead, he headed toward the bridge, intent on giving his crew new orders to head to *Manruvia*.

As soon as he entered the bridge, Mikel headed toward Commander Sutter. "Commander, please make haste toward *Manruvia*. The pursuit of the Black Rose will have to wait. As soon as we're within an hour of landing, please contact me via *Skalldari*. For now, I'll be in the recreation center."

The commander saluted, his face showing his concern for the sudden change of plans though he didn't ask questions. "As you say, Prince Logann. It will be done."

As Mikel left the Command Deck, he heard Sutter shouting orders to his crew. Mikel knew without a doubt that he'd miss this ship, its people and the battles they engaged in with the Black Rose. Here he could see the difference his people made as they rescued the slaves she and her people captured to use as breeders.

Thinking about the Black Rose did naught but anger him. Without a doubt, he knew she was behind the coup on his home world. He didn't know who had poisoned his father, but he would. Sooner or later, that person would be caught and suffer the consequences. But he didn't doubt the culprit was nothing more than a pawn in her agenda. He would take Brantiff's words to heart and look beyond the obvious.

Shaking his head, Mikel wove through the waters, allowing his body the freedom it had been too long denied. Faster and faster, he swam. Here he could relax, could embrace the other half of his soul. Even knowing that Maryann was somewhere on the ship waiting for him, he was reluctant to leave the sanctuary of the holographic ocean.

Mikel grinned. He couldn't wait until after her transformation, until she could join him as they frolicked in the water together. There's nothing like making love in the water, he thought to himself. He couldn't imagine how much better it would be with his destined mate. And just like that, his cock hardened. Thank the Goddess, that in this form, he could hide his erection from the others swimming nearby. Unless he pulled his cock out of its protective pouch, no one would be the wiser.

Again, he sped up, twisting and weaving through the water as fast as his body would go. Beneath the sea, there was a sense of freedom that walking on land never gave him. It lightened his spirits and renewed his faith. As he swam toward the surface of the turquoise water, his heart beat faster in his chest. His entire body quivered in joy.

He knew then his mate had come to him. Even though he could breathe underwater, his lungs felt starved for air. Knowing that she was so close, that soon she would be his mate in fact, that within minutes he could be sinking into her flesh becoming a part of her, as she would become a part of him, filled him with happiness. By the Goddess, he couldn't wait.

Mari, the Goddess of the sea, was said to bless the couple if they mated for the first time in the waters of *Manruvia*. Though they weren't on his home planet, he hoped mating here would suffice, because no way could he wait two more days before making love to her. The last week had been a living hell. Never before had he been so sexually frustrated—not even when he'd first reached his sexual maturity and reveled in the sexual act, exploring all his sexual fantasies with the pleasure nymphs on the Verunian home world.

Mikel couldn't help but wonder if Maryann was waiting for him on the shore as desperate to make love to him as he was for her. He knew that once they landed on *Manruvia* there would be many challenges to face. There would be opposition to their mating, for she was human and not one of his people, something no one in the royal line had ever done. Not only that, but he had to discover who'd poisoned his father and take up Triton of Ascension, something he'd not had time to prepare for.

He had two days to cement the fragile bond building between them—two days to tie Maryann to his side, both emotionally and physically. As Mikel broke the surface of the water, he laughed in absolute joy. Two days was plenty long enough.

His gaze immediately zeroed in on Maryann where she lounged on the shore. Seeing Maryann with her head tossed back, her face tilted up toward the sun and a smile of contentment stretched across her face, filled Mikel's soul with peace. Nothing made him happier than knowing his mate was happy. Maryann's auburn hair fluttered in the soft breeze, looking sexy and tousled as if she'd just been thoroughly fucked in bed play.

Knowing that she realized he swam nearby and remained on the shore looking as though she enjoyed their people's sanctuary—aware that soon he'd make her his—encouraged him to close the distance between them quickly, even though watching her while she remained unaware was a pleasure in itself. He'd have plenty of time to watch her from afar—after he sealed their bond.

As THE SUN WARMED her face, Maryann's thoughts turned to Mikel, something they'd done with increasing frequency over the last week or so, much to her chagrin. Thank the Goddess that the *Abacine* suit no longer plagued her with sexual arousal. Not to say that the idea of mating with Mikel didn't arouse her. Shockingly it did, especially considering all she'd been through at the hands of the Black Rose.

But now arousal simmered just below the surface, merely waiting for him to encourage it to fever pitch once again. She didn't know whether that was a good thing or not. Either way, her time to get used to the idea of taking someone to her bed willingly had run out. It was time to make Mikel her mate, in fact, time to make love to him.

Off to her right, Maryann heard a loud splash. Without looking, she knew Mikel was nearby because the connection between them sparked to life. She could feel his happiness, his joy at seeing her sitting on the shore waiting for him. It would take getting used to knowing she could feel everything Mikel did, knowing he could feel her emotions as well.

That didn't bother her as much as she thought it would though. It could end up being beneficial knowing what mood her husband was in before ever seeing him, therefore knowing when to avoid him and when to soothe him.

Maryann almost chuckled at the thought. She couldn't imagine herself in that role, but she didn't doubt she would more often than not want to ease Mikel if something were to bother him. That's the way Eve and Taliff Shi'Lan were, as well as Hunter and Amy Shi'Lan—something to do with the strength of the mate bond between the pairs, no doubt.

Anxious to know what Mikel looked like in his merman form, Maryann turned her head, just in time to see him explode out of the water, do a forward flip, then dive beneath the waves. In that one instant, she was stunned out how absolutely beautiful he looked.

His lower half shimmered, his scales ranging from the lightest silvery blue to the brightest teal and aqua she had ever seen. With the sun shining down on him, he seemed to glow. She sucked in a breath, awed at his beauty. His chest gleamed, water rivulets running down his washboard abs.

Even now, when she could no longer see him, she could still see him in her mind's eye. His long hair hung to his shoulders in reckless waves and he'd been laughing in absolute joy. She'd never forget this moment, never forget seeing him so happy and carefree. She had a feeling those moments had been few and far between in his life—like hers. Maybe that would change—maybe not. Time would surely tell.

Lost in her thoughts, she hadn't realized Mikel had come to shore until his shadow blocked out the sun and water dripped onto her thighs. Meeting his gaze, she wasn't surprised to see the arousal in his eyes. She'd felt it from the moment their link snapped back in place once she'd settled herself on the shore. What did surprise her was the very large erection just inches from her mouth. Instead of feeling fear as she expected, she had the insane urge to lean forward and take him in her mouth.

"Do it," Mikel growled.

Maryann blushed. She couldn't help it, not knowing he'd heard her thoughts. Their bond must be growing stronger, she thought, because he was definitely picking up more than her emotions now.

Maryann quirked her eyebrows, not quite willing to submit to him yet. Let him work for it, work for her surrender. Besides, out of the corner of her eye she could see others swimming in the distance and she didn't want others to watch them making love. Maybe after she was secure in her relationship and her reactions to Mikel that would change, but for now, she wanted privacy if she were going to be intimate with him.

Energy built around him. It wasn't something she could see. She felt it, sensed it was there more than anything else. A strange sound emanated from him. A low, keening vibration caught the attention of everyone in the huge chamber. He opened his mouth and strange sounding words came out, though somehow, she knew what they meant.

All within hearing must listen. All within hearing must obey. Leave the cool water. Leave your Mother's warmth. Leave your prince and his woman and return another day.

Chapter Six

MIKEL LOOKED AT HIS WOMAN WHILE HE WAITED FOR THE OTHERS TO obey his command. Under normal circumstances, he wouldn't throw his people out of the recreation room as the ocean was a solace to them, but not today. Today however, his need to make Maryann his in every sense of the word overrode his compassion for his shipmates. They'd just have to wait until tomorrow to feel the welcoming hold the sea provided them.

Today, he wanted the place reserved for them alone. Here, he'd finally make Maryann his mate, join his body to hers in as close to the proper setting as possible while still traveling through deep space.

Mikel watched Maryann swallow nervously, then look away only to dart a sneaking glance at his erect cock. He chuckled when her face turned pink in embarrassment. How he had lived so long without this bond with another, he had no idea. Now that she was a part of him, he couldn't imagine a day where he wouldn't want to hear her thoughts or feel her emotions.

Maryann licked her lips, then raised her head, looking him straight in the eye. "Why did you send everyone away?"

Wrapping his hand around his erection, Mikel slowly began to stroke his cock, from the base to the head and back down again. Up. Down. Up. Down. His slow, rhythmic movements drew her gaze once again to his raging hard-on—right where he wanted it. "You know why I sent them away, Maryann. It made you uncomfortable having them nearby, knowing what I'd want from you—what we both want. They can come back tomorrow."

He nearly laughed when he watched her look down the shore in both directions, nibbling her lip in indecision. He knew she'd not been with anyone other than her rapists so he could understand her hesitance at lovemaking in a public location. She was new to intimacy after all.

How would she take it when she learned that it was common to come upon a couple mating out in the open on his world, that his people were comfortable making love out in the open or in the sea where anyone could stumble upon them at any time? It might be wiser not to mention that part of his people's customs until after they'd sealed the mating. He didn't want anything to run her off, not after waiting so long to find a mate of his own.

At close to nine hundred summers, most of his friends and peers had long ago taken mates. It took battling Hunter Shi'Lan's sister, the Black Rose, to bring him to the one soul that matched his own. He wouldn't lose her—not to his own stupidity and not to the political intrigue that would surely surround them once they reached *Manruvia,* and would most certainly not lose her again to the Black Rose. He'd defy Mari, the Goddess of the Sea herself, to keep Maryann at his side.

As the silence between them lengthened, Mikel couldn't help but wonder what Maryann's next move would be. Would she balk at making love near the sea his people craved or would she enthusiastically participate? He couldn't wait to find out.

After another quick glance in every direction, Maryann tentatively reached out and trailed her finger down the length of his cock. Mikel's stomach muscles clenched. His thighs trembled. Just that slight touch and it became nearly impossible to stand still so she could have free reign over his body. For now, he'd let Maryann control the pace of their love play—for as long as he could stand to anyway.

When she wrapped her hand around his erection just above his own hand, he almost came. His breathing grew harsh and sweat ran in rivulets down his spine. By the Goddess Mari, nothing had ever felt so good and all she'd done was grip him. How much better would it feel once he finally sank his cock into her? He had no idea, but he couldn't wait to find out.

When she hesitantly began to slide her hand up and down his cock, he gritted his teeth and dropped his hand. To keep himself from reaching out and pulling her against his body, he fisted his hands down by his sides. It took all his control not to clench his hands in her hair and pull her face to his jutting shaft so she'd take him into her mouth. Soon, he promised himself. Soon.

Maryann's stroking grew firmer, the feel of her hand more sure around his cock. It took only a moment to realize she knew just what her touch did to him. Though it pleased him she used their bond, he knew he wouldn't withstand her touch for long—not without coming entirely too soon.

Knowing he was but moments away from losing what little of his control remained, Mikel stepped back, forcing Maryann to let go of his aching cock.

"*Skalldari*," Mikel growled, his gaze intent on Maryann, "Place the Royal *Manruvian* Mating Bed five meters to the right of my position and far enough back that it stays dry. Then lock the doors so no one may enter."

"As you command, Prince Logann. Processing."

When the ceremonial bed materialized several meters behind Maryann, Mikel bent over, scooped her off the sand and stood in one continuous motion. When she nestled against his chest, placing her ear against his thudding heartbeat, he nuzzled the top of her hair, inhaling the sweet smell of *Tupa* Blossoms in her hair, which only enhanced Maryann's already exquisite scent.

"Wrap your arms around my neck, *vasha*."

Maryann complied immediately. Her hard nipples scraped against the rough hair of his chest with each step he took toward the bed. It was torture despite the clothes that separated her flesh from his. He couldn't wait to once again feel her body pressed against his, skin to skin, with no barriers between them. Just thinking such thoughts sent more blood rushing to his cock, causing it to throb and bounce against her bottom.

With the need to possess her riding him mercilessly, he quickened his pace, reaching the bed in seconds. Gently, he eased her down onto the bedding, then placed a tender kiss across her forehead before trailing his lips over her cheek, down her neck, before finally reaching the pulsing hollow at the base of her throat.

Maryann moaned, writhing beneath him as eager for his touch as he wanted—no, needed—to touch her.

"Please, Mikel."

"Please, what? What do you want, Maryann?" he asked, needing to hear her pleading for his touch.

After swallowing nervously, Maryann met his gaze. Her eyes were heavy-lidded and smoldering with arousal. "Please, Mikel, kiss me."

"That wasn't too hard, *vasha*. Now was it?" Not waiting for a response, his mouth covered hers hungrily. His tongue traced the soft fullness of her lower lip before demanding entry. He kissed her like a man possessed, devouring her. His tongue dueled with hers, thrusting and parrying, demanding her surrender.

When her body relaxed against his, he softened his kiss, coaxing rather than conquering. His body was on fire for her, raging at him to complete the mating. With trembling fingers, he began to unbutton her blouse with one hand while the other tangled in her hair, holding her head imprisoned so he could continue to ravage her mouth with his. By the Goddess, he couldn't get enough of her—not enough of her taste, not enough of her spirit and definitely not enough of her body.

After slipping the last button from its buttonhole, Mikel broke their kiss. Maryann mewled her displeasure at the sudden loss of his mouth against hers. He wanted—no, needed—to know what she was feeling. With shaking hands, he spread her blouse apart, leaving her heaving chest open to his gaze, but he wanted to see more of her. He wanted to see everything. After popping the front clasp of her bra open and pulling the lacy cups away from her breasts, he stared in awe. He swallowed. Hard. Unable to speak aloud, he used their telepathic connection instead. *Open your eyes,* vasha.

Without hesitating, Maryann's eyelids fluttered opened. He sucked in a breath at the naked emotion displayed in her eyes. Passion and need, desire and trust, all evidence of the strengthening bond growing between them. He could get lost in her eyes, lost in the passion and desire he could so easily see there. For so long he'd waited for his mate, his perfect half, and in Maryann, he'd finally found her. He could hardly believe it—could hardly believe she was the one, but the evidence was looking him right in the eye.

MARYANN GASPED AS HE stood before her, glorious in his nudity. His blond hair gleamed in the sunlight like a halo and his aquamarine eyes glittered with passion as he oh so slowly lowered himself over her body. With his every masculine curve plastered against her feminine ones, her pussy began to spasm with need.

"Now I have you exactly where I want you, Maryann. And there is nothing you can do about it."

"Who said I'd want to do anything about it? I like where I'm at."

Mikel chuckled. "Hmmm...You're sassy. I think I like that in a mate," he whispered as his lips slowly grazed her ear, her neck, until they finally slid down to the base of her throat.

He gently nipped her at her pulse point, then swirled his tongue over the tiny wound. Goosebumps pebbled across her skin in reaction. She arched into his touch, desperate to feel his lips glide further down her body.

Mikel's mouth drifted down past her neck until he reached the top of her breasts. When he flicked his tongue over her rigid nipples, Maryann moaned. Again and again, he stroked her hardened peaks while gently rasping his teeth against them. When she thought she could take no more, he eased away from her nipples and swirled his tongue on the underside of her breasts, his obvious intent to drive her absolutely crazy.

After taking each of her nipples into his mouth one last time, he released them with a pop before moving down her belly to her navel. "Goddess, Mikel. What are you trying to do to me?"

"Turnabout is fair play, *vasha*."

"I've been meaning to ask… What does *vasha* mean?"

"It's a term of endearment. It's 'dear one' in *Manruvian*."

Again she leaned into his touch. She needed to come and she needed it now. "Please, Mikel. Stop torturing me already. Let me come."

Goosebumps once again rippled across her skin, her every nerve ending felt on fire and still he methodically trailed his lips past her belly, her pussy, until he finally reached the inner thigh of her right leg. He nipped her, leaving his mark on her pale skin, then eased the tiny ache with his tongue before he drifted lower down her body. Maryann screamed her displeasure when he skipped over her pussy. She was desperate to feel his tongue delving into her aching cunt. But no, he was bent on seduction and torture, she was sure of it.

His lips slowly trailed down her thigh, her calf, then to her ankle, all the time ignoring her pleas for mercy, her cries to ease her need. After suckling on the toes on her left foot, he moved to her right, kissing and nipping his way up her right leg, nipping and swirling his tongue around to the back of her knee and up her inner thigh. Whoever taught Mikel the ways of lovemaking knew the proper ways of seducing a woman, of that there were no doubts.

Maryann thought she'd die if he didn't stop this slow act of seduction. Mikel looked up into Maryann's eyes and gave her a slow smile before dropping his head, then he carefully eased her thighs apart. With exaggerated slowness, he leaned forward and softly blew on her pulsing clit. He did everything in slow motion, as though he had all the time in the world—at least, that's what it felt like to her passion-fogged mind. By the Goddess, what she wouldn't give for a good, hard, quick, fuck. To hell with seduction. She could just scream in frustrated agony. As far as she was concerned, seduction was overrated.

Then scream, vasha.

When she thought she could take no more, he took her clit between his teeth and gave it a slight tug. Maryann did scream, then her entire body shook with frustrated longing. She was so close to climaxing, she knew that one more good tug on her clit and she'd explode. She couldn't stop the rumble of contentment that erupted from her chest—

didn't want to. She was so close to climax, she'd beg to come if she had to. If she didn't get off soon, she might just kill him if he didn't kill her first. But damn, the wait just might be worth dying over. "Please, Mikel. Let me come, please."

"You must learn some patience, Maryann. The more drawn out the lovemaking is, the greater the pleasure you will feel in the end."

"Ughhh... I can't last much longer, Mikel. I really can't. You've made me wait long enough as it is."

Mikel lips tilted up in a carnal smile. Pure deviltry lit up his eyes as though she'd dared him with her statement.

"You'll take whatever I give you and love it, *vasha*. I could keep you on the edge for hours if I wanted and in the end, you'd thank me."

His touch gentle, Mikel spread her thighs further apart with his fingers, exposing her pussy to his gaze. "You have such a beautiful pink cunt, *vasha*. I can't wait to taste your woman's cream."

He put his words to action and bent his head to her woman's mound. A deep moan rumbled from his chest as he stroked her pussy with his tongue. He swirled it around and around her erect clit and between her pussy lips as he lapped up her dripping nectar.

Oh, Goddess. The pleasure was so intense, unlike anything she ever felt before in her life. None of the experiences in her past could compare to this. What she'd suffered at the hands of the Black Rose had been a violation of the worst sort where this was a celebration of life, a man claiming his woman and a woman staking a claim on her man.

Unable to stay still under Mikel's tender assault, Maryann began to squirm. Determined to keep her still, he gripped her by her thighs and held her immobile as he continued to eat at her without mercy, until she was nearly incoherent, begging him to stop, pleading with him not to.

He must have realized she could take no more, for he eased away, gave each of her thighs a tiny peck, then lifted her by her waist and flipped Maryann gently onto her stomach.

He quickly slid into place behind her, replacing his lips with his throbbing cock. Slowly he stretched her tight pussy as he sank into her silken depths. He eased himself in and out ever so gently, in and out, in and out, until he reached full penetration.

Once sure he'd seated himself fully inside her, he started to thrust with ever-increasing force. She could feel every vein in his cock, every beat of his heart, every emotion in his soul through their joining. Never had she thought to feel such exquisite sensations with and for another.

Maryann met each stroke with one of her own, frantic to feel that connection, to feel his balls slap against her ass when they came together. She could feel his cock sliding through her pussy as though it were her own, feel her pussy clasping his cock as though she were the one thrusting inside him. The sensations were so intense, so overwhelming, but she wouldn't stop them for anything. And each thrust carried her closer and closer to climax.

She was so close to coming. It was time to take matters into her own hands. Knowing instinctively just what to do, she clenched her inner muscles around his engorged shaft, making the fit just that much tighter. His thrusts became stronger, his groans rumbled in his chest even louder. Within seconds, he drove her over the edge of the world. The pleasure was pure, explosive and more intense than anything she could have imagined possible.

Her thoughts fragmented as his hands and lips continued their hungry search of her body even as his thrusts grew still stronger, still deeper, if that were even possible. All she could do—all she wanted to do—was hold on and enjoy the ride as explosive pleasure invaded every cell of her body. Lassitude began to seep in, but still Mikel forged through her pussy, striving to reach his own completion. Their connection forged a circle of tremendous completion. She thought she might collapse with pleasure. All she could do was take it as all her nerve endings seemed to fire simultaneously. How could anyone survive such sensations?

Unable to hold back his release any longer, Mikel stiffened and Maryann felt the ropes of his come jet deep inside her sheath. The pleasure was unbearable and seemed never-ending. Finally, unable to hold herself up any longer, she collapsed onto the bedding, dislodging

Mikel unceremoniously in the process.

Mikel collapsed onto the bed next to her, then quickly took Maryann into his arms as he rolled onto his side, spooning with her. While her heartbeat slowed and the silence spread over them like a warm blanket, Maryann drank in the comfort of his steady strength. She felt the joy of being cherished as a mate as she lay safe within the security of Mikel's arms, rather than the fear of being the victim that the Black Rose had made her. It felt so good to be held so snugly against his side. Turning over, she buried her face against the corded muscles of his chest and took the time to breathe in his scent.

"Are you okay, Maryann?" he asked.

Mikel's voice sent another round of ripples through her. Her clit twitched in response. How could she still be horny after he so thoroughly ravaged her body? "Hmm...never been better," she murmured, though the strange tingling on her face and the burning sensations below were giving her second thoughts. What the hell was up with her burning crotch? And why the hell was her the skin around her eye itching? Was Mikel contagious? Was she catching some fishy disease or something?

Mikel, what the hell did you do to me?

Chapter Seven

Mikel laughed. He couldn't stop the chuckle even though he knew his mate didn't find her current situation the least bit funny. He wouldn't if it were happening to him. How to tell her what was happening were perfectly normal without making her madder than his laughing had already made her?

Maryann, the only affliction I have is my addiction to you. And what you're experiencing is normal if, a bit uncomfortable. It will pass shortly.

Uncomfortable! You Ass. This is more than uncomfortable. Getting your teeth cleaned is uncomfortable. Wearing thong underwear is uncomfortable. This burns like a son of a bitch. This is more than uncomfortable. What the hell is happening to me?

Hoping to calm her down through touch, Mikel began making small circles on her back with his hand, soothing her the best he could. "Your body is going through the conversion, *vasha*. You knew of this beforehand. The burning in your body is your cells adjusting, forming the necessary cellular changes so that once you're exposed to the *Manruvian* waters for the first time, you'll be able to shift and breathe under water as if you'd always been one of us. The itching around your eye is your mating mark forming. It is how our people will know on sight that you are my mate. No one will doubt it once they look upon you."

"Well, you should have warned me. It hurts, Mikel. A little warning of what to expect would have been nice."

"Noted. There won't be any further surprises if I can help it. I plan on having a full partnership with you, Maryann. I saw the damage that

Eve suffered when Taliff treated her as less than an equal. I won't do the same to you. You are my other half, the one woman I've waited for most of my life. I won't make the same mistakes he did."

Maryann snorted against his chest. "No, you'll make different ones."

Mikel sighed, aware his mate still felt slighted by his lapse. "If my mother had told me of the pain of transformation, I would have told you, Maryann. I regret that I did not ask her when we spoke earlier. But she had much on her mind." Immediately he could sense her compassion and her sense of shame, quickly followed by regret.

"No, you were right not to bother your mother over our mating. Your mother's wellbeing as well as your father and his health and the safety of your people should be your main priorities right now. What's happening to me is trivial in comparison."

"Nothing about you is trivial, *vasha*."

Maryann must have liked that response because he felt her smile against his chest, felt her happiness through their bond. As Maryann's breathing grew slower, he eased his strokes along her back until he felt certain she drifted asleep. She needed to rest for the coming days ahead. As a matter of fact, so would he. His last thoughts as darkness descended upon him were of his mother and the heartbreak she must be suffering. If anything were to happen to his mate, he didn't know what he'd do, how he'd cope and they'd only been mated mere hours compared to the hundreds of years his parents had shared.

"Red Alert! Red Alert! All crewmembers report to your designated areas. This is not a drill. I repeat. This is not a drill. All crewmembers report to your designated areas. This is not a drill."

Maryann woke up gasping, her heart pounding in her chest. She didn't have to look to know that Mikel also had woken thanks to the alarms. She could feel it through their bonds. Throwing off the covers, they simultaneously sat up and started for the edge of the bed.

Mikel held his hand out for her and pulled her to her feet. At that point, it didn't matter if they were on the beach or in his private quarters, naked or fully dressed, she needed answers. Looking up into his eyes, she didn't miss the grim determination and worry she saw there. Swallowing past her fear, she knew the Black Rose was still out there, still kidnapping victims for breeding purposes. She straightened her shoulders. "What's going on, Mikel? I can feel you talking to someone even though I can't hear exactly what you're saying."

Mikel slowly ran his hand through her hair, while squeezing her right hand with the other. "There is a ship approaching at high-velocity and heading to intercept us. The commander has ordered all crewmembers to ready for battle in case we must fight our way through to continue our trip to the *Manruvian* home world. It's a precaution just in case the Black Rose or her allies are foolish enough to attack a Royal *Manruvian* Battle Vessel."

Running a trembling hand through her hair, she took a step away from her mate, reluctant to end their time together despite the possible danger. She couldn't keep Mikel from his duties—fighting by his people's side was what he was meant to do and she'd not stand in his way, no matter her feelings. "Oh... Okay. Then we better get dressed so you can do whatever it is you do. Don't you think?"

Just then she felt something beneath her skin begin to ripple and move as though something were trying to break free from her skin. Her whole body began to tingle, to burn. Frightened, she lifted her gaze to Mikel, knowing he could feel exactly what she did, that he, too, was experiencing the same sensations. "Mikel, what's going on?"

Mikel shook his head, his eyes mirroring her confusion. "I'm not quite sure, it almost feels like..."

Before he could finish his thoughts, the *Abacine* material they'd absorbed during the binding ritual erupted from their bodies, covering them from neck to toes in the thin silvery material. "Oh no, not again." Once again, something else could control their bodies and she didn't like that one bit. "Why is this happening, Mikel?"

Mikel's brows pinched into a frown as he held out his arm, his gaze intent on the material that now covered their bodies, protecting them. She could feel his confusion, his wariness.

"I think with the ship alarms sounding off and your request for clothing, the suits have decided it might be best to shield us from danger. It's only a guess as no one has been able to actually communicate telepathically with the sentient material."

That seemed to make sense, but she would have liked some warning before it actually happened.

"I, too, would have liked preparation for this. In all my life, I've never heard of this happening before and I've lived a considerably long time."

Maryann nodded. Though she'd like to know how the *Abacine* could rematerialize, now wasn't the time to question it. They might be headed into battle and that was by far a more important matter. *Well, at least we have clothes on, skintight though it is,* she thought to herself.

She could feel her face heat under his perusal. Her nipples immediately grew hard under his heated stare. Dropping her gaze, she swallowed, then blew out a long breath. Wiping her palms on her thighs, she straightened her shoulders, then raised her head, staring him dead in the eye. "Then perhaps we should find out just who is heading our way so that we can figure out why the *Abacine* has reacted this way once the possible danger has passed."

Nodding, Mikel once again clasped her hand in his and, after quickly glancing down the shoreline, as though looking for danger. "Skalldari, please transfer my mate and I to the command deck immediately."

"Processing."

In not much more than an instant, they found themselves on the Command Deck of the *Victory*. Maryann could feel the tension in the air like a living thing. The crewmembers' faces were grim, determined. With her hand still in Mikel's, she followed him to one of the stations where a female crewmember furiously typed at a very advanced looking computer. The keypads were touch sensitive, not real keys—like something out of a sci-fi movie.

She could feel Mikel's concentration, his tension, through their bond, and knew he was reading the symbols scrolling across the screen in purple and green flashes. Even if she knew the language, it flickered across the screen too quickly for her to even see what the characters were. *What is troubling you, Mikel?*

There are two incoming ships and both are refusing to answer our communiqués. I cannot not think of any good reason our requests for the ships to identify themselves have gone unanswered.

Behind her, she heard someone shouting orders to raise the shields. Maryann's stomach clenched. Fear ripped through her. The fact that the Black Rose might be about to attack had her legs feeling weak and her palms sweating. No. She would not cower before that evil woman again. Even if she were taken again, she'd fight back with everything in her. She wasn't a victim any longer. She'd never be a victim again.

Mikel grimaced, then reached for Maryann's hand again, giving it a small squeeze. *All will be well,* vasha. *This ship is the finest in the Manruvian* fleet. *It would take much to damage the* Victory. *Even if we were under assault by our enemy, I'd die before I'd allow you to be taken from me.*

No. If I were taken, you'd live and fight so you can rescue me later on. I couldn't live with myself if you sacrificed yourself for me. Your people need you. Besides, if she didn't break me before, she won't the next time either.

Rage blasted through their bond. Rage and fear. *There won't be a next time.*

Rather than argue with her mate, Maryann shook her head and kept her gaze focused on the viewport. She at least wanted to face whatever headed their way. Better to know what they faced rather than hide away, fearing the unknown.

Dropping her mate's hand, Maryann walked toward the wall of *transonami* that passed as the viewscreen. The vastness of space seemed never-ending. She could see no stars, no planets, nothing but absolute darkness. Maryann cleared her throat, knowing that getting answers were the top priority right now. "*Skalldari*, how long before they get here?"

"At their current speeds, the two vessels will reach us in four point three two minutes."

Nodding, she turned to Mikel who still had his gaze glued to the computer in front of him. "Any idea yet what kind of ships are heading this way and whether there's a way to determine who is on the ships?"

Mikel quirked his brows, then tilted his head to the side. After a few moments, a slow smile spread across his face. "*Skalldari*, as soon the ships are close enough, use the prototype Genome Scanner we'd intended for locating the Black Rose. The database has every known species listed so we should be able to determine just who we're facing."

"It will be as you ordered."

"Three minutes until the ships drop out of folded space, Prince Logann." The commander's voice held no trace of fear, just iron determination to face whatever headed their way.

As Maryann's gaze traveled around the Command Deck, she couldn't help but find the *Manruvian* people impressive. She could feel their courage, their conviction like a living thing. They truly were prepared to die for their people, for the other victims of the Black Rose. She didn't know how she could feel the crewmembers—maybe due to her bond with their prince—but she definitely felt connected to them.

"Two minutes until contact."

Maryann could hear the steel in the commander's voice, the strength in it and knew that this is why the rest of the crew seemed so steady. They were feeding off their commander's own emotions. Tension mounted as everyone waited for *Skalldari* to determine who was headed straight for them.

"That should give us enough time to mount some sort of defense once she discovers who the incoming ships belong to and what their offensive capabilities are."

Maryann nodded, feeling oddly calm, knowing deep in her heart that Mikel and this ship and its crew would fight to their last breaths to prevent the Black Rose from seizing any more victims as breeding slaves.

"One minute until contact, Prince Logann," muttered the commander.

"Arm all weapons, Commander," ordered Mikel. "I'd rather be

prepared if they start shooting right away."

"High Prince Logann, I have discovered the identity of the ships heading toward us. They are…"

But before *Skalldari* could even finish speaking, a familiar voice broke out over their Command Deck's communication system.

"Gee, that's some welcome. And I thought we were friends."

Maryann almost laughed when Eve Shi'Lan's sarcastic voice blasted through the nearly silent room. That could only mean that her mate, Taliff Shi'Lan accompanied her. They'd never be apart, especially during times of war as they were both lethal in a fight. Lethal and mated.

"Prince Logann, you can count on *Chantrea* as your ally. Permission to transport aboard the Victory? Both the *Wanderer* and the *Vengeance* are at your disposal." That had to be Hunter Shi'Lan. Who else would have the power and the authority to say such but the heir to the throne of *Chantrea*? And if Hunter were here, that meant that Amy was nearby as well, because like the younger Shi'Lan brother, Hunter would never go anywhere without his mate, as Amy herself was once a victim of the Black Rose.

Chapter Eight

At the first sound of Eve's voice, the tension that built inside Mikel eased. Then, when Hunter pledged their help, he knew things were looking up. Hunter was his closest friend, his staunchest ally next to his own family members. He knew the ferocity with which the *Chantreans* would fight to stand by him and knowing they'd be watching their backs as they approached *Manruvia* did much to calm him.

"It is good to hear from you, my friends. But why the silent approach?" Mikel knew Hunter and Taliff wouldn't approach in such a way without a damn good reason. They'd not put either their people or the *Manruvians* carelessly at risk without a very good reason.

After a momentary hesitation, Hunter cleared his throat. "There is much to tell you. Perhaps it would be best if we do so in person."

Mikel had known Hunter Shi'Lan for many, many years, knew every inflection in his voice. Despite his friendly tome, Hunter was clearly furious. That didn't bode well for whatever they needed to tell him.

"Please be welcome, High Prince Shi'Lan. Have your crews transport your retinue to the Royal Quarters. Maryann and I are famished. I'll have a meal prepared and sent to us and we can discuss what's brought you here while we catch up."

"Sounds good. We'll be there momentarily."

As soon as Hunter ended his communiqué, Mikel turned toward his mate, then the rest of the crew. After grabbing Maryann's hand in his and giving it a light squeeze, he turned toward the commander. "As soon as I know what's going on, I'll be sure to let you know. Hunter wouldn't go through these lengths to prevent others from hearing what he has to say unless it was critical to the safety of our peoples."

"I understand, Prince Logann. And may I take this opportunity to congratulate you on your mating. We've long waited for you to find the other half of your soul. It's truly a blessing."

"Thank you, Commander Sutter. Please have the mess hall send a meal for six to my quarters as soon as possible."

"Absolutely, consider it done."

Entwining his fingers with Maryann's, he slowly led her from the Command Deck. "*Skalldari*, transport us to our quarters so we may dress before our visitors arrive. When Hunter, Taliff and their mates are ready to join us, send them directly to our private dining room."

"As you command, Prince Logann."

Within moments, they were in their quarters. His gaze strayed toward his bed and he really wished they could retire there for the next twenty-four hours rather than have to put clothes on and entertain—even if it was his closest friends coming to call.

There's nothing I'd like better either. I have a feeling that once we reach your planet, the time we have to spend with each other—learning each other—will be in slim supply.

Mikel's heart stuttered in his chest, then sped up. That was the first time Maryann has initiated a conversation with him using their new mate bond, the first time she truly embraced that which connected them and his soul rejoiced.

"When the others leave, we'll just have to take up where we left off. It will be another day before we reach *Manruvia, vasha*." Knowing if he didn't step away from her, they'd never get dressed and meet with the *Chantreans*, Mikel let go of her hand. "Well, we'd better get dressed. I imagine the others will be here momentarily."

When Maryann sighed and he could feel her disappointment through their mate bond, he almost gave in to his need to take her back to his bed, to make love to her through the long hours left of this trip. Only knowing Hunter wouldn't have shown up requesting a personal meeting without a dire reason kept Mikel from surrendering to his heart and body's desires. And when a flare of arousal from his mate swept through his body, he knew that she'd been merged with him, with his thoughts completely.

Knowing that as soon as the meeting with the *Chantreans* was over he could take his mate, Mikel stepped away from Maryann and headed toward his closet. He'd had *Skalldari* supply him with some clothes for Maryann several days ago in anticipation of their joining, so at least he could give her something to cover her body. Their *Abacine* suits had dissolved into their bodies as soon as they'd returned to their suite and, with his raging hard-on, the sooner they were dressed, the safer they'd all be. Seeing her lush breasts quivering with her every breath, or her gorgeous ass another moment, he couldn't guarantee he wouldn't sweep her right back into bed, despite his duties.

Not trusting himself not to grab his mate and take her like his instincts demanded, Mikel stopped several feet from her and held out the clothes *Skalldari* had provided for her. He'd asked the sentient ship to provide clothing that she would feel comfortable wearing, and by the look of joy on her face when he handed her the pair of jeans and soft blue sweater, *Skalldari* had chosen well.

When Maryann clutched them to her chest and smiled up at him as though he'd given her a priceless treasure, he knew he'd slay water dragons for her if she but asked it of him. He loved her—would love her forever. She was his and soon, once the others left, he'd take her back to the Recreation room and make love to her beneath the water, completing their mating and her transformation.

As Maryann clutched the jeans and sweater to her chest, she allowed her gaze to travel over her mate, regretful he would soon cover all that naked flesh. With his back turned to her, his luscious ass beckoned her to cop a feel. She didn't get to explore him nearly enough earlier and if there weren't others arriving shortly, she might just have tried her hand at seducing him, something she couldn't have imagined doing even a week ago.

Mikel had taught her that love play between mates was nothing like what happened to her at the Black Rose's hand while she'd been a prisoner. She'd felt no pain, no shame, no fear, just unbelievable, unending pleasure. Licking her lips, Maryann watched fascinated as the muscles in his back rippled and bunched as he stepped into his trousers. Heat and longing burned through her body, leaving her trembling in need.

Swallowing her groan of frustration, Maryann dropped her gaze from her mate and quickly began dressing. Mikel had the right idea. If she didn't get dressed and get out of the bedchamber, she might just jump him and unfortunately now wasn't the time to be screwing like monkeys—or Merfolk as the case may be.

Within seconds after Maryann fastened her jeans and pulled on her sweater, a chime rang. "What's the chime?" she asked, though she was pretty sure she knew exactly what it meant.

"That's Hunter announcing they've arrived. Several times over the years we've had to meet this way, without notice or warning. That's his signal that he's waiting."

"Why didn't he just come in here?"

Mikel's husky chuckle had goose bumps pebbling across her skin.

"In case there was a crewmember in here, it's his way of being anonymous. Our peoples each have their enemies, it's not always good to announce a visit to all and sundry while meeting with your allies. It's a good way to die at the end of an assassin's blade."

Nibbling her bottom lip, Maryann nodded, seeing the wisdom in such a precaution. She wouldn't want Mikel walking into a situation that might be dangerous either and now that he was about to be crowned the king of *Manruvia* she couldn't help but worry that he'd be an even bigger target for assassins than ever before. That thought did not put her at ease, especially considering they had no idea what Hunter and Taliff Shi'Lan were there to tell them.

"Well, let's get in there then and find out what they have to tell us. The more information we have, the better for us."

When Mikel gripped her hand and led her through the main sitting room and through another door on the far side of the room, Maryann pushed away her anxiety. Though the *Chantreans* might be bringing bad news, she was looking forward to seeing Amy Shi'Lan again. If it hadn't been for Amy and her mate, Hunter, she would have died at the hands of the Black Rose. She'd never be able to adequately thank them for rescuing her, but maybe one day she'd be able to do something for them as equally important.

Together she and Mikel entered their private dining room, determined to face whatever the Shi'Lans had to say. She would not let her mate down. Not now, not ever. Besides, she'd missed Amy, Hunter's wife. Even though they'd not gotten to spend much time together after her rescue, she knew that Amy and Eve were both women she could trust, two women in which she could confide. Somehow, she knew in the coming days, she'd need that.

As soon as they entered the room, Hunter Shi'Lan, a tall *Lionese* male with long red blond hair and the body of a fierce warrior, approached them. Though she'd feared Hunter when she first met him, she could never forget that it was this man and his mate who had saved her from a life of sexual slavery. For that, she'd always be thankful to them. Without their intervention, she never would have survived the rapes and torture that the Black Rose and her followers inflicted on her. Without them, she'd never have survived, never had been brought to Mikel's ship, never have met her mate. Nothing she could do or say would be adequate thanks for that.

Grasping Mikel's forearm in a warrior's embrace, Hunter pulled her mate into his arms for a short hug before stepping back. Hunter's eyes seemed to twinkle as he looked from Mikel to her and back again. A blazing smile spread across his face when he stepped forward and traced the mating markings around her eye.

"Congratulations on your mating. May the Mother Goddess bless you with a long and happy life and a passel of beautiful babes."

Blushing at the thought of just how they'd go about making those beautiful babes, Maryann couldn't bring herself to look into Hunter's knowing eyes. Dropping her gaze from his, she focused on the others in the room. Amy Shi'Lan, Hunter's mate, a stunning red-haired beauty had her arm tucked into Eve's, their heads pressed together as they whispered to one another. Taliff, Hunter's younger brother and the head of his security forces, watched the pair with amusement, his amber eyes twinkling. He looked so relaxed she could almost pretend that they weren't there for a clandestine meeting rather, but simply a companionable dinner amongst friends.

"What news brings you here, Hunter?" Mikel asked. "Not that I'm not happy to see you and your family," he assured him.

Before he could answer, the door chimed, announcing a visitor. "It seems our dinner has arrived. Perhaps we can speak of this during the meal."

Hunter nodded, then walked toward his mate, grasping her fingers in his hand. "Come, *moya*," he whispered, leading her to a chair.

Maryann could see the love Hunter had for Amy. It was in his touch, his voice, his every glance. After seating her, he gently pushed her chair up to the table. Across from them, Taliff was doing the same, seating his mate as though she were the most precious treasure in the room. Someday she hoped that she'd find that same soul-deep love with Mikel. Already she couldn't imagine living her life without him and they'd only been mated mere hours.

As if sensing her worry, Mikel bent down, lightly grazed her lips with his. His kiss was tender, filled with quiet joy. *How can you doubt how much you mean to me,* vasha? *You are my one, and by the end of this eve, you'll never doubt my love for you again.*

Maryann's gaze searched his. Did he mean it? She'd find out soon enough. If only the meeting were already over. She had a feeling tonight would be life altering and she didn't know whether to be afraid or exhilarated.

Once everyone was comfortable seated around the large oval table and the crewmembers serving their dinner had withdrawn from the room, Mikel met Hunter's gaze. "Tell us," he softly ordered, though she could hear the steel in his words.

Nodding, Hunter pointed toward his brother. "Perhaps Taliff

should begin with the explanations."

"Two days ago I received an urgent summons from my father to attend him in his quarters. At first, I thought perhaps he or mother had taken ill. But within minutes of his summons, I knew that we had to get here as soon as possible."

Mikel frowned.

Maryann could sense Mikel's worry through the bond, his confusion.

"What did he have to tell you that made you drop everything to race across the star system?"

Taliff swallowed, then looked to his mate, Eve. When she nodded in encouragement, Taliff sighed. "Father had a visitation by the Lady Goddess Alana. She warned him that unless the *Chantreans* accompanied you to *Manruvia*, the Black Rose would spread across the galaxy, enslaving millions before moving onto other star systems."

Maryann trembled, remembering all too well the shame, pain and degradation she felt at the Black Rose's hands.

"What are you to do besides accompany us?" Mikel asked.

Maryann wanted the answer to that as well.

Taliff shook his head. "That we don't know. She didn't say. But knowing what it felt like to be her prisoner, knowing what the victims we rescued had gone through, he didn't even think about refusing. Within six hours of the Goddess's, visit, Hunter and I had assembled our crews and left *Chantrea*."

Nodding, Mikel turned toward Hunter. "Is there anything else I should know?"

"Only that according to Father, your mating and coronation celebration will proceed on the very eve you return home. Another demand of the Lady Goddess, apparently."

Maryann's eyes widened. "What? Already?" By the Goddess, she wasn't prepared. She'd only just mated with Mikel. The thought of taking up the role of queen so soon terrified her. As Maryann's thoughts raced with fear, a soothing wave of warmth poured through her.

Be calm, vasha. *You'll do fine. You think I wanted to lead my people so soon? I'd rather my father be whole and healthy, leading our people himself than have to step in because of his illness.*

Put that way, she felt ashamed for allowing her fear to overwhelm her. Mikel might lose his father and she was only thinking about herself. What must he think of her?

I think everything of you, Maryann. You've been through hell and the last week hasn't been the easiest on you. I don't expect you to handle all these changes without getting scared.

You should. Maryann swallowed, then looked at Eve and Amy. "So will you all be present at the ceremony then?" Goddess, she hoped so. She wanted some friendly faces around her when she stepped into the role of queen.

"If that is your wish, of course we'll be there," Amy promised.

As soon as she heard Amy's reassurance, some of the tension eased from her body and, when Mikel leaned down and placed a tender kiss on her cheek and ran his hand through her hair, she allowed her fear of the unknown to dissipate. For now anyway. "Good. Then let's eat. I'm absolutely starved."

As she dug into her food, a husky chuckle rippled through her mind, sending tingles down her spine. *Yes, eat hearty my mate. You'll need your strength for what I have planned for you this eve.*

Chapter Nine

Just over an hour later, Maryann found herself once again in the Recreation room. Somehow, she'd thought they'd spend this night in their quarters, but for some reason Mikel had insisted they return here.

Looking up into his eyes, she gasped. The hunger there was almost palpable. His desire reached out to her, beckoned her to succumb to the pleasure she knew he'd lavish on her. Her voice quivering, she asked the one question uppermost in her mind. "Why are we here when we could be in our quarters christening the bed there?"

"Because it's here that we'll complete the mating, beneath the water."

Maryann shook her head, confused. "In the water? I can't breathe underwater, Mikel. I can't stay under as long as you."

Mikel smiled.

Her heart clenched. By the Goddess, how could anyone not melt into a puddle when he smiled like that?

"Of course you can, *vasha*. Already you've had enough of my seed to initiate your first shift."

Holding out his hand, Mikel beckoned her.

"Come, join me beneath the sea, Maryann, and become mine completely."

When still she hesitated, he squeezed her fingers, then brought her hand up to his lips to kiss her palm.

"Trust me, *vasha*. I'd never do anything that could harm you."

Glancing at the waves caressing the shore, a strange longing filled her. Could she really shift into a mermaid, swim beneath the waters at her mate's side? She trembled, both excited and wary. Well, she wouldn't know until she tried. With a reluctant nod, she returned Mikel's smile. "Okay. But you better not let me drown," she warned.

Chuckling, Mikel led her toward the water. "Never, *vasha*. I'd protect you with my life." Soon they'd reached the water, where Mikel slowly turned her to face him. "'Tis time, love. Remove your clothes and I'll show you my world."

Unable to deny him, she lifted the hem of her sweater and tossed it to the white sand. Having been in a hurry earlier when she'd dressed, she'd not put on a bra so her breasts were completely bare. When Mikel groaned and licked his lips, her nipples tightened into hard points just begging for him to suckle.

"Now the pants," he ordered, his voice raspy and heavy with need.

Desire unfurled within her. Her gaze drifted over him as she worked the zipper of her pants. As she shucked her jeans, she watched in awe as Mikel did the same. As he lowered his pants and his cock emerged, she wanted nothing more than to drop to her knees and take his length into her mouth. By the Goddess, what had gotten into her? In a matter of hours, she'd turned into a sex fiend.

Once she'd kicked free of her jeans, she watched fascinated as Mikel's cock bobbed in front of her. She barely noticed that he once again had his hand held out waiting for her to take it.

"Come, *vasha*," he whispered, his voice a velvet seduction she had no desire to deny.

Entwining her fingers with his, she let him lead her into the warm water. It swirled around her legs, caressing her like a thousand fingers. Further and further, he led her out into the ocean. When the water reached her neck, she began to tense up, fear of the unknown pressing against her.

Blue-green eyes glittering with hunger, Mikel cupped her head with a big palm, sunk his fingers into her hair and slanted his mouth over hers. The moment their lips met, fire raced through her. All thoughts of drowning disappeared. So lost in his kiss, she didn't even realize he taken them into the depths of the ocean, that water covered her completely, that she could breathe despite the fact his lips were sealed to hers.

Only when a strange tingling began to work its way down her spine and spread to her legs did she realize that he'd taken them below the water. Frantic now that she knew there was no air to breathe, she started to thrash against him.

Calm, vasha. *You can breathe. The gills behind your ears are processing the oxygen you need.*

She could barely hear him, never mind understand what Mikel was trying to tell her. Only when he latched his mouth once again to hers was she able to calm down enough to process the words he'd said.

Are you all right, love?

I-I think so. What's wrong with my legs? Why can't I move them?

There's nothing wrong with your legs, love. I'm going to stop kissing you and you can look down. You can breathe just fine, vasha, *and I'll be right here if you need me.*

Maryann could sense his worry, his concern that she might freak out again. If she weren't so scared, she might have laughed. Gathering up her courage, she finally dropped her gaze from his and quickly looked down. Awed at what she'd become, she gasped. Where her legs had once been, now a mermaid's tail swayed in the water. Scales of the lightest rose pink and silver covered her lower body. With each movement of her tail, the colors seemed to sparkle and dance beneath the waves.

You are beautiful, love, absolutely perfect. I've never seen a more lovely Manruvian *in all my years.*

Pleased beyond words, Maryann continued to grip Mikel's neck as she stared at her tail. *Somehow, even knowing what you are, knowing that I'd transform after the mating, I still hadn't realized this could really happen,* she admitted.

When his hand gripped her chin and raised it so she could once again look into his eyes, she felt lost, trapped in his gaze. So much hunger and fire burned there, but something else, too, something else she'd never expected to find—tenderness. Slowly, as if he had all the time in the world, Mikel lowered his head to hers, sliding his lips against hers before nipping her bottom lip until she opened her mouth so he could deepen their kiss.

Tongues mated and dueled as they tasted each other. Pressing her chest against his, her nipples scraped against him, sending shards of fierce pleasure to her pussy. By the Goddess, she wanted to make love to him, wanted to feel him sink his shaft so deep into her she'd feel every delicious inch.

With her new body, she felt like a virgin again, unsure what to do, how to proceed. She had no idea how Merfolk mated, how part A fit into slot B.

Mikel broke their kiss and chuckled. *Envision your human legs, love, wrapped around my waist. Picture them clearly in your mind and it will happen.*

Will I still be able to breathe?

Of course. You're only partially shifting. Trust me, vasha.

Looking into his eyes, she smiled. She did trust him. With everything inside her, she knew that he'd never do anything to intentionally harm her. Following his instructions, she focused on her legs, envisioned them wrapping around his waist so that she could feel the heavy weight of his cock pressing against her aching core. And when her tail transformed into her own two legs, she did exactly that.

Make love to me, Mikel. Finish the claiming, she begged, somehow knowing that until he came inside her again, she wouldn't be completely his. And completely his was what she wanted to be.

WHEN MARYANN WRAPPED HER legs around his waist, pressing her woman's mound against his aching cock, Mikel thought he'd die. Unable to stop himself from taking her, claiming her as she demanded, he lowered his mouth to hers. Lips and tongue met, dueled, stroked one another until both were gasping and groaning, desperate with their need. When her nails dug into his scalp and her fingers wrapped around his hair, he lost all semblance of control.

Wrapping his arms around her waist, he slowly lifted her until her gate was poised above his aching shaft. With a powerful lunge, he seated himself fully within her gripping sheath, desperate to feel her clasping around his cock as he forged inside her. She groaned loud and low and the huskiness of the sound rippled through him like an electric current. He had to move and he had to move now.

With more speed than finesse, Mikel lifted his mate by her waist, then pulled her back down onto his throbbing erection. Over and over, he thrust inside her, using the rhythm of the water currents to increase her pleasure. His lungs labored and his pulse raced as he pounded in and out of her cunt. His pace was quick and hard, ruthless in his determination to make them both come.

Before long, they were heaving and sweating, writhing and grunting despite the water surrounding them. The force of his thrusts grew stronger, the penetration deeper and still they fucked, long and hard, desperate for release. Seconds later, he heard her scream out her climax through their bond and it nearly sent him over the edge with her. He thought he could last longer, bring her to another blistering climax, but when her clenching pussy tightened around his cock, it milked him of rope after rope of scalding hot and sticky come. And as his seed splashed against his mate's womb, he knew. In that moment, he knew that they'd been blessed by the Mother Goddess of the Sea. An heir would come from their joining this night and he couldn't have been happier.

As their heartbeats slowed and his mate grew limp against his chest, he gathered her in his arms and slowly made their way toward shore. It was time to take his mate to bed, to wrap himself around her as she drifted off to sleep. They needed their rest, for tomorrow they'd arrive in *Chantrea*. He only hoped that the Black Rose was far from his world, hiding instead from her enemies. But somehow, he knew, that wasn't to be. Soon, they'd battle again. Far too soon.

Chapter Ten

Rage whipped through her. The desire to kill, to destroy filled her body, her very soul. How could they? Everything had gone according to plan. Everything.

The *Manruvian* king lay helpless, his people saddened at the imminent loss of their leader, unsure what to do, what to believe. Now the heir, Hunter's friend and ally Mikel had thwarted her. How could this happen without her finding out? Some of her followers would pay with their lives for failing to tell her that the heir had taken a mate and now would be king.

Her followers had infiltrated all portions of *Manruvian* society and were even now awaiting on word to attack the helpless king and his queen so she could take control of *Manruvia* with ruthless and deadly efficiency.

Now, in a matter of hours, Mikel would be crowned and all her previous plans to kill the weakened king would be for naught. Once the power in the Trident of Ascension was transferred to the heir, he would be nearly unstoppable unless she made other arrangements.

Letting out a roar of rage, it took all her control to keep her beast leashed. No. Not yet. But soon all would be hers. She was the Black Rose and before this day ended, blood would seep into the seas and *Manruvia* would scream out its anguish as she destroyed everyone in her path.

Let them try to fight her. Let them think they had the upper hand, but within hours, when all the Royals lay dying by her hand, no one would dare rise up against her. The *Manruvians* would regret ever helping the *Chantreans*.

Laughing with anticipation, Haeda Shi'Lan, the *infamous* Black Rose stared down at the planet below. Let them have their ceremony. By night's end, not a soul in the palace would have the strength to fight back her forces. By dawn, *Manruvia* and all her resources would belong to her.

Knowing what must be done, the Black Rose headed toward the communications terminal. She had a spy to contact on the planet below and she knew just how to defeat her enemy. No one could stop her now. No one.

Chapter Eleven

Looking around the spacious chamber where she'd been shown to change for the coronation ceremony, Maryann couldn't help but chuckle. Dressing room hell, this room was larger than her living room back on Earth. With black marble floors and pink and ivory veined marble walls, it was the epitome of luxury. The ceilings were painted to look like the *Manruvian* sky at dawn and the hard floors were covers with furs of every imaginable shade.

Then there was the furniture. Who ever heard of furniture in a dressing room? But this one had a chaise lounge covered in a pink silk like material, a huge marble vanity with a cushioned bench. Not to mention the huge wardrobes filled with gowns in every style imaginable.

Hell, she couldn't believe the coronation and mating were tonight. Within minutes of their arrival in the palace, Mikel's mother, Vandora, had shown her to this chamber, letting her know that the Ascension ceremony for Mikel needed to be held right away to thwart an uprising if that were the plans of those that had poisoned her mate.

Maryann fidgeted. She just couldn't help it. In mere minutes, she would be crowned the queen of *Manruvia* and she felt clueless as to how to act. Of course, that wasn't the only thing making her so completely uncomfortable either. As she looked down at herself, she grimaced at what the *Manruvians* considered the proper dress for this event. Topless, she wore nothing but a skirt of cream-colored pearls. No underwear to hide her sex. No shirt to hide her breasts. Nothing except a mini-skirt of pearls and her new mating mark—the ring of pink and silver stars circling her left eye.

Looking into the mirror, she couldn't help but feel self-conscious. The *Manruvians* were such a beautiful people. She'd yet to see a plain woman or an average man. They were all drop-dead gorgeous and she couldn't help but feel like she'd never belong. Once again, she would live with another species, though at least this time she could shift. How was she ever going to be a good queen to their people if she couldn't even get up the nerve to walk out of their room to join her mate in the Ascension ceremony?

You'll do fine, my love. You are a beautiful woman. My woman. My mate.

Maryann smiled, couldn't help it really. She could feel the sincerity in Mikel's words. He truly did think her beautiful. That didn't mean she felt better about walking out there so everyone could see her practically naked.

All they will see is my love for you, vasha.

Her heart clenched. By the Goddess, she wanted to believe him—believe that he could truly love her. But she'd been broken inside for a long time, maybe too long, and didn't know if she'd have the strength to be what he needed. She didn't know if she had the strength inside her to be a good queen to his people, to be what they deserved, or what he deserved.

Have faith, Maryann. The Sea Goddess, Mari, would not have brought us together if you didn't have the strength to carry the roles expected of you. Now, come to me. Join me. Become my queen and rule by my side.

Maryann hesitated. Looked at herself one more time in the mirror. *Are you sure this is what you want, that I'm what you want?*

Of course, I'm sure, love.

Maryann nodded, then heaved out a sigh. She could do this. She would do this. *Okay, I'm ready. Just tell me what to do.*

My sister, Valla will be in to escort you to the Throne Room. I'll be waiting for you there, as will my mother and the rest of the Manruvian

Elders. *The ceremony will be broadcast through every home on* Manruvia *so they can see for themselves the proof of the mating and the coronation, as we become their new king and queen.*

Licking her lips, Maryann ran her hand through her long auburn hair one more time, then grinned. If only her mother could see her now, she'd never believe that her once awkward shy daughter would soon become royalty. Hell, she almost didn't believe it herself.

Before more doubts about her ability to be a good queen could surface, she heard the door to the dressing room open.

Valla, the youngest *Manruvian* princess—of which she learned there were three as well as two male siblings—entered the room. With golden blonde hair that hung nearly to her waist and the delicate, almost ethereal beauty of her face, Maryann couldn't help but feel less than pretty in comparison.

Such nonsense, love. You are who I want, will always want. I love everything about you. One day, you'll believe that. I promise.

She felt a gentle hand on her shoulder. There was kindness and a quiet joy in the young woman's aqua eyes.

"You will make a fine mate and a wonderful queen. There is purity in your soul and great strength in your heart that no one can challenge. Have faith in the Goddess Mari's wisdom. She chose you as Mikel's mate for a reason."

Maryann swallowed past her fear. "Do you truly believe that?" Mikel's sister just smiled at her, but there was a touch of sadness in her gaze.

"I do. If I were to ever meet my mate, I couldn't imagine not embracing the joy of such an event. We are gifted with only one perfect mate, one soul who is a complete match to our own. It's a blessing that I hope to one day have for myself."

Nodding, Maryann twitched her pearl skirt, settling it lower on her hips, then ran her hands down in thighs in nervousness. "Okay then. I guess I'm ready. Let's do this."

"Just remember, you are already mated to my brother, your soul and his already joined. This is only a formality. In his heart, you're already his, already queen to our people."

"I'm ready then. Piece of cake."

"Piece of what?" Valla asked as she opened the door.

They left the dressing chamber that led into the royal suite that she and Mikel would be sharing as of tonight. Apparently, it used to be his mother and father's room, but because of the upcoming ceremony, they moved to another suite, one not earmarked for the king and queen of *Manruvia*. Maryann chuckled. "It's just an old Earth saying meaning this will be easy."

Valla nodded, then stopped, turned and looked at her, her gaze serious. '"Just follow your heart, Maryann, and all will be well."

Before Maryann could reply, Valla started once again down the long hallway. After several more turns down the marble hallways, they reached a set of wooden doors that had to be at least ten feet tall. The mahogany colored doors were beautiful, covered with magnificent carvings of Merfolk, water nymphs and even sea dragons.

As soon as they approached the door, it slowly swung open, welcoming them to enter. She didn't know how she knew that, but somehow she could sense the welcome in the air and it eased her nervousness somewhat. As her gaze darted around the opulent chambers, the beauty and majesty of not only the people but the surroundings awed her. Everywhere, men and woman wore gowns and togas in colors of such amazing shades from silver to pink, white to vibrant reds, blues and greens and everything in between.

The throne room's ceiling was also covered with paintings of mythical creatures and some she'd already been privileged enough to meet including the *Chantrean* Lions and the *Manruvian* Merfolk. A thousand ivory candles or more hung suspended from the ceiling as if by magic, lighting up the room and lending it a mystical air. After taking a few more seconds to stare in awe at her surroundings, Maryann's gaze found Mikel's as he waited patiently for her at the head of the room.

Wearing white fitted trousers similar to riding breeches and a deep blue sleeveless tunic trimmed in silver piping, he was the sexiest man she'd ever seen. His ash blond hair hung to his shoulders and gleamed beneath the candlelight. His blue-green eyes practically glittered with heat and love. His mouth—by the Goddess—his mouth had her anticipating their mating night. He stood there so straight and proud, waiting on her as if she were the most important person in the world.

You are the most important person in my world, vasha.

And somehow, she knew that. Through their bond, she could feel his love for her, his complete faith that only she could stand by his side throughout their lives. She'd never thought to find someone who'd love her just for herself. On Earth she was the human girl living among *Chantrean Lionese* shifters. After her kidnapping, she became just another one of the Black Rose's breeding slaves, raped and tortured day after day in an attempt to impregnate her.

Since meeting Mikel, she truly felt whole and independent for the first time in her life as though she was destined for more than mediocrity and that in itself was a blessing. But most of all, she felt loved, and though she'd yet to speak the words to Mikel, she loved him as well. She just hoped she didn't fail him or his people.

You will not fail us. It's an impossibility. They'll come to love you as much as I already do.

Warmth spread through her chest. As she looked on her mate and slowly made her way toward him, her soul felt lighter. Her steps grew quicker and it took all her control not to race down the aisle and jump in his arms. By the Goddess, how had her feelings changed so quickly? Just a week ago, she'd gone out of her way to avoid Mikel, blaming him and everything around her for forcing her into a mating she didn't want. Now she couldn't imagine her life without him.

With both her mind and heart now at ease, Maryann closed the distance between her and her mate. Whatever happened next, she knew without a doubt she'd be at his side and only death would ever separate them. Even then, she'd spend eternity with him even once they were no longer on this mortal plane.

MIKEL'S HANDS SHOOK. HIS heart thundered in his chest. Finally, all would acknowledge their mating. No one would be able to take her from him after this. No one.

Wearing naught but pearls from the *Sea of Ishima*, his mate approached with her head held high. By the Goddess, she was so beautiful to him. With her wild mane of auburn hair, breasts that over filled his hands, hips that were made for a man to grip while in the throes of passion, he felt nearly overwhelmed with happiness.

As he continued to watch her approach him, his heart felt too full for words. He couldn't wait until she was his completely, couldn't wait until he could get her alone again. First though, he had to get through the ceremony. After that, he'd make love to her throughout the long night.

Just thinking about the night ahead had his cock hard and aching. By the Goddess, the ceremony couldn't be over fast enough for him. He watched his mate approach him, her head held high despite her embarrassment at her nudity, her gaze locked to his. At that moment, the pride he felt for her, for her strength, her integrity, her courage, filled him to overflowing. He knew in that moment, he could have chosen no greater queen for his people. And when his mate took that final step to reach his side and reached for his hand, twining her fingers with his, he knew he'd do anything, be anything, to always have this woman at his side.

He could feel Maryann's nervousness through their bond, knew she worried about what would happen next. If he could have told her, he would have. All he knew for sure is that the Trident of Ascension would be passed to him this day. What happened after that, what the ceremony actually consisted of, he had no idea. He thought he had all the time in the world to ask his father about the ceremony, but that didn't happen. He was just as in the dark about the upcoming ceremony as she was.

When chimes began to ring through the hall, growing louder and louder as the music went on, he knew he'd soon find out. Squeezing his mate's hand in his, he looked down into her worried eyes and smiled, letting her see inside him, feel his conviction that this was meant to be, that she was meant to be by his side right now and forevermore. As her tension eased and her lips tilted up into a shy smile, he knew he'd do anything to keep that smile on her face.

Sudden silence filled the throne room. Not a person whispered. An air of expectancy filled the chamber. As the silence lengthened, even Mikel began to grow tense. Beside him, Maryann trembled. He could feel her discomfort that now that the room had grown silent, all eyes were on her. Yet she didn't cringe, didn't drop her head in embarrassment—she just continued to gaze into his eyes as though gathering strength and courage by looking into his soul.

Before he could consider their connection further, two priestesses entered the chamber through a hidden door behind the thrones. One carried an ancient text, the other the Trident of Ascension. It glowed with a strange green light. He could feel the power of the Trident even from a distance, even without touch. It beckoned him. He wanted to reach out and grasp it in his hands, not to wield the power he could feel emanating from it, but because of an insane belief that once he held the Trident something momentous and life changing would occur. What, he had no idea.

The two priestesses moved toward them until they stopped directly in front of them.

"We are the priestesses of Ikaria, sent by the Mother Goddess of the Sea, Mari, to ordain you as the new rulers of the sea. Kneel, Mikel Logann of *Manruvia* and Maryann Wilson of Earth, and receive that which awaits you."

Nodding in acknowledgment, Mikel gripped Maryann's hand tighter and slowly eased them down until they were kneeling before the Mother Goddess' priestesses.

The young priestess carrying the ancient tome moved forward first and began to read. "The Mother Goddess created life for her people in hopes that they would thrive. She gifted them with all the emotions of humanity—love, passion, joy, happiness as well as envy, jealousy, fear and others. Long ago, when her children were but babes, she knew that strife and hardship would one day enter their lives. Knowing that her children would one day suffer under the hands of cruelty, she chose a protector for them, a warrior of unequal strength in both body and heart. For thousands of years, the line of Logann has protected her people, her children, from enemies within as well as enemies without. Today, another Logann will pick up the mantle of leadership with his mate at his side. Her compassion, her courage, her spirit and her love will ensure that the Protector will always remain grounded, will never seek to wield the power of the Trident to abuse."

Next to her, the older wizened priestess stepped forward, lightly placing the three prongs of the Trident against his shoulder. "On this day, the Priestesses of Ikaria on behalf of the Mother Goddess of us all bestow upon you all the power and responsibilities of her people."

Heat the likes of which he'd never felt before surged through his body. A thousand bolts of lightning zinged through him, firing nerve endings, causing muscles to bunch and spasm as the power of the Trident of Ascension roared through him. Beside him, Maryann's fingers tightened against his, her body also quivering under the onslaught ripping through them. Connected as they were through the mate bond, he had no way to protect her from the fire burning in his body.

When he thought he'd not be able to take any more, the heat began to cool, soothing his body and his mind. Strange warmth settled in his chest, filling him with foreign emotions and thoughts. Like the mate bond between him and Maryann, he felt connected, but instead of to one soul, it was to thousands. He could feel the hearts of his people, their worries, their joy, their passion, their anger. Thousands upon thousands of others were now a part of him. This then was the power of the Trident, the power to sense the emotions and thoughts of his people, to gauge their needs, their desires.

Beside him Maryann trembled. By the Goddess, he'd never imagined just what the Trident could do. No wonder his father had led his people with wisdom and an uncanny ability to gauge his people's hearts.

It's almost too much, Mikel. How did your mother and father cope?

How did they not drown beneath the tide of emotions bombarding them?

Mikel moved closer to his mate, pulled her into his arms so he could surround her with his body, let her feel his emotions until her panic began to fade. *They had each other, as we do. Together we'll do what we must.*

He could feel his *vasha* gaining strength and courage from his words, could sense her determination to help him lead his people with honor.

"Rise King and Queen Logann. Embrace your joined destiny."

With Maryann's hand still gripped in his, Mikel and Maryann turned to face those attending their ceremony. Raising their joined hands above his head, Mikel looked out across the faces of his people. Their expressions were filled with a myriad of emotions from awe and caution to joy and envy.

Knowing that the weight of the future rested upon their shoulders, he straightened his spine and stepped forward, walking down the center aisle with his mate until they stood in the center of the room.

"Thank you for joining us on such an auspicious occasion." Looking down at his perfect mate, Mikel allowed a heated smile to spread across his face, letting her see both his desire and his love. "Join us in the Royal Ballroom where tables have been laid out for a feast in celebration."

And as the people surrounding them broke out in applause, Mikel led Maryann out of the room, knowing full well that somewhere in the crowd surrounding them, someone was planning their demise. Knowing the emotions of his people definitely had its advantages. He now knew to be on his guard for an imminent attack—something he wouldn't have known even an hour ago.

Chapter Twelve

Seated at the raised table set aside for the royals, Maryann gazed across the crowded ballroom. On her left, Mikel sat tense, as though prepared for battle. Surely, he must sense what she did. Tha someone was relishing the idea of ending the Logann line of rule.

Yes, vasha. Though I would have preferred to celebrate our joining this night, I fear that danger is all around us.

Maryann exhaled, thankful it wasn't just her. Getting used to all the emotions and thoughts of the people surrounding her was overwhelming at best. Learning to interpret the sensations bombarding her would take a long time, she imagined. At least Mikel would be by her side.

Always, vasha. I'll always be by your side.

Within minutes of being seated, a barrage of servants began carrying in trays loaded with glorious smelling food. Her stomach rumbled, telling her emphatically that it'd been entirely too long since her last meal. While servants laid out bowls of soup in front of them, others went around filling golden, jeweled goblets with something that smelled suspiciously like Cranberry Juice or something very similar.

As Maryann lifted her glass, an eerie sense of wrongness spread through her, a sense of danger that she'd never experienced before. Shaking her head over such nonsense—too much stress the last few days had to be messing with her mind, she thought—she pressed her mouth to the lip of her glass. As soon as the liquid touched her lip, her entire body froze. She couldn't move, couldn't open her lips, couldn't speak.

Mikel!

Startled, Mikel gripped her arms. *What is it,* vasha?

I can't move. I can't move. What's going on?

Mikel tensed. His aqua eyes began to glow with power and rage. *Poison. The drink is poisoned. The* Abacine *inside of you is protecting you.*

Maryann's eyes widened. *Just my drink? What about yours?*

Lifting his goblet to his nose, Mikel inhaled as though savoring the drink's bouquet. *Mine as well. Did you see who filled our glasses?*

Yes, it's the male at the end of the table to our right. He's filling your youngest brother's glass.

Rage whipped through their bond. Even knowing that her mate would never hurt her, it surprised her to sense so much anger in him. Since her rescue, Mikel had never shown he had a temper, that he could be violent.

No one harms me or mine. No one.

Finally, after what seemed forever, Maryann's arm twitched. Apparently, the *Abacine* that she'd understood the warning it had given her and released some of her body's control. Slowly, Maryann lowered her glass, pretending she'd taken a huge swallow of the liquid. If someone had gone out of their way to poison them, she couldn't let on that she knew of their plan.

Good, now I just have to warn the others not to drink whatever they'd been given. I'll not lose any more of my family to this poison when already my father lies in a coma and my mother stays by his side, grieving over the potential loss of her mate.

How will you tell everyone not to drink from their glasses when you don't know that this servant is the only one out there intent on killing you?

Good question. Any ideas, vasha?

Maryann tipped her head back and closed her eyes, quickly considering and rejecting thoughts and ideas as they tumbled through her mind. She'd do naught to harm either her mate or her people. *What if you tell them that I'm expecting and that because I choose not to drink during my pregnancy, you'll do the same. Since time is a celebration of our mating, no alcohol will be served.*

Startled eyes met hers. *How did you know that you already carry my heir, Maryann?*

Maryann swallowed, had no idea what to say. She couldn't believe it. *What? I'm pregnant?*

You mean you didn't know?

Maryann shook her head. *No. Oh my god. I'm pregnant.* She didn't know whether to laugh or freak. She had no idea how to be a mother. Was he happy about it? She had no idea.

You've made me happier than you can imagine, Maryann. I knew the moment you conceived, the moment my seed granted life. I planned to tell you tonight once we returned to our suite.

Something inside her eased. Though she hadn't planned to have children quite this soon into their mating, she couldn't regret it. *Well then, I suggest you tell them to remove the wine. I want us to live long enough to enjoy our child. If they planned to poison us, there must be a reason.*

Of course. They must plan to attack tonight while we are supposedly incapacitated.

Standing up, Mikel raised his arms above his head and clapped them together. Even above the noise of the crowded room, the clap thundered, echoing through every corner of the ballroom. All eyes turned toward them, waiting for whatever he had to say.

"I have a joyous announcement. We planned on waiting to share this with you, but decided not to wait any longer."

Reaching toward her, Mikel gripped her hand and pulled her into his arms.

"My mate and I have been blessed by the Mother Goddess, Mari. Already our heir lies safely nestled in your queen's womb. To honor her decision to avoid anything that may harm our child, no alcohol will be consumed tonight for I'll not let her feel left out of this celebration."

Though there were some groans of disappointment that their wine would be taken away, the crowd appeared to be both stunned and awed that the royal couple had been blessed already. An overwhelming sense of happiness spread through the room, almost overshadowing the hatred she could feel. Besides the servant that poisoned them, she couldn't pinpoint where that hatred came from, but she knew more than one person in this room had planned tonight's treachery and that did nothing to set her at ease.

Turning to the servant who had poisoned their glasses, Mikel waved toward the full goblets on their table. "Please, take away the wine and bring out enough Vicuña Juice for everyone."

From across the room, Maryann met Eve's gaze. Her and Amy had decided to stay for the reception, not only because they were her friends, but because they were telepathically connected to their mates, who awaited word on their ships if an attack occurred during the celebration. At her slight nod, Eve touched Amy's shoulder, then whispered into her ear.

Good, they would warn Taliff and Hunter who would in turn notify the *Manruvian* fleet that currently circled the planet, cloaked in preparation for battle. At least they weren't totally unprepared for such an attack. The last day in space, plans were made, allies contacted. No one wanted the Black Rose to spread her misery any farther than she already had. They would stop her. There was no other choice.

As the servant left the room, Maryann tensed, knowing full well that as soon as the traitor found a place where he couldn't be seen, he'd report to the Black Rose that their plan had failed. Whatever happened after that wouldn't be good, of that she had no doubt.

As soon as the traitor disappeared, Mikel tensed. It wouldn't be long now. With her plan a failure, the Black Rose would be enraged. Mikel searched the room for Lucas Logann, his cousin and Chief of Palace security. He had to warn the man before all hell broke out. When his gaze landed on Lucas, he wasn't surprised to find a servant pressing her breasts against the male's shoulder. Lucas was known far and wide as a lover of woman. A night didn't go by that women didn't offer themselves to him, desperate for the pleasure he loved to lavish on them.

Lucas, as much as I'd love for you to enjoy your pursuits this eve, it will have to wait. The wine has been poisoned, probably with the same compound that sickened my father and I fear an attack is imminent.

Lucas's gaze clashed with his, anger blasted through their mental link. After a moment's silence, Lucas nodded. *I understand. Armed guards will arrive shortly. I've already called them.*

Good. Be prepared for anything. We have no idea how many traitors are involved. Mikel's gaze dropped to Maryann. After running his hand through her wild mess of auburn curls, he looked up, once again meeting Lucas's gaze. *Protect the queen at all costs. Not only is she carrying my heir, but I honestly don't think I could survive without her.*

Understood, cousin. After whispering in the servant's ear and sending her off with a pat on her ass and a smile, Lucas stood and made his way toward the dais and the royal table. *I'll guard her myself.*

But before Lucas could even reach their side, a shrill alarm pierced the chamber as the walls and floors began to quake. Chaos erupted. Shouts and screams echoed through the room. Chairs and tables were overturned as men and women raced for the ballroom doors. Beneath his clothes, the *Abacine* erupted through his skin, covering him from neck to ankle. Beside him, Maryann's did the same. Pulling her into his arms, he looked toward the exits, knowing they'd never get out that way. Knowing that time was of the essence, he glanced at Lucas who was still trying to make his way toward them. *Contact* Skalldari. *I want her to lock on to Maryann and me and send us to the command bunker beneath the palace.*

Lucas nodded, then raced toward the exit to their right where a computer panel was recessed into the wall. From there he could contact the orbiting ships as well as their forces here on the ground. Just as he reached the hidden panel, a squad of the Black Rose's followers transported into the center of the room. They dressed in all black, hiding their faces behind hoods and masks, which could not cover the evil in their souls. Only one stood out so completely that Mikel almost stepped back, the viciousness and blackness of her soul beyond anything he'd ever experienced.

Without seeing her face, without looking into her eyes, Mikel knew that that one could be no other than Haeda Shi'Lan, the Black Rose herself and his mortal enemy. She was responsible for his mate's suffering, her pain. And for that alone, she'd die.

After whispering a kiss against his mate's cheek, he rubbed his thumb across her bottom lip. *Get below the table, Maryann, and don't come out until I give the all clear.*

No. I'll fight by your side, not hide beneath the table trembling in fear.

Mikel grimaced. He didn't want her in any more danger than she already was.

Dammit Mikel. I know what you're about to do. I can help you, lend you my strength. Don't shut me out.

Fine, give me your hand and sink into our bond. We'll do this together. He only prayed that nothing happened to her.

Focusing on the Black Rose, he did his best to ignore the shouts and screams as laser blasts from her weapons pierced flesh. He knew his people were being slaughtered, unarmed as they were, and that he couldn't allow.

Mikel searched inside himself and embraced the gifts he'd so long kept hidden, even from his parents. Since childhood he had felt the untapped power curled in his soul, a power so great he feared he'd one day hurt those around him if he didn't learn to control it.

Unlocking the barriers he'd placed around his gift, he fully embraced the darkness inside him for the first time. Heat poured through his veins. His muscles twitched, seemed to grow. His skin burned as though heated by the summer sun. His vision blurred and still he focused on the woman that had caused the hurt to his mate. Using his newfound powers to sense others, he latched on to her thoughts, searching for a way into her mind.

Disgust washed over him as he sensed the glee his enemy felt as those around her fell beneath the onslaught of her attack. Deadly rage infused him. No more. Burrowing into her mind, he loosed a bolt of psychic lightning through her mind.

The Black Rose gasped, clutched her head.

Her gaze lifted, searching for the cause before settling on him. He smiled grimly and sent another shaft of pain through her, doing his best to cripple her. He felt his strength weaken, knew he couldn't keep this up for long.

Suddenly power swept through him, warmth. He squeezed Maryann's hand, knowing that she was lending him her strength. He redoubled his attack even as his legs began to tremble.

Again the Black Rose gasped. She dropped her weapon, gripped her head and fell to her knees.

Her body twisted in pain and still Mikel kept up the attack. A feline roar of rage ripped from her throat. He could sense her trying to shift, trying to latch on to her beast and he couldn't allow that. Forcing more power through the link, he pummeled her mind, determined to finally defeat her. She squirmed and thrashed atop the floor. He didn't let his gaze leave hers, imprisoning her with his stare.

Seemingly from out of nowhere, a small sonic grenade hurtled through the air, heading straight for their table. Only Maryann's gasp warned him in time. Wrapping his arms around her, he knocked her to the ground, shielding her body with his own. The blast of sound waves rocked the table above them, sending pain shooting through his mind. He covered Maryann's ears with his hands, doing his best to shield her from the debilitating sound until the attack stopped. His nose began to bleed, dripping into her hair, but he didn't release his hold on his mate. Darkness beckoned, his body demanding he shut down, escape into unconsciousness until the pain ceased, but he wouldn't give into it.

Already nearly a minute had passed. A few more seconds and the weapon would stop its attack. He only had to hold out a few more seconds.

Finally, blessed silence filled the room. Only the moans and muffled cries of his people could be heard. Lifting himself from his mate, he quickly ran his hand over her body, searching for injuries. When she only smiled and pulled him down for a hug, he thanked all that was holy that she'd not been hurt during the attack. Once positive that she'd been unharmed, he stood up on shaking legs, wiped the blood from his nose and surveyed the chaos surrounding them.

His gaze scanned the room efficiently, searching for his nemesis, but he didn't have to be told she'd escaped. He could feel it. The foulness of her soul no longer pierced his mind. Shaking his head, he reached down for his mate, pulled her into his arms. Looking around the room, he was filled with rage and sorrow at the destruction surrounding them. Too many of their people had been injured in this attack.

She may have gotten away, Mikel, but at least she felt pain before doing so. We'll find her.

Mikel dropped his gaze to his mate, beyond thankful that she was at his side. He could feel his mate's worry through their bond, wasn't surprised by her next question.

But until then, she'll continue to harm others. I've never felt such absolute malevolence before. How many more will she kill before she's finally brought to justice?

I don't know, Maryann, but I do know this. Eventually, she'll be caught and her life will be forfeit. Until then, we'll continue to fight her, continue to search out those she's taken. I've not forgotten my promise to Eve to find her brother and until he's returned to her and all the other victims are rescued, that's what we'll do.

Maryann nodded, then looked around the room. When her gaze settled on Eve and Amy Shi'Lan, her eyes lit up with joy. *At least they are safe.*

Mikel winced. *Thank the Goddess. I wouldn't want their mates to come after me if they'd been injured. I doubt I'd survive it.* Knowing that the Black Rose had probably attacked the entire city, he gripped Maryann's hand in his. *Now, let's see what we can do to help our people. Especially now, they need us.*

At Maryann's nod, they left the dais and spread out, comforting the injured as best they could as they awaited medical attention. After an hour of helping the injured, his gaze sought out hers. Happiness infused his soul. No matter what they'd face in the coming years, he knew that with Maryann at his side, they could get through anything. With a smile lighting up his face and heart, he walked up to his mate and pulled her into his arms.

Come to bed with me, vasha. *Tomorrow, we'll rebuild. Tonight, I want to celebrate our future.*

Rising up onto her toes, Maryann wrapped her arms around his neck and placed a tender kiss on his cheek. *Then take me to bed, love. I'm all yours.*

Epilogue

Ryan Morgan held on for dear life as the small ship left the shuttle bay. A blast from a laser cannon rocked the larger ship as they exited. He managed a quick glance over at his companion as another blast rocked the craft.

"We're going down!" Anna screamed into her communications device. "Dear Goddess, we're going to crash on this planet and we don't even know where we are to call for help."

"As long as we're away from the Black Rose, I don't give a damn where the hell we are," Ryan said with a snarl. "Nothing could be worse than staying on that ship." He was tired of being poked and prodded—sick of the drugs they injected him with. He didn't know if he could have endured another woman's scream as she was repeatedly raped in an attempt to impregnate her. He gave Anna a meaningful look. "Even death was preferable to that hell." He jerked his head toward the others. "I think our friends would agree."

Glancing back, the other three women he helped to escape merely nodded their agreement with thinned lips. He wished he could have taken more. Still, four women out of the Black Rose's grasp were better than none.

Fire blazed over the nose of the shuttle as they forced their way through the layer of atmosphere.

"Shit! I don't see anything down there but water." Anna fought with the steering lever, trying to regain control of the ship. "I can't… Brace yourselves for impact and try to find something that floats. We're going in and going in hard," she called over her shoulder.

Ryan gripped the arms of his chair and kept his eyes glued to the window in front of him. He was a dead man, plain and simple. He glanced over at Anna again. "You know, as soon as that glass breaks, we're goners."

"It's not glass. It won't break." Anna gave him a tight smile. "The dampeners should slow us down at least a little and afford some protection. My main concern is water temperature." She glanced back at the others, then back at Ryan.

And whether or not everyone could swim, he thought.

What seemed like forever really took less than a minute, including their conversation. Strange how falling several thousand feet could take so long.

The dampeners held. Damage from the impact was minimal and, thankfully, no one was injured. The women screamed at the bobbing of the small craft. None of the women could swim. They were nothing but big cats, so he could understand their immediate fear—but fear had to be overcome. How in the hell would he save them? He *was* a water baby. He'd been more comfortable in the water than out all of his life, despite being part feline. *And* he was an award-winning swimmer. But none of that explained how he'd keep them all from drowning. He glanced through the transparent hull just in time to see a large fin disappear.

Anna opened the hatch. Two of the women held cushions that would keep them afloat, if they were lucky. That still left two to keep above the surface. He sighed. He didn't have the heart to tell them they were dead already.

"On the count of three, we all need to jump from the shuttle as fast as we can. The force of our leaping out and the loss of weight will cause the ship to spin, take on water and sink. Understand?" They nodded. "One."

The women moved closer to the hatch, two in the doorway and two just behind.

"Two."

The women grasped their cushions in white-knuckled grips and braced themselves for their jump.

"Three!"

He and Anna pushed the first three out, then leapt from the shuttle together. The water closed over their heads as the shuttle capsized and slipped below the surface as predicted.

Something large brushed Ryan's side. *That's it. I'm shark food now. I hope they at least wait until we've all drowned so we don't have to feel them ripping us apart.* He exhaled, hoping to quicken the inevitable. His eyes flew open when soft lips pressed against his, forcing air back into his lungs.

A strange beauty stared into his eyes, her golden hair floating around her face in a long, tangled mass. It covered her shoulders and chest, hanging well past her... Ryan blinked, then smiled. Now he *knew* he was dead. He was seeing mermaids!

About the Author

Bonnie Rose Leigh has been enthralled with the written word since childhood. When she ran out of things to read, she created her own stories. Now, she is a multi-published author and lives in a small town in Upstate, New York. She spends most of her time on the computer either writing or visiting with friends. When not busy on the computer, her free time is consumed with reading. It doesn't matter what genre the book is either, though she is partial to romance novels. Her favorite after-hours hobby is sprawling in a chair with a book clutched in her hands and a cup of cocoa sitting nearby.

Bonnie would love to hear from each and every one of you. Make sure you subscribe to her monthly newsletter or check out her blog as it will be updated regularly with release dates, excerpts and online appearances. And, as always, feel free to drop her email if you have any questions, concerns or just want to chat and she'll get back to you as soon as she can.

Bonnie's website address is located at:
www.mybonnierose.com
She can now also be found on MySpace at:
www.myspace.com/bonnieroseleigh

Bonnie's other books
Available at eXtasybooks.com

Binding Lena
Tempering Zoe
Sheltering Abby
Loving Jordan

Coming soon

Waiting for Willow

Serving Sera

Two for Twila

The Protector's Jewel

Made in the USA